PHILIP GOODEN is the author of *Sleep of Death* and *Death of Kings*, the first two novels in the Nick Revill series. A contributor to various short story anthologies, he also works as an editor, most recently on a new edition of Arthur Conan Doyle's *The Lost World*. He lives in Bath, where he is currently working on his fourth Nick Revill mystery.

Praise for the Nick Revill series

'The witty narrative, laced with puns and word play so popular in this period, makes this an enjoyable racy tale.'

Susanna Yager, *Sunday Telegraph*

'The book has much in common with the film Shakespeare in Love – full of colourful characters . . . [but with] an underlying darkness.'   *Crime Time*

Other titles by the same author

Sleep of Death

Death of Kings

Alms for Oblivion

THE PALE COMPANION

PHILIP GOODEN

CARROLL & GRAF PUBLISHERS
New York

Carroll & Graf Publishers
An imprint of Avalon Publishing Group, Inc.
161 William Street
16th Floor
NY 10038–2607
www.carrollandgraf.com

First published in the UK by Constable,
an imprint of Constable & Robinson Ltd 2002

First paperback edition published by Carroll & Graf 2003

ISBN 0–7867–1176–0

Printed and bound in the EU

Library of Congress Cataloging-in-Publication Data is available on file.

Turn melancholy forth to funerals;
The pale companion is not for our pomp.

A Midsummer Night's Dream, I, i

Waxing Crescent

The murderer straddled the prone body. He watched his victim closely, alert for the slightest sign of life. There was a twitch from an outflung arm, a spasm in a sprawled leg. The man who was still standing raised his club in the air, ready to bring it down once more on his victim's head. But there was no need. The other was safely dead, and all those little shifts and shivers were no more than the dregs of life departing from him. A dark thick red pooled from where his skull had been stove-in.

The murderer, who had been wholly absorbed in his task up to this point, now began to take in his surroundings. Dusk was falling. Shadows were gathering in corners. He glanced uneasily to the right, then the left. There! What was that crouching in the underwood? Whose were those gleaming eyes? Did they belong to a beast of the field – or a human witness? He moved uncertainly in that direction before some sound spun him round to face danger from the opposite quarter. He lifted his club, then lowered it once more.

He waited. Flicked a glance down towards the corpse. Started to realize the need for concealment. Awkwardly, still clutching the club tightly enough to throttle it, he bent down and nudged and tugged the body towards a nearby bush. No time to dispose of it properly. He would leave it to be buried in the maws of kites and crows, of bears and wolves. They would do his filthy work for him.

The murderer left the body part-hidden under the foliage. He turned round and, stooping slightly, began to exit from the scene of his crime. He walked on tiptoe, as if frightened the ground was going to swallow him up. Suddenly he halted.

Slowly . . . slowly . . . he directed his gaze upward as the realization struck home. Above was the arch of the sky, a deep darkening blue. The murderer had been looking in the wrong direction all this time. His yellow beard jutted out from his chin. If I have an enemy, his posture seemed to say, then that enemy is looking down on me from above. At this moment. While I have been thinking myself invisible, he has been watching me. My every move. Worse, he has read my every thought and inspected the chambers of my heart. He has seen my hollowness, my arrogance and anger. Everything was conveyed in the murderer's huddled shoulders, in the limp helplessness of the club swinging between his knees. He seemed to be at once looking upward and downward, to be apprehensive and abject.

Now fear and dread overcame him. He turned back to regard the evidence of his crime, improperly concealed. Tremors ran through the murderer's frame. He made to fling the club away but the haft of it seemed to stick to his hands, to refuse to be released. Then he made to fling himself away. He turned in circles which grew wider and wilder by the instant. He spun round until he collapsed on the ground. Only then did the club fell from his nerveless fingers. He clutched his face with his hands.

What have I done? God hide me from the knowledge of what I have done, from the knowledge of myself.

Oh hide me from God.

But it was no use. At that moment God entered from the right.

At first the murderer, hands covering his face, could not see his Maker. Then, becoming aware he was not alone, he peeped between parted fingers.

God spoke.

He said: "Where is your brother?"

The murderer scrambled to his feet, looked at God in amazement. What brother? his look seemed to say.

But God, undeceived, repeated the question.

"Where is your brother?"

"I know not," said the murderer. "Am I my brother's keeper?"

"What have you done?" said God.

And the murderer followed God's eyes as he looked towards the bush where the body was barely concealed.

"The voice of your brother Abel calls to me. The voice of your brother's blood calls to me from the ground."

The murderer said nothing but tumbled to his knees. As God's sentence fell from his lips, Cain's head slumped forward until his forehead was resting on the ground with his body arched awkwardly above.

"Now you are cursed by the very earth which has opened her mouth to receive the blood of your brother Abel. You are cursed among men, Cain, and the earth shall no longer sustain you. You will be a stranger to it."

Cain's entire body now pressed down on the ground. Our first murderer seemed to be clasping his mother, the earth. But God was unyielding.

"You will be a fugitive and a vagabond on this earth. No place shall be a home to you."

"All men will turn against me," moaned the man on the ground. "All shall curse me, and one will slay me."

He raised his head to look imploringly at his Maker. His beard, bright yellow, the sign of Cain and Judas Iscariot, seemed to gather the last flecks of the disappearing light.

"Not so," said God. "You are doomed to wander out your days and no man may end them before I have determined. Whoever kills Cain, vengeance shall multiply seven times over on that man's head."

And in the gathering dusk God moved forward to put on Cain the mark of sin whereby all men would know the first murderer for what he was and that his punishment was God's alone, not to be usurped by humankind.

God extended his thumb to brand Cain on his forehead.

Then somebody laughed.

It wasn't a pleasant laugh but a wild, mocking cackle. It came from somewhere to my left and nearer the front. God stopped in his progress towards Cain and seemed put out. Darkness was closing in fast and the crowd was a mass of blocky shapes and shadows. The stage in front of us was unilluminated. Obviously, the Paradise Brothers had expected to arrive at the end of their Cain and Abel drama before night closed her curtains round all of us. I doubt that they had so much as a single torch or brand between them. They were bare, unsophisticated fellows, these three players – but for all that, they had a kind of authority. The Paradise brother enacting Cain, for example, had presented a nice mixture of rage and bad conscience. God too had been well personated, although the player's appearance helped. He had a great white beard and a stern brow. Now he gazed into the gloom that filled the market square as the laughter rang out once more, laughter that was raucous and disturbing.

At first I'd thought the cackle was a sign of impatience with the drama unfolding on the makeshift scaffold which was erected in a corner of the square. Someone who'd grown tired of the familiar Bible tale of brother-bashing, and was eager for a jig or a spot of bawdy instead. Certainly, in London the audience wouldn't have permitted so many minutes to pass without a dance or a dirty joke. But then that's the city for you, and we were in the country.

Now there was a disturbance in the crowd as someone pushed his way right to the edge of the scaffold and hoisted himself onto the platform before turning outwards to face the audience. God stood where he was, his right arm held out ready to give Cain his mark. The fratricide still knelt, his forehead tilted up to meet his brand of punishment.

And, even as I waited to see what was going to happen

next, I wondered at the inexperience – the *greenness* – of this little company of players. That they could be put off their action by the mere fact of someone getting up on their makeshift stage. That they did not roundly tell this individual where and how he might dispose of himself. We of the Chamberlain's Company occasionally encounter persons – drunks and show-offs mostly – who believe that our Globe customers prefer to see *them* rather than the players. These people, who want to usurp our places on stage, are soon seen off by an outstretched arm, an outstuck foot or a ribald remark.

But here in the market square these country players were transfixed. Like the crowd, they were waiting to see what the intruder would do next. Even the actor playing dead Abel had twisted round from his position at the edge of the platform to see what was happening. Jack Wilson, standing next to me, nudged me in the ribs in a this-is-going-to-be-good gesture. The individual who was now standing centre-stage staggered slightly and produced a bottle from the folds of his upper garments.

I felt disappointed. A man playing drunk can be amusing enough on the boards but a real drunk is a different kettle of fish, the more tedious in proportion as he believes that what he has to say is of any importance.

Sure enough.

"Snoffair. Snorright. Snoffair."

He stopped, perhaps to allow us to ponder the wisdom of his words.

Jack Wilson whispered in my ear, "He thinks it's not fair, Nick."

"And not right, Jack."

Then, looking round at God, the newcomer proceeded. "Snoffair. You respek Abel 'n' his burnt off'rins yet Cain and his fruits you do not respek."

"He says God doesn't respect – " whispered Jack.

"Shut up," I said. "I can understand drunk as well as you."

"His fruits you – do – not – respek – no," said the man, menacing his Maker with the bottle in his fist. The white-bearded God retreated a step or two. His frown deepened. By now, Abel was upright once more, the side of his face streaked with the sheep's-blood which gave colour to the first murder. The trio of players – God, Cain and Abel – looked affronted. Perhaps I'd been wrong in supposing them green. It was rather that they weren't prepared for interruptions of any kind. They were obviously used to being watched and listened to in respectful silence.

"Fruitsh!" declaimed the drunkard, getting into his slurring stride now and spitting over those lucky enough to be close to the stage. "Fruitsh he hearned honesht by sweat hizbrow and work hissand. Cain ish simple man, Cain ish farmer."

He waved his arm towards the individual who had the part of Cain, and for a moment I wondered whether he'd mistaken the player for the person.

"Me – simple man – farmer – like Cain."

"That's right, Tom," yelled someone to my right. "We know you."

"Why does God not respek farmers? Why does he not respek Cain here?" enquired our plaintive drunk.

"Cain was a killer," hissed someone to my left.

Various noises (assenting, dissenting) from the crowd.

"Shall I tell how he does not respek us?"

More cries and whispers.

Now, this was a group of country folk in the market square. To an outsider, they might appear as so many hobs, clods and clowns. But they seemed to me to be urging on our friend Tom in the expectation of a good show. In this respect at least, they were very like our London audiences at the Globe.

"Thish what he does. When we want rain – sends drought. And when we want shun . . . whassee send?"

He paused as if expecting a reply. When none came, he

said with satisfaction, spluttering over the front rows, "Rain – hail – tempesht."

By now, it was almost completely dark in the square. I'd been wrong to suppose the players didn't possess a torch between them, for suddenly a couple of brands flared up at the edges of the stage. I don't know who lit them and wondered that they wanted to illuminate the proceedings. The smoky brands cast a lurid, wavering glow over Cain and Abel and God who had grouped themselves uneasily about farmer Tom.

"God does not deserve our praise – "

At this there was a collective intake of breath from the crowd. Tom appeared to be on the edge of a blasphemous remark. I was slightly uneasy myself. Next to me, I sensed Jack tense where he stood.

"Not our praise, I shay, but our – "

He got no further because Cain clubbed farmer Tom from behind. This was the very weapon with which he had murdered his brother in play (though not in jest) and if it was not a full-fledged cudgel but a trumpery thing for the stage it was nonetheless weighty enough to fell the farmer. Tom dropped his bottle, pitched forward and almost toppled off the scaffold.

In the darkness there was a stirring.

"Leave him be!" shouted one and another said, "He speaks true."

"You've done for Tom."

This was not the case, fortunately. Almost straightaway Tom pushed himself upright and gazed groggily round as if uncertain where he was or how he'd come there. Then, regrettably, God intervened. Feeling perhaps that he had been slighted by the farmer's words, he came forward and pressed his thumb onto the hapless Tom's forehead, to leave there the mark of fallen, sinful man. But Tom took exception to this treatment and swung out at God with his fist, and at once bedlam broke loose on the stage as the Paradise Brothers piled onto the protesting farmer. They were big men. Arms and legs flailed, there were thumps and groans and oaths.

This was the moment the crowd had been waiting for. The moment when the pieties of drama were finally sent packing by the pleasures of riot. A bunch of onlookers clambered onto the swaying stage to assist in the confusion. Bodies tussled in the dark, illuminated by the flaring torches. The few simple props – a handful of branches representing the underwood where Abel's body was hidden, the canvas rock behind which God had bided his time – were soon being employed as weapons in the fight. Some of those who hadn't yet joined in were obviously considering doing so, while others were trying to hold them back, and smaller scuffles were breaking out around us.

I tugged at Jack Wilson's sleeve.

"Time to leave," I said.

I'd seen enough trouble in the streets of London – with her apprentices steeped in liquor and her superannuated veterans with no skills but those of riot – to know that the best place to be in a brawl is elsewhere.

"Let's wait and see what happens," said Jack.

"No, Jack," I said.

"It's getting interesting."

"No, Jack," I repeated before saying in a manner that, in retrospect, might have been a little lordly. "Nothing interesting can happen. These people are rustics and bumpkins. Just look at them. Witness their taste in plays. Witness the way they have responded to one."

"What was that, my friend?"

The voice came from my right. A thick voice. A rustic, bumpkinish voice.

"Nothing at all," I said, shifting to the left and leaving Jack, if he was so inclined, to face the music. But the press of people and the darkness made it difficult to find my way out and I felt myself being grabbed by the collar.

"Repeat your words, friend," said the voice over my shoulder.

"Let me go first."

"What, and have you run off into the dark. Repeat your words."

The grip on my collar tightened. I could feel the gentleman's raw breath on the back of my neck. I was aware that the two of us were rapidly turning into a little knot of interest for those whose attention wasn't fixed on the stage.

"Which words?"

"The ones about us country folk."

"If you already heard them why do you want me to repeat them?"

"Because – I – say – so."

With each word, he jerked me violently backward and forward by the collar.

"Very well," I said, trying to be dignified about it. I was about to offer some crawling apology to him and his rustic ilk when a silly idea seized me. Though at first I'd wanted to get as far away from the stir in the square as possible, now I felt aggrieved that my words (admittedly slightly injudicious ones) had been snatched out of the air by some eavesdropping yokel. Why should I apologize to this oaf, even if he was breathing down my neck and twisting my collar? Why shouldn't he have the benefit of my real opinion?

"I said that my friend and I were surrounded by individuals of a certain stamp, to wit – "

"I'll to-wit you, my friend, if you don't speak plain English."

" – to wit, clods, hobs and lobs . . . ouf . . ."

He kneed me in the back and I fell forward onto the cobbled ground.

"I haven't finished . . . louts, clouts and clowns . . . ooh! ah!"

That was when he kicked me in the ribs.

And some of those roundabout joined in. Whether they'd

heard what I said and were genuinely offended or whether they simply saw a man curled up on the ground and couldn't resist laying into him, I don't know. As kickings go, it might have been worse. They kept stepping in each other's way so their feet got tangled up and then in the dark they missed me and struck one another. Two or three of them were women, no doubt as provoked as the men by my aspersions on their rusticity.

There's another thing. I'm a player (Nick Revill, at your service) and a player has to know how to take punishment both simulated and real. Why, once when I was doing a brief stint with the Admiral's Men and watching a rehearsal – ever eager in those days to pick up any tips I could – I tumbled out of the gallery of the Rose playhouse and into the groundlings' area. I sustained nothing worse than a few bruises and a burst of applause. And when a player thwacks a player on stage with sword or club, although the blows may not be meant they are not altogether innocent either. So I knew that the secret in a situation like this, where one could do nothing to help oneself straightaway, was to remain supple and passive.

"What – do – you – say – now?" came a voice that I recognized through the roaring in my ears as that of my initial assailant, raw breath.

I said nothing. I tasted blood in my mouth. I wondered what had become of my friend Jack Wilson.

My muteness must have satisfied the little knot of men and women because I sensed them draw back from me. The circle became ragged as one or two quit the scene, perhaps ashamed at what they'd participated in and wanting to avoid trouble. This was my chance. I staggered to my feet and limpingly made off.

No-one tried to stop me. The square was still crowded and thumping noises and swearing continued from the stage. Evidently the battle between players and people wasn't over.

I slipped down one of the lanes that led from this public space.

I didn't know Salisbury. The inn where we of the Chamberlain's Company were putting up for the night was somewhere on the edge of the city but exactly where I couldn't have said. Jack Wilson and I had arrived in the market-place during the last hours of daylight and our attention had been caught by the preparations for staging an open-air drama in a corner. We'd stayed to watch, even though the action unfolding on the bare scaffold was the fustiest, mustiest morality stuff, all to do with Adam and Eve and Cain and Abel. To give us all a taste of what we might expect, the play was preceded by some kind of sermon from the bearded, furrow-browed figure who was later to take the part of God (and whose name I subsequently discovered was Peter Paradise, leader of this fraternal threesome). He hectored and ranted and called us "brothers and sisters" like a puritan. He told us we were accountable to none but God and to have no truck with earthly power and wealth. That's all very well for you, I thought, carting your few paltry possessions from place to place and no doubt living on crusts doled out at back doors, but some us have got livings to make and patrons to please.

Several times Jack and I sneered at the backward taste of the inhabitants of this town. If it hadn't been for the surprisingly high quality of the playing we'd have gone off to join our fellows at the Angel Inn. But a professional always takes pleasure (sometimes of an envious kind) in watching another professional, even when he's working with inferior material. So it was in this case.

Because we were only a little short of midsummer the west yet glimmered with some streaks of day. But then I remembered that we'd entered the town from the east, which was the side the Angel lay on, so I changed course and turned down another street and then once more until I found myself back in the market-place. Usually I have a good sense of direction, know my east from my west, &c., but the beating I'd sustained at the hands (or feet) of the locals had muddied my brain. Warily, I skirted the square. The fighting seemed to have stopped but people were still milling about in the gloom. I spat to clear my mouth of blood. One side of my face felt raw where it had scraped the cobbles. I wasn't hurt – or not much – but I'd be glad enough to get back among my fellows and to slide into bed. Though not before I'd roundly rebuked friend Wilson for his flight from the field.

Fortunately, there was one way to establish my rough whereabouts in the town. There is a great church here in Salisbury, greater than any such edifice in London, indeed the greatest church I have ever seen. As tall as Babel tower, it looks roomy enough to house half the town. Its spire shoots heavenward like an arrow, as if impatient to be rid of the earth. Crossing the last few miles of downland that afternoon, we'd kept our eyes on the spire glinting in the sun and guiding us to our destination for the night. This mighty church lies a little to the southward side of the town. So, I reasoned, if I kept it on my right hand I'd be able to find my way back to the street of the Angel Inn. There were a few passengers out and about in the side-streets but my recent experiences of how they regarded outsiders – admittedly, an outsider who had said some provoking things – made me reluctant to ask for directions.

Down the end of the road which I was now travelling I could glimpse, above the roof-tops, the arrow-like spire, its slender form slipping upward into the twilight. So ... if I crossed into this small street ... and then turned left ... no, right ... or perhaps straight across and down that alley? I gasped as a sudden pain seized me in the side. I was not hurt, not much hurt, but I had to rest for a moment to recover from the insolence of the beating I'd received. If I got my hands on that raw-breathed fellow who'd kneed me in the back and then encouraged the bystanders to add their pennyworth, he'd know what it was to ...

All at once I found myself on my knees in the middle of the highway, retching. A yellow and red taste in my mouth. Bile and blood. But not much. Ah, that was better. Nevertheless, I needed to stop for a moment to consider the way forward, or rather the way back to the Angel Inn, otherwise I'd be wandering around Salisbury until daybreak. There was a convenient doorway . . . yes, that one over there, with a sheltering porch. I crawled on hands and knees to the porch and hid myself in there.

It was dark, it was secure, and I must have fallen asleep for a few moments, because the next thing I knew was that a light was hovering in the air in front of me.

I put up my hand to shield my eyes. The lantern was shifted to one side but a firm, dry hand grasped mine and pulled it away from my face.

"Let's have a look at you."

Through half-closed lids I was aware of a large looming face.

"Ah yes," it said.

"What?" I said.

"You are not from these parts."

"Oh God, you're not going to beat me up too?"

By now I'd fully opened my eyes and realized that my question was absurd. Crouching down in front of me was a man of middle years with a greying spade beard and mild grey eyes. He was wearing a nightgown. I was able to see so much because, in addition to the lantern which he'd placed on the ground, the door to the house was open and there was another figure in the entrance, dressed in white and holding a candle.

"I . . . I was on my way to the Angel Inn. Perhaps you can direct me to it?"

I made to get up, and the man hooked his hand under my arm and helped me to my feet.

"The Angel is in Greencross Street. A few dozens of paces from here."

"Thank you, then I'll be on my way."

But I made no move and I don't think the grey-bearded man expected me to.

"Will your company be anxious that you're late?" he said.

"Company?"

"Your fellow players."

"Not them," I said. "As long as I'm there for the set-off tomorrow morning they'll not trouble themselves about where I am tonight. They'll think I've found me a – "

Some sense of delicacy made me break off, and the grey-beard said, "In that case you'd better come inside and take some refreshment. Can you walk unaided?"

"Thank you, yes."

"Follow me then."

He led the way into the house, the figure with the candle having by this time disappeared. He ushered me into a parlour, delaying in the passage for a moment to call out "Martin!" Candles were already burning on a table where a pile of papers and a clutch of pens were neatly arranged. I guessed I had interrupted my host in the middle of some business. He motioned me to a nearby chair. As I sat down I groaned involuntarily.

"My dear sir, you are hurt."

"Not at all," I said "or only slightly. A loudmouth's penalty."

"There's blood upon your face. A little blood."

"Only mine."

A stocky man appeared in the doorway.

"I can offer you cider," said my host, "or perhaps purging beer would be better for your case."

"Cider," I said rapidly. I wasn't at all sure what purging beer was and didn't like the sound of it.

The grey-bearded gentleman gave the order to the servant and then sat down at the table. He pushed a couple of candles nearer to me, apparently for my convenience but really, I think, to make a more careful assessment of what he saw.

"You were about to ask who you had the honour of addressing," he said.

I was, but even so his quickness took me by surprise and I simply nodded.

"My name is Adam Fielding, citizen of Salisbury."

This time I nodded more slowly.

"Nicholas Revill," I said formally. "I'm – "

I stopped because he'd raised his hand.

"Wait."

He leaned forward and squinted through the candle-smoke. As he cast his grey eyes up and down my front I became a little uneasy at his scrutiny. I wanted to wipe away the blood from wherever it was staining my face but didn't move.

Then he sat back and smiled.

"Don't worry, Master Revill. It's only a little occupation of mine."

"What is?"

"To, ah, see what someone is before he speaks what he is."

"And what do you see, sir?" I said, prepared to humour this kindly gent.

At that point Martin returned with tankards of cider for his master and me. Fielding waited until the servant had gone and I'd had my first sip. Until I tasted the cider I hadn't realized how tired and thirsty I was.

"This is made from my own apples. Pomewater. But you were asking what I could see."

I nodded, then abruptly remembered that he'd mentioned my "company" on the doorstep. How had he found out about them?

"Well, Master Revill, you are a player, one of a travelling group newly arrived from London and currently lodging at the Angel Inn on Greencross Street."

I almost spilled my cider.

"Don't be alarmed," said my host. "This I knew already. I am a Justice of the Peace for this town. One of our duties, as you surely know, is to license and superintend the visits which players make."

"We are not playing here, your worship," I said, to show that I knew the proper form of address for such a dignified gentleman. "We're only travelling through."

"No, the only company licensed to play these many weeks is the Paradise Brothers. They put on Bible stories and old morality pieces."

"I know. I saw them in the market-place."

"And you belong to the Chamberlain's Company, so I imagine you'd have little time for the kind of thing which the Paradise Brothers present."

"They are – professional enough," I said. "How do you know I belong to the Chamberlain's?"

"No magic," said Fielding, although I sensed that he was enjoying taking me a little by surprise. "In a town like this, probably a small town to your London eyes, a Justice of the Peace makes it his business to know what is going on. Besides, the sister of my man Martin is married to the landlord of the Angel."

"Oh," I said, vaguely disappointed. "So that's it then."

Again the parlour door opened. This time it was the figure who'd stood, candle in hand, at the front doorway while I lay slumped there. She crossed the floor and moved towards where I was sitting. She was wearing a night-rail that concealed her shape but her face in the diffused light had a youthful sweetness, a quiet beauty. She carried a tray containing a bowl of water and a small pot and one or two other items.

Fielding had his back to her but smiled to hear her approach.

"My dear," he said, "this is Nicholas Revill, who has fetched up on our doorstep. Master Revill, my daughter Kate."

I made to rise, but she put a restraining hand on my arm.

"Please, Master Revill, stay still. I can see that you are tired – and that you have injured yourself."

Ah, the softness and understanding of women!

"My own fault," I said, "the injury, I mean."

Kate the daughter placed the tray on the table. She dipped a cloth in the bowl of water and dabbed at my face to clear the crusted blood. I bore up bravely, though in truth I might have withstood her ministrations for longer, much longer. I could smell her sweet breath. All this while Adam Fielding, her father, gazed approvingly at her and her actions. When she'd done with the cloth, she turned once more to the table and dipped her fingers into the small pot. She smeared the unguent on one side of my face, explaining that it was a tincture for bruising and cuts, made with plantain leaves. It stung slightly. But this too I might have borne for longer, much longer. Her slender fingers seemed to have a healing touch of their own. I could sense the warmth of her body beneath the white night-rail she wore.

I wondered whether she was doing this of her own accord or whether her father had sent her off to fetch these salves when he first saw me at his door. I rather fancied – that is, I hoped – she was doing it of her own accord.

"There," she said.

"Thank you," I said, wondering whether to make some crack about how I'd been looking for my night's lodging but had found the Angel in another guise and place. However, I kept my mouth closed, perhaps because her father was still looking at us though he had so far said nothing. Also, there are some women who are immune to my wit.

"I'm going to bed now, father," she said. "Don't stay up too late talking to our visitor."

This remark, which on paper looks rather impudent, even from an adult child to a parent, was delivered fondly and received with an indulgent smile by Fielding.

When she'd gone, he said, "Now where was I?" but in a

way that suggested he knew exactly where he was. Sure
enough: "Ah yes, I was telling you about yourself. Humour
an old man if you would. There's more, you see."

"More, sir?"

"More, Master Revill. Let us see. You are not originally
from London but have lived there for a year perhaps. Your
roots are in the west, further west than here . . ."

"From a village near Bristol. And it's two years in London,"
I said, a little aggravated that my voice still betrayed my
origins. Fielding must have a good ear.

And a good eye and brain as it turned out.

"You've been walking today at the front of your company,"
he continued, "with the wagon full of props and costumes
trundling at the rear, where it was probably accompanied by
the more senior players. You, though, would have kept pace
with a fellow player of about your own age."

"Go on," I said, half smiling and sipping at my cider.

"You also thought occasionally and fondly – but not over-
fondly – of she whom you had left behind."

I sat up a little straighter at this.

"Because you are away from the city, thoughts of your
parents most likely crossed your mind too – "

How on earth did he know that?

" – particularly of your father, the parson."

At this I almost dropped my tankard on the floor.

I didn't have to voice the question which appeared on my
face.

Adam Fielding, Justice of the Peace, looked gratified at the
effect he'd produced.

"You have an informant," I said hopefully, "not a servant's
sister but a cousin or a grandfather in the church perhaps?"

He shook his head

"Then how?"

"It's surprising how much information we give away gratis
and unawares, Master Revill."

"I said nothing, next to nothing, your worship."

"There's no such thing as saying nothing. Let me explain. I know already that you are a member of the Chamberlain's Company spending the night here at the Angel. Therefore you must have completed your journey to Salisbury this afternoon. I'm familiar with the disposition of travelling companies, how the costumes and so on are borne in wagons while the poor players stumble along on foot."

"We players are the least of it," I said. "Our tire-man tells us again and again that people pay to see his robes, not our bodies."

"As a youthful member of the Company, you'd have walked a bit quicker than average. And it's unlikely you'd walk alone. Players are naturally gregarious. Also, I can see that the chalk kicked up from the way is still dusting your shoes while your front and leggings are pretty clear of marks – which certainly wouldn't have been the case if you'd been walking at the back. There you'd've had to contend with all the dust thrown up by the others."

"Well and good," I said. "But how did you know my thoughts – some of my thoughts?"

Fielding smiled and took a long pull from his tankard of cider.

"The woman you left behind, you mean?"

"Oh there may be one," I said, thinking of my whore Nell.

"Any young man who's been in London a year or so will have furnished himself with a paramour – unless there's something strange or unnatural about him. And there doesn't look to be anything strange or unnatural about you, Master Revill."

(Was this a compliment – or a slight slight? I couldn't tell.)

"When he's away, a young man's mind will naturally turn to the girl he's left behind. On the other hand, after that year or so with her and on a journey out of the city he will be ready for other adventures too. He'll consider her fondly – but not over fondly, I think."

"I – yes, you've described my state almost exactly," I said, remembering how little, really, I'd thought of Nell on our three days' tramp from London, and becoming almost ashamed of this.

"That's because I've been in it myself," said Fielding. "I too left a woman behind when I quit the city for the first time."

"What happened to her?"

"Ah . . . " was all he said.

"You said my father was a parson."

"I was right?"

There was something almost touching in his eagerness to be proved correct.

"Yes, you're right enough, he was."

"Was?"

"Both my parents perished when the plague struck our little village . . . I was away at the time."

"And so you were preserved."

"It was God preserved me, my father would have said. But how did you know his calling? You must have secret powers of divination."

"No magic, no mystery. You confirmed my guess by your surprised reaction when I mentioned it. But even before that, you said you'd come from a village near Bristol. Now, you're obviously an educated young man, and education in a village is normally confined to the offspring of the parson, the squire or the schoolmaster."

"So why shouldn't I be the squire's son – or the schoolmaster's?"

"You might have had the schoolmaster for a father. But the squire, I think not. Forgive me, Master Revill, if I say that the son of a man of, ah, substance will usually find himself discouraged from joining a band of players."

"True enough," I said. "There's not much respect in playing even nowadays – or much revenue either, for a squire's son."

"So why do you do it?" said Fielding, looking at me shrewdly over the rim of his tankard.

"I'm not sure. Perhaps the best I can say is that it's with me as it was with my father, a calling."

I regretted the words almost as soon as they were out of my mouth and was only glad that none of my Company was about to catch them. I could already hear the scorn which such high sentiments would receive – and deservedly.

"Though not such a high a calling as your father's. You will save no souls from the eternal bonfire," said the Justice of the Peace. "Nor will you guide any up that steep and thorny path to salvation."

"I leave that to others, like the whatyecallem Brothers in the market-place this evening. I'm content merely to divert people on the way up or down, whatever their destination. It's none of my business."

"Well, that is what you think now," said Fielding.

"And what I also think now, sir, is that I have an early set-off to make tomorrow morning so, if you don't mind, I should be on the way back to my inn and my fellows. Not that they'll trouble themselves over my absence – "

"Because they'll conclude you've found one of our Salisbury whores for the night," said Fielding.

I coloured slightly. "I forbore to say it on your doorstep but yes, that's probably what they would think."

"I thank you, Master Revill, if you were protecting my daughter's ears but I think she would have been amused rather than otherwise."

I stored away this piece of information for future consideration (and possible use) while I rose from the table. Adam Fielding accompanied me to the door, making small host-like queries about my well-being. He told me how to find my way to the Angel Inn and then shook my hand.

"I'm surprised you haven't asked where we're going tomorrow," I said. "Or perhaps you know already."

"I do," he said. "In fact, I will be there myself at the appointed time."

"The appointed time?"

"I look forward to seeing you, Master Revill, on midsummer's eve."

"And your daughter?" I said, greatly daring.

"Oh, I am sure she will be gratified to see you too."

Since he'd indirectly answered my question I said no more but gave him good night and walked off in the direction he'd indicated. Light seems to tease the sky even in the middle of a fine June night and so I found my way to the Angel with ease. The house was shuttered and dark, and I had to rouse one of the ostlers who was sleeping in a crib near the horses, and accommodated rather worse than his charges. In exchange for a half-penny the boy showed me the whereabouts of the back window which was kept unclasped for late-returning customers.

My Company was divided between a couple of rooms on the upper floor and I gratefully climbed into the bed which I was sharing with Jack Wilson. In other circumstances, he might have heard my opinion of his cowardly behaviour in the market-place but he was asleep, or pretending to be. In any case, I told myself, if it hadn't been for my unfortunate encounter with the local who took exception to my description of him and his kind, I'd never have met Adam Fielding, Justice of the Peace, or his daughter Kate.

The next morning we made the early start that was customary on tour. This was my first expedition out of London but after a few days on the road I'd rapidly grown used to the pattern. We woke, dressed, swallowed our bread and ale, and set off soon after first light. We walked for most of the morning, pausing towards midday for refreshment in a tavern (if one happened to lie in our path) or finding a sheltered or shaded spot and making do with whatever small provisions we carried. After a short rest – more for the luckless horse which pulled our wagon than for ourselves – we continued our journey for the better part of the afternoon, aiming to reach that night's destination in time for an early supper. Eating done, our time was our own. If we found ourselves in a town or even a large village we might walk around, looking to be diverted. This is what Jack and I had been doing when we'd stumbled across the Paradise Brothers' presentation of the Cain and Abel story in Salisbury market-place.

All the time I'd been watching that simple morality piece I'd thanked my lucky stars that I was with a great company like the Chamberlain's. We didn't have to wander about, enduring make-shift scaffolds and a paucity of props, together with country audiences who could afford no better. No, when the Chamberlain's Company went touring we didn't set up in any old hole or corner, but played the greatest towns, the grandest houses, the finest audiences. Nor did we have to endure the law's delay or the insolence of office in the shape of self-important justices and aldermen imposing terms and conditions on what might or not be enacted in front of *their* citizens. No doubt they weren't all like that – indeed, my new acquaintance Adam Fielding didn't fit the description in any way. But in the country one has the expectation that everything is going to be a little slower and more awkward. Why even the rain in the shires hasn't quite got the greasy polish of the London variety!

You may see from the above that I am truly country-born and bred.

Every company of players must tour, however. Why should a good thing be confined to the capital? There are more practical considerations too: you can be driven from London for a time, by an outbreak of plague or by the Council's equally plaguey edict. You might want to withdraw yourself briefly from the easily-sated gaze of the Londoner, knowing that he will welcome you the more avidly (though without showing it, of course) on your triumphant return. And sometimes a company of players has a very particular commission to carry out. So it was with us as we proceeded north-west of Salisbury.

I liked to imagine that our players' tour had something in common with a royal progress. No huge entourage or strings of sumpter mules of course. But still a ceremonial advance across the land, the breathless expectation of town and village, the gratification of the inhabitants, their sense that something special had descended to touch their mundane lives. Or so I liked to imagine . . .

However, if you'd actually seen us as we trudged along the the trackway which crossed the wide plain to the north of Salisbury, you might have thought we were no more than a band of tinkers. In the middle of our group lumbered the wagon containing the properties, the stage-cloth and other necessaries. These items, as I'd said to Adam Fielding, were considerably more valuable than mere players, and were carefully stowed and protected from the weather by tar-coated canvas sheets. Up on the wagon sat William Fall, the 'carter' and also one of our Company, who claimed this high position by virtue of the fact that his late father drove for a livelihood. He frequently stated that he would have earned more money by carting than playing the boards. To the carter fell the additional responsibility of caring for the horse, except when we put up at an inn where it became the ostler's charge. Our nag was familiarly called Flem – on account, I suppose, of its being a Flanders draught horse. But the name was fitting because it wheezed and coughed a great deal, and altogether behaved as though this journey might be its last.

Beside William Fall sat one of the two seniors on the tour, each man taking it in half-day turns to relieve his trudging feet. This morning, as we headed out of Salisbury, the reserved Richard Sincklo was sitting next to Fall. It was the responsibility of this high-up traveller to ensure we were going in the right direction – no great task so far since the road from London to Salisbury was clearly enough marked, and at this time of year there were plenty of groups moving both ways. For this last stage in our progress, when we were wandering a little off the beaten track, Master Sincklo had taken care to establish our precise route before we left the Angel.

Our walking group split into contingents fore and aft of the wagon. The younger ones tended to stride ahead and the older and wiser to lag behind, at least in the day's beginning. So I frequently found myself in the van with my friend Jack Wilson.

This sunny morning I teased and twitted him about his desertion of me on the previous evening and he took it all in good part. In truth, I wasn't too troubled. At the cost of a few cuts and bruises, I'd made the acquaintance of a Justice of the Peace and his dark-haired daughter, been soothed by her healing hands, and been told that we were likely to meet again. That, combined with the prospect of the special performance which we were to give in a few days' time, gave a glow to the midsummer morning. The view ahead was fair. I even took a quiet pleasure in being back among hills and dales after an extended stay in the city. Not that I'd ever admit to it of course . . .

"Hills and dales" wasn't exactly the right description of the terrain we were crossing. The land to the north of Salisbury is high, flat and bare. It is curiously dotted with mounds and long low shapes, as though the earth were a green quilt pulled over an ill-made bed. The sky is huge. Overhead sing the invisible larks while clouds of butterflies and other tiny summer creatures dance attendance on you.

Jack nudged me and said "Look", and I thought at first he was trying to distract me from mocking him. But then my eyes followed his pointing finger and I stopped dead in my tracks. Several hundred paces away to our right there stood a great pile of stones. In the morning sun, they reared up like the dark ribs of a giant's house or lay on the ground as if that same giant had tossed them carelessly aside as unsuitable for his purpose. Some of them, with upright posts and lintels laid haphazard on top and the sky visible between, were constructed like titanic doorways. Gazing longer at these mighty stones, I realized they were arranged in a kind of circle: this was no chance collection but one put there for a purpose, and by a race of beings which was mightier than any in our current fallen world. I grew a little afraid in the openness of the plain, until I heard a laugh from the wagon which had by now drawn level with Jack and me.

"You know what those are?"

It was Richard Sincklo sitting up beside Will Fall. Serious, reserved Richard seemed amused at my amazement.

"No," I said. "I have never seen anything like it."

"I first passed this way many years ago," said Master Sincklo. "I too wondered at the standing stones."

He looked round. By now, the whole band, near enough twenty of us, had gathered round to hear Master Sincklo's explanation.

"They say," he said, "that those stones were brought from Ireland by Merlin the wizard in the time of King Arthur."

"Why?" said someone.

"To commemorate those who had fallen in a battle," said Sincklo.

"So they do," said someone else.

"It's a story that will do as well as any other," said Richard Sincklo, clapping Master Fell on the shoulder as a signal to prod Flem into motion once more. Our little caravan moved on.

I stayed behind for a moment to stare at the stone circle. I didn't altogether believe Sincklo's explanation, but I didn't disbelieve it either. During the time of King Arthur, many extraordinary things had fallen out in this realm. At that moment, a cloud flew across the sun and darkened the stones further. Now they looked like teeth.

I shivered slightly, and ran on to join my fellows.

But that was not the end of the morning's strange sights.

We walked a little further and descended from the high

plain. We entered a wooded place, and the path narrowed so that the company naturally straggled out. After the airiness of the plain the forest felt enclosed, the full-leaved branches almost closing in over our heads. Beams of sunlight slanted through where they could manage it. Now I was trailing in the rear of the group, the nearest man a couple of dozen paces to the front. All at once, with a prickling sensation on my nape, I became conscious of being watched. If you're a player this is a well-honed response, and generally an agreeable one. Or at least not disagreeable. This time it was definitely unpleasant. I glanced furtively over my shoulder and then, rebuking myself for cutting such a shifty figure, stopped and turned round to make sure that I was indeed the last of our ragged procession. Behind me the path curled innocently round a corner.

But there was nothing, nobody.

By the time I'd turned back again, the one or two players to the rear of our group had moved out of sight round the next bend. I was, for the moment, all alone in the wood.

I put on a little speed to catch up with the fellow in front, Laurence Savage I think it was. Not wanting to appear anxious or winded, I walked on just a bit more briskly, head erect, shoulders tense, looking straight ahead. Still the prickling sensation continued. Despite my quicker pace I couldn't catch up. The track through the wood took on a more snaky quality, with a new curve every few paces. The trees clustered more closely, as if trying to blot out the pale thread of path which separated them. At every bend, I hoped to come on a straight stretch and glimpse the diminishing backs of my friends. But all I gained was a few more yards of empty path hemmed in by walls of green.

Then I wondered whether I'd somehow wandered off the right path onto some side-track. Yes, that must be it, of course. I stopped, breathed deep and listened. Listened for someone shouting, speaking, laughing. For the creak of the wagon or the wheezing of the luckless Flem, sounds which must surely carry back to me if the company was just ahead. Nothing, only the leaves rustling and the sound of something sliding in the undergrowth. I must have lost the right path, I told myself, though I couldn't remember where it had forked. However, it should be simple enough to retrace my steps and . . .

For some reason the image of the mighty stone circle which we'd seen on the plain came into my mind. And with that came the thought of the beings who had built it, no ordinary men to be sure.

Then I saw it.

Saw it move in the corner of my eye.

Something whitish among the trees, off to my left.

I tried to tell myself that it was a trick of the light. I moved a few steps forward. The white shape moved with me, on the edge of my vision.

I stopped. So did the figure.

With a great effort of will, I turned to the left in order to confront it head-on. I peered into the woods. Their innards were flecked with light where the sun penetrated, and there were infinite shades of green among the darker tones. Was it one of these, or a chance grouping of them, which I'd taken for the shape?

I cleared my throat, wondering whether to ask if there was anyone there. I stayed silent, not wanting to appear foolish. Then, considering that it was foolish to worry about appearing foolish (after all, who was there to witness me?), I said: "Who's there?" The words came out less crisp than I intended. But there was no answer, to my relief, and I did not repeat them.

Once again I strode off, and once again the white form gathered to my left and kept pace with me, slipping and sliding among the trees as I walked increasingly fast down the path. Now I started to run, forgetting myself and forgetting too that I had taken a different path from my comrades and that each bound must be taking me further away from them.

My only instinct was to break clear of this accursed wood and reach the open spaces of the plain. But the frequent bends in the path made it hard to get up speed and all the time I could see – or feel rather than see – the pale shape in the woods gliding along smoothly beside me. Sweat began to run down into my eyes and that, combined with the twistiness of the path, caused me to blunder several times into bushes and overhanging boughs.

Then, just as panic was about to leap on my shoulders, I came to a clearing. And there, lounging in scattered groups, were my fellows in the Chamberlain's. I had been following the right path all the time! The property wagon stood in the centre of the glade while a hobbled Flem grazed nearby. Since there was no tavern on the road, this was evidently the place we'd decided to halt for our midday rest. The repast was simple, in fact the same as breakfast, a little bread and ale. The sun shone down on our pastoral scene. All that was missing was a warbling bard or a shepherd tootling on his reedy pipe.

So into the glade bursts a red-faced, dishevelled Nicholas Revill. A few faces turn but most are too busy chewing or chatting. Some have already laid themselves down for a nap.

I stumbled into a group that included Jack Wilson and Laurence Savage, who had been the hindmost man in the column apart from myself.

"Why, Nick, what's the matter with you?" said Laurence. "Are you all right?"

Jack grinned, perhaps not displeased to see me discomfited. (I'd spent much of the morning ribbing him about his flight from the market-square.)

"Yes," I said breathlessly. "Fine."

"If you didn't look so hot and bothered, I'd say that you must have seen a ghost," said Laurence Savage.

"I – I thought there was something in the woods."

Jack and Laurence and a couple of the others gazed back at the point where the path entered the clearing. On either side the blank green walls of the wood returned their stares. A gentle breeze ruffled the topmost branches. Overhead the sky was clear and calm. The eye of heaven beamed down benevolently.

"What sort of thing?" said a third member of the group, Michael Donegrace, one of our boy players.

"Oh I don't know," I said, slightly embarrassed now. "All imagination, I dare say."

And indeed now, sitting in the open with my friends and fellow players, and helping myself to some of the proffered bread and ale, and feeling the sun drying my sweaty face while my heart and lungs settled back into their normal rhythm, I did consider that it was all imagination. (Probably.) For sure, when I'd actually scrutinized the trees, I had seen nothing. A man alone in the middle of a wood, even on a fine summer's morning, may see and hear all sorts.

"I expect it was the gentleman you had the discussion with in the square last night," said Jack. "A woody spirit if ever I saw one. He probably wanted to continue your talk – with the aid of a branch torn from the nearest tree."

The others laughed, and I saw that my little escapade had got round the circle. Only Nick Revill shooting his mouth off again. And now he says he's seeing things in the woods. I decided to keep quiet.

I smiled, joining in the laughter against myself, shrugged and lay down on the grass. The sun warmed my face and, at intervals, the breeze cooled it.

After a while our rest was finished so we rose and resumed our walk.

Nearly there, Richard Sincklo informed us. He had surrendered his position on the wagon to Thomas Pope, another of the seniors, as we covered the final stages of our journey.

We arrived a couple of hours later. The woods had thinned out but we had not returned to the open uplands of the first part of the day. Rather we'd passed through more comfortable-looking pastures and a small village called, someone said, Rung Withers. I don't know how he knew this. A few of the locals came out to gawp and we waved cheerfully back. Eventually we came to the borders of a large estate and knew without being told that this was our destination.

In the distance we saw Instede House. It was set on a slight rise in the ground as if to say, look at me. To one side there glimmered a little lake.

"Do you suppose that our Queen has slept here?" said Laurence Savage to me as we paced together behind the property wagon.

"I don't know. I suppose she has. They say she's slept in every great house in the land."

"That is why these great men build such great houses," said Laurence. "So that she may find a palace wherever she turns in her kingdom."

"She will not be journeying much more, I think," I said.

I thought of the ageing figure I'd been presented to a few months previously.* The greatest of ladies – but also now an old woman. I was awed at being in the same chamber as our sovereign. But even though I was tongue-tied much of the time, I could see that close beneath her silver skin lay the skull. No, our Queen Elizabeth would make no more drawn-out progresses through her realm. For some reason, I forbore to talk about my interview with the Queen. It was partly because of what had happened afterwards but it was also because – as I knew from my friend Nell's sceptical reaction – that people's first inclination if I mentioned it was to disbelieve that a mere player might be summoned to meet the sovereign. Yet, such things we'd talked of in our brief discourse, the Queen and I!

"Sorry?" I said. Wrapped up in my memories, I hadn't heard Laurence's words.

"I said, this is the imposthume of much wealth."

* see *Death of Kings*

He waved his hand in the direction of Instede House, which however steadily we marched towards it didn't appear to be getting much larger. Not that it wasn't large enough already. It glinted like a jewel on our horizon. Now we were passing the little lake.

"I don't quite – "

"Master Shakespeare's words, not mine. The imposthume of much wealth and peace. You remember Hamlet?"

"How could I forget him?" I said. And then the lines came back to me, something said by Prince Hamlet near the end of the action as he's about to depart for England. On the subject of Fortinbras and his reasons for going to war. As if too much prosperity and tranquillity cause men to hanker after their opposites. Wondering if I was ever to be allowed to escape from that play, I quoted our playwright's own words:

"'*This is th'imposthume of much wealth and peace,*
That inward breaks, and shows no cause without
Why the man dies.'"

"Why, Nicholas," said Laurence, "you have them off pat."

"A proud swelling," I said, regarding the great edifice before us. "Yes, I suppose that would describe it."

"A monstrous carbuncle," said Laurence.

"But an elegant one," I added.

"No doubt," he said. "A fair testament to foul pride and vanity. Elcombe's pride."

I was taken aback to hear Laurence Savage speak in this fashion. Despite his surname, he was usually the mildest-mannered of men. He had a round inoffensive face, with an incongruous cowlick of dark hair falling over his forehead. His features were oddly characterless – one of the things that made him good on stage, I suppose. When he spoke, his words were almost invariably gentle, even appeasing. Witness the way he'd enquired whether I was all right after I stumbled out of the forest. By a paradox familiar to players, his personal mildness made him fitting for dark roles, parts such as the poisoner, the smiler with the knife, the man you would not suspect.

So his comments about Lord Elcombe's "foul pride and vanity" took me by surprise. Since Elcombe, the owner of Instede House, was our patron for the moment, and we were dependent upon his hospitality and goodwill for the next few days, it seemed unwise – or at least premature – to speak in such critical terms of the gentleman. I was curious at the causes of it, particularly as I knew next to nothing of our host.

"What do you know about Elcombe?" I said as we walked up the long straight ride leading to Instede House.

"Know?" replied Laurence. "I know that he is a great man, which is to say a proud one. He is the possessor of this fine pile before us, which he inherited from his father though I believe he has mightily improved it. The said father was a youngster at the court of the old king and cut from the same cloth as that luxurious monarch."

"It was another age," I said.

"Then to bring you up to the present," resumed Laurence, "the current Lord Elcombe possesses an older son by the name of Harry and a younger one by some other name. The said elder son is contracted to marry a young woman whose name I cannot at present call to mind if I ever knew it, and the nuptials are to take place in a few days' time, and an obscure company of players called, let me see, the Chamberpots has been invited to participate in the nuptials, or rather in the revels which are to garland them, by putting on a performance of a play by someone or other, Master Shakeshaft or Sceneshift, is it?" He paused for breath. "There, will that do?"

"Well enough," I said, "though you have omitted the name of the play."

"Oh, a *Madsinner's Night's Dram* or something similar."

"Almost to the letter," I said. "But where is the foul pride and vanity here? I do not see it. The son of a rich man is getting married. Banquets and feasts will be had, and crumbs will fall from his table, and poor folk like we players will stoop to gather them up. Now tell me if you know anything else of Lord Elcombe, besides all this which is common knowledge?"

"I have no knowledge which is out of the common," said Laurence evasively. "Except one thing perhaps."

I waited, knowing that this is the surest way of getting a man to tell you you a secret. There was a pause, then Laurence asked an odd question.

"Do you know who is playing your Demetrius?"

Now, the part I was playing in our play (*A Midsummer Night's Dream*, of course) was that of Lysander, one of the young lovers who flee to the Athens woods. There are a brace of young men, Lysander and Demetrius, as well as a pair of girls – Hermia and Helena – for them to fall in and out of love with. The *Dream* is stuffed with lovers but you'll recognize us, boy and girl both, by our youthful, unfledged quality. I didn't know who was playing Demetrius, as it happened, but assumed that it had to be one of the four or five of our Company whose looks and general address fitted them for the part.

So I said to Laurence, "No, I don't know who's Demetrius. It's not you, is it?"

Laurence almost laughed at this, which I took for a negative. (In truth he would have been most unsuitable for a young lover.)

"Who is it then?"

"Ah."

"Tell me, Master Savage."

What I didn't know about three minutes before, and hadn't lost any sleep over not knowing, abruptly became very important. Forgetting my recent belief that the best way to get information is not to press for it, I badgered Laurence to tell me: who was playing Demetrius, my co-sufferer and rival in love?

"Ask Richard Sincklo," he said. "He'll tell you."

"Which means that you could, just as easily."

"No, you ask Sincklo, it's his job."

And with that I had to be content, even though the question continued to nag at me.

Like a hill which you've been walking towards for hours and which seems to grow no larger and then suddenly swells to fill your vision, so it was with Instede House. All of a sudden we entered the formal gardens that were laid out around the mansion. Once, great houses were built like castles – in fact, once great houses *were* castles – and it is perhaps a measure of the fat and pursy times in which we live that powerful men feel safe now and no longer need to fence themselves in with moats and battlements. Concealment has been replaced by ostentation. Maybe I was infected by Laurence Savage's impatient, even contemptuous attitude towards Instede and its owner, for these were among the first thoughts that went through my mind as we covered the final distance towards the house.

The great oblong face seemed more glass than wall, although the cold sheen of the windows was offset by the warm stone of the frontage. At the corners were little towers: slim, elegant features that my lady might have sketched out for the builders after they came into her mind while she was lounging in bed one morning. Before we could get too near to the main entrance, a liveried figure approached our little convoy and spoke to Master Pope, who was sitting up on the wagon beside William Fall. No doubt the servant was enquiring after our business. Anyway, we changed direction and moved parallel to the house and then turned again to go down one flank of Instede. It was like circumnavigating some island in the main, I imagine, searching for a favourable landing-point. I have been in some of London's great houses – have even been a guest in one or two – but they seemed pinched and constrained in contrast to this magnificent edifice. Eventually, after rounding yet another corner, we fetched up at an entrance which was suitable for players and other riff-raff. That is, it was slightly less grand than the rest.

We found ourselves in an inner courtyard. Our seniors, Messrs Sincklo and Pope, now engaged in earnest conversation with a stick-like individual whom I took to be a steward. I stood back with Laurence Savage and Jack Wilson and the others, happy enough to wait for instructions. Oh, we knew our places.

Eventually, the property wagon drawn by Flem was led off by one of the servants while the steward beckoned us with a haughty long-armed wave to attend him. Sincklo and Pope went first and we followed. We entered by a low doorway, which restricted us to single file, and then almost immediately started to mount some stairs. I've never climbed so many stairs in my life. One flight was succeeded by another until it seemed as though we must be due to scrape heaven. At last we fetched up in a long dusty dormitory which, by its slanting ceiling, roughcast walls and squinty windows, occupied the very topmost storey of Instede. Lines of trestle beds stretched down both sides of the room. This, we gathered from our superior conductor, was our place. His name was Oswald Eden and it was apparent from his words and manner that he had a low view of players.

"Well, gentlemen, dispose yourselves as you please. You are generously housed here, above your deserts though it may be."

He had a dry voice, like dead leaves scraping across a yard. His arms, I noted, were almost abnormally long. They fitted his stick shape.

"Account yourselves fortunate," added this magnanimous man.

I was surprised that our seniors didn't bridle under this treatment. If Master Shakespeare or Dick Burbage had been with us, surely they would have put the fellow in his place. Why, they'd only have to tell him that we had played – and played regularly – before the Queen and her Court to assure him of our quality. And after all, we weren't interlopers; we had been *invited* down to this remote (albeit grand) pile. But Sincklo and Pope seemed to accept the steward's high-handedness. Perhaps it amused them. But me it angered, and I said as much to Laurence Savage.

"The man is often mightier than the master," he replied. "Though in Elcombe's case the master is mighty enough."

Anyway, the steward soon left us alone to settle into our new quarters. At the top of this great house the air hung hot and heavy, where it had been stewing all day underneath the leads. Motes of dust swayed idly in the sun's beams. It was the kind of afternoon that seems a rehearsal for eternity. Two or three of our number lay down on the narrow beds to resume their interrupted woodland sleep. But Richard Sincklo would have none of this and soon called us to order.

"Gentlemen," he said, "welcome to Instede. I know that Lord Elcombe is a good friend to us players and to the Globe playhouse, and would wish me to say so on his behalf."

"That's more than he knows," said Laurence Savage to me in a fairly audible aside.

"We must remember," continued Sincklo, "that although we are accustomed to be the centre of attention, the cynosure of all eyes, for as long as we're here at Instede we are a side-show to the principal attraction. We are in this place to assist at the celebration of a wedding and cannot expect to be centre-stage."

I wondered whether he was saying this to excuse the off-hand treatment which we'd already received and which was probably a foretaste of more off-handedness to come. Richard was a rather formal, cautious man, apt to think before he spoke and to speak only when necessary. I suddenly saw that staying and playing in a great man's house might not be the simple proposition I'd imagined. Leading a band of players into what was a kind of foreign territory might require the skills of an ambassador. Perhaps this was why the Burbage brothers had selected Sincklo to be our senior on tour.

"Nevertheless," he continued, "I know that I can depend on the Chamberlain's to give a good account of themselves whatever the circumstances. We are here to practise our craft and to earn our living. We are here to spread our good name even further abroad and to justify the sharers' trust in us."

At this, he nodded in the direction of the other senior, Thomas Pope, who was himself one of the sharers – that is, an individual who had put up some of the cash to buy the Globe when our Company moved south of the river. Thomas smiled and slightly inclined his head at Richard's words. I felt my heart swell to be a member of this fine Company in which men could give and receive compliments with such grace.

At the same time there was a little niggling in my mind as I continued to wonder what Laurence Savage had meant by his cryptic remarks concerning the part of Demetrius in the play. However, this was not an appropriate moment to ask Richard Sincklo, who continued: "We have a chamber on the ground floor of this great house which has been put at our disposal for practice and rehearsal and, though we are all tired and dusty at the end of a long day's journey, our craft will be tireder and dustier still if we do not attend to it. After all, it's several days since we last rehearsed. So I say to you that we shall begin our business in half an hour."

Such was the discipline and good-will of our band that there was not even a murmur of protest at what Sincklo had said, although inwardly no doubt quite a few (like me) were regretting being called to arms quite so soon. As often happens in rehearsal the tiredness dropped off me like a snake's skin. Jack Horner took the part of Demetrius. I knew, though, by the manner of his playing and by his frequent recourse to the scroll containing Demetrius's lines that this was not *his* part. He was standing in for someone else. I could have asked Jack but our friendship had somewhat cooled of late, and I didn't want to give him the impression that I didn't know what was what. Equally, I could have spoken to

Richard Sincklo but he was preoccupied and furrowed-looking. I decided to leave the question since it would be apparent enough who was playing Demetrius when we got down to the real rehearsals. It was a little mystery I would have to live with for the time being.

Anyway, by the end of our practice I could have run through ten more plays and a dozen jigs to round them off with. And this despite the fact that I have a not inconsiderable part in the play. I shall say more of both play and part (really quite a big one) later on in the story. What I want to relate now concerns what happened later that evening.

As Master Sincklo described, we'd been provided with a chamber on the ground floor of Instede House. Once our play practice was done we were fed and watered, or rather aled, in a neighbouring room. In the glow of a rehearsal which has gone off properly – and with that pleasant tiredness which is well earned and soon to be relieved by a good night's rest – and in the consideration that the Chamberlain's Company's stay on Lord Elcombe's great estate might, after all, be a satisfactory affair – I felt like taking the air late on this summer's evening before climbing the stairs toward heaven and my trestle bed.

I asked one or two of my fellows to join me but, since I really wanted my own company, was glad enough when they refused. Jack Wilson anyway preferred to leave me to my own devices after the previous evening in Salisbury. "God knows what you'll stir up this time, Nick," he said. "Well, I won't look to you for help," I said.

I walked out into the warm air. The formal gardens and working parts of the estate were obviously on the other quarters of Instede House because, from where I was standing outside the courtyard at which we'd first entered, the land dropped away towards a wooded area. I was facing west and the sun filled the sky with his evening benediction, drawing a few golden strands of cloud after him like a king going into exile. (That was a rather fine poetic figure, I thought; perhaps

I should drop it casually in the hearing of someone like Master W.S.) Shading my eyes with my hand, I could see beyond the wood a low line of hills. Somewhere over there, and not so very many miles distant, was the village of Miching, where my father had preached from his pulpit, where I had played as a child, where my mother had summoned me indoors to bed at about this very time on a summer's evening. And now, stolen from me by the plague, they were there no more and I would never again be welcomed home by them this side of paradise.

Unexpectedly, I felt water come into my eyes. I dabbed at them and walked off down the gradual slope which led away from Instede and towards the woods. It is odd how even at moments of ease and content, perhaps especially at such moments, darker thoughts will come to shadow us. To dispel these I deliberately turned my mind elsewhere.

Item: the excellence of my Company and how they were like a family to me, supplying what the plague had taken.

Item: she whom I had left behind in London. So I asked myself what my Nell was doing at this instant. This very instant. A bad idea. Because she was most likely plying her trade in Holland's Leaguer, just as I'd been plying mine in the rehearsal room. A mixture of jealousy (at the thought of the customer who was occupying her now) and regretful lust (that I was not in his place in her bed) overtook me.

Well, business is business, as she would say ... only business.

Instead of Nell, I summoned up images from the previous evening. The kindly keen-eyed Justice of the Peace, Adam Fielding. His beautiful dark-haired daughter Kate, she of the soothing hands and ointments. Instinctively I raised my hand to touch the bruised, scraped places on my face. And that made me remember the stir in the square and the performance of the Cain and Abel story by the Paradise Brothers. An appropriate appellation for a travelling band which dealt in old Bible tales. I wondered whether they'd been drawn towards such subjects by their name alone.

All this time I was making progress across a sheep-cropped area of grass and towards the woods which lay on one side of the mansion house. I paused, turned around and gazed up at the great palace on its knoll. From this angle it looked even grander and more imposing. The sinking sun struck the windows and they gave back a dazzling return. One or two diminished figures were moving around the side of the building. My attenuated shadow stretched out impossibly far in front of me.

I turned back in the direction of the wood and entered the trees' own long-drawn shadows. Either my eyes were still affected by the sun's glare or there was actually something there, because I saw – or thought I saw – and for the second time that day – an object moving in the darkness among the trunks. Not white, but a gloomier flickering shade. I stopped, blinked and looked again. I almost made to return to the shelter of the great house with the excuse that we had a long day of rehearsal on the morrow, that there was no require-ment to walk any further, &c. It also occurred to me that I'd had enough of this nonsense. If an energetic and straight-thinking young man was going to be frightened by some silly shifting shapes among the trees, then it was a pretty poor look-out for all concerned.

I walked on, tasting again my panic of the afternoon and determined to face down my fears.

A rough path led from the field into the wood and it was apparent from the beaten-down grass that feet often wandered this way. Perhaps it was a trysting-place for the lads and lasses cramped up in the servants' quarters of Instede. I threaded my way through outcrops of bush and briar. Once inside the wood, I hesitated, to let my eyes grow accustomed to the gloom. It was old, this pocket of woodland, much older than the house. The lower branches of the oaks and elms writhed overhead. Mossy, misshapen trunks clustered on every side. After the heat of the day it was cool in here. The airs of evening were stirring, bringing with them the pungent odour of wild garlic. A hidden stream murmured in my ear. There were animal rustlings and whirrings. These were familiar sounds. They posed no threat. By now I was able to see quite clear. I wiped my sweaty palms on my shirtfront and breathed deep. The best way – the only way – to overcome fear is to walk up to that old rascal and face him down.

"Hist!"

"Jesus save us!'

I would have jumped clean out of my shoes if I could. As it was, I stumbled backwards over a fallen branch. Winded, I lay on the ground looking up at the splinters of light among the topmost branches. A strange face thrust itself between me and the view.

A disordered face, with straggly grey hair and a beard all grimed and leaf-strewn, and exhaling reeky breath from a toothy hole of a mouth.

A figure dressed in animal pelts and skins tied about his person.

A wild man of the woods!

I must have screamed or shouted in terror, even as I frantically scrambled to my feet, for this weird individual backed away in alarm and lifted his hands protectively in front of his face. His evident fear helped me to get the better of mine.

For an instant I wondered whether he was a man at all, but his apprehensive posture and (to be candid) his smell even at a distance persuaded me that I was not dealing with a wood-spirit or demon.

I have heard of these feral beings – unfortunates abandoned at birth, suckled by wolves and raised among the beasts, and who scarcely know themselves to be human. Men who, when they perish in the winter's cold, have no gravestone to mark the place where they fall and only a veil of dead leaves to cover them.

He lowered his hands from his face. They were oddly crooked, like animal paws – or, with their long nails, more like claws. Then, still keeping a distance between us, he said, "Well, sirrah. What are you doing in my territory? Have you come to spy?"

In the dimness of the wood I stared at this wild figure, from whose bewhiskered mouth emerged sensible, if slightly threatening, sentences.

Out of my own mouth emerged nothing. I was too surprised to speak.

"Well then?"

He crept a couple of paces towards me while I retreated. He had a strange, swaying movement. I was frightened of tumbling over backward again and having him on top of me. Him and his reeky breath.

"I – I – am . . ."

"Out with it!"

Something in his peremptory tone, incongruous in this dishevelled, rank-smelling figure, struck me as absurd. I nearly laughed out loud and then thought better of it.

"Nicholas Revill is who I am," I managed to get out finally.

"And who might Nicholas Revill be? Is he a spy?"

"No spy but a player in the Chamberlain's Company. We are newly arrived from London to – to this place here. We are the guests of Lord Elcombe."

I jerked with my thumb in the general direction of Instede House.

"What do you play, sirrah?"

"We play the words that are set down for us."

He nodded at this deliberately unilluminating reply, seeming to think about it. I took the opening to ask him a question, "Now that I have given you my name and trade, as the phrase goes, you must give me yours."

"Who am I?" he said curiously, as if he'd never heard the question before. "I? Some call me Robin."

Well, that name fitted one who flitted and bobbed about in the greenery, although the breast of this one was dun-coloured rather than red. It also brought to mind the thief called Robin Hood. And that character called Robin Good-fellow in Master W.S.'s *Dream*, he who is jester and attendant to King Oberon in the same piece.

"But I have no trade," he added.

"Oh I would say you have not," I said, humouring this odd fellow and casting my eyes up and down his ragged outline.

"Does a lord need a living?"

"As you say."

"I am the lord of all this little land," said Robin the wood-man. "Look around you. I am master of what you see."

At this moment I wasn't able to see very much but I nodded and said soothing things and wondered how quickly I might escape from this individual's company.

"Master . . . Revill, is it?"

"Aye, Nick Revill."

"I can see by your looks that you do not altogether believe my words. [*This remark – which was right enough – took me aback a little because my own eyes couldn't have read a face. The fellow's must be adapted to the darkness under the trees.*] And it is late for you to be out, Master Revill. But if you return tomorrow I will show you my kingdom."

"Tomorrow?"

"Come to me when the sun is directly overhead," said Robin. "I have things to show you."

"Very well."

"You may leave my kingdom now, Master Revill," said this scarecrow in the dusk.

"Thank you, your majesty – Robin."

I almost bowed my way of his "court" in the woods, half in jest but half struck too by the earnestness of the man.

Maybe I would go back next day, for my own amusement – and instruction. It's a player's duty, almost, to study those among whom he finds himself.

By the time I exited the woods only a few fragments of day remained to the sky. The great bulk of Instede House blocked half the horizon in front of me, with little flickers and gleams of light signifying some of the windows. A young moon lolled low on the earth, as if unwilling to make the effort to hoist herself higher in the heavens. I hastened across the short turf which separated the wood from the bank on which the house perched. At one point, I thought I heard someone breathing quite close by, a kind of sighing, and I looked round and went a little faster. I had had enough of woodland shapes, sounds and spectres for one day.

It didn't take long the next morning to establish the identity of the weird man in the woods. The cold reception we'd received from Oswald Eden the steward on our arrival was thawed out by the warmer manners of some of the lower servants. In conversation with one of them, Davy by name, I happened to let slip that we'd recently played before the Queen and the Royal Court in Whitehall. After that he was like warm wax in my hands, even if the notion of Whitehall was so unfamiliar to him it might as well have been on the moon.

Anyway, what I learned was straightforward and confirmed what the wood-man had told me the previous evening. Robin was indeed his name; he had no other that anyone knew.

How long had he dwelt among the trees? I asked.

Oh, since time immemorabilial, sir, replied Davy. He was like a whatdyecallem? an anchor? or was it a helmet? Living off all by himself and away from the haunts of man.

He meant an anchoret or an hermit: I gently corrected Davy.

So he did, sir, ah what a fine thing was letters and learning in the right hands!

And what did Robin do down in the woods?

Do? – why he talked to squirrels and toads and attercops.

Attercops?

Spiders, sir. Didn't they know that word in Whitehall town, them with all their letters and learning?

He said he was lord of the wood.

He *was* lord and master in the wood just as Elcombe was lord and master there in Instede House.

And Lord Elcombe, didn't he mind this, ah, wild man saying such things?

He was harmless enough, sir, Robin was harmless enough. And there were some said he brought good luck on the house.

Very well, I said.

He should be looked after, said Davy. And he was looked after, was Robin.

No doubt, I said.

I still had it in mind to go back and visit Robin later that day. It was curiosity and that player's itch to observe his species in all their manifestations which prompted me. And a dangerous itch it turned out to be.

Meantime, we of the Chamberlain's-in-the-country had further rehearsals of *A Midsummer Night's Dream* to fill our mornings, although it was hardly a new play for us. Indeed, I was one of the few who had *not* taken part in a previous performance, and even I had seen it when the Chamberlain's were still based north of the river in Finsbury. You might think rehearsals were hardly necessary. And if it had been an everyday *Dream* at the Globe it would not have received much attention. But this was a special performance, not quite the equivalent of playing before our Sovereign Lady but not so far beneath it either. Lord Elcombe was a valued patron of the Chamberlain's and a friend to some of our seniors. Players and their companies can never have too many friends – for the reason that we have several very potent enemies like the watchers in Council, or the puritan, or, worst of all, the plague which canters in on a pale horse to close us all down.

So we need friends, the more powerful the better. And there were few more powerful than Elcombe, possessor of a good slice of Wiltshire as well as of a grand Whitefriars mansion in London. When such a man invites you to perform at his son's wedding and offers to pay you handsomely for the privilege, you don't hesitate.

However, as I've said, we knew the *Dream* pretty well. Even I knew it. So perhaps it wasn't surprising that my mind wandered in the rehearsal room when I wasn't being called on to spout my lines and make my moves as Lysander.

Something to do with my part as one of the young lovers caused me to remember, in the long intervals of practice, how only a few days before I'd been at home in London town and talking to Nell – my whore and my good friend – about this strange, fantastical piece of Master Shakespeare's.

She and I were in my lodgings south of the river. Not the fourpenny-a-week upstairs hole belonging to the witch-like sisters where I'd shivered and suffered during the last winter, but a more commodious establishment nearer to the Globe playhouse. My room was on the second floor of a house in a street called Dead Man's Place (why it had this unfortunate appellation I don't know). Perhaps because of the ill-omened street name, rooms there were not hard to rent on favourable terms. In addition, I'd caught the eye of my landlord, one Master Benwell. He looked me up and down at our first meeting, not once but many times. When I told him that I was a player – a revelation not always guaranteed to cause delight – he licked his thin lips. I speedily concluded that he was, in all likelihood, a gentleman who preferred the male gender and the back door. Certainly he liked to talk about such things. He fired questions at me, hinting that the Chamberlain's was a hot-bed of sodomy. I was about to get on my high horse but realized how his prying interest might be turned to my advantage. From a starting-point of one shilling and three-pence I bargained him down to 1s a week.

This was more than I'd been paying in Broadwall, but the room in Dead Man's Place, though not ample, was much better than the one in the Coven. In exchange for a reasonable rent it was understood that I'd provide him with little snippets and snatchets of tittle and tattle to do with the Chamberlain's Company.

So this shilling chamber in Dead Man's Place was where I was lying with Nell on an evening in June. Once our more pressing needs had been met, she started to ask me about where we were going on tour, and what we were going to do there, and who for, and how much we'd earn by it, and whether I had a big part this time ("What do you mean, this time?" I said), and a dozen other questions which came tumbling out at once.

"One at a time," I said. "I can only answer one at a time."

I was subjected to a rigorous catechism which I pretended to be wearied by but which, in truth, I took pleasure in answering. Doesn't every man enjoy talking about the mysteries of his craft – and if he does not, he has no business practising it, I think.

"Is that it?" I said after many minutes. "You will leave me with no energy for anything else."

"Almost there, Nick. Tell me this too. Are you all going to the country? Or are some of you left behind in town?"

"No, 'we' are not all going," I said, slightly annoyed. What was she thinking about? Her trade? "Shakespeare and Burbage and Heminges and most of the seniors remain here."

"So the children are being let out to play. How will they fare?"

Strangely, the same idea had occurred to me but to hear Nell voice it out loud was somehow aggravating.

"If by that you mean that we are not capable of conducting – "

"It was a joke, Nick."

"We are to visit Instede House at the personal invitation of Lord Elcombe, I'll have you know."

"Hush. Save your passion for later."

"You're in danger of dousing it."

"Then tell me of the play, this Midsummer Nightmare."

"*Dream.*"

"Dream. See how much you have to tell me still. And talk of your part in it."

Even if she was only being conciliatory at this instant, Nell did like to hear some account of the plays in which I participated. Inevitably she hung about the playhouses in the way of business but, equally inevitably, she did not much attend to the action on stage. (I'd tried to prohibit her from attending the Globe when I was playing there at first and she eventually told me I had no more right to regulate her trade than she had to regulate mine.)

So I lay flat on my back, eyes fixed on the lumpy plaster of the ceiling, and started to give my *Dream* narration. Nell snuggled up beside me. In fact, my narrow bed didn't permit of any relation other than snugness.

I told her of Hermia and Lysander, the Athenian lass and lad in ancient times, who are in love with each other. I told her that I played Lysander while young Michael Donegrace took the part of Hermia. All would be well were it not for Egeus, Hermia's hard-hearted father, who is compelling his daughter to marry another man, one Demetrius. I told her how this same Demetrius is already loved by another woman, Helena. Of the elopement of Hermia and Lysander (Donegrace and Revill) to a neighbouring forest; of the pursuit of them by Demetrius and Helena. Oh, the love-tangle that ensues! For in this charmed wood wander Oberon and Titania, no mortal man and wife but king and queen of the fairies, and they too are engaged in a love-dispute, just as the mortals are.

"It's not easy to follow," said Nell.

"It's not meant to be," I said, although I considered that my outline had been quite lucid, all things considered. "It is a love-tangle. Unless you have confusion you can never arrive at clarity."

Nell slipped out of bed, and I assumed she intended to use the jordan in the corner. Instead of the expected tinkling, however, I heard her rummaging about on the small table where my few effects were untidily piled. I gazed at the lumpy ceiling through drowsy eyes. In a few moments she slipped back in beside me. She waved something white before my face.

"Write it down."

"What?"

I opened my eyes wider. She was clutching a piece of paper and a stub of pencil.

"It will be easier for me to understand, Nick, if you write it down."

"But you can't read."

"I am not altogether unlettered," she said, with a touch of indignation. "There is someone teaching me."

This was news to me. I was wide awake by now.

"Someone?"

"One of . . . the sisters."

She meant one of her co-labourers in the field of flesh that was Holland's Leaguer. God save us, a pedagogue-whore, I thought, and then banished the description as unworthy.

"*I* could have taught you," I said. "I have offered."

"But you prefer me as I am."

"Of course I do."

"Ignorant and unlettered?"

"Well not exactly . . . not at all, if you put it like that."

"Then you would have me different?"

"A little, I suppose."

"See," Nell said triumphantly. "Now write down the names of the people from your Nightmare."

I wasn't even sure what argument we'd been engaging in here but it was apparent she considered herself the winner, while I was tangled among the toils of her logic. To avoid further discussion, I sat upright in bed and scribbled down the names of the characters, firing off miniature arrows like a demented Cupid or looping them with little hearts to show who went with or after whom. Then, to make it complete, I added some of the others parts as well, the rude mechanicals &c.

When I'd finished, she snatched the paper and pored over it.

"There. Ell . . . why . . . ess – Lysander. That's your part. And you have drawn a heart which encloses aitch . . . eee . . . arr – Hermia! So that's who *you* love. And here is Dee . . . mee . . . trius and, er, Helena. And the arrow shows that she is chasing Demetrius. And, Nick!, what is this word? Is it what I think it is?"

She could hardly speak for laughing. I looked at where her finger was jabbing at the page.

"Nell, you would be safer to learn from an absey book than one of your sisters of the flesh. You'll find no rude words in a child's primer. No, that's Puck, not what you think it is."

"Oh," she sounded faintly disappointed. "Who's Puck?"

So I explained about Robin Goodfellow, and that part of the lesson was done. And then we had a joke or two about Bottom before concluding our business together.

Post-Puck, I saw her on her way along Dead Man's Place. It was still light on this fine June evening. I did not like to walk too many paces with Nell through the public streets, particularly when, as now, she was dressed in what might be termed the colours of her guild (viz, red). This was partly because I had a strange reluctance to be taken for one of her customers and partly because I felt that I might be impeding her trade. If I wasn't entitled to block a whore's business in the playhouse, I certainly had no right to obstruct her traffic in the street.

Nevertheless, she seemed in an unusually fond and clinging mood as we parted. Probably because we wouldn't see each other again until I returned from Wiltshire. It was the first time I had been right out of London since my arrival in the spring of 1599. Nell too was country-born. Like me, she had come to seek her fortune in the great city. It was one of the things which had brought us together.

"I have your paper," she said, pecking me on the cheek several times.

It took me a moment to realize what she was talking about.

"When I want to be reminded of what you're doing I shall look and see that you are chasing that boy called Hermia."

"You'll not learn to read much from that," I said.

"Have a good Dream," she said, departing. "You see, I have remembered your title."

In the event, Nightmare would have been more apt.

The image of Nell as she walked down Dead Man's Place, her taffeta dress flickering like a fiery candle on that summer evening, recurred to me as I sat on the side of the practice chamber in Instede House. The sun poured through the high windows and glittered on the polished oak of the floor. In the centre of the room, Thomas Pope was exchanging a few words with Laurence Savage and the others playing the "rude mechanicals", Nick Bottom the weaver, Snug the joiner *et al.* At this moment Pope was discussing with Laurence and the rest the exact turn or flavour to give to the closing scene, even if they had been through it a dozen times before. Thomas wasn't at all as grave a senior as Richard Sincklo, indeed he was someone who usually spoke his mind without reserve. He had a deserved reputation as a comic player (and now took the part of Puck, jester to Oberon and all-round mischief-maker). For all that, there was an authority in his words, and he had the knack of providing suggestions and even criticism without giving offence. This made him especially useful in his role of "guider" for our *Dream.*

We'd reached the point when the clowns come forward to play out the tragic tale of Pyramus and Thisbe for the diversion of the Athenian Court, of which I as Lysander was an insignificant part. They are such poor journeymen players, these clowns, that they make a mockery of what is serious in love, and at the same time give unintended instruction in how *not* to play. Any fool can play badly, and usually does. But to play badly well . . . ah, there's an art to that.

Laurence crouched down to peep through the parted fingers of Sam Smith, who (in the *Dream*) was playing the part of Tom Snout the tinker, who (in the Pyramus and Thisbe diversion) was playing the part of Wall, lying flat on the floor with his arm and hand awkwardly crooked up in the air. Never have lime and rough-cast been so funny. But not on this occasion.

Usually, Laurence would have levered himself down with cumbersome comicality to the low "chink" provided by Sam's splayed fingers. But before he could begin this movement his attention was arrested by a group which had just entered the room. I saw him straighten up. Over his broad, undemonstrative features there passed a shadow, like the cloud which crosses a summer field. I remembered that later.

I turned to look at the door. Four figures, three men and a woman, were standing just inside the entrance. The whole of the players' company had paused. Those of us who didn't already know these people for who they were guessed their identity.

"Please continue," said Lord Elcombe.

So the clownish interlude went on, with Laurence Savage peeping through Sam Smith's digits and lamenting that he could not see his Thisbe. A number of us, however, rather than watch an already familiar scene, took the occasion to examine our hosts. I had plenty of opportunities in the days to come to grow familiar enough with Lord Elcombe, and his family too. But I'll describe them here more or less as they first struck me.

Elcombe was a tall, thin man of middle years, soberly dressed in dark clothes which, though rich in their working, lacked any ostentation. His face was narrow with close-set eyes and a hooked nose jutting out over a small mouth. He was clean-shaven. His wife beside him – or she whom I supposed his wife – was near as tall as her husband. There was a kind of drawn beauty in her face, and though she shared her companion's courtly bearing her features were softer than his, the lips fuller, the nose less imperious.

To one side stood two younger men whom I took to be their sons. I presumed that the one who looked less young, or maybe just more careworn, was the groom. This was Elcombe's first son and heir, Lord Harry Ascre (pronounced Ascray), to give him his family name. Some offspring seem to be a rough draft of a mother or father, as if paradoxically the child had come first; some appear as a more refined version of either parent. But this one looked like a pale shadow of both. As tall and pinch-faced as his parents, I guessed he was about my age; but hoped that I would never have to carry around such a haunted look. His complexion was a chalky white and the dark rings under his eyes testified to sleepless nights. The other son, Cuthbert, might have been drawn from an entirely different source. He appeared healthy and well-fed, and though not plump in the face he lacked the drawn look of the others.

This quartet of father, mother and sons looked on as the lamentable saga of Pyramus and Thisbe drew to a close, with Pyramus stabbing himself in the (mistaken) belief that his Thisbe had been mauled by a hungry lion, and Thisbe stabbing *herself* because her Pyramus has stabbed himself in the (mistaken) belief that . . . Well, you get the picture. It is a tragic tale of young love confounded by accident, mischance and parental opposition. By the end of the interlude, we of the Chamberlain's had to wipe our eyes. To clear away the tears of laughter. No matter how many times we've watched this scene in rehearsal or even participated in it, we've always been overcome by the skill of Messrs Savage and Smith and the other "mechanicals" – and the skill of the writing. I will go further. It is the brilliancy – yes, there is no other word – the brilliancy of Master W.S. to seize on the idea that the language of love is separated from the language of absurdity by a wall considerably thinner than that which divides the two would-be lovers. In fact, sometimes they're the same thing. The lover drools and dotes, and is a sport to his friends.

What I'm saying, is that this is a *comic* scene.

Laughter is appropriate.

Naturally, those of us who weren't engaged in spouting our lines at this moment were casting surreptitious glances at Lord and Lady Elcombe and their sons, to see how our playing was being received. We're in for a rough ride at Instede, I thought, if this is the regular mood of our patrons. The only one who seemed to be appreciating our efforts was Cuthbert. He was almost slapping his thighs. He even seemed to be mouthing some of the lines along with Laurence and the rest. He knows the play well, I thought. And just at this point a little suspicion crept into my head.

To itemize the rest of Elcombe clan: a small smile had incised itself on Lord Elcombe's small mouth, as if he acknowledged our efforts but did not want to betray himself by any excessive mark of approbation. His wife looked fairly straight-faced and strait-laced. While, as for Harry their son . . . I've seen people bored by comedy, I've seen people scarcely able to hold their water for being convulsed by it, but I don't think I've ever seen anyone brought to the edge of tears (real tears, not those of laughter) by the absurdity of two lovers played by a weaver and a bellows-mender. Yet this is how the young man seemed to be affected. Standing slightly behind his parents and brother, he raised his hand to his eyes and wiped at them several times as Pyramus or Thisbe launched into some lament for their perished partner or into a tirade against the malevolence of fate.

It's a comedy, for God's sake, I wanted to tell him.

When Pyramus and Thisbe had done their dying, with much last-gasping and writhing around, they stood up again and took their bow. Lord Elcombe clapped politely, while his

Lady did nothing much and their elder son looked as though he was about to run out the door at any moment. Cuthbert was the only one to show a full appreciation. Give me an audience full of Cuthberts, I thought (though I didn't know his name at that point). The seniors Thomas Pope and Richard Sincklo went forward to present themselves to our patron. I was pleased to see some smiles break out at this point, otherwise I'd have begun to wonder what we were doing in this place. An altogether warmer mood stole over the group, and after a moment Lord Elcombe himself stepped forward and, with a curious circular motion of his arm in the air to draw our attention, he spoke to us.

"Gentlemen all, you are welcome at Instede. You must forgive us if we are somewhat distracted with preparations for our son's nuptials and do not give to the players the honour that is their due. But we are sensible of the honour that you do *us* by your presence. One or two of you are familiar to me from the old days but I see that there are many fresh faces in the Company. To you in particular a hearty welcome."

It was difficult to imagine this gentleman being hearty about anything but he nevertheless came to join us, to shake hands with some and exchange pleasantries with others. Lady Elcombe remained talking with Richard Sincklo and Thomas Pope. Their gloomy-looking son had disappeared while the more cheerful Cuthbert was mixing gladly with the players.

I was standing next to Laurence Savage and, referring to Elcombe, said, "There, you can hardly say that this is ungracious behaviour."

"You do not know him."

The shadow that had earlier passed across his face now reappeared.

"And you do?"

I was curious to know what it was about Elcombe that Savage didn't like.

"I do not know him in the sense that you mean, Nicholas. He is not my drinking companion or my friend. How can a mere player aspire to that? But know him in other ways, I do."

I waited but he was obviously disinclined to say more. Before Elcombe had reached the part of the chamber where we were standing, Laurence shifted to avoid having to speak to the nobleman.

I turned to look through the window. Outside was a glorious summer morning. I turned back and found myself face to face with our host. Someone close by, possibly Jack Horner, said in the way of introduction, "Nicholas Revill, my lord", and I made the gesture of a bow.

"Your servant, Master Revill."

"My lord."

"You're new to the Company, are you not?"

"Since last autumn, my lord. My first acting part was in Master Shakespeare's *Hamlet*."

"And what did you enact, hm?" said Elcombe. He had clear blue eyes which, because of their colour or their close-settedness or both, somehow gave the lie to his warm questions. Or perhaps it was that I'd been listening too closely to Laurence Savage.

"Small parts. A poisoner, an ambassador."

"But you are grown to greater things in this midsummer dream?"

"Lysander. One of the lovers."

"One among many," he said with a sideways movement of the lips which could have been read as a smile.

"Willing and unwilling," I said.

"What do you mean by that, hm?" said Elcombe.

I'd meant nothing, or next to nothing, but was now forced to lay some foundation under my words.

"The play is full of lovers both voluntary and compelled," I said, seeing the owner of Instede House staring hard at me, no trace of a smile now. "Like . . . like Titania and Bottom. The Queen of the Fairies doesn't *choose* to fall in love with an ass. Or – to take the case of my own Lysander – watch how mischievous Puck squeezes magic juice over my eyelids. So that when I wake I shall fall in love with the first person that I see. That is what I meant by involuntary love."

"Caused by a juice or a potion, hm."

He had an odd, interrogatory trick of ending his words with a "hm". Maybe it was that which provoked me to go on.

"Ah, my lord, I think that – "

"Yes?"

I hesitated because I'd been about to say what I thought Master Shakespeare meant by this business of juices and potions, when the notion of explaining the playwright to someone else (and that someone a lord of the realm) suddenly struck me as presumptuous. However, thought is free and W.S. wasn't here to contradict me – so I plunged in.

"I think that Master Shakespeare is showing us that it is human to chop and change in love, so that we sometimes love a Hermia and the next day, the very next hour perhaps, love a Helena instead. And that love can even make us descend to love a Bottom or an ass . . ."

"Go on," said Elcombe, putting up a good pretence of being interested in a poor player's views.

"But because we are sometimes unhappy at our inconstancy . . . [*God help me, what was I talking about?*] . . . in order to, er, keep our consciences clear we have to imagine the potions which cause us to be inconstant. And then after that we must conjure up the fairies and sprites who will make us take them – all so as to compel us to do what we would do anyway."

I halted like a man reaching the end of a race, then added, "If you see what I mean."

Lord Elcombe looked thoughtful. I wasn't surprised. I probably looked thoughtful myself, trying to work out what I'd meant. Sometimes you don't know what's in your mind until you say it out loud.

"So you think love is stronger than will?" he said. "That it may operate against what we truly want or intend to do? Hm?"

"To be sure, sir."

"Come, Master Revill. That's a fiction, and fiction is all very well for poets and for plays like this one which you have in hand. But tell me the truth now. You have been swept away by love, have you, and rendered powerless?"

"Well . . ."

"You have been pierced by Cupid's dart, hm?"

I had been indeed – once. So I wanted to answer: yes, when I was eight I fell hard for a cottager's daughter who was a year or two older. But fear of sounding ridiculous prevented me.

"Well, er," I mammered, "not exactly if you put it like that . . ."

What had I done to deserve this scrutiny? All the facility of a moment ago had deserted me. I felt myself growing a little warm about the face.

"You will have to talk to my son," said Elcombe.

"Is he a . . . er . . . philosopher?"

(I'd been about to say 'lover' but stopped myself at the last moment. In any case, which son was he referring to?)

"No, but he would be a player – if he were not already a gentleman."

I glanced across to where the relatively sleek Cuthbert was laughing and discoursing with my fellows. Ah yes. Suspicion confirmed.

"You know the play, my lord?" I said, mostly to change the subject.

"Well enough to think that it would be a fitting garland for my older son's wedding, Master Revill."

And with that and a slight inclination of the head, he withdrew his cool blue gaze and moved off to chat with some of my fellows. While the above dialogue was going forward they had been glancing at me curiously from time to time.

I felt relieved to see the back of Elcombe. But at the same time obscurely pleased to have been singled out for conversation in this way.

I had to face some questioning over our dinner, and some jokes about rubbing shoulders with the high and mighty. But it was only for form's sake. In truth, we of the Chamberlain's were used to aristocratic company. In fact, on this country occasion we were privileged to be joined by the high and mighty on stage. The mystery of who was to play my love-rival Demetrius was soon solved. I'd half-guessed that Cuthbert, Elcombe's younger son, was more than merely whiling away the time in our practice room. Sure enough, he was soon introduced to me as the newest – albeit temporary – member of the Chamberlain's. Since we were to share several scenes, Cuthbert was put in the experienced hands of Uncle Nicholas.

Now, I've no quarrel with the aristocracy dressing up and spouting lines as long as they don't tread on our toes or take away our custom. And, in truth, we weren't in a position to refuse this young man. That Cuthbert should play the part of Demetrius in *A Midsummer Night's Dream* had obviously been settled between the Elcombe family and our seniors before we left London. My first impressions were favourable enough. Though the son of a nobleman, and therefore never likely to be in the position of having to scrape a living (and certainly not in the ungentlemanly business of the playhouse), Cuthbert seemed modest enough as well as responsive to instruction. He was the humblest of apprentices. Actually, he appeared to believe that players were hung about with clouds of mystery, that their jokes were funnier, their thoughts more elevated and their farts more perfumed than ordinary men's.

In short, I'd thought we'd probably get along fine. I did wonder, though, whether he was getting paid at our rate of a shilling a day for his performance. Or was he paying us for the privilege?

A morning's playing gives you an appetite. Today's dinner, like last night's supper, was calculated to satisfy it and all of us, except Cuthbert who'd withdrawn to more refined quarters, fell on our pigeon pie and mutton. There was no sign of

Oswald, the haughty steward who'd "welcomed" us the previous day. Perhaps he was unwilling to sully himself by further association with rag-tag players. At least his master showed a more accommodating face.

We had more work later, of an ambling kind, when we were due to go out and prospect the ground where the *Dream* would be played – for this was going to be an outdoors performance, with the sward for stage, the woods and fields for hangings, and the stars above for our roof. Richard Sincklo told us to be in attendance on the south side of the house at three in the afternoon. Once on our space, we'd pace out the area and mark off the boundaries enclosing what would become the short-lived kingdom of the players. Thomas Pope would consider how best to incorporate whatever we found there to our advantage, such as paths and hedges and little irregularities in the ground. But between times the post-dinner gap was our own. I remembered that I'd made a half-promise to Robin, the man of the woods, that I'd allow him to show me his "kingdom" among the trees.

Well, no harm in it, I thought.

As a player I ought to be interested in humanity in all its guises, I thought.

Too much thinking, I thought.

Once again I crossed the grassy space between one side of the great house and the wood where Robin lived. The sun shone benevolently on my head and a spacious afternoon peace sprawled across the landscape. It was weather to bless all life. I recalled the drunken farmer who'd clambered up on the makeshift stage in Salisbury. What would he say to this even-tempered climate? No doubt, he'd find fault. Too little of one thing, too much of another. Farmers are like that. Then, as if to confirm that farmers are by no means alone when it comes to perverse fits of feeling, I suddenly missed the smells and sights and sounds of the capital. The sweet stench of the river, which particularly tickles your nose on warm summer days like this; the boiling crowds of apprentices, moving like packs of dogs through the streets; the everlasting peal of the church bells and the coarser peal of the orange-sellers and other street-hawkers. And I was pleased to miss these things because that must mean I was on my way to becoming a true Londoner. Why, I was even missing the sly insinuations of Master Benwell, my landlord. I missed Nell also, and our sessions in Dead Man's Place and elsewhere. But I could not have put my hand on my heart and answered yes to Elcombe's question about Cupid's dart, at least not in relation to her.

By now I had entered the wood once again and a profounder hush folded itself about me. I paused. I felt oddly at ease. As though this wood posed no danger.

"Master Revill."

"Robin," I replied.

He appeared seemingly through the trees. But in truth I'd nosed him out before I'd seen him.

"You have come."

I bowed slightly.

"So that you can show me your kingdom," I said, "as you promised."

He put himself into that queer crouching posture which I'd observed on first meeting him and beckoned me on with a curved hand. There was something dog-like about his attitude. By the clearer light of day I saw that he was covered not so much with whole animal pelts as with fragments of fur and hide crudely stitched together. Parts of his body which in the evening gloom had looked clad, like his arms and knees, were in fact bare but all weathered and besmirched. Leaves clung to his beard and a single jay's feather protruded, by design or accident, from the thatch of his head.

Robin again beckoned me with his hooked hand before turning and moving off into a denser part of the wood. I glanced back at the reassuring bulk of Instede House through the outer fringe of trees. Someone called out in the distance, the shout resonating in the quiet of the early afternoon. I followed Robin. He wove his way among the undergrowth and pursued a route that was apparent to him alone. At one point we came to a boggy patch and then a stream. Robin's feet were unshod – though a cursory glance downwards might have deceived you into thinking he was wearing shoes, so filthy-black and hardened were his feet to look at. I would normally have trodden carefully, in my townee's way, but was forced to follow my leader through the squelch and wet. I made some involuntary noise as the water rose over my shoes but Robin was silent. From time to time he glanced back to see that I was still with him.

We must have been moving for five minutes or so. I'd spent most of the time looking down, trying to avoid the damp places and the tiny pits and falls which Nature scatters everywhere for the unwary. When I glanced up again, Robin's brown-grey shape had vanished.

I sighed inwardly. I was getting used to being lost in the woods.

"Hist!"

The sound came from by my feet. I looked down and eventually discerned a darker shape on the forest floor. The feather still stuck straight up from his head. Then the head was withdrawn to be replaced by that beckoning, curved hand. Wherever he was going he evidently expected me to follow.

I crouched down. There was a large ragged hole torn out of a bank of earth and fallen leaves. Patches of sunlight fringed its edges but within it was earthy-dark. Just as the vixen has her earth, and the conies their warrens, so does Robin the wood-man have his home in the ground. Well, what had I expected? A fine mansion perched among the tree-tops with a perspective in every direction? Some cosy cottage with Mistress Robin, a dimpled dame, in attendance? Only in a story.

What I faced instead was a hole. And a decision. Do I follow this strange man into his lair? What if he is in the habit of luring young players and other passengers into his den, there to club them to death and roast their mortal remains over a fire for his supper? What if he imbalms them, and keeps them for his winter provender?

Only in a story, I told myself. A story fit to frighten children on a winter's night.

I remembered what Davy the servant had told me too. Robin was harmless enough. Some said he brought good luck on the house.

I eased myself into the hole, sometimes crouching, sometimes on hands and knees, feeling my way forward down a tight tunnel. Damp penetrated my leggings. There was a slight gleam of light a few yards ahead. The passage stank, though whether this was its natural smell or the smell of its occupant I wasn't sure.

"Hist, Master Revill," came from up ahead.

I scrabbled along the passage, suddenly frightened that the mud-ceiling was going to come down and bury me. I emerged into a tiny hollowed-out area which – as I realized when my eyes gradually grew accustomed to the light (or lack of it) – had been formed under and to one side of the clustered roots of several great trees. The earth must have washed away naturally or been scooped out by Robin so as to form this hide. The spaces between the twisting, diving roots had been filled with branches plaited together and then covered with a kind of mat of leaves. But a small quantity of light was still admitted, enough for me to see my host squatting in the opposite corner.

"You are welcome to my home," he said.

I would have bowed but I was already hunched over.

"Most gracious."

"I can offer you water," he said, without moving from his squatting position with his arms hooped over his knees.

"I do not drink it, thank you," I said.

I didn't drink it neither, or not much, and certainly not from the green-mantled pool he most likely obtained it from.

"Flesh I cannot offer you," he said solemnly. "Flesh I do not eat."

So much for my childish fantasies about being killed and roasted! I settled myself down on the leaf-mould which passed for flooring.

"To kill even the meanest creature," he continued, "is to injure one of our fellows."

I must have looked automatically at the strips of squirrel and rabbit and God-knew-what-other fur and hide which patched his begrimed body for, seeing my glance (he had very acute sight), he said, "I have not harmed a living creature. I take only from those who no longer have need of covering in this cold world. It is no sin to borrow from the dead."

It might have been the dank air of the den but I started to feel shivery. Something tickled at the back of my neck and I reached up to brush it off.

"No, no, flesh I do not eat. They know that."

"They?"

"My dependencies."

He waved a bedraggled arm to the left and for a moment I wondered what he meant, then realized he must be referring to Instede.

"So they bring me only turnips and green sallets, and goosegogs and raspberries . . ."

What had Davy said about this man, that he should be looked after. Perhaps this was what he meant.

". . . on silver trenchers."

Looked after because he was mad, no question of it.

"That is no more than you deserve," I said.

"A king does not go foraging," said this muddy man.

By now my eyes had grown used to the near-dark and I could study my host. My intention was to bring this dialogue to a speedy close, however. Poor Robin was plainly out of his wits, and though one may learn something from the mad it is limited. He had once been a handsome man, with a strong, long face. Hunger and exposure had sharpened his features, so that his nose was like a pen. Deep scars and embossed scabs were visible through the grime on his face and arms and legs. This was unaccommodated man himself, a poor forked being.

Again I felt shivery. A spider, one of Davy's attercops, suddenly lowered itself in front of my eyes.

If part of Robin – the kingly part – was mad, another part seemed aware of his predicament because he now said, in a tone of sadness, "I was not ever thus."

I waited, for revelation.

"No lord of a shrunken kingdom was I, but of many acres. Of dale and forest and mead. I could have ridden across them from dawn to sunset without dismounting."

"Where was . . . where is . . . this kingdom?" I said gently, noting the poetic way he'd described it.

He tapped his skull with crooked fingers.

"Safe and sound in here."

He laughed a quite pleasant laugh, not the mad cackle you might have been expecting.

"Where none can seize it," he said.

Or see it, I thought.

"You don't believe me, Master Revill."

Again, that acuteness! I squirmed uncomfortably on the dank and dirty ground.

"You have your treasures in mind," I said, noticing how the jay's feather stood upright from his hair.

"Oh I have them here too," said Robin.

All this time he had been squatting, hugging his knees with his arms, an awkward position which I couldn't have sustained for more than a few minutes. Now he reached behind him in the dimness of his lair and brought forward a small leather-covered box. He fiddled with some kind of hasp. He struggled for some time, his nails scraping on the surface. Eventually he half-opened the lid. I couldn't see what it contained. Alternately glancing up at me and then down at the box, he started to rummage awkwardly inside it. I imagined he might bring out a bit of dried bat's wing or a withered chaplet of flowers but instead there was the rustle of paper. His eyes flicked up and down, the whites unnaturally bright in the gloom.

Finally, he extracted from the box four or five discoloured sheets of paper. Pushing them close to his face, he seemed to scan them in search of a particular item. Then, selecting one, he held it out to me but without letting go of his side of it. There seemed to be some writing on the sheet but, so dim was the interior of the hole under the trees, that I couldn't make anything of it or even see which way up the sheet was meant to be.

"Yes," I said, nodding slowly (and all the time thinking furiously about how I could extricate myself from this ridiculous business), "yes, I see what you mean."

What had I done to earn the privilege of a peek inside this crack-brain's head? Had I offended Genesius, the patron saint of players? Was he now giving me a little lesson in the cost of showing too much curiosity about my fellow man?

"There's more, Master Revill," said Robin, carefully returning the unreadable sheet to the leathern box.

"I'll take your word for it."

"You're not the only one to have seen my treasures."

"I expect not."

"He's seen them too."

"Who?" I said mechanically.

"Oh you know," he said. "You are familiar with him."

"I don't know who you're talking about."

"He is clever," Robin said. "He does not wear the badge of his tribe."

I stayed silent for the simple reason that I could think of nothing to say – and also because I was unwilling to provoke him to further nonsense.

He too said nothing for a moment, and then began to sing in a tuneless up-and-down way.

When the devil came up
And walked the lea,
Who was he looking for?
Me or thee?

I couldn't stand up in this damp, dirty-smelling hole but I made to back out, on hands and knees, down the earth passage by which I'd entered. I'd had my fill of the smell, the talk, the papers, and now the sing-song. But I wasn't quick enough. Robin's scrawny arm shot forward and he grabbed at mine. I felt the bone of his fingers scrabble at the flesh of my arm but he didn't have sufficient control of his hand to take a firm grasp. He leaned forward and his breath buffeted against my face.

"That's who," he said. "You know him. You've seen him."

He meant no harm, I am sure of that, no harm. He did not have it in him to do harm. With his feeble frame, he was no threat. Even so, I rebelled at the hand which was scraping at my arm, and pulled away. After that I might have pushed at him or kicked him, I'm not sure which, I was so eager to get out of this stinking, mouldy house. Desperation gave me strength and I heard him gasp as my shove winded and overtoppled him. I took off backwards down the little tunnel and out into the air.

Once on the exterior of the bank, I didn't stop but crashed and blundered my way out of the woods. As I ran I raised my arm to my face and smelled at it, as if Robin might have left his scent on the place where he'd tried to hold me.

Surprisingly soon I came out into the open at a point a little distant from where I'd entered the wood. All was calm. The sun shone uninterrupted on Instede House and its grounds. From the angle of the light I guessed it was about three o'clock. Quickly I made my way round to the southern side of the building where I expected to find my fellows gathering to inspect the playing-area for our *Dream*. And sure enough there they were, and Revill was the laggard once again.

Two or three heads turned towards me and stared. Too late, I realized that I was probably stained and odorous from visiting Robin's hole. Richard Sincklo was gathering everybody about him. I ran up in time to catch his first words and stood there picking off some of the fragments of earth on my clothing. Cuthbert, the younger son of Lord Elcombe, was on the far side of the crowd. He was evidently in earnest about his playing.

"Here is our spot. This green plot shall be our stage," Sincklo said, opening his arms wide. Everyone smiled in recognition of the line.

"And a hawthorn brake for a tiring-house?" said another, supplying the next one.

"*We* shall be better housed," said Sincklo. "I have Elcombe's word for that."

Then Sincklo moved away and he and Thomas Pope, using small wooden pegs, marked off the extremities of our playing-area. While they are so employed and while we players are hanging around, doing not much (a usual enough state with us in rehearsals), I shall attempt to give you an idea of the arrangement of the grounds of Instede House, since they are material to this story.

The operative parts of the estate, such as the stables for the work-horses and the farm and the brew-house, were dismissed to a distance of almost half a mile or more away on the northern side, rather as a great lady might disdainfully wave off a stinky petitioner. Also on that side but much closer to the house were the kitchen garden and the wood yard. On the western edge of Instede lay the slope and cropped turf and the wild wood where wild Robin lurked, and beyond these rose the low hills which caused me to think of home. The eastern aspect, the one towards which we'd made our slow approach the previous day, and the southern one where we now stood while Sincklo and Pope pegged out the plot – these were what you might call the ornamented fringes of the edifice. To continue with the analogy of the great lady, the gardens hereabouts were the jewels and brooches which she wore close about her person and which were designed to show her to advantage.

In this ornamental part, there were alleys and arbours, beds and bowers, even a few little brooks and bridges to cross them but which somehow seemed to lead nowhere. There was a complete pleasure garden with high hedge of hornbeams round it. Every so often windows and arches had been cut through the pleated hedge so that one had teasing glimpses of the interior. At first glance I thought that someone was inside there at this moment, watching us at play, but a longer look told me that it was merely a piece of statuary or painted wood, gleaming whitely in the afternoon sun. Just when the eye got tired of all this clutter and close ostentation, relief came in the shape of parcels of plain turf, green plots like the one which was to be our stage.

Since nothing seemed to be going forward then, I lay down on the edge of the grass plot and rested my head on my clasped hands. I closed my eyes. From somewhere near at hand came the soothing trickle of water. The sun kissed my face and helped to drive away the smell of mould and worse which still lingered about my nostrils from Robin's lair. What an odd fish! With his animal pelts and his leathern box of papers and sing-song about the devil. And an alarming one too: I still felt the touch of his curved, bony hand on my arm. I resolved not to visit Lord Robin again. This was not a difficult resolution to make (or to keep). In future I must confine my time in Instede House to the Company's business.

So to work, I thought, feeling a mid-afternoon drowsiness overcome me as I lay on Lord Elcombe's sward. Talking shadows crossed my closed lids and I heard little sighs of pleasure as others, following my example, eased themselves down on the grass nearby. My companions were in the middle of a discussion.

"I tell you, they say he doesn't want to," said a voice which I identified as Will Fall's, the driver of the property wagon and occasional player.

"Says who?" came another voice (my friend Jack Wilson's).

"Yes, how do you know?" said Michael Donegrace, the boy who played Hermia.

"Oh there's a girl in the kitchens . . . " said Will and tailed off so that the other two might join him in his low laugh. Will was well-known in the Company for the frequent exercise of his – well – will. At least according to the way he told it.

"A girl in the kitchens," echoed Michael Donegrace. "Have you shown her your roasting-jack yet, Will?"

"Seriously though," said Jack Wilson. "And we must not talk too loud about the groom. His brother, whatsisname? – Cuthbert, is over there."

"Audrey of the kitchen says – "

"Audrey!" spluttered Michael Donegrace. "Ha, catch me playing an Audrey."

"Do you want to hear me or not?"

"Tell us, Will," said Jack, "I apologize for my young friend here. He is still of an age when names cause him to snigger in the back of the class."

"No, it's simply that I abominate rusticity," said young Michael in a fluty townee's voice. "Audrey – such a *country* name."

"Abominate away if you want. There's nothing wrong with Audrey," said Will Fall, with a touch of pretend indignation. "A good plain name – to suit a good plain girl."

"As long as she's not too good, eh."

I could visualize the nudge which Donegrace gave to Fall at this point.

"I shall soon bring her to the test under that heading.

Meanwhile, you will hear what she told me whether you like it or not. Because it has a bearing on our fortunes as players."

The other two said nothing. My own ears, lulled by the usual banter of my fellows, pricked up at this point.

"Briefly Audrey's tale is this. That the wedding which we are here to help celebrate would not be taking place at all if the wishes of the young man were to be consulted. That this is all Elcombe's doing. That he is a high-handed father who has more or less found his son a bride, instructed him to marry and will march him to the priest if necessary. And afterwards march him to the marital bed and so on. In short he'll do everything but perform the final duty of the groom."

"Not high-handed," said Jack Wilson. "Normal. Only the poor are free to choose."

"Why does the father have to force the son's hand in marriage anyway?" said Michael. "Is the girl ugly? What's her name?"

"I don't see what her name has to do with it, but it is Marianne. Whether Marianne is ugly or beautiful or something middling I rest in ignorance, not having seen her."

"Ask your Audrey, she of the kitchen."

"Ah, there, young Michael, you betray your inexperience," said Fall, who had only a few years' advantage over Donegrace. "You do not ask one woman to comment on another woman's looks. They are predisposed to find each other unpleasing in that regard."

"I stand corrected, and ready to kiss your arse *in that regard*. I've played dozens of women but evidently can't speak for my sex. And you still haven't told us anything, really."

"Listen then." Fall's voice dropped. "The reason for this marriage is not far to seek. It is that Marianne Morland comes from a wealthy family. Her father is a great merchant in Bristol, and his money comes in with every tide. Think of the size of her portion, think of what more her father may be happy to agree to in the way of a settlement if it means allying his daughter with one of the greatest families in England."

"So it's all money then."

Michael Donegrace sounded disappointed. Obviously he was young enough to believe in true love.

"It's always money," said mature, cynical Jack Wilson.

"But look . . . " said Michael, and with my eyes still shut I could imagine the boy waving an arm at the grand house and the fine grounds and the general splendour that lay around us.

"A couple of years ago our host lost the farm of sweet wines," explained Jack. "Which meant that the little payment he received on each cask brought over here – and if you put it all together that's a fair flow of cash – was diverted elsewhere. Meaning that the Queen was displeased with Elcombe for some reason or that she wanted to reward someone else instead. So he has lost revenue from that source and others besides."

"You are well informed, Jack," said Will Fall, echoing my own thoughts.

"I keep my ear to the ground," said Jack, "rather like Nicholas Revill over there who's pretending to be dozing but in fact listening to every word we say. His ear is close to the ground indeed. In fact, he looks as though he's spent some time recently *under* the ground."

I sensed them looking in my direction so lay very still, trying to keep from grinning.

"And furthermore, since we're talking of Elcombe and his means," said Jack, showing off his wordly knowledge of money matters, "a great place such as this is a great devourer of revenue. Why, if I pluck up some grass here it's as if I'm pulling up twopenny pieces. While the stones of this great house might as well be made of gold."

"There's your answer then," said Will. "That is why Elcombe is so eager to push his son into the marriage-bed. He's in desperate need of revenue."

"He ought to encourage whatsisname Cuthbert to go on stage then," said Jack. "He's sure to earn his weight in gold that way, I don't think. But seriously, there's a bigger mystery. Why is his elder son reluctant to be pushed into marriage? For sure, if this girl, whatsername Marianne, is rich – or if her father is, which comes to the same thing – and provided she's not absolutely ugly or totally a shrew – why shouldn't he be as eager for it as his father is? If someone compelled me to marry a wealthy woman, I wouldn't scruple too much about her looks. If very wealthy I wouldn't scruple at all."

"They say – "

"*They?*"

"Not Audrey this time but some of the other women in the place where she works . . ."

"You have been busy, Master Fall," said Michael Done-grace, half in mockery, half in envy. "Picking up tasty gobbets in the kitchen."

"Be sure I shall leave the scourings to you when you grow man enough to use your roasting-jack."

"Tell us, Will, what is it they say?" said Jack.

"They say . . . they don't know why the master's son should be unwilling to leap into such a rich bridal bed."

The other two groaned in exasperation and, lying on my back with the sun pressing down on my face and limbs, I joined them in spirit. Will Fall was only teasing, however.

"But there are stories. For example, that young Harry has no liking for women but prefers boys. So, Michael, you should parade past him in full fig."

"And a fig to you, Fall. To your face, thus."

"They also say," continued Will, "that Lord Harry has such a great hatred for his father that he would do anything to spite him – and that if it wasn't for his even greater fear of the man, he would have refused long ago to marry his father's choice of bride."

"I can see that he might be a fearsome man," said Jack thoughtfully. "Elcombe, I mean. Someone not to be crossed.

Look, Master Nicholas over there agrees with me for he's moving his noddle slightly – or perhaps it's just the breeze wagging at its emptiness."

I realized that I had unawares been nodding my head at Jack's description of Lord Elcombe as fearsome. Those close-set clear eyes. The long head and hard stare. Yes, a man not to be crossed. Since it was no more use pretending to be asleep, I stirred into reluctant life and sat up. My comrades were lounging a few paces from me.

"You've been spying on us, Nick," said Will Fall.

What had Robin the wood-man asked of me? *Is he a spy?*

"Oh Will," I said, "we know that you have no secrets from the world but are eager to tell everyone your doings and more besides. If everybody was like you there'd be no need of spies. All the same I've been most interested to hear your kitchen gossip."

"More than gossip, Nick. Supposing this wedding was called off and we players sent home with a few groats and our tails between our legs?"

"Won't happen," said Jack. "Not with all the arrangements made. Besides it would leave whatsisname Cuthbert with nobody to play with."

"Isn't there another possibility with Elcombe's son?" I said. "Besides this loving boys or hating his father."

"Which is?"

"That he loves another woman rather than the one his father has chosen."

"This is no play," said Will. "This is not the *Dream*."

"I tell you," I said, "there *is* another woman in the case. I have even seen them conversing close together."

At this, the other three sat up a little straighter and waited for me to enlighten them.

"She is not of his class, I think. In fact she is far beneath him. She has a red face and coarse features and thick limbs but that is on account of her trade."

"A washerwoman?" said Fall.

"No, she works among great heats and odours and the clanging of metal."

"In a forge?" said puzzled Donegrace.

"No," I said. "In a kitchen . . ."

"Oh I see where you are headed," said Jack Wilson.

". . . and her name is – let me see – I have it somewhere in mind – ah yes, Audrey."

I would have gone on to add one or two choice remarks about this kitchen-piece except that Will Fall launched himself in my direction and started to pummel me. After I'd thrown him off and we were lying side by side, panting slightly in the sun, Will said, "Seriously though, Nick, do you know anything?"

"About your Audrey?"

"About the woman he really loves."

"Nothing at all," I said. "But, admit it, it's as least as likely as any of the tales you brought back from your kitchen-piece."

And here the business of gossip was interrupted by the need to play. Richard Sincklo and Thomas Pope had finished their pacing and pegging out of our stage and now all that was required of us was to enact W.S.'s *Dream* on the green. Or rather to work out our exits and entrances as a preliminary to the first rehearsal *in situ*. In the playhouse, or indeed any indoor area (such as Whitehall Palace where we'd played the previous winter), there is a comfort in knowing where your boundaries are, your fixed points of entry and disappearance. Also, indoors, there are places to hide away from the eyes of the audience. But in an open pastoral setting like Instede there is no such easy concealment. The nakedness of the player, which one may feel even in a snug indoor space, is greatly magnified when the only margins are greenery and sky. True, there were three or four trees fringing the playing-space between which some painted hangings could be strung, and there was a box-hedge to one side. These would have to do for our shelter and our transformations.

Anyway, this conversation of Jack's and the others set me thinking about the forthcoming marriage and whether any of the speculations about young Harry Ascre might be correct. Certainly, the young man hadn't looked happy when he appeared in our rehearsal chamber with his parents. Was his white-faced, sleepless look the mark of love-sickness? Had he watched the farce of Pyramus and Thisbe with watery eyes because he was actually affected by the death of those clowns in love? I couldn't put myself in his position. Not so much because I'd never really suffered from love-sickness (that question of Lord Elcombe's: *You have been pierced by Cupid's dart?*), but because I couldn't imagine what it would be like to be heir to a great house and a vast swath of land and a title. Or to be directed by my father to marry someone against my wishes, if that was actually young Harry's case. What Jack Wilson had said was right, though. In a wealthy family, the older son had little choice.

That there was something wrong in the situation was confirmed for me later that same afternoon. All of us were released by Thomas Pope after practising our entrances and exits several times over on the green. Once again we had an hour or two to spend as we wished, pursuing rustic girls in the kitchen or wild men in the woods, lying on our beds on the upper floor, poring over the scrolls containing our parts – what you will. Having several days to prepare *A Midsummer Night's Dream* was a June holiday for us and I began to see why companies liked to leave the city in mid-year. The rush of plays in London, where one piece is being rehearsed in the morning, another played in the afternoon, and a third scanned for next week, leaves you breathless. Here at Instede we had time to sit and stare, walk and talk.

And talking of walking. I stayed behind on the green when most of my fellows vanished after our practice. I had a mind to explore some of the nearby walks and arbours. Perhaps I was trying to imagine what it would be like to be heir to a great house after all. My curiosity was particularly roused by the garden enclosed by a high wall of hornbeams.

I ambled through the nearest entrance. And halted there for several moments, breathless. For, inside the hornbeam-enclosed garden, there was stored a cornucopia of scents and shapes. I shaded my eyes with my hand, as if to protect my sight from the dazzle. Even though there was no one to say I shouldn't be here, I had an uneasy sense of trespassing. Directly ahead was a massy white marble fountain with figures of nymphs and sea-monsters twining around its base. On a pedestal in the centre of the basin stood Neptune, looking newly risen from the waves, his trident still dripping stone weeds. I peered over the thick rim. Dark finny shapes lounged in the depths, carp perhaps. Clouds of minute aerial creatures clustered over the water. I wandered round the fountain, running my fingers along its cool rim. To either side were narrow paths fringed with lavender and rosemary. A sanded walk stretched ahead to a little rise in the ground on which stood a summer-house, large enough to accommodate a yeoman farmer and his family. Standing in front of it was a low sun-dial whose sharp-pointed brass gnomon told me that it was after five in the afternoon. Round the face of the dial were engraved the Latin words *tempus edax rerum*, and I nodded sagely in agreement with the poet Ovid, whose words these are: time is indeed the devourer of all things.

This pleasure garden was parcelled up into precise areas marked off by paths or low hedges. Stone seats had been provided in sheltered, out-of-the-way corners. Black obelisks were grouped in pairs like impassive sentries. Statues of nymphs and fauns and of quite unaccountable creatures were dotted about. With the sun beginning to slip down the sky, the shadows were massing thickly at the base of the hedges. I wondered which members of the household took their ease in this garden. The place was immaculately tended but queerly devoid of activity, of human presence.

But while I stood gazing round, my nose and eyes assailed

by the sights and scents, I caught a different noise beneath the plashing of the fountain and the humming of the bees. It sounded like someone talking softly to himself, a continuous low mumble broken by occasional sharper sounds. Recalling my earlier resolution that whatever was happening at Instede House was really no concern of N. Revill, my first instinct was to steal out of the hornbeam garden. So I turned away from the summer-house and walked back towards the Neptune fountain. But as I passed one of the many little bays which had been created out the low box hedges that crossed and re-crossed the garden, I noticed a figure sitting on a stone seat. He was in shadow and must have been very still for me not to have seen him earlier. He was bowed forward, with his hands covering his face. His whole posture bespoke gloom, even despair. Through his clasped hands there poured an indistinct stream of words, expressive of anger or lamentation, I couldn't be sure which. Every so often his voice rose in a little bark, possibly a curse or a protest. I'd recognized him almost straightaway as Harry Ascre, Lord Elcombe's son and the subject of our gossiping speculation on the lawn. Seeing him in this state made me feel for a moment ashamed of the light-hearted way we'd played at shuttlecock with his misery. For misery it certainly was.

I crept on. But he must have somehow sensed my presence because Lord Harry chose that instant to look up from between his parted hands. His face was chalk-white and forlorn. He gazed at me incuriously, then buried himself in his hands once more. I did not wait to hear whether he resumed his grumbling lament. Rather I hastened to get out of the garden.

Thinking about it afterwards, what was almost as disturbing – and as inexplicable – as his distress was the fact that he hadn't challenged me for trespassing in the garden; or, at the least, that he hadn't attempted to hide what he was feeling. And yet here was a man due to be married within a few days!

*

Two things happened the next day, apart from the continuing round of play preparations (for us) and marriage arrangements (for the rest of the household). It was a Friday and those who regard the day as unlucky will have their fears confirmed when I tell what occurred.

Sometime in the morning we heard that the Paradise Brothers, the holy little trinity which Jack Wilson and I had seen perform in Salisbury, had fetched up at Instede with the intention of playing out their Bible tales to any who would come and watch. The Brothers were not housed in the main building, I'm glad to say; we would have taken that ill. Rather they were accommodated in some outbuildings by the brew-house. Nor were they expected to have anything to do with the wedding celebrations; we would have taken that *very* ill indeed. But the servants of the house and any of the field-workers were permitted, if they had time on their hands in the late afternoon, to slip off and be entertained by the story of Cain and Abel or Noah and his Ark. I couldn't understand why these people were tolerated on the estate until I heard that they were there by the allowance of Lady Penelope, Elcombe's wife. She apparently considered it edifying for the household menials to be instructed with pious drama.

Perhaps I was a bit touchy on this topic, although rivalry between acting companies is natural and inevitable. It was true that the Paradise Brothers' presentations had a force and effectiveness about them, but of a crude sort. Where, in their thumping dialogue and straightforward tales, was to be found anything approaching the supple beauty of Master Shake-speare or even of our lesser writers like Edgar Boscombe and Richard Milford? Why didn't the Paradise Brothers deal with real people – with kings and dukes and clowns and the like – instead of Abraham and Isaac? Didn't they realize that they were living in the seventeenth century! Anyway, there was no reason why the paths of our two companies should cross as long as the Brothers stuck to their outbuildings and their rustic audiences and left the palaces and nobles to us.

The other event of that Friday was more serious than the arrival of a pack of pious players. In fact, it was the real beginning of a catalogue of misfortune and worse.

From what Davy, my informant in the household, had said I gathered that Robin the wild wood-man was regarded as a species of walking charm – albeit a somewhat shaggy and smelly one. His continued presence in the woods of Instede was thought to confer good fortune on the house. It was apparent that Robin was treated almost like a sprite or sylvan deity by some of the less educated members of the establishment. They left offerings for him once or twice a day, those little items which he'd referred to, the turnips and sallets and goosegogs, according to the season.

The kitchen drabs took it in turns to convey food to the edge of the wood, carrying it not on a silver salver, as Robin had claimed, but on a simple wooden trencher. Every day they left the food on the stump of a felled tree, at the same time retrieving the empty platter from the previous day. It happened that on this Friday afternoon it was the turn of Audrey, the kitchen girl that Will Fall had his lecherous eye on. She walked down the slope from the house and across the cropped turf towards the dark bank of trees, with her trencher loaded with scraps of fruit and green stuff. She was one of the more intrepid of the drabs and sometimes watched the wood-man take his food. Today, on this Friday, she wondered whether she might go so far as to call out "Robin!" Or better, to whisper it. She didn't want to alarm him. He was harmless, everybody said so. And if he wasn't . . . well, she trusted to a pretty pair of heels. But would he respond? Even a dog responds to its given name. That would be something to take back to the servants' hall. She might even tell the story of her daring to Master Will Fall, that gentleman player from somewhere in the east.

In the event, Audrey did not have the opportunity to see whether Robin would respond like a dog to the calling of his name. Once she'd placed the trencher of food on the stump and tucked the empty one under her arm, she made to turn towards the thornbush where she'd successfully hidden herself on previous occasions. Then she screamed. Dangling before her face were two objects which she had some difficulty in identifying. She knew only that they were ill to look at. There was a strong, disagreeable smell in the clearing. Then the objects gradually resolved themselves into familiar items: a pair of feet – blackened, curled and scabbed feet. Fearfully she glanced up. The feet belonged to Robin, who was hanging by a rope from the branch of an elm tree. His face was even darker than usual. A swollen tongue extruded itself from his mouth.

Waxing Gibbous

The death of Robin had a lowering effect on the Instede household. I would've said that it cast a shadow over the wedding preparations but there hadn't been any great signs of joy to these beforehand, and they went forward without interruption. No, I mean that it made the servants' hall a gossiping, troubled place from which all kinds of stories and rumours spread through the estate. As newcomers, we of the Chamberlain's were largely unaffected by the death. (For some reason I kept my two encounters with the man to myself.) Nevertheless, an episode like this gives a disagreeable tinge to everything for a day or two. And these same days should have had a midsummer bloom to them. Ever since we'd arrived at Instede the mornings had dawned clear, warm and bright. Throughout the day the sky was scarcely blotted with a single cloud and, when evening approached, the golden glow of day seemed to gather itself round the great house in fold upon fold. The death of the wood-man sat oddly with all this warmth and tranquillity.

I spoke to the servant Davy about the stories concerning Robin's death – or rather he sought me out to tell me of them.

"Some say he hung himself up because he had run mad in the woods."

Remembering Robin's half-crazed behaviour and his strange talk, I had to agree that this seemed the most likely explanation. How long would I have lasted in such circumstances without going out of my wits? However, the simple explanation obviously wasn't good enough.

"Some say he was hung up, sir, because he saw things he oughtnter."

"Who hung him up, Davy?"

"The fairies and the woodwoses and other creatures of the forest."

I thought of the fairies in W.S.'s *Dream*. Airy beings whose very names (Cobweb, Mustardseed) signified their lack of size and strength.

"I do not think so, Davy."

"Begging your pardon, sir, but what do you fine people from Whitehall town know about country matters?"

I told him that I stood corrected and asked what other stories were doing the rounds.

"There is one among our fellows, Kit he is called, says he was the – the devil's own in human form, was Robin, and that the old gentleman came to collect his dues. We do not pay much heed to him because Kit says that of anybody he does not like, and he does not like anybody. He wishes them all to . . . go and see the aforementioned gentleman. Even so . . ."

"Yes," I urged Davy, seeing that there was something he was reluctant to utter.

"Even so, sir, Audrey of our kitchen says that she glimpsed Robin's feet when he was a-hanging from the tree. And one of them was – was cloven. She says."

Davy looked round apprehensively at this point. His shoulders hunched and a shudder passed through his diminutive frame.

"There, Davy, I can put your mind at rest – and Audrey's mind too. I saw Robin's feet and, though somewhat blackened and hard, they were human feet."

"Are you sure, sir? The . . . person I was referring to . . . is a cunning gentleman."

"Robin was as human as you or me, almost," I said, realising that this wasn't exactly complimentary or reassuring as soon as the words were out of my mouth. "Anyway, you told me before that he was harmless and so on. That he brought good luck on the house as long as he was in the woods."

"I don't know what to think, sir. I leave that to those up in Whitehall town."

"Very well," I said.

But it was not very well. Something about Robin's death troubled me, in a different way to that in which it disturbed people like Davy, and it took me a little time to realize what it was. The wild man of Instede woods was speedily buried a matter of hours after he'd been cut down from the hanging tree, not in the consecrated ground belonging to Rung Withers church, the one which stood nearest the estate, but in an unmarked spot on the far side of the woods where he'd spent his strange life. As a suicide he was lucky – if one can ever call the dead lucky – to avoid interment in the public highway at night. Lucky to avoid the stake through the heart which, they whisper, is sometimes the final obsequy of the self-slaughterer.

Some of the workers from the estate farm, under the direction of their bailie, took down the corpse, wrapped it in a winding-sheet, dug a shallow trench and covered the remains with the freshly turned soil. I believe that the Rung Withers parson said some words over the makeshift grave. I do not know what they were – he could not have read the office because Robin had quit this life in such a way as to ensure his eternal damnation – but they would surely have been a comfort to Robin's soul as well as a testament to the Christian spirit of the parson.

I remember my own father burying a man whose body had been recovered from our river. The villagers of Miching said that he had thrown himself in on purpose to drown but my father would have none of it and insisted that the young man had lost his footing and been swept away by the torrent. Yet it was summer and the banks were dry, the river low and sluggish. Neverthless, said my father, since none of us was there to see him fall and since he had given no notice of his intentions, he deserves Christian burial and will continue to do so as long as I'm parson in this place. It seemed that the gentleman at this church was cut from the same cloth as my father.

Anyway, poor Robin was duly dead and buried – but not forgotten. In fact the sense of his presence seemed to grow larger in his corporeal absence.

Stories continued to fly about the place, the kind of thing which Davy had repeated to me, that Robin had been set swinging by the wood-sprites, that Old Nick had come to claim his own, &c. The question which snagged on my mind, however, had to do with a more practical consideration. It wouldn't have occurred to me if I hadn't found out by chance that the halter which he'd been wearing when they cut him down had been preserved. The bailie of the farm, an oily individual by the name of Sam, had loosened the rope from off Robin's neck, coiled it up and kept it as a prize.

I'd heard that the rope from London's Tyburn tree was often chopped up into little lengths and then sold by the hangman for several shillings apiece, it being supposed that the sweat and grease of the man on the gibbet had peculiar life-giving properties. I'd even heard that those who despaired of a cure at the hands of a physician would sometimes pay – and pay highly – to be allowed to hold their infected parts against the raw and reddened neck of a man newly cut down. I'd heard of these things, I say, but this was the first time I'd ever encountered the practice.

It turned out that Sam the bailie wasn't yet as advanced as his London counterparts. He was keeping the rope with which poor Robin had turned himself off, true, but not with the aim of profiting by another's misery – or at least not profiting unduly. Rather he was charging the simple folk on his own farm, as well as others on the estate, a mere halfpenny to gaze on this fatal cord and a full penny to touch it. What claims he made about it, I don't know. Perhaps that its touch would cause the blind to see and the halt to walk without limping. Or perhaps he was merely building on that secret delight which we all have in seeing (and sometimes touching) those items which are linked to death. I dare say he extracted a kiss or a grope from some of the women. He was an oily man was Sam. This knowledge I had from Audrey of the kitchen via Will Fall, her beau.

When I heard that the bailie had saved the cord with which Robin had suspended himself, I paid him a call. He lived in a tiny two-storey house near the farm, from which he kept a close watch on all the doings of his workers. He stayed a little aloof from them, to enhance his mystery, and his house was set behind low hedges. He expressed surprise that a gentleman player from London should be interested in examining a suicide's rope. Maybe he thought we were surrounded by the hangman's impedimenta all the time up there, stumbling over scaffolds, running into ropes, and would think nothing of a country hanging. Anyway, Sam the bailie didn't hesitate when I showed him my penny and, after securing the outside door to his downstairs room and slipping the coin into a practised pocket, he went straight to a coffer in a corner. This he unlocked, blocking my view with his back. From the coffer he produced, with a touch of ceremony, an item wrapped up in some kersey cloth. He bent forward to lay it out on the floor in a patch of sunlight, and wheezingly peeled away the coverings to reveal a grimy, tangled length of rope. After this he stood back, as proud as if he'd just given birth to this mortal coil.

"You may touch, Master – ?"

"Nicholas."

"You've paid your penny, you may touch."

I wasn't that eager to finger the rope but I did get down on hands and knees to peer closely at it. I felt my skin crawl slightly and my neck began to itch in expectation of the cord. Without straightening out the rope, I estimated its length to be about five or six feet. One end had been cut through, but not cleanly. A few strands of fibre frayed out. There was a crude but effective knot securing the noose at the other end. It didn't look as though it would have given even under the weight of two men. I thought of Robin's thin raggedy frame, swaying in the summer airs. Standing up again, I made a business of extracting a whole sixpence and holding it aloft so it caught the light which streamed through the small grubby window. The room was close-pent, airless. Sam was on the alert to meet my requirements.

"I have a question or two."

Even as I said this, I wondered why I was saying it, why I was going to this expense to establish how Robin had met his end. Sixpence was no great matter but it was still half a day's pay. I placed the coin in Sam's greasy palm. We stood with the coil of rope between us.

"You cut him down?"

"Not I personally, Master Nicholas. But the men under my direction."

"Can you describe how you did it? How they did it."

"They cut him down, is all."

"But how? Sixpennyworth of how."

Sam paused. His oily brow furrowed. I believe he considered that I was deriving some queer pleasure from his description.

"Oliver climbed up the tree and then out along the branch from where the body was hanging. He had to come down again to get a knife."

"Why?"

"The rope was tied about the branch with a knot. The knot was too fast to be untied. Oliver fumbled with his hands but he could not unpick it when all the time he was trying to keep balance on the branch. I saw the rope must be cut and I told Oliver so."

"He used a knife."

Sam nodded, as though he was humouring a slow child.

"Whose?"

"Why, his own," said Sam, looking at me in puzzlement (and indeed I could not have said why I was asking some of these questions). "He had taken it off his belt when he first climbed the tree. A man can fall on his own knife."

"He found it easy to climb the tree?"

"Not so much, but he is young and limber. He likes these feats."

"And then?"

"Then Oliver cut the cord, though it took some time because his knife needed sharpening."

Sam gestured at the rope lying in the sunlight. That explained the frayed end.

"Who else was present?"

"There were two others who held – held Robin's legs."

"Why?"

"We did not want him to fall in a heap on the ground."

"Of course," I said. "That was thoughtful of you."

"Not me. We had Brown with us. Brown told us."

"Ah," I said, wondering just how much of a crowd had attended this deposition. "Brown?"

"The parson of Rung Withers."

"The one who also attended when you buried Robin, and said a few words?"

"He's an odd one," said Sam. "To care for a poor worthless body."

"Just one more thing, Sam, for my six pennies. They're saying it was the wood spirits who did this or – or something else."

"Thought is free," said Sam.

"Yes," I said. "But let us suppose that Robin did this to himself. How do you think he did it? How did he hang himself?"

"He climbed the tree, Master Nicholas. He fastened one

end of the rope about the branch and the other end about his neck and then he fell off into the empty air."

I admired the touch of poetry in my friend's answer but the rest of it left me dissatisfied. However, I asked nothing more in this line.

As I was making to leave, Sam said, "Have a look in the barn before you return to the big house."

"Why?"

For answer, Sam tapped the little protruberance that served him for a nose.

"Do you believe in this?" I said, glancing down at the dirty rope on the floor. It seemed to swell and writhe under my gaze. The room grew hotter.

"There are things in the woods which might drive a man to despair."

"No," I said, reluctant to make myself clear, "I mean – that touching this cord will bring luck and so on."

"Thought is free," he repeated. "Go on. You have paid."

I bent down and touched the rope with my fingertips then turned quickly about and, after fumbling for a moment with the door, walked out of his dwelling and into fresh air. My fingers burned.

Outside all was calm. The afternoon sky was cloudless. Farm buildings were dotted among clumps of elm and sycamore. I wondered why Sam had directed me to go to the barn. It was easily identifiable as the largest of the buildings hereabouts. The path to it was scuffed and rutted. As I drew nearer I heard someone speaking inside in low, even tones but was unable to make out what was being said. The double doors to the barn were wide open. At the far end among the shadows stood a pale figure. I wondered that a man could stand so tall. Then something thickened in my throat, for the figure was not standing but swaying slightly from side to side. I blinked and rubbed my eyes but the image did not disappear. I felt my gorge rise. Even so, I continued to advance towards the black, gaping entrance with an almost mechanical tread.

I halted on the threshold. I wasn't the only one drawn by this spectacle. Knots of people stood about in the interior of the barn. They were looking at a man hanging from a rope which was attached to a beam. The body, clad in a white smock, swung gently from side to side. The tie-beam creaked under its weight.

"Well," said Will Fall, "I thought it was nearly as good as the real thing."

"I have never seen one," I said, "and I'm not sure I want to either."

"No true Londoner then, Nicholas — not until you've been to Tyburn and seen someone turned off. My father would drive me miles to see the sight."

I'd been told this before: that I was no true Londoner until I'd done or seen something . . . usually something unpleasant, even if exciting. My normal response would have been to shrug it off or make a joke of it. But this afternoon I felt unequal to laughter. The session with Sam the bailie had left a bad taste. My fingertips still tingled from touching the rope with which Robin had hanged himself. Then to witness, immediately afterwards, the body of a man swaying from the beam of a barn, watched by an appreciative crowd as if it really had been a Tyburn turn-off. No, I didn't see much to applaud here.

"What you should do," said Will Fall, his voice dropping low and glancing behind him, "is take along a wench, especially one who has not yet come round. There's nothing they like more than to see a man turned off. Even better if he struggles somewhat. It's more efficacious than a love-philtre. You'll hardly have time to find a dry patch of earth."

"I'll remember that," I said, wondering if Nell had ever been present at an execution.

Will looked behind him once more. Audrey, his "wench" from the Instede kitchens, knew her place and followed us at a respectful distance. She was red-faced in the sun. She it was who had discovered the swaying body of Robin the wood-man, and gained a certain fame thereby, particularly with the claim that one of Robin's feet was cloven. I wondered that she had any desire to see the scene re-enacted in play. But there is no accounting for human taste – and, more particu-larly, no accounting whatsoever for the leanings of the female half. As Will Fall showed by his next comment (he was unable to shift off the subject of women and executions):

"And for the effect on a woman of a full hanging and drawing and quartering . . . just think of that."

"You've seen one of those?"

"I live in hope."

"We need more traitors," I said.

"Aye, we do," said Will eagerly, oblivious to my irony. "More common traitors. These noblemen like the Earl of Essex are no good. They lose only their heads, not their bowels and all."

I stared ahead across the fields. We were walking back towards the big house which, from whatever angle you approached, dominated the scene. Inside the barn I'd found, in addition to the hanged man, Will Fall, our carter-player, making up one of the onlookers and accompanied by his drab Audrey. Plain described her fairly. Whether she was good or not there was no knowing. She cast frequent cow-like glances in his direction. If she was still good then it was a condition she wouldn't enjoy much longer.

As you've probably guessed, what I'd witnessed through the open doors of the great barn was no real hanging but the mere simulation of one, though quite good enough to deceive the eye from a few yards off, especially when played in shadow. The "victim" was supported by quilted belts and straps fastened around his chest and under his arms, the whole apparatus being concealed beneath the white smock he wore and being connected at the back of his costume to a dark cord hanging from the rafters. The noose circling his neck was a trumpery thing, more like string and probably made of flax for safety's sake (so that it would have snapped if it had borne any weight), yet because of its light colour it stood out against the gloomy interior of the barn, as did his white garb. All that was required to top up this desolate picture was a deal of face-pulling and the sounds of strangulation on the part of the dangling man – in short, the kind of effect which every player loves (there is a child in all of us). After that he merely had to swing gently. It wouldn't have been comfortable to maintain this position six feet above the ground for long but you can endure much for the edification and amazement of the crowd.

This hanging was the conclusion of yet another drama penned and performed by the Paradise Brothers, the players who'd so recently fetched up at Instede and who were allowed to remain here through the sufferance, perhaps even the active encouragement, of Lady Penelope Elcombe. This time the brothers – of whom there really were three (aptly named Peter, Paul and Philip) – had chosen to enact the story of Judas Iscariot's betrayal of our Saviour. So, for the betterment of the Instede workers, they told the sorry tale of the thirty pieces of silver, the treacherous kiss in the garden, the despair of the renegade, and his self-slaughter dangling from an elder tree. This had gone down well, I gathered, particularly the hanging. As Will Fall had said, it was nearly as good as the real thing. And the Instede workers probably welcomed it the more because they didn't have the benefit of all the amenities and diversions enjoyed by Londoners: to wit, regular hangings, and occasional drawings and quarterings as well.

At the end of the hanging – that is, after Paul "Iscariot" Paradise, again wearing the yellow beard he'd sported in the part of Cain, had swung up there for long enough – the leader of this holy trinity, Peter Paradise, stepped forward and sermonized and harangued the rustic audience, just as he had the Salisbury townees a few nights before. Once more he "brothered" and "sistered" us puritan-style although real puritans would have had nothing to do with the drama, even of this pious Biblical kind. I wasn't entirely clear what the God-player was talking about, but he seemed to be attacking greed and money – and cupidity and lucre – and, just in case the point hadn't been driven home, avarice and coin. Judas Iscariot, you see, was tempted by thirty pieces of silver. Observe into what an abyss of despair his money-lust had tipped him. Begone, greed! Avaunt thee, avarice! The day will come when the rich man shall be expelled from his castle, and the poor man come into his own.

I wondered to hear all this. Like the talk in Salisbury it sounded faintly seditious. Did Elcombe over in his palace know – or more to the point did his wife know – that a company of player-preachers were uttering heresies about money and property on the edge of their fine estate? Perhaps fortunately, most of what he said seemed to go over his audience's heads. They were only there for the hanging, after all. Whether he was understood or not, Peter Paradise, with his natural white beard and furrowed brow, was a powerful speaker. He thundered. And he was a powerful man too. As a whole, the trio were well able to look after themselves; I remembered how "Cain" had clubbed Tom the farmer, and the brawl which had ensued.

I wondered also whether the holy brothers had heard of the stir on the estate over the hanging of Robin and were using it to their own ends. If so, I didn't in any way blame them for this . . . they were merely behaving like players in all times and places, setting themselves afloat on the current of the moment, the one that was flowing past their door. Otherwise it seemed too much of a coincidence that they should have picked on Iscariot's tale at the same time as a man had strung himself up in the woods.

If he had strung himself up.

This was the question that my visit to Sam the bailie hadn't answered. If anything, the visit had deepened my doubts. In pursuit of this problem I went down to examine the spot where Robin's body had been discovered. I quickly identified the elm, not by any markings on the tree itself but because of the scuffed, disturbed ground around its base. The branch was easy to identify too. It was long, straight and relatively low. Still hanging from it was the little stub of rope, cut through by Sam's man when he'd been unable to undo the knot. The air was warm but I shivered.

Nothing of what I saw there hardened my doubts into certainties. But it didn't allay them either. The trouble was that I could do nothing practical with my suspicions. Our seniors Richard Sincklo or Thomas Pope would probably have been receptive enough if I'd talked to them, but they wouldn't have been able to do anything either, even had they been so inclined. We had no real foothold in this place. We were guests of Lord Elcombe, but paid guests, relatively lowly ones at that with a task to perform. Whatever happened on his estate had nothing to do with us. And the suicide of an eccentric who dwelt in the woods, odd and unsettling as it might be, would surely be forgotten soon, especially when there were great matrimonial matters to attend to.

Except that it showed no signs of being forgotten. The stories about Robin being strung up by woodwoses or sprites or fetched off by Old Nick did not abate but became a distraction at a time when the hearts and minds of everyone at Instede should have been devoted to the nuptials of Harry and Marianne. Someone in authority – presumably Elcombe himself – evidently decided that enough was enough and called in help from outside to try to clear up this business.

I learned of this in a roundabout way the next morning. I was wandering about the eastern side of the estate, near the margin of the little lake which lay by the approach to the great house. Sun glittered off the water. I wondered whether Elcombe had had the lake dug or whether it was already there, conveniently at hand when the house was built. The diverting pretence that all these acres were mine, never a very convincing one, was hard to sustain for more than a few moments, and my mind was free (*videlicet*, idle). So generous was the provision which had been made for the Chamberlain's preparation and rehearsal time at Instede that we found ourselves with several spare hours of the day to fill. The *Dream* and the wedding were still some days hence. So there I was wandering, slightly mopish, in these sunlit grounds, book in hand, and thinking of Master W.S.'s Hamlet, who also wanders about the chambers and grounds of a great palace, book in hand, and much more than a little mopish. I was word-perfect in my part as Lysander the lover. If we'd been in London I would've been furiously learning my lines for the next day's play, and the day after's, and the following week's too. But here in the country there was no urgency.

In the absence of work, my thoughts drifted like the thistledown which floated through the haze. I had no kitchen-piece to pursue, although I was beginning to wonder whether I shouldn't find myself some occupation of that sort, as two or three of my fellows had.

Country matters.

"Master Revill."

I looked back. A woman was approaching across the sward.

My heart started to beat faster and my bowels to do a little dance. Afterwards I couldn't have sworn that I hadn't been thinking of her at that very moment, and that she had arrived pat.

"Master Revill," she called again, but softer. She was wearing a small-brimmed hat and had to shield her face with her hand so as to see better.

I smiled as she drew closer. At least I hope I smiled. I was, to be honest, a little flustered.

By day she was even more beautiful than by the candlelight of her father's house. Her hat provided a little shelter from the sun but left her face largely open for my timorous inspection. Her complexion had that natural whiteness which only a young woman can achieve without artifice. She had her father's eyes, grey and penetrating but in her case they were softened by a touch of amusement, even mockery. Her lips were firm and red. Her nose was more assertive than shrinking, yet still delicate enough, even if it confirmed her as a woman of decided opinions. Or so it seemed to me. I hadn't even started to look below her fine neck yet, except in the most general, fleeting fashion. Staring would have been ill-bred. I didn't want lower myself in her eyes by lowering my own on her.

I was, of course, already half in love with her and I hadn't even said a word yet!

"Mistress . . . Fielding," I eventually stumbled out with.

"How are your cuts and bruises?"

She made to put her hand up to my face, to the places where only a few days before she'd touched me with long white fingers and soothing ointments. But to my regret she withdrew the hand, obviously considering that this would be rather a familiar gesture in broad daylight.

"Much better," I said. "In fact I'd forgotten about them – thanks to your ministrations."

"My father told me how you'd acquired them."

"Oh, it's not worth troubling about," I said, embarrassed to recall my unwise words in the Salisbury market-place and surprised that Adam Fielding knew the story. I thought I'd taken care to not tell him. However, he was obviously the kind of man who made it his business to know everything.

"What must you think of us down here?"

"I come from down here myself – or not far away."

No doubt she already knew this too from her father. The idea that they might have discussed me was not unpleasing.

"Anyway I've seen much worse in London," I said airily. "Up there . . . mobs of apprentices roam the streets like wolf-packs looking for honest citizens to insult and foreigners to injure."

Her grey eyes widened and, pleased with effect I was producing, I plunged on.

"There are cast-off soldiers and sailors, desperate men who know no way of life but fighting or threatening to fight. There are places you'd be afraid to tread by day let alone at night."

Her eyes widened further. Too late I noticed they were tinged with mockery.

"Strange, Master Revill, that I saw so little of this when I was last in London a few weeks ago."

"You probably didn't visit the right places," I said lamely.

"The wrong ones, you mean. But then my aunt lives quite close to the city walls."

"I am not lucky enough to be connected with anyone on the other side."

"The other side? You make it sound like the hellish river Styx."

"Right enough," I said. Not only was she beautiful, she was also quick and resourceful in conversation. "There are many Charons, though, who will transport you across to the south side, which is where I am. And my Company as well."

"Where the soldiers fight and the apprentices fester?"

"You take it lightly, Mistress Fielding, but there are places where I would not be happy to see *you* wandering, at any rate by night. Even if you are no stranger to London."

"It's good of you to be so concerned for my welfare, Master Revill."

"Nicholas, please, if you will agree that I can call you Kate. And I'm merely repaying the concern you showed for *my* welfare when you dressed my wounds."

She made no direct answer to this but turned slightly to one side, as if to indicate that she wished to move on. I fell in step beside her. We ambled in the direction of the Instede lake. The sun dazzled off the water. As we walked I cast covert glances at her, but (believe me) in no lascivious spirit. Her neckline was low enough to interest but not to overexcite. She was wearing a farthingale which defined a small, delicate waist.

"What do you read?" she said, glancing at the closed book in my hand.

I might have answered with the words my lord Hamlet uses when he is questioned by Polonius – namely, words, words, words. But I said, "A volume of verse by one of our playwrights."

"Our?"

"At the Globe playhouse in London."

"It is Master Shakespeare you mean?"

"No, Kate," I said, a little surprised at her knowledge, "not Shakespeare but a lesser light. A new writer in fact. One Richard Milford who had some luck with a piece called *A Venetian Whore* earlier this year. His success on the playhouse stage has encouraged him to turn his hand to poetry, and call it *A Garland*."

Richard Milford had given me the newly published book just before we'd left for the country. He handed over the volume, still crisp from the press. I could have sworn there was water in his eyes. It was obviously a solemn and proud moment for him, although I must confess that these little mysteries and sentiments of authorship are beyond me. Anyway, Milford trusted my judgment and wanted my approval, despite the differences we'd had from time to time.

"A direct title, that *Whore*," said Kate. "A London title. I don't know how that would go down here. So what does he deal with on paper?"

"What all poets deal with in their first volumes," I said.

"Love?"

"Just so."

"Is he good?"

"He has something," I said guardedly. "A little something."

"Read me something of what he has then," she said. "A little something."

"Let's sit down. I can't walk around and read aloud."

We reached the margin of the lake. Stone seats had been placed at irregular intervals round the banks. The stone was warm to the touch. We sat at opposite ends of a seat. I flicked through the volume although I already had an idea of which one I was going to read to her. Finding the page, I started without any throat-clearing preliminaries.

When suns shall set their final time of all,
And stars no longer light us with their fire,
The moon herself withdraw from night's fair hall,
And darkness universal us enmire,
Grieve not, o world – for one torch still remains.
This, seen but once, will all that's lost restore,
Turn Nature's course and break nocturnal chains,
So 'stablish light on earth for evermore.
Thy beauty 'tis which can this feat achieve,
And, for a wonder, work it from the grave.
For though foul death must us of thee bereave,
There yet remains a glory shall us save.
They who read my words in praise of thee
Will never want a light by which to see.

I looked up slyly, shyly, to watch how she was receiving this sonnet by Master Milford. Not that I was very concerned about Richard Milford's words. All readers like to be complimented, as do all players, but not so much on the matter (which isn't theirs) as on the delivery. Kate was looking at me intently. I was unable to read her eyes but saw the smile which tugged at the corners of her firm mouth.

"That is very typical, I think," she said.

"Do you know his work? The book's only just come out."

"Typical of poets. That they should welcome the end of the world and universal darkness . . . as long as it provides them with a conceit about a single light remaining."

"Extravagance is natural in love poets," I said, feeling slightly defensive on behalf of young Milford. "They imbibe it with their mother's milk. You don't have to take what they say so seriously."

"Oh I think you do."

"You do?"

"This seriousness is not about she who he loves, all he is serious for is himself."

I began to feel I'd made a wrong move in reading to her. What I'd wanted was to establish a mood, a mildly melting mood, not to initiate a discussion on the principles of love poetry. However, she persisted.

"See at the end of it where he says . . . what is it? . . . *They who read my words in praise of thee . . . Will never want a light by which to see.* And by the way, if there're no lights left in the world how could anyone see his words to read them, however brilliant they are? In any case what he's praising there is not her beauty but his own writing. Isn't it, Nicholas?"

"Well, yes, I expect so," I said, impressed by the way she'd memorized the final couplet after a single hearing, and thrown by her somewhat masculine application of common sense to the fragile world of the love-lyric. She obviously had something of her father's clear intellect. "But remember what inspired him to write in the first place. Her beauty. Cause and effect."

"Oh," said confident Kate, "I don't suppose there was a woman in the case at all. He was writing his poem to the empty air."

"That doesn't mean he doesn't mean it," I said.

"No," she said, "but it doesn't mean he does either."

"If you say so," I said, seeing we were going nowhere and tapping the binding of the book. "I know the gentleman but not quite well enough to question him on these things."

"There," said Kate, and I was reminded by her small smile of satisfaction of my friend Nell and her pleasure when she bested me in argument.

"One thing I've learnt, Kate, from this."

"Yes?"

"That I shall not be writing you a love poem."

To my surprise she said nothing to what was intended as a piece of provoking banter but coloured slightly. Quickly, I moved to talk of something else.

"You are visiting Instede for the wedding?"

"I'm with my father. He is on other business now. There was a man died here a few days ago."

"On Friday last. He hanged himself from a tree."

"But I believe there are many stories about how he died," she said.

"Yes," I said. "Stories credited by the simple folk on the estate."

"Therefore Lord Elcombe, learning that the matter would almost certainly be enquired into, requested my father to look at the manner of this man's death and pronounce on it in order to calm such speculations."

"As a Justice of the Peace his word is bound to carry weight," I said.

"Everyone knows my father," said Kate. "He is respected the length and breadth of the county."

Her face softened. I remembered the way she'd spoken to him in their Salisbury house, mildly chiding and affectionate. Perhaps she had no other love in her life but him.

"Isn't this more of a job for a coroner?" I asked, genuinely curious.

"You'll have to ask my father that. But I know that it wouldn't be worth a coroner's while to look into it. They get nothing for a suicide."

"Well, the man who died certainly had nothing, nothing at all. He lived wild in the woods and was fed by members of the household. They believed that for as long as he lived down there he brought good fortune to the house."

Kate glanced over her shoulder at the glittering palace on the rise.

"It's still there," she said.

"I met the wood-man, met him twice, he was a strange creature, he wore animal skins but no shoes," I said in a rush.

"He gave you an audience?"

"Yes, it was exactly that. He said he was lord of the wood, just as Elcombe is lord of Instede. His name was Robin."

"After Robin Hood."

"He was as ragged as the redbreast is in a hard winter," I said. "Can I talk to your father about him? I have something to say concerning his death."

So Kate Fielding conducted me to her father, the Justice of the Peace. When I expressed surprise at her familiarity with the house she told me she'd been a visitor to Instede ever since she could remember.

Adam Fielding and his daughter were much better quartered than we Chamberlain's men on the top floor. It was apparent from the comfort of their apartment that Elcombe had a high regard for his guests and that he was earnest in his desire that Fielding should put a stop to the gossip and rumour about the death of Robin. I waited in an antechamber while Kate went ahead to prepare the way with her father. After a few moments she reappeared and told me to go in, saying that he had already seen us together. This main room faced east and looked out over the lake where we'd so recently been sitting. That Fielding was aware of our approach merely confirmed my impression of him as a man who made it his business to know all. The windows were open and sweet smells of summer sidled into the room. Fielding was sitting at a small table and making some notes. He looked up from his writing when I entered.

"Your worship," I said, bowing quite low.

"Master Revill . . . Nicholas," he said. "I was wondering when we should meet again."

"The honour is mine, sir."

"You will not deny me some share in the pleasure of

renewing our acquaintance, I am sure. Sit down, please. This is not my house but the servants are mine to command. Is there anything you require?"

"No thank you."

"You are well looked after here too, I hope."

"Above our deserts, some would say."

Some, like Oswald Eden, I added to myself.

"It would be a different story for each of us if we were looked after according to our deserts. Kate says you have something to tell me."

"Yes, sir. But first could you inform me . . . why you are here? Forgive me if that sounds impudent. I don't mean it to."

Fielding paused for a moment as if gathering his thoughts then spoke. "A man has died in the grounds of this place by his own hand, it appears. Yet there are plenty of tales flying about concerning the manner of his death, and foolish talk of devils and wood-spirits. This would be unwelcome enough at any time but particularly now when all hands and eyes are meant to be directed towards the wedding. So Lord Elcombe has asked me to do what I can to set people's minds at rest. It is, in any case, a situation where the law would – and should – have its say. Men ought not to die unregarded, whoever they are. Will that do?"

"Thank you."

"But you already know this? Kate has told you."

"I needed to hear you say it, sir, since I'm not certain how welcome my words are going to be. They may not give much authority for devils or wood-spirits but they won't set anybody's mind at rest."

"Since I am just arrived, Nicholas, you shall be my first witness. Speak on."

So I told him.

He listened intently. I spoke precisely. Everything about him, from his manner to his square-cut beard, from his profession as Justice to his cool grey eyes, suggested a preference for neatness and order. After I'd finished – it didn't take long – he steepled his fingers.

"Why do you think no one else has noticed this?" he asked at last.

"I don't take credit for any special perspicacity, your worship. It may be that others did notice but said nothing because Robin himself was, as it were, beneath notice. He was a strange man in the woods. Scarcely human in a way."

"What exactly was wrong with his hands?"

"I don't know. I suppose that long exposure to the elements had caused them to turn inwards like that or perhaps they had been so from birth. They resembled animal paws more than human hands. He could clutch at things but he couldn't grasp properly. Certainly he would not have been able to weave the knot which I saw on the noose."

"Two knots in fact," said Fielding. "You said that the rope was secured about the tree as well as around his neck."

"And the tree was not so easy to climb. Sam the bailie told me that one of his men had had some difficulty getting up it when they went to collect the body. And he is young and fit."

"Whereas Robin was thin and ragged by all accounts."

"Yes."

"Without much strength!"

I thought of the way he'd scrabbled at me in his underground shelter.

"Little enough."

"But sufficient, it seems," said Fielding, "to shin up a tree, crawl along a branch, balance astride it somehow and stay up there for however many minutes it took to fasten the rope first about his neck and then to the branch – or the other way round – and make all secure enough so that neither knot should give."

I said nothing, wanting him to come to his own conclusions.

"And in your opinion, Nicholas, he could have done none of these things?"

"I don't know. He was nimble in his own way, scurrying along the ground like an animal. He might have climbed the elm and the rest of it."

"You looked at the ground below the tree?"

"Yes," I said, a little gratified at my own thoroughness, "but it did not reveal much. Or anything at all, except that a number of people appeared to have stood on that spot."

"When they took down the body."

"It would seem so."

"Seems and appears. Seems and appears. But nothing is certain."

"No, your worship."

"You mentioned the rope. What was troubling about that?"

"Robin fastened his garments, if you could call them that, with bits of thread and twine. Where would he obtain a rope to hang himself with?"

"The house?"

"The servants brought him odds and ends of food. They would surely have balked at a halter."

"Perhaps he kept one for just such an eventuality," said Fielding, "like Hieronimo in that piece by Thomas Kyd."

"*The Spanish Tragedy*," I supplied almost without thought but pleased to be reminded of the safer world of the stage.

"Except that this is no fiction," said Fielding grimly.

"There's more," I said. "I didn't mention this before because I wasn't sure how you would respond to what I've said so far but . . ."

"Yes."

Fielding again fixed his penetrating gaze on me as I described in more detail the second visit I'd made to Robin's domain and the way in which the wood-man had showed me his lair, and the leathern-covered box. And the papers inside it.

"Which you couldn't read?"

"He didn't give me a chance. He wouldn't let them out of his hold. Anyway there was little light to read by inside his hole."

"You've been back to retrieve them?"

"No."

"What are we waiting for then?" said Fielding, rising for the first time from his writing-table. He grabbed a brocade doublet from the chair-back. "Come on."

He lead the way out of the room. I followed dutifully. There was no sign of Kate. Like his daughter, Fielding was familiar with the lay-out of house and grounds and within a few minutes we were on the western side of Instede and descending the slope towards the woods. He slackened his pace to allow me to catch up.

"You can show me the tree as well."

For the second time I stood under the elm from which poor Robin had hung. I pointed up at the guilty branch – a gesture which was hardly necessary since the convenience of that limb made it the obvious choice for the would-be suicide. And then there was that small, dirty stub of rope waggling off the branch. I thought of a birth cord and felt momentarily nauseated. At the base of the tree were twigs and leaves, now losing some of their sappiness, and presumably torn off by Robin himself when he climbed up or by those who'd cut him down.

Adam Fielding, dressed as he was in fine doublet and breeches, squatted on his haunches and examined the ground below the branch. Evidently he couldn't see enough in this position for he soon got down on all fours, bringing his nose close to the forest-floor like a dog. He pushed aside some of the little accumulations of grass and leafage which had piled up there. He scooped up several handfuls of loose soil and let them trickle through his fingers. Then he got to his feet again and approached the base of the tree as if he was going to subject it to an interrogation. He pushed his face at the bark and walked around the tree several times. I stood by, uncertain what was required of me and unwilling to disturb him in his devotions. Eventually he stopped.

"Look here, Nicholas."

I crossed over to where he stood.

"This would be the place to climb up from, no? This knot here would allow you a foothold, and you could hoist yourself up using that cluster of twigs, could you not? In fact, from the way they're bent down it looks as though someone has already taken this course. And then you might take hold of that branch round the corner . . . and so on . . . and so up . . ."

For an instant I thought Fielding was going to follow his own directions (I've rarely seen a more vigorous man, given his middle years). Then I was afraid that he might ask me to climb it. I don't mind climbing trees but part of me revolted slightly at the idea of scaling one which had been employed in a hanging. However the Justice's mind was already shifting elsewhere.

"Now, Nicholas, you must take me to this strange man's – what did you call it? – hole."

This was easier said than done. When I'd followed in the naked footsteps of Robin I had taken little heed of the path through the woods. For some time Adam Fielding and I blundered about in sun and shadow, stooping under branches and skirting dense clumps of undergrowth. The longer we spent in the wood the bigger it seemed to grow. I began to have an inkling of how Robin might regard it as a "kingdom". On several occasions I thought I'd identified the hollowed-out bank standing next to a line of large trees. But each time I failed to find the entrance to the elusive earth. I started to sweat and grow worried. Some bird which I couldn't have named began to make noises that sounded mocking, a kind of rippling ha-ha-ha.

I wasn't so much discomfited by not uncovering Robin's hole as by the notion that I was wasting Fielding's time. After all, it was I who had sought him out because I was troubled by the manner of the strange man's death. I'd offered to show the Justice something which could be material in the case, and it was plain that I didn't have the least idea what I was about. He was silent, probably because his patience was running thin.

I wiped my eyes. Suddenly across the corner of my vision there flickered that white form which I'd first glimpsed in the woods some miles outside Instede. I turned to catch it – and it was gone. I felt dizzy. I grabbed a branch to support myself. Fielding was behind me. My mouth was open to say, or rather to stammer out, "Did you see . . .?" but it was apparent from his settled expression that he'd seen nothing. Perhaps it was imagination; safer to put it down to imagination.

"Nicholas?"

"I'm sorry, sir, but I am not sure where this place is. The wood is bigger than I supposed."

"Let us abandon the search for now. It's nearly dinner time, anyway."

I agreed reluctantly.

"I rather think the way out must lie in this direction," said Fielding, taking charge. We moved off to the left, like two gents out for a late morning stroll, although from time to time we were forced to go in single file.

"Tell me about your play, Nicholas. I trust the rehearsals are going well and so on."

"Well enough, your worship. We are unused to having so much time at our disposal. In London we'd already've played the *Dream* a couple of times before a congregation and be engaged in something else by now."

"Congregation?"

"What Dick Burbage calls our audiences. Congregations."

Fielding laughed. He had a pleasant, unforced laugh.

"Because the playhouse is the temple where they do their devotions? Where they come to worship their idols?"

"I am sure Dick means nothing disrespectful by it."

"And I am equally sure he does. At least I hope he does."

Knowing Master Burbage's combative attitude to most things, I could only agree.

"You miss the press and hurry of your London life?" Fielding asked.

"The country is well enough in its way and I'm glad to be here, but as to missing London, if I'm honest I do. Perhaps we should be staging a city play to relieve this itch of mine. *A Midsummer Night's Dream* is all palaces and woods."

"Like Instede," said Fielding. He paused before continuing, "And in this *Dream* you must be one of the lovers."

"You have seen Master Shakespeare's play?"

"Yes, in – let me see – '95, when it was played in . . . I cannot recall the name of the place . . ."

"The Theatre? Near Finsbury Fields."

"Over there. My sister-in-law lives on the north side of the city," he added.

I remembered that Kate had mentioned her aunt while I'd been trying to impress her with London wickedness.

"The Chamberlain's Company are better lodged now in the Globe playhouse," I said, "though some would say that we're in a, ah, less respectable district."

"Respectability again, Nicholas. Anyone would think you were my age. The day a player becomes too respectable is the day he dies, in his craft at least."

"You are right, sir," I said, though such sentiments were surprising in the mouth of a magistrate. "And to answer your question, I do play one of the lovers, Lysander by name. While for my co-rival in love I am privileged to be playing alongside Cuthbert, Lord Elcombe's younger son."

"So he plays at playing."

"Oh, he is quite in earnest about it, I think. Wait!"

I stopped, for we were passing the spot where Robin had had his lair. Almost certain of it, I looked about. Yes, there was the tall shoulder of trees rearing up to the right while below was a leaf-strewn bank. I crouched down. Straight in front of me was the dank hole that led to his hide-away.

"It is here."

Fielding crouched down beside me.

"I found it when I wasn't looking for it."

"That happens, sometimes," he said. Then, "Go on. I'll wait here. You know what it is you're searching for."

Since I'd started this particular hare running, I had no choice but to see it through. So I set off down the earth passage, slightly reassured by the weighty presence of a Justice of the Peace to my rear, but apprehensive nonetheless. Even in my short crawl through the malodorous tunnel I had the notion that Robin would be waiting for me at the other end, raggedly dressed in the pelts of small animals, earth-mouldy. That bony hand which could not clutch. The talk which did not make sense.

Then I emerged into the hollowed-out space where he'd lived. It took some moments for my eyes to get used to the deep gloom. Light broke through the leaf-matting in threads and tiny spoonfuls. A little low creature scuttered behind me. Root tendrils tickled my face. To my overtaxed mind, it seemed that someone sat sighing in the corner. The white form which I'd glimpsed moments before. Or the ghost of Robin perhaps. His true self but incorporeal. Everyone knows that a violent despatch makes for a restless spirit.

Just find it, Revill, and make your escape before the woodwoses get you too and string you up from the nearest tree.

What was I looking for? Ah yes, the little leathern box that I'd been shown. Or rather, not the box so much as the papers which it contained. Papers which Robin – a man near the edge of his wits if not toppled off them altogether – considered important. I moved forward on my knees, sweeping ahead warily with my hands. Almost straightaway, in the near dark, I struck something. Touch and a dim sense of sight gave me an oblong box with some kind of hasp on it. I scooped it up and backed out of that place as fast as my hands and knees would carry me, bringing down clods of earth as I exited.

The sun was most welcome on my face after my immersion in the gloom. Adam Fielding was standing by the entrance. He looked pleased to see me. I held out the box to him.

"No, Nicholas, it's your find. Complete your search."

I examined the box. It was less than a foot in length, about half that in width and a couple of inches deep. It felt light but, when shaken, something shifted inside it. Where the leather cladding hadn't turned black it was green from damp and mould. The hasp was stiff and rusty but not secured by any kind of padlock. Hands slightly trembling, I opened the lid. Inside were several sheets of grimy paper, close-packed and crammed on top of each other. To my horror, as sunlight struck the interior of the box, these sheets of paper started to shift about like living things. They quivered and heaved up and down as if the box was going to vomit out its contents.

"Jesus!"

Repelled, I dropped the box instinctively. The lid snapped off as it hit the ground and the sheets of paper slithered out. From beneath the pile scrabbled and crawled several of the largest beetles I'd ever seen. Their backs, iridescent in the sunlight, showed a glossy green. Speedily the beetles lost themselves amongst the grass and leaves. Feeling foolish, I bent down to retrieve the scattered papers. They were creased and chewed-looking as well as being badly mildewed – to the extent that if anything had been written on them in the first place it was surely now obscured for ever.

I held out the sheaf of filthy papers to Fielding, as if to say: see, something was there inside the cavern after all, that box and these its dirty contents. The Justice took them and, with less delicacy than I'd shown, raised them to his nose before wiping at the smutted, greasy surface of the topmost sheet. His expression showed nothing.

"Is this everything that was in the box?" he asked.

"I don't know," I said. "He only showed me one or two sheets and even those I couldn't see clearly."

"What did you think these would prove to be?"

"I've no idea," I said, rather abjectly. "But I suppose I believed them to have a value — like most items kept in a box."

"As legal documents, deeds of title, and such?"

"Yes . . . perhaps." I hesitated. "Robin talked to me of having had great estates once, of lands that it would've taken him a day to ride across. I don't think he'd always lived here."

I indicated the hole in the ground.

"So you consider this to be some kind of story, Nicholas, in which he'll turn out to have been a great man."

"Not necessarily," I said, though that had perhaps been a notion at the back of my mind. "But it was obvious that what he was now was not what he had been once."

"No, he was half out of his wits by your account."

Adam Fielding gestured with the bundle of papers at the earth-hole from which I'd just emerged. When looked at in that way, Robin's talk seemed to be indeed the fruits of long solitude and privation.

"This is thin cheap paper," said Fielding. "Not intended to last. No lawyer would commit anything to it. There might have been some ink markings here but they are diluted over or washed away beyond recall."

He handed the sheaf back to me. I must have looked disappointed for he added, "You have done well, Nicholas, to recover these. If you would be so good as to take the box and put those back inside, I'll ensure that it is kept safe."

"But it's worthless."

"Not worthless. Its value is not apparent at the moment, that is all," said Fielding cryptically.

I squatted down to retrieve the box and its separated lid and then made to return the papers to the beetle-free interior. Something caught my eye. Adam Fielding had already moved a few paces off and was examining the environs of Robin's dwelling.

"Sir," I said. "Your worship."

"Adam, you may call me," he said abstractedly.

I felt a tiny surge of pleasure at this mark of familiarity.

"Adam, there is something here after all."

He was by my side in a moment. I jabbed with my finger at a word which was distinguishable near the bottom of an otherwise blackened scrap of paper. It was scrawled in thick, crude letters.

It was a plea.

It read: MERCY.

Demetrius was calling me a coward, for hiding my head in a bush. Then Puck retorted, in my voice:

> *Thou coward, art thou bragging to the stars,*
> *Telling the bushes that thou look'st for wars,*
> *And will not come?*

Thomas Pope, our "guider", had the part of Puck. He presented an aged sprite with just a touch of malevolence about him. As I listened to him speaking in "my" voice, I wondered whether I actually sounded like that, whether he had me off pat. We cannot hear ourselves, or only indirectly in the aping of others. It's like trying to catch a glimpse of the back of your head in a glass.

Finally I, as Lysander, drooped to the ground, overcome with weariness. I was closely followed by Demetrius, Helena and Hermia, all of us led to this spot by Puck, here to be cured of our love-sickness or, rather, of our misdirections in love. The ground was dry and the air warm. We were meant to have got lost in a fog but that would exist only in our – and our audience's – minds. No fog now, but golden warmth. On this June evening one could happily fall asleep lying on the turf.

We were practising again for the *Dream* and not so distant prospect of the real thing on midsummer's night. The ample rehearsal time was justified now by the presence in our band of Cuthbert Ascre, who played Demetrius. In fact, Cuthbert had proved quick and adept at learning his part. He was a natural, in the good sense. If he hadn't had the prospect of an idle life in front of him as a great man's younger son he would have made a most acceptable addition to any company. True, he found our jokes too amusing and he hung onto our seniors' words as if his life depended on them, but all of us have been guilty of these faults, and much worse ones, in our 'prentice days. Perhaps I was disposed in his favour because we shared so much time on stage. Because he regarded me as an oracle on the subject of plays and players, he badgered me with questions, something which, though it can be irritating, is also flattering.

As well as Cuthbert, we'd taken on other temporary members for this performance, in the shape of several children who'd lately arrived at Instede with their families for the wedding celebrations. The great house was beginning to fill up with guests, who appeared to my easily-dazzled eyes to fall into three types: grand, grander and grandest. I've performed at court in Whitehall Palace but somehow this seemed an even more splendid and lavish concourse. Some of the exalted visitors nevertheless had sufficient share in our common humanity to have brought themselves – once or twice anyway – to perform the act of generation. It was the children of these lords and ladies, knights and their dames, who were to swell our numbers, by appearing at various points in the action, dancing in a ring, bearing lighted tapers, singing in their piping trebles.

I marvelled at the skill and diplomacy with which Thomas Pope and Richard Sincklo marshalled their small charges, combining firmness with kindness and patience. At the same time I realized that performing in a great man's house was never going to be straightforward. You do not have that freedom of decision and action which comes from treading your own boards.

As Pope was instructing these little eyases in their movements and gestures at the close of the action, the rest of our company took their ease on the fringes of the playing area. Earlier on in the evening I'd spotted Adam Fielding and Kate observing us from the side. Their presence, hers in particular, gave a spring to Lysander's (and my) step. Now, however, they were nowhere to be seen. Instead, Cuthbert Ascre came to join me and resumed a conversation, or rather a question-and-answer session, we'd been having earlier.

"You were telling me about your early days with the Admiral's, Nicholas."

"I served a kind of apprenticeship with them. I played little things, attendant lords, third murderers. But they are a good Company."

"Not as fine as the Chamberlain's though?"

"No, it is the general opinion that we carry it away."

"So you are at the pinnacle."

"For myself, I am at the bottom of a hill or at best on its lower reaches, Cuthbert [*you may see by this that we were already on good terms*]. But it is the highest hill in the region and, though the way up is steep and winding, I am resolved to reach the top."

"That is highly poetical, Nicholas. You should write it down. And your ambition as a player speaks well for you."

"Your father," I said, encouraged, "he is a friend to the playhouse also?"

"He is, but not through a liking for the art for its own sake, I think, or not so much. He took his cue from Her Majesty. Queen Elizabeth stayed here several times when I was small. I can scarce remember her, though she did give me a silver pin."

"I know that the Queen is a votary at the altar of the drama," I said – without adding that I'd met her and that we'd discussed plays, among various matters.

"Votary at the altar, hmm . . . Anyway, my father realized that players enjoyed the highest possible patronage and that it might advantage him to befriend them too. This is what my mother says."

I was a little embarrassed by the openness of Cuthbert in describing his father's motives. Almost disappointed too. True, where the Queen led others were bound to follow, but it is agreeable to be liked for one's own sake. Since Cuthbert was evidently in a mood to be confidential I thought I'd press him on another question.

"Your mother also is a supporter of the drama," I said. "I understand that those wandering players on the estate-farm are here by her allowance."

"You mean the Paradises? Oh they have connections here, yes. By your tone I can see you don't approve of the 'wandering players'."

"I saw them first in Salisbury and was surprised when they fetched up here."

"They're not really brothers. They just call each other that."

"And their audiences as well," I commented. "Brothering and sistering away like mad."

"They've visited us with their Bible stuff before. My mother believes that everything should be for our instruction and edification Accordingly, she hopes to improve the conduct of our workers by allowing them to watch plays in which punishment is always meted out to wrong-doers and despair overtakes the sinner."

"But that's what happens in any play," I said. I kept quiet about the little speeches and sermons with which Peter Paradise prefaced or rounded off their performances.

"My lady mother would say that not all drama is blessed with the tinct of scripture. It is not specifically designed to elevate or frighten."

"I'm not sure if that's what was happening when your labourers were watching Judas hang himself the other day in the barn. I think they were simply enjoying a spectacle. It was elevation in a strictly limited sense."

Cuthbert grinned gratifyingly at my little word-play on elevation, then said, "But spectacle is the business of players, isn't it, whether they're wandering or fixed?"

"May I ask you a question?"

Cuthbert looked at me. Underneath the friendly, easy-going exterior, there was a shrewdness about him, an inwardness. Before us, Thomas Pope continued to put the little sons and daughters of the great noblemen through their paces, as they danced in circles on the green or held up imaginary tapers to the declining sun. I noticed two or three of our company, in particular Laurence Savage, casting frequent glances in Cuthbert's and my direction. I supposed that there was a certain resentment when the son of our patron fastened on to so junior a member of the Company.

"Would you act, if you were free to do so?"

"I *am* acting in the *Dream*, Nicholas – although of course I would never claim to be the equal of any of you."

"For a living, I mean."

"Very well. Perhaps I would. If I was free. But I am not free. To be born to all this, even if it will never be yours, is to be born in a cage."

"A cage with golden bars and a marble floor."

"Oh yes, and fine views and so on. But a cage nonetheless. I tell you, Nicholas, I would give much to be as free as you are."

To be envied (and especially by the scion of a wealthy house) for something you've hardly ever considered, is a disconcerting experience. Free! Yes, free to worry about where your next month's rent will come from, if your fortunes turn Turk. Free to find your lodgings in a ditch should you fall out of favour with the audience or the shareholders!

I said none of this, but instead asked another question which had been nagging at my brain.

"Your brother Harry, is he not free either?'

The changed expression on Cuthbert's face made me realize I'd overstepped the mark. At once, there was a chill between us.

"I am not sure what you mean."

His voice had something of the aloofness of his father's.

"It was nothing," I said lamely. "A foolish remark."

He seemed to accept this as a species of apology, but the closeness which had been between us moments before was dissipated in the cooling evening. Perhaps it was fortunate that the practice drew to a close at this point, with Thomas Pope himself rounding off the action by delivering Puck's valedictory lines. Before we dispersed Pope spoke to us all, consulting the notes he'd made during the rehearsal. As I've said, he had the gift of offering criticism in the guise of encouragement. He had some comments, of a shrewd but generous sort, to make to Cuthbert Ascre and I noticed that my new friend (if that's what he still was) accepted the guider's advice like a meek boy.

I was trying to fathom Cuthbert's remarks about "freedom" and wondering whether I'd really offended him by the query about his brother when I was suddenly assailed by Laurence Savage. For once, my co-player lived up to his name. An angry redness suffused his broad, equable face. The livelihood of the Chamberlain's was threatened on two fronts, he said furiously. Over there was a bunch of vagabonds living in a barn and presenting crude Bible tales which brought the refined art of playing into disrepute. And on the other hand – and a much worse hand it was too – here was the disgrace of a jumped-up sprig of the nobility's using his father's money to procure himself a place in a professional troupe of players, so that he might strut, mince and mumble his way to the sycophants' applause. And what made it worse, a great deal worse, was that members of the same troupe – supposed professionals – bowed and scraped in front of the said sprig, and told him that he could do no wrong but was a very fine actor indeed, yes sir, no sir.

I tried to interject that, in reality, Cuthbert Ascre — "if that's who you're referring to," I said disingenuously — was a capable player who deserved his place in our *Dream* on merit, that he didn't present any threat to us Chamberlain's, that as far as I knew no money had changed hands, &c. But Laurence only grew angrier at me. So it's Cuthbert now, is it Nicholas, Cuthbert Ascre, well, I noticed you on the grass grinning like an ape and exchanging compliments. What would you have me do with him? I said. Turn my back and never speak to him again? Yes, said Laurence, that's what you should do, Nicholas. We may have no choice about whether he's in our play or not, considering his father used his stinking money to secure him a stinking place, but we do have a choice about whether to talk to him or not, about whether to kiss his arse or not. Have no truck with fellows of that sort, I say.

Only afterwards did I understand that Laurence Savage was not attacking Cuthbert Ascre, or at least not primarily. He was furious to see me, and no doubt Thomas Pope and others, consorting with and complimenting the son of a man whom, for some reason, he loathed: Lord Elcombe.

Adam Fielding remained at Instede during these wedding preparations while he continued his investigation into the death of Robin the wood-man. Kate remained too, and I was always on the alert to catch a glimpse of her or to exchange a few words. Each time I sighted her, my heart beat faster and my palms turned slippery. If she was similarly affected by my presence she didn't show it. She maintained the same light, slightly mocking look and manner; she was always quick in converse; she did not ask to hear more poems by Richard Milford or anyone else. Yet, despite this apparent distance, I found myself thinking of her — or rather, her image wandered unannounced into my mind — at odd moments during the day and as I lay wakefully on my crib in the players' dormitory at the top of the house. Though, if I'm to be honest, it wasn't at *odd* moments that she occurred to me, but *frequently*. I caught myself mooning and moping about. I sighed often and, if I noticed myself doing it, sighed more emphatically. It seemed to me that my appetite grew less hearty and that I slept little during those short summer nights. These are some of the indisputable signs of the lover, ones which I was pleased enough to cultivate. Yet my thoughts were pure enough, and my mind shied away from imagining the two of us engaged in anything more reprehensible than chaste kissing. Well, relatively chaste.

Of my friend Nell back in London I did not think much at this time – except to consider that she was still there.

My most reckless imagining in respect of Kate was to picture the two of us together, Nicholas Revill and Kate Fielding, united and living happily ever after. Hymen must have been hovering in the Instede air (even if the white-faced Harry didn't look eager to pluck down his share of that god's train). So quick do love and unreason rush ahead together that I went so far as to approach Kate's father in the way of marriage – albeit in my mind only. How would a Justice of the Peace look upon having a poor player as a son-in-law? Not very favourably. It would be different, of course, if I was further advanced in the craft which I practised, higher up that steep hill which I'd mentioned to Cuthbert Ascre. If I was a Globe shareholder, say. But I was not long out of my 'prentice period. No, I would have to do something very pleasing – or very clever – to influence Adam Fielding. To make him consider me as a suitable match for his daughter.

As you'll have observed, this calculation left entirely out of account Kate's feelings for me. Perhaps this was because I feared that she didn't really have any, or nothing that extended beyond courtesy and womanly concern. Maybe I thought of winning over her father because that seemed a less difficult task than winning *her* over.

With this in mind, when Adam Fielding asked if I'd be present at a formal conversation with Lord and Lady

Elcombe, I was pleased enough to agree but baffled as to why he needed me.

"Because, Nicholas, I'd value your eyes and ears in this matter."

This was gratifying, naturally, but I worried about what cover he would offer for my presence.

"None is necessary," said Fielding. "As a Justice, I may press you into service if I wish. Anyway, it was you who first saw that there was something untoward in the manner of Robin's death. You have won the right to share in my discoveries, if there are any."

"But Robin was – somebody of little account," I said, somehow surprised that this matter should be taken as high as the Elcombes.

"And so his death may go unexamined?"

"Of course it shouldn't, but . . . sir . . . Adam . . . is this timely?"

"No, and nor is death," said Fielding, "if we wish to get profound now."

"The house is all in a stir with this wedding. I hardly think that Lord and Lady Elcombe will be happy to answer your questions at this time."

"Again, my title and position carry some weight. And I am long familiar with this couple. They will not grudge half an hour, believe me."

So it proved. We were summoned to attend on Lord and Lady Elcombe in their lodgings, a large assemblage of rooms on the second floor commanding fine views over their property. I was still not accustomed to the size of these Instede apartments, into the smallest of which you might have fitted my bedchamber in Dead Man's Place several times over. Nor had I recovered from my surprise at the sheer quantity of light which flooded through the great windows. Coming from a city where, at least in less prosperous quarters, sunlight seemed to be doled out in miserly parcels and to fight its way through the smoky air before penetrating one's squinty windows, I was dazzled by the splendour and openness of the Instede interiors.

Before we had our interview with the Elcombes, Fielding instructed me that I should say nothing unless asked but should watch and listen carefully. My youth and my training as a player would come in handy, he claimed, since I would doubtless be able to recollect what was said more accurately than someone of his advanced years. I was to write down what had passed as soon as possible after the encounter was done. I did as instructed (still hoping to win the Justice's favour) and what follows is my record of this dialogue.

We were ushered in by one of the manservants. The Elcombes sat stiffly side by side, as if they were to be painted. The long face of the master of Instede was unrelieved by any softening mark. For all her drawn beauty, his wife shared his stony features. After we were bidden to sit, the questions began.

Adam Fielding: Thank you for agreeing to see us.
[*A slight inclination of the head from Elcombe, a small smile from Lady Elcombe*]
Adam Fielding: Master Revill is here in my service.
Lord Elcombe: Master Revill and I have already met. He was generous enough to instruct me in the true meaning of Master Shakespeare's *Dream*.
[*Master Revill blushes furiously and wishes he could hide himself under the rich carpet which covers the floor.*]
Adam Fielding: May I remind you, my Lord, that you requested my presence at Instede in order to enquire into the death of he that was called Robin.
Elcombe: What have you discovered, sir? Enough to put to rest the whispers and rumours that run about the place? Hm?
Fielding: With your permission, I will come to that in due course. First, I would like to establish one or two things about the dead man.
Elcombe: I will answer if I can.

Fielding: Who was Robin?

Lady Elcombe: A man without a master. A man without a place to house his head.

Fielding: I mean, my Lady, where did he come from? He was not born in your woods, surely? Master Revill says he was a man who had once been something . . . different.

Lady Elcombe: Then perhaps Master Revill should be answering your questions, since he knows so much.

[*She looks at me with a cold look and I wish to burrow further under the carpet. But Lord Elcombe puts out a placatory hand in his wife's direction.*]

Elcombe: I can satisfy your curiosity to an extent, sir.

Fielding: No mere curiosity, my Lord. I speak with the weight of the law on my shoulders. A man has died and I am charged with discovering why.

Elcombe: So be it. Robin was the son of a woman who was born on the estate in my father's time. She was not strong in the head. She hardly knew herself. She was tolerated here out of charity.

Fielding: What happened to her?

Elcombe: She moved away from here. She is in another country.

Nick Revill [*under his breath*]: And besides the wench is dead

Elcombe [*who evidently has sharp ears*]: The young player knows his Christopher Marlowe. Master Revill is probably right. She is doubtless dead. She left this place many years ago.

Fielding: While Robin remained behind, to fend for himself in the woods?

Elcombe: No. She vanished from here when he was not full grown. So did he. Merry must have taken the brat with her.

Adam Fielding: Merry?

Elcombe: So she was called – on account of her ever-laughing countenance.

Fielding: She was a cheerful soul.

Elcombe: A simple one. I said that she was weak in the head. She gaped for any reason, or none at all.

Fielding: And Robin? Her offspring. He must have come back to Instede at some point.

Elcombe: When he returned nobody knows, but it was as a grown man. I did not discover that he was here until he had been dwelling in the woods for some time ... perhaps a matter of years.

Fielding: But someone in your household must have known?

Lady Elcombe: Of course. Do you think that we are aware of everything that goes on in the holes and corners of this estate?

Fielding: Why did he return?

Elcombe [*with a kind of sneering smile*]: Perhaps he thought that he was coming home. I do not know, sir, and he who could have told you has now gone out to make his home in the dark.

Fielding: Who was Robin's father?

[*Lord Elcombe looks abashed at the question. My Lady merely looks – daggers.*]

Elcombe: When I said that Merry gaped I was referring to her mouth, permanently open in mirthless mirth. But it could as well have been said about her other parts. Why, man, any fellow on the estate might have covered her, or any passing vagrant for that matter.

[*Nicholas watches Lady Elcombe carefully to see how she responds to her husband's coarseness but she is too busy staring at Fielding's reaction.*]

Fielding: I see.

Elcombe: I am not sure that you do, sir. The plain fact is that I know next to nothing about this individual. I merely required you to come to Instede and quieten the more foolish gossip about his death. No more than that.

Fielding: The requirements of the law may not be consonant with your wishes, my Lord. Have you ever picked at a fraying thread on a sleeve ...?

[*The noble Lord and Lady regard Fielding and each other with bafflement and then irritation.*]

Elcombe: To the quick of the matter. What have you discovered that makes you so riddling? Hm?

Fielding: Nothing.

Lady Elcombe: Nothing?

Fielding: Because there is nothing to discover. My opinion is that Robin the wood-man was as you have described his mother, that is, somewhat addle-pated. I believe that a period of many years living in the woods curdled whatever few wits he was born with, and that one fine morning he slipped a cord about his neck and so slid into the next world. Be assured that I shall do my best to spread this version of events among the more impressionable members of your household, my Lord.

Revill: But –

Fielding: Yes, Master Revill?

Revill: No matter.

Elcombe: So there was nothing out of the way in this person's death?

Fielding: That is my opinion.

Lady Elcombe: Could you not have told us this direct, sir? Did we have to be troubled with your questions?

Fielding: I wished only to clear my mind, and now I see that I have cleared yours as well. However, I must apologize for having taken up your time, especially at this delicate and propitious moment for your family.

Lady Elcombe [*with the merest touch of graciousness*]: Now that you are no longer our inquisitor, perhaps you and your beautiful daughter, Justice Fielding, can revert to being our guests.

Elcombe: And Master Revill can go back to his playing, hm.

Fielding [*standing and half-bowing*]: My Lord and Lady.

[*Nicholas Revill also stands and does a small bow before following the Justice of the Peace from the chamber. He says nothing. He can think of nothing to say.*]

As soon as we were outside the door and out of earshot of the hovering manservant, I turned to Adam Fielding.

"Sir, Adam, did you mean all that?"

"All what?"

"How can you say that there was nothing out of the way about Robin's death? After I showed that he could not have tied a knot in the halter. Or climbed the elm most likely. And after we found that case of papers."

"Steady, Nicholas, steady. You are growing heated."

"But you left several things unexamined."

In my urgency I forgot the normal courtesies due to this grey-bearded man.

"No, it is you who are leaving things unexamined," said Fielding. "Tell me what happened with Robin."

"Well, I don't know – "

"Ah, you don't know. Why not, exactly?"

"I wasn't there when he died."

"You weren't there when he died," Fielding repeated with irritating deliberation. "Just so. Tell me what you think happened, then."

By this time we'd emerged into the open. We continued to walk, in the direction of the lake. The day was like all the days of that June, warm, fresh, untarnished.

"I . . . well . . . all right. I believe there was foul play in this matter, I believe that Robin was helped to slide into the next world, as you expressed it in there."

"You understand Latin, Nicholas? But of course you do, you're the parson's son from Somerset. So I ask you in that tongue: *cui bono?*"

I could not understand the question – not its meaning, which was simple – but the purpose of it. Also, I couldn't understand Master Fielding's rather distant, even mocking manner. Had I spoken so much out of turn during our interview with the Elcombes?

In case he should think my Latin was feeble, I quickly said, "You ask me 'for whose good is it?', 'to whose advantage?' "

"When we're looking at an apparent crime, we must ask not merely how it was done, what instruments were used, who might have carried it out and so on, but one question above all the rest: *whose good does this serve*? Who might benefit from it?"

"And since nobody benefited from Robin's death, there was no motive for anybody to do away with him."

"You've said it for me."

"But . . ."

"You must admit, Nicholas, your own reasoning has a certain force."

"Have you considered another possibility, sir?"

"I have considered many. Go on, though."

"That he was . . . murdered . . . to silence him, to shut his mouth for good."

"What was he going to say that was so dangerous? From your own account, when he did talk he didn't make much sense. And if you're hinting that he was in possession of some mortal secret, which I think you are, was there anyone to listen to him and, if there was, then why did he remain so long alive and untouched in the woods? Why put an end to him now at what is, to say the least, an inconvenient moment?"

"What about the evidence of the halter and the knot? Or the papers in the box?"

"Which were smudged and unreadable."

"There was one word left on them – mercy."

Fielding laughed, to my discomfort. "Oh, mercy. Well, you can't build a house out of a single brick. The papers were spoiled and will never be restored and therefore must be left out of the question. As for the rope, you said yourself that you weren't there when he died. How can you know precisely what he was capable of doing? Men may achieve extraordinary feats if driven to them by despair – or any other great passion."

"Well . . ."

"I think we really must leave this now, Master Revill. Kate and I can revert to being ordinary guests at this wedding while you – "

"Can go back to playing, I know," I said, unable to keep a touch of asperity out of my reply. We had arrived at the margin of the lake and the stone seat where I had so pleasantly dawdled away the time with Kate a couple of days before. "Only one more thing, your worship. At the beginning, when I first came to tell you of my suspicions and concerns in this business you seemed to share them. And when you came with me to examine the place in the wood where Robin's life was ended you acted as if you too believed there was something unexplained in the matter."

"Oh, there is always something unexplained if you look hard enough. As for what I was doing in the woods and before . . . it is called keeping an open mind."

"And now?"

"If your mind be open too long, Master Revill, anything may fly into it. Beware."

Full

We were invited to a marriage feast. But of course we had to sing for our supper. The feast preceded the *Dream*, the evening performance of which was the reason we were at Instede. And a great feast it was, even if it was meant to be no more than a prologue to greater post-nuptial ones.

The early evening sun streamed through the ample windows of the Instede banqueting hall, and the wax candles which had been placed in silver holders at regular intervals down each table remained unlit – no doubt they were there in case of a sudden eclipse. We of the Chamberlain's occupied a low to middling position in the hall, from which we were permitted to glance up at the high and mighty beings on the dais, who included bride, groom, their parents &c. Below us were the lesser folk from the estate and its environs. As I've noticed in the playhouse, however, nobody wastes time inspecting his inferiors. All eyes were fastened upwards. So large was the number of important guests that the high table was, in fact, three tables: the main one many yards in length and with two shorter ones angling out from it at either end. The diners occupied one side only so that they might gaze over the rest of the hall, something which they did from time to time but in an abstracted, distant way.

This was our first opportunity to study the bride, and – given what we'd heard about Lord Harry Ascre's unwillingness to grasp his fortune (in any sense) with both hands and the consequent speculation about the reasons for his reluctance – study her we did. Our questions about Marianne's appearance were soon answered.

Questions such as: *Had she two heads?* No.

Did she squint? Not that one could see.

Was her complexion as pocked as a nutmeg-grater? From a distance, she looked to have a fetching mixture of red and white in her cheeks, with the latter as predominant as it should be in a young lady of good breeding.

Her shape then, her proportions – was she spectacularly unpleasing in that regard? Again, no. From where I was sitting with my fellows, Marianne Morland seemed gracefully but not ungenerously built. Jack Wilson and Michael Donegrace and I commented on the cut of her gown, or rather on the way in which it teasingly revealed her cleavage – a style that was appropriate to the unmarried woman which she could still (just) claim to be. In fact, we decided that, if asked, any one of us would have been prepared to consider her as a match for himself, quite aside from the matter of the large portion or dowry which came with her.

What of Harry Ascre, the reluctant bridegroom? During the last few days leading up to this marriage eve, he'd been looking slightly less gloomy. I'd glimpsed him about the place in the company of his brother Cuthbert or with some of the great guests, and had even noticed the odd smile, the occasional grin softening his haggard features. So I'd begun to discount that memory of him in the hornbeam garden, hunched up, muttering madly, as well as the gossip concerning his willingness or otherwise to be married. Perhaps all grooms-to-be endure such moments of doubt and anxiety. What did I know? (I only knew that if I were to have the prospect of marrying, say, Mistress Fielding, I would endure many throbbing days and sleepless nights beforehand.) But whatever it was that had been making Lord Harry more cheery during recent days had now evaporated. The old, drawn look was returned to his features. Sitting at the top table in the banqueting hall, he seemed sunk inside himself. I hoped for her sake that his bride did not take this as a personal slight, and by her smiling she seemed to say that she did not.

The bride's parents, the Morlands of Bristol, were seated beside their hosts, Lord and Lady Elcombe. These Bristolians had the sheen of money. Just as the good huswife protects a piece of furniture by frequent waxing and shining, so this couple – plain only in their names, Master Martin Morland and Mistress Frances Morland – had been buffed with wealth until they shone. You felt that nothing could touch them, or rather that they would have remained unmarked by anything placed on them, as it were. The chief guests, lords and ladies, filled the remaining seats on the dais. The grandest of them had whole counties for names: Devons and Cornwalls, Surreys and Rutlands. The less grand were named for mere cities or towns: your Winchesters, Exeters and Derbys. I was somehow pleased to see Justice of the Peace Fielding sitting up there with his daughter, even though we hadn't spoken since our argument of a couple of days earlier. Whatever coolness there'd been during the interview with the Elcombes, it evidently hadn't affected his standing at Instede House. Kate too looked cheerful and at her ease, chatting with Cuthbert.

The tables immediately below the dais were occupied by knights and their dames, together with individuals such as the kindly-looking parson Brown (the one who'd overseen Robin's interment) and the local schoolmaster. Also stationed here were the noble little children due to play the sprites and fairy attendants in our *Dream*. Like more than one or two adult players I've known, it seemed that they were mostly too excited to eat anything before the performance.

There may have been holes in Elcombe's purse – and according to Jack Wilson, this was a main motive behind the Elcombe–Morland marriage – but it was apparent that the host wanted to demonstrate that his resources were almost without limit. Even the tables of we less elevated folk were covered with the finest linen, and we ate and drank with and from silver and glass. Men servants only were used to fetch and carry, since everybody knows that they're more costly than women on occasions like this. These servants were attractively liveried in a grey, marbled worsted that subtly signalled money as well as the good taste which knows how to spend it. I detected my lady's hand here.

As for the food . . . we'd heard that a master cook by the name of Cox had been brought down from London, together with two undercooks, specially for this feast and the ones which would follow the wedding. And as for the food they produced . . . what herds, gaggles and shoals must have breathed their last for our pleasure! The choice on the high tables would have been much more lavish than what was offered to us, but even we were provided with veal and conies and goose and capon – and that was just to start with. I would have been content with cheat-bread and ale to accompany all this – I've still retained my country preferences and, anyway, never have much of an appetite before a performance – but we were given manchet to sop up the juices and claret to wash it all down with. As a second course, we were plied with lamb and kid, pheasant and pigeon – oh, and tart and butter and fritters and custard and fruit.

They say that banquets are meant to inflame the senses, or at any rate the lower urges, and this must be doubly true of those celebrations which frame a wedding. For the first time in several days I caught myself thinking of my whore Nell and wishing that I had her at hand, so to speak. And this despite the fact that I was due to perform, in quite another sense, in a hour's time. Perhaps these stabs of lust were inspired by the kissing-comfits which suddenly appeared in profusion on the tables and which made one think of their breath-sweetening purpose and then of reasons why one might wish one's breath to be sugared over. Together with the comfits came suckets, both wet and dry, and some tantalizing little mounds of sweetened cream which worldly old Jack Wilson told me were known as 'spanish paps'. They were delicious.

But I was able to get my own back on Jack when we were presented with more sweets in the shape of escutcheons or arms. It was the design on the shield which baffled Jack and which, with my fondness for puzzles, I was able to elucidate. The brightly coloured, candied device featured a large yellow L-shape nestling in a kind of curved hollow. "It's a rebus," I explained, "a pictorial pun on the family name. El-combe. Here's the 'ell', and it's resting in or just above this curved hollow – or 'combe' as it's sometimes called. Hence, Elcombe."

I waited for Jack to congratulate me on my cleverness, but unaccountably he just said, "You should have been a school-master, Nick. All I'm interested in is what it tastes like. And when I put this in my mouth, so, I am in a manner nibbling on our host."

"Eating him arms and all," I said, pleased with my pun (which, by the by, also went unremarked).

All around us was laughter and chat, the clink of cutlery and glass. From a far corner emanated the soothing sounds of lute and hautboy, as sauce to our eating. Even at our comparatively lowly station in the hall there was a restraint in manners. I saw no one wiping his or her lips with a hand; rather each diner used a glowing white napkin to dab delicately around the mouth. There was no unseemly jostling to plunge one's knife or spoon into the serving mess contain-ing the meats; instead it was the attitude of after-you-sir-no-you-first-madam which predominated. Of course on the top table they had individual serving dishes, that was how special they were.

But we of the Chamberlain's were not permitted to sit long over the feast, picking every last morsel from between our teeth and draining the final dregs from the cup of pleasure. We had to attend to the pleasure of others, namely the Elcombe and Morland families and their guests. At a discreet signal from Thomas Pope, we got up from our seats. I was half impressed to see Cuthbert Ascre also rise from his privileged place on the top table, when he realized that we were leaving. He is a proper player, I thought, and wondered whether he had not been absolutely sincere when he rued that he was not "free" to act. Did he really want to escape from his gilded cage of rank and wealth? Of course the scion of a noble house *could* act, as long as he remained unpaid. But once coin entered the question, well, then the well-born had to bow out. Playing isn't that respectable – yet.

Outside, the declining sun shot his beams over our playing area and the banks of seats which had been erected to accommodate the bottoms of top persons. Above was the limitless blue arch of a fine summer evening. Off to one side was the pleasure-garden enclosed by the hornbeam hedge. We were to begin our *Dream* at eight o'clock or thereabouts. The action would finish as darkness began to fall. The glimmers of a midsummer's night would attend Oberon and Puck's closing words, their visages flickeringly revealed by the flare of torches, as they called down blessing on the newly married couples and required indulgence from the audience. Then the noble little children would parade and troop, holding tapers and singing their own epithalamium.

A shiver ran through me, a shiver of expectation and, just a little, of apprehension. I'd played outside on only a couple of occasions and never before with the Chamberlain's. Of course, it was what some companies did all the time, those companies which were perhaps less fortunate or gifted than ours and were without a house to call their own. I thought of the Paradise Brothers (would they be in attendance tonight, to see how it should be done? I wondered), they who carried their properties from town to town and enacted their tales of the Bible on makeshift stages in market squares.

Playing outside feels more ... dangerous than playing

inside. Not because of the obvious things like wind and rain, mere inconveniences which might keep an audience away or carry off our words into oblivion. Rather, I can only describe it as enhanced sense of exposure. There's no barrier between the player and the great wide world, even the overhanging firmament itself. Man in all his heroic littleness standing against the sky and the stars.

And if this sounds like arrogance or simple absurdity – well, maybe it is.

Enough cut-price philosophy. You can get that free in any tavern.

Canvas screens had been slung between some of the trees on the edge of the playing area, and it was in the shelter of these that we changed and did our face-painting. We had brought no tire-man with us to straighten out our costumes or to tell us of our infinite insignificance in comparison with what we were wearing but Jack Horner, who had relatively small parts in the play, had elected to smooth each man's lappets and tighten his points – or at least to indicate to us what was needed in the way of smoothing and tightening. Perhaps Sincklo had requested that he do this. Jack was doubling as Egeus, the tyrannical father of my Hermia, and Philostrate, the master of the revels at Theseus's Court. As such he appeared at the beginning and the end of the action but not in between. He cast a cursory glance over me and pronounced that I'd do.

"Thank you, Jack," I said.

"Delighted, Nicholas," he replied before moving on.

Cuthbert Ascre presented himself for Jack's approval, and I observed that Horner was rather more courteous with our patron's son. I saw Laurence Savage observing it too. I was still smarting from his recent attack, when he'd not minced his words in telling me to have nothing to do with Cuthbert. We hadn't spoken since.

"Tell me, Laurence, is it only the father that you hate? Or his sons as well?"

I don't know why I said this. I suppose that I wanted to

demonstrate, in a roundabout way, that I wasn't the only one to show civility – or, as Laurence would put it, arse-licking – to an Ascre.

Laurence was in his rough garb as Bottom. And roughly he replied, "Am I required to like this family?"

"No," I conceded. "Of course not. But ever since we arrived here, in fact as we were walking together up the road to Instede, you've made it absolutely clear that you loathe Elcombe and all his works."

"And you wonder why?"

"That would be my question, if we were still friends."

I was glad to see a kind of softening come over Laurence's featureless features and hoped we might re-establish our usual cordial relations.

"Very well, Nicholas. We have a few moments before these high and mighty folk come and plant their posteriors on the seats."

From the shelter of the canvas screen we could see the great company come trickling from the house. The Devons and the Cornwalls. The Winchesters and the Derbys. All of England came rolling towards us, in little. Some of them drifted in the direction of the enclosed garden to take a stroll before the play. There was laughter and shouting in the golden air. I wondered how many of our audience, bellies already full and heads rapidly filling with winy fumes, would be able to resist the lure of sleep.

"Let me enlighten you," he began. "I have a story to tell. There was once a woman who lived near Cheapside. She had two sons, one of them scarcely beginning to walk and the other . . . well, the other old enough to be beginning to know how the world works. There'd been three other children in between these two, to fill up the spaces, but they'd all died. And her husband too had died not long since, just after the birth of the youngest son. He'd been a glover and in the way of things she was allowed to take over his business when he went. But the business was debt-ridden and anyway she lacked the skill or the will to carry on the trade. It quickly declined and was bought for a pittance by a man in the next street who had long been a rival of her husband's. The widow didn't mind too much. She was handsome enough, particularly when dressed in black, and could expect to marry after the appropriate period of mourning had passed. In the meantime, though, with two children to provide for, she had to turn her hand to small jobs which she considered to be beneath her. Laundering and the like. After the mourning period was over the offers of marriage didn't come in, not in the quantity or the quality she'd hoped for. Perhaps the prospective husbands were put off by the gossip about debt, or perhaps it was her pride that did it, she was a proud woman. I believe there was one man who'd been turned away early on who she'd've been glad enough to accept later when times got hard, when things got desperate."

All this time while Laurence Savage was talking in a low, confiding tone, I nodded away and looked understanding though I couldn't see what any of this had to do with Lord Elcombe.

"Things grew desperate, as I say. This little trio had to shift to some tumbledown tenement near the Fleet Ditch, and there the widow struggled to keep the black clothes on her back and the white shirts on her children's. Well, one fine morning these two surviving sons, the small one who was walking quite sturdily by now and . . . the other one, were outside in the street. Perhaps the older son was amusing his little brother by drawing shapes in the dirt with a stick, perhaps he was teaching him to count the number of rats that crawled about the bank, and showed no fear of man or beast. Those rats, by the by, looked much more thriving than the poor benighted humans who lived on the banks of that stinking current."

"Yes, I know the place and do not like it," I said. "What happened?"

"Ah, Nick," said Laurence, "we shall have to wait for the conclusion of the story. Look."

He gestured at the bank of seats erected in front of the playing area. They were all full now except for a central section which was to be occupied by the bride and groom-to-be and their families. I'd been so absorbed in Laurence's tale that I'd almost forgotten the audience – but not quite. No actor quite forgets his audience.

"We are both on in a moment," said Laurence Savage, sliding away. I was momentarily annoyed, almost suspecting him of deliberately pausing at this point in his narrative to make me more eager to hear the rest of it. I still couldn't see any connection between Lord Elcombe and two little Savages – for it was certain that the older boy was Laurence himself, wasn't it? – playing by a filthy London stream. But now these speculations were put to one side as Master Thomas Pope came round in his Puckish guise to give us, each and every one, some last word of encouragement. I noticed that he was especially solicitous to the company of noble children who were to open the action with a fairy procession and a dance before the appearance of the adult humans. By this time, with a little fanfare, the Elcombes and Morlands had taken up their places and so we had our cue to begin.

Before I entered, and while Theseus and Hippolyta were talking of the snail-paced approach of their wedding, I cast my eyes swiftly across the audience, trying to place Kate Fielding. Yes, there she was, next to her father. Both of them were sitting above and to one side of the Elcombe clan. I felt a little shiver run through me which, I swear, was less to do with apprehension over the coming performance than it was connected to Kate's presence. She had never seen me act before, although as soon as this notion occurred to me came the counter-idea: why should she care whether she'd seen me before or not? And then I was able to give no more time to my heart for I had to step out onto the golden green and play the part of the anguished lover, Lysander.

> *Ay me! For aught that I could ever read,*
> *Could ever hear by tale or history,*
> *The course of true love never did run smooth . . .*

And so we began. The lovers' crossed fortunes, their wanderings in the forest whose mazy windings show the tangled paths we humans tread in pursuit of our desires, the intervention of Oberon and Titania who have the powers of gods and the appetites of mortals, the quite different contribution of the rude mechanicals to the love debate – all of this surely served as a fitting dessert course to the banquet they (and we) had just enjoyed. Master Shakespeare's words are sweet enough but there is in them the tartness of observation and experience.

As the action of the *Dream* unfolded, the heavens above us gathered up the day's gold and stowed it away in night's dark trunk. But because it was midsummer the process seemed infinitely slow and gentle. Even as we drew towards an end, with all the confusions and cross-purposes resolved in wedding and celebration, there was still a sheen of light in the west while on the opposite side the moon – pale companion to our revels and almost at the full – gazed coolly down.

After Thomas Pope as Puck had spoken his final words – *Give me your hands if we be friends, And Robin shall restore amends* – the noble troupe of children once more danced and sang, their burning tapers making stately circles in the twilight. The applause which Puck had solicited was duly given, the more generously perhaps because so many of the audience's little darlings were on show, and the whole company bobbed and bowed on the moonlit sward. This is what it means to play before the quality. No whores and pickpockets, no swearing veterans or unlettered apprentices; instead there is taste, balance and restraint. I couldn't have put up with it for too long but, once in a while, it's a pleasant experience.

"How was I?" said Cuthbert Ascre to me as we gathered "backstage" behind the canvas screens. The area was fitfully illuminated by a couple of flares; the moonlight did better service. Here we changed back into our day clothes and Jack Horner took charge of our costumes. Because we were touring we were less lavishly garbed than we would have been at the Globe and, as usual in these circumstances, most of us were wearing a mixture of our own garments and Company property. The waning light of evening, by comparison with the bright glare of afternoon in the London playhouse, also allows one to make do with less in the way of face-painting &c.

"How was I?" Cuthbert Ascre repeated, impatient for opinion like all beginners. "Was I good?"

"Very good," I said. "We'll make a player of you yet."

I was not straining to pay a compliment or not by much. Cuthbert really had shown a natural fluency as Demetrius, my rival in love. In that mood of easy jubilation which comes at the end of a successful performance, Cuthbert was as open to my praise as I was ready to give it. I could see his face glimmer with pleasure in the flickering light.

"Oh, this has given me a taste for it, to be sure. I could throw up my fortunes now, such as they are, and go on the road – with your company."

"We would be delighted to have you," I said, wondering what Laurence Savage or any of us – would make of an aristocratic companion but willing enough to indulge Cuthbert for a moment.

"But that's a fantasy," he said, as if reading my thoughts. His face suddenly took on a harder cast. "My father would never permit it."

"I didn't know you were serious."

"Nor did I," he said. "But why should I be constrained to play a part I do not wish?"

I presumed he meant the part of a younger brother, usually a pretty thankless role in the real world. Trying to lighten his newly clouded mood, I said, "If you were a member of our company you'd find yourself playing plenty of unwelcome parts. Look at me, for example. I've only been with the Chamberlain's a short time, yet I've been poisoned twice, torn asunder once and stabbed three times at least. The rest of the time I've stood around as an ambassador, or a soldier, or a member of council. That's when I haven't been skulking in the bushes as a murderer. There's no great romance in this. Villains and placemen are my meat and drink."

"And lovers."

"I am only lately graduated to them."

"But Nicholas, that is exactly what I would choose. To be one day the murderer and the next his victim. To be the victor in battle, then the vanquished. Or the shop-keeper who sells poison on a Monday and the lovelorn youth who swallows it on the Thursday."

I saw that my attempts to play down, as it were, the appeal of the playhouse were serving only to inflame him further and leave him with a sense of what he could never have, at least as long as his father stood in the way.

By now most of our company had wandered away from the area to mingle with the lords and ladies of the audience or, in a few cases perhaps, the men and maidservants. I was eager to be off myself, perhaps to catch up by accident with Kate Fielding and to have her opinion of what she'd just seen. I saw there was no placating Cuthbert Ascre who seemed to growing gloomier by the instant. So, assuring him that he'd made a fine Demetrius – no, really, an excellent performance – I sped off into the gathering darkness.

Almost immediately I ran into Kate. Literally. I didn't recognize her at first, nor she me.

"Take care, sir," she said.

"Oh Kate, Mistress Fielding . . ."

"Master Revill, is it?"

"The very same."

"Well, you are obviously off somewhere in a rush. Don't let me detain you."

We looked at each other in the moonlight. Not too far

away torches flickered, while soft voices and laughter blended in the mild air.

"No . . . I'm not. Nothing that can't wait. Did you enjoy the play?"

"Yes. I saw it first some years ago in the city, but it's better suited to this sylvan setting."

"Where we may all imagine ourselves to be lovers in the woods of Athens?"

"Some of us perhaps."

"Of course, I forget. You don't believe in love poetry. You think that poets are just writing to the empty air."

"And you think, if I remember correctly, that even if they are that doesn't mean that they don't intend their words to be taken seriously."

It was gratifying, of course, to have my own opinion recalled and quoted back at me, even if we were speaking in a rather combative spirit.

"Well, perhaps you're right," I said. "Who was it said that the truest poetry is the most feigning?"

"Your own Master Shakespeare, I believe."

"I think I have found you out . . . Kate."

"How so, Master Revill?"

"You see, you know the lines, you know the ideas and opinions of our poets. That tells me one thing. Under this guise of pretended indifference or even contempt for love poetry, you are really in thrall to it. Admit that you are a devotee in your closet of the latest volume of sonnets, that you pine and sigh with the lovesick – in spirit of course."

"Really, Master Revill, you must change out of your costume. If you are still speaking as the impassioned Lysander."

"Perhaps I am speaking in my own part," I said, wondering how much longer I could continue without breaking cover. Did I dare to confess openly what I felt towards her? My heart pounded and there was a roaring in my ears. On the edge of my vision the light from the torches seemed to swim in the soft, mothy air. So, I noted (and a part of me was still sufficiently detached to note that I was noting it), this is what it means to be in love. These are the symptoms of the sickness.

I was about to open my mouth to make some declaration, which might have changed everything (or more probably left everything just the same), when I sensed rather than saw another figure approaching through the dark.

"Cuthbert," said Kate.

"Kate," said Cuthbert.

"Did you like my Demetrius? Good, was I?"

"I have never seen a finer lover, coz."

"I was a little worried at the start but I soon got into it. My friend Nicholas here assures me that it was an excellent performance."

"Oh yes," I mumbled. "Very good."

"Tell me, Nicholas, when we were searching for each other in the mist . . . when you were chasing me, you know, with your sword . . . don't you think that if instead of coming in from that side, the effect would have been better if . . ."

"Well, you must excuse me now," I said, slipping away from them. I was half-relieved to be quit of Kate's company for I feared her mocking reception of the stuttering declaration of love which I'd been about to make. And, though glad enough to see that Lord Cuthbert had recovered his good humour, I didn't want to be exposed to his ideas on how the *Dream* performance might have been made sharper or funnier. Let him bend Kate's ear for that.

But the ear-bending wasn't finished for me either.

For I'd no sooner reached the company of my fellows, who by now had finished receiving the personal plaudits of the audience and were making up for the drink-deprived hours we'd endured while performing, than Laurence Savage reminded me that I hadn't heard the end of his tale of the two boys.

"Very well, Laurence," I said, a little impatient even though

I'd been eager enough to hear its conclusion earlier on. "But can we get one thing clear. No more mystification if you please. You're talking about yourself and your brother and your mother, aren't you?"

"How did you guess, Nicholas?"

"Get on with the story."

Taking a swig at some of Lord Elcombe's ale, Laurence launched into the second half.

"As I was saying before I was interrupted by the play, these two boys of a poor widow-woman were together one day on the margins of Fleet Ditch. All of a sudden the little one, the one who had only lately learnt to walk, loses interest in what his brother is doing and sets out on his sturdy legs to examine something which has caught his eye on the other side of the street, something glinting in the sun, I dare say. Meanwhile the big brother is distracted for an instant, perhaps caught up in some day-dream. He is not looking after his charge."

Laurence, still in his garb as Bottom, paused to slurp again at his tankard. It was evident that the scene he was describing was unfurling again before his eyes. I would have told him to hurry it up but something in his grave, determined expression suggested that it would be safer to hear him out in silence.

"All at once, round the corner of this stinking thoroughfare come a pair of horsemen riding as if the devil were at their heels. The older boy hears them before he sees them and makes a plunge to save the little one from being knocked to the ground and trampled upon. But he is too late. The child is struck by the hoofs of the leading horse and again by the hoofs of the second. The rush and frenzy of their passage throws the little boy against the wall of the tumbledown tenement. The older boy feels the heat and draught of these frantic travellers and their mounts and does not at first realize what has happened to his brother. In front of him is the empty roadway with the ditch beyond. He turns round and sees crumpled against the black wall a pile of clothing. Though the street is always filthy he hadn't noticed that particular mound of rags earlier and he wonders how it came to be there. Then he understands."

Laurence paused again to swig his drink. I saw his eyes moisten. He was sweating heavily. His cowlick of hair was glued to his forhead.

"I ran across and picked up the bundle in my arms. Thomas was dead, of course, several times over. If the first blow from the horse had not finished him then the second would have done, or the third or the fourth – and after that to be thrown violently against a brick wall. His brains were near dashed out. My mother, she emerged from the house, drawn by something or other. Perhaps I was crying out or screaming, I don't know. And we took the little form back inside and laid him down on the chest which served as our table. He was not yet a year and a half."

Laurence Savage gulped before resuming. "I had lost other brothers and sisters before – that is not much, provided they go early. But this one I had just got used to. Thomas his name was."

"Oh I am sorry to hear it," I said, "but even in a case like this we still have judgement here. Surely those who caused your brother's death were brought to account."

"They were not," said Laurence. He grinned but it was a very grim grin. "They were too rich and powerful, or rather one of them was."

"No-one is above the rule of law," I said piously.

"Wait. Later that day, while the bundle lay wrapped up in his cradle, his last resting-place before the grave, a man came calling. A gentleman judging by his voice and manner. He explained to my mother that he had heard of our misfortune and that he came to offer condolences. More than condolences, as it turned out. Because even as he spoke he drew forth a leather pouch and casually tipped its contents onto the very chest which my brother's body had so recently occupied. I couldn't help noticing how my mother's eyes were drawn towards the little pile of silver or how she responded to the visitor's manner. She had always been vulnerable to smooth tones, to an easy address. As I said before, I was old enough by now to know how the world works.

"Our visitor gave her to understand that the money he had so carelessly disbursed was hers on condition that she made no fuss about the dead child – or no more fuss than might reasonably be expected from any woman who lived in circumstances like ours. What he meant was that any family inhabiting one of the Fleet Ditch hovels had not much more entitlement to life than the rats which crawled about its banks. Every third day some infant fell from an upper window or was drowned in the stinking channel or was trampled underfoot. There was nothing out of the way in this. In return for not taking the case before the coroner, my mother would receive a further payment in three months – by which time Thomas would be safely underground and forgotten. Our visitor didn't say this but it's what he meant."

"Who was this gentleman?"

"I discovered later that he was Elcombe's steward, Oswald Eden, the very man who is still in his employ and who greeted us so warmly when we arrived the other day. He was the second horseman in the street who rode down my little brother. The two of them, master and man, were no doubt going somewhere on pressing business. Elcombe has a town house near Whitefriars."

"But it was an accident," I said mildly, and looking round half fearfully to see whether this great man or any of his immediate family was in earshot. The grander members of the party, however, had shifted indoors while we poor players and a handful of lesser guests remained scattered about the playing area. I'd have wagered that none was engaged in so earnest a dialogue as Savage and Revill.

"An accident," I repeated.

"Oh yes, Nicholas, it was an accident. Half the children in the borough succumb to such accidents, falling, dropping, drowning. Or if they don't go that way then the plague will catch them out. Nothing remarkable, nothing *particular*."

I had it in mind to ask why, then, it was so particular with him. But tact prevented me. Anyway Laurence went on to supply the answer, unprompted.

"My mother hesitated for an instant then she reached out a hand for the silver on the chest, realized that the pile of coin was just too large to be contained within a single clutch and so stretched out both hands and scooped the money into her apron, which, by the by, still carried slight traces of my brother's mortal remains. That is the picture of her which lodges like a beam in my mind's eye and cannot be dislodged. My mother tipping money into her spread lap. By comparison, the action of Lord Elcombe and his steward was a mote, a speck of dust – though I hate them both for it and will do until my dying day."

I had never seen Laurence Savage in such a mood. Usually the blandest of men, he was now red-faced and sweat-streaked. As he uttered those last words, he seemed for once to fit his surname. Then, in a more relenting tone, he said, "After all, what else can you expect of the rich and powerful but that they will ride roughshod over all who are in their way. It is my mother who I cannot forgive. All her pride dwindled to a pile of coin."

"What happened to you after this?"

"It is easily told, Nick. My brother Thomas was buried and forgotten. After that our fortunes seemed to change. A few months later another visitor, not Oswald but a man with a cast in his eye, came calling with a second packet of blood money. My mother accepted it of course and soon after that she received a proposal of marriage. It was from the very glover who'd bought up my father's shop. Perhaps he was waiting for her to be a little stretched and strained by circumstances, in order that he might wear her more easily. So we returned to the shop and the business which we'd lost scarcely a year earlier. My stepfather was an unpleasant man, and it is some consolation to know that my mother was not happy with him. He beat me, as was his right, until I grew too large and he was afraid I might hit him in return. One day, encouraged by his fear, I did. Then I ran and ran. Until one day, another day, I fetched up on the shores of the Chamberlain's Company as an apprentice."

I had no idea that Laurence's history was so, well, dramatic. I looked on him with new eyes.

"So now you know why I hate Elcombe and all that he stands for. Wealth and power."

"Why did you agree to come and play the *Dream* at Instede then?"

"I am a player, Nick. No doubt you recognize the breed. I thought you were one yourself. We'd play in front of Old Nick himself, wouldn't we, if we were paid for it and the shareholders told us to get on with it. Anyway, I didn't realize that I would feel so . . . bitter towards this great nobleman until we actually came within sight of his fine pile. And I was amazed to see Oswald himself still in his master's employ, still the same arrogant, high-handed bastard. Little did he think that the boy in the Fleet Ditch house who watched him spill his silver on a chest would one day turn up at his master's country seat."

"I don't suppose he noticed the boy at all, Laurence."

"The man is often mightier than the master," he replied. "No, he probably didn't even see me. Then or now. And talking of now, if you'll forgive me, I have some drinking to do."

Laurence blundered off in search of more ale, leaving me to reflect on all I'd heard that evening: Cuthbert Ascre's resentment of his father because Elcombe apparently stood in the way of his younger son's pursuit of a player's life; Laurence Savage's contempt for the Instede's owner's wealth and casual power. When these things were put side by side with Harry Ascre's seeming reluctance to marry, a course he was compelled to follow by his tyrannical father, it seemed as though no man had a good word to say for our patron. I thought of that cold, hard stare, and told myself that I wouldn't like to be on the wrong side of it.

I looked around. The moon cast her pale shroud over the scene. By now, the playing area and the banked seating beyond it were almost deserted. Most of my fellows had disappeared. The Elcombes and the Morlands, together with their guests, had long since repaired indoors. No doubt the bride-to-be had already been ushered to her bed with all the ceremony due to her last night on earth as a virgin. I assumed that she was one; but a bigger assumption was that Lord Harry would be willing to deflower her on their first night, or any other one for that matter.

We of the Chamberlain's were due to stay on at Instede for another couple of days, to attend the wedding as something between guests and servants, and to provide diversion after the celebrations in the shape of some song and dance as well as a little masque. But our chief business at Instede was complete. This stirred mixed feelings in me. On the one hand, I'd be relieved to be away from a place that – for all its space and lavishness – seemed to contain more than its fair share of human turmoil and unhappiness (mind you, a wedding is a great provoker of those very items). And, of course, I'd be glad enough to return to my adopted city with all its stench and stir. But leaving this country meant leaving behind Kate Fielding. No, not leaving behind ... that implied some connection between us. Simply leaving. For she had not yet given me the chance to make my feelings clear and – even though I feared that I might not gain an inch with her – I knew that if I departed without making some declaration of my passion I would regret it for the rest of my life.

So I climbed wearily up the stairs to our upper dormitory. Some of the trestle beds were already occupied and a medley of snores and other unguarded night-sounds filled the moonlit chamber. Unlacing my boots but not bothering to remove anything else, I lay down on my own lumpy bed and tried to sleep. The house would be stirring early for tomorrow's wedding. But I didn't consider that. Images of Kate kept filling my eyes. Kate calling to me as I wandered by the lake, Kate debating love poetry, Kate tending to the wound on my face.

In the pre-sleep time various silly courses of action slipped into my head. Perhaps I should injure myself in her presence to elicit her sympathy and to compel her to attend to me again? No, she'd see through that in an instant.

Perhaps I should write her a love poem, instead of relying on the words of Richard Milford? No, she'd see through *that* too.

Had she admired my performance as the love-sick Lysander? She'd said she liked the play (in truth, it'd be difficult to dislike it) but she had not said a word about *my* performance. When Cuthbert Ascre turned up she'd complimented him, hadn't she – but perhaps she was just being polite. After all he was only playing at playing. He needed reassurance. But so did I, something whimpered inside me.

I must have fallen asleep in this feeble, self-pitying mood for the next thing I knew I was coming awake with a start, dazzled. For an instant I couldn't remember where I was. The moon was glaring almost directly on my face. Squinting, I observed her shining unashamed at me through the small window opposite. Why had I woken? Around me were little noises, sounds of shifting, but no evidence that anyone else was awake. Without knowing why, I rose and walked towards the window, skirting the bed of one of my fellows. The boards were rough under my stockinged feet. The window was tight shut against the contagion of night. I tried to peer out but could see nothing except the moon's white eye warped by the thick glass.

There is a line in our play – I mean in Master W.S.'s *Dream* – where Snug the joiner asks whether the moon is due to shine on the night of their performance of Pyramus and

Thisbe. Bottom and Quince consult an almanac to discover that, yes, the moon does shine. The mechanicals, like good improvisers, think to use this light, gratis. Bottom says, "Why, then you may leave a casement of the great chamber window, where we play, open, and the moon may shine in at the casement."

Well, on cue, the moon had indeed risen for the latter part of the Instede *Dream*. And now the moon was shining in through a line of small casements. Our dormitory floor was at the very top of the house, its mean window-apertures hidden behind a parapet. Between the window and the parapet was a space of a couple of feet or so. The casement opened inwards. I tugged at the catch and, after a little rusty resistance, it gave. The night air was fresh on my face. I glanced round at my sleeping companions. For some reason, I did not wish to be observed as I slithered through the little window and tumbled awkwardly into the standing-space between casement and parapet.

Once outside, I stood upright and held firmly onto the coping stone. Some of the previous day's heat still radiated from the wall behind me but the lead-lined guttering was cold underfoot. I guessed that it was about one or two in the morning. By the calendar it was midsummer's day but there was not yet any sign of lightening in the east. Rather, the moon queened it over the night. A few thin shreds of cloud were scattered across the heavens, scarfing the stars. An owl hooted. I peered over the parapet. I seemed to be standing on the edge of a dizzying cliff, gazing down at a strange landscape in which objects were blanched and transfigured. The space where we'd played out the *Dream* was almost directly below. At one end were the rows of seating. At a little distance was the garden enclosed by the hornbeam hedge. The plashing of the fountain carried through the soft air. A dog barked in the distance.

By craning out and round I could look down the flank of the building and see, beyond the little turret on the corner, the moonstruck trees where Robin had lived and died. I thought of the odd way in which Adam Fielding had suddenly decided that the woodman's death was natural – or as natural as suicide is permitted to be. And shifted my gaze back to the enclosed garden which, from this height, had a queer resemblance to a chess board. For one thing it was neatly quartered and then re-quartered by paths and low hedges, and the light was strong enough to cast flat black shadows among the pale, illuminated segments. For another, the statues and obelisks, the Neptune fountain and the summer-pavilion, had taken on the aspect of chess-pieces disposed for a game. Or rather they appeared like pieces abandoned half-way through a game.

I blinked in the moonlight. Blinked again. For it looked to me as if one of the figures in the central part of the garden was moving. A white form flickered, was still, flickered again. My skin crawled. Then a piece of shadow appeared to detach itself from a larger area of darkness and to move towards the shifting white shape. To stop, then move forward. To stop, then move forward once more. Everything about it signified stealth, or worse. The figure in white was surely unaware of the creeping but resistless progress of the dark shadow. I wanted to cry out a warning. But I also wanted to stay quiet, to duck down below the parapet. My mouth gaped but, as in a dream, no sound emerged. Then it seemed as though the white and dark shapes met, swirled about, coalesced. Through the night there came a thin shriek.

At almost the same instant the moon was obscured by a rag of cloud. It was like the snuffing of a candle. By the time she'd re-emerged, the scene had changed again. There was no shifting figure, white or black, in the enclosed garden. Night and silence only. No more.

I waited, but somehow sensed that whatever had happened was over and done with. Nevertheless I stood there clutching the parapet for several minutes more. Then, cold and fearful, I climbed back inside, taking care to close the casement silently, and tiptoed across the splintery boards to the trestle bed. I lay down and closed my eyes. The moon no longer shone direct on my face but shot her beams into a far corner of the long room. Whereas earlier I'd been preoccupied with thoughts of Kate, now it was the image or the series of images I'd just seen which filled my head. The secluded garden, laid out in its squares of moonlight and shade, the blurring, coalescing figures. That thin shriek.

There was a game going on here all right, but what was it? Who were the players?

I slept for a couple of hours. When I awoke a grey light was seeping into the dormitory, displacing the moon's brilliance. Birds were singing. Remembering what I'd seen and heard in the night I was inclined at first to put the whole business down to imagination. Perhaps I'd not even woken and got up but dreamed those actions as well (as one can sometimes dream that one has awoken from a dream). And if I *had* actually crossed to the casement and exited onto the roof leads, then what had I witnessed? Night shapes, the cry of a hunted animal. No more. So I convinced myself and turned over for another hour's uneasy slumber.

But there was a game going on, and a deadly serious one too, for a little later that morning – as Instede House was beginning to stir for the midsummer marriage of the heir to the estate – the body of Henry Ascre, Lord Elcombe himself, second holder of that title, was discovered in the hornbeam garden. He appeared to have been pushed, with great violence, onto the sundial which stood near to the summerhouse. The first person to see Elcombe (the first person apart from his murderer, that is) was one of the gardeners. He discovered his master sprawled atop the dial, his arms outflung and his legs splayed forward of the stone pedestal. The gardener didn't recognize him at first. He probably thought that one of the guests at the wedding, or more likely one of those riff-raff players, was sleeping off a night's drinking in a peculiar and highly uncomfortable position. Then, as he drew nearer, he saw the bared teeth and fixed heavenward stare of his lord and master.

He was puzzled by a black triangular object which was resting on his lordship's chest. It was only when some of the other servants, together with Oswald the steward, came to see and then to shift the corpse that they realized what the object was. The tip and the tapered end of the long brass gnomon, whose innocuous shadow served to remind onlookers of the passage of time, had pierced his heart. Elcombe had been shoved and then probably held down on the dial with sufficient force and fury for the point not merely to enter his back and heart but to burst out, all black and bloody, through his chest. The metal had buckled under the stress but not before it had done its job.

'*tempus edax rerum*' read the legend round the sundial. In Elcombe's case the words had proved all too true: time is indeed the devourer of all things.

It might, I suppose, have been considered an accident. It could have happened that Elcombe – maybe set on by an excess of wine the previous evening (although it was hard to envisage such a steely man being overcome by anything so mundane) or maybe driven by some strange rage or by self-forgetfulness – had slipped and fallen onto the sundial in his garden, and been run through by the point of the timer. It might even have been that, in his anguished struggle to free himself, he had merely succeeded in pushing the brass dagger deeper into his body.

But the hand of man seemed a more likely culprit than the point of a dial. And so it proved when young Harry Ascre, he who was due to be married that midsummer's day, wandered down one of the walkways in the garden while Oswald and the servants were recovering from their first shock and terror. They were mutely contemplating how to detach the body from the sundial's tip and bear it indoors. Ascre was dressed simply in shirt and breeches. He appeared confused. All over his shirt and hose were gouts of blood, his father's doubtless. Questions were put to him but he refused to respond – or was unable to. He stood there, mouth slightly open, not looking (as was noted at the time) in the direction of his father's body. Then he made to wander off again, for all the world as if he was out for an early morning stroll on the morning of his marriage. Oswald gave orders for him to be apprehended and two or three of the burlier servants seized their master's son and heir and bore him inside, where they secured him in a chamber on the ground floor before returning to help with the corpse.

I can hardly begin to describe the numbness and then the turmoil which descended upon Instede House as the news of Elcombe's murder spread. Any death must cast its shadow over a feeling neighbourhood. We'd seen that with the recent demise of Robin. But this, the second violent death in little more than a week, was not to be compared to the woodman's departure. Where the one man had slipped into a feral condition almost beyond the human world, the other had been at its very heart. To vary the figure, he was like a great wheel from whose spokes depended hundreds of lesser folk, from gardeners to brewers, from cooks to gamekeepers. Whether Lord Elcombe was loved or loathed, or whether he simply left people cold, was beside the point. He – or his position – ensured that many men and women and their children too were kept sheltered, fed and clothed, in exchange for their labours. To have him die, and especially in such difficult, violent circumstances, was to feel the world tremble under one's feet.

Even we players felt keenly the loss of a patron. We were in his house by his invitation and, whatever this courtier's motives for favouring the Chamberlain's Company, we couldn't be anything but grateful for his notice.

Nor was this uncertainty, into which all of Elcombe's dependants had been thrust, the worse aspect of the situation – or rather it was one among several aspects which vied with each other for worstness.

There was first of all the private grief of the family, Lady Elcombe and Cuthbert Ascre. Penelope remained closeted for most of the day with parson Brown. Cuthbert vanished from sight somewhere. As well as the normal shock of death, the mother and brother must have been tormented by the fact that the destroyer of Lord Elcombe shared their own flesh and blood. There is a particular horror in the crime of parricide.

But there was no end to the horrors. For this was no ordinary day at Instede. Some of the grandest people in the land had gathered to celebrate the match of Harry Ascre to Marianne Morland. Now the groom's father was violently dead, foully dead, and the groom and Instede heir was incarcerated in the great house which was, in name at least, his own. The division and hatred at the heart of this great family had been brutally exposed for the world to see.

There was no question of the marriage proceeding now, of course.

Before the day was out most of the guests had slipped away, with stony or tear-stained faces. The Devons and the Cornwalls, the Winchesters and the Derbys: England quit Instede. As if in mockery or defiance of human concerns, the sun shone down unblinkingly on the departing groups. I myself saw the Morlands as they were stepping into their coach. We have a natural appetite to watch how others bear their distresses – at least if we do not know them well – so I observed with quite an appraising eye that mother and father Morland had lost some of the gloss they'd worn at the previous evening's feast. Their attractive daughter I couldn't see since she was wearing a veil. But as she climbed into the elaborately carved coach she stumbled and her mother caught her under the arm. Suddenly my heart went out to this girl, someone I'd not even spoken to or been within ten yards of. Who knew whether she'd chosen Harry Ascre for a husband or – a thing much more likely – he'd been chosen for her by her title-hungry parents. Who knew whether she was a willing bride or merely a resigned one?

From what I'd noticed at last night's banquet there didn't seem to be much between the prospective husband and wife, no fond glances, no hungry looks, no quick clasps. Whatever the state of their hearts, her present suffering and situation were painful to contemplate; and assuredly much more painful to endure. To wake on your wedding morning in the fever of expectation and then to discover that everything had been violently snatched away. To return to the parental home, matchless and mateless, with the future perhaps clouded for ever . . . to grieve for a dead father-in-law and, much more, for the husband who would most likely be accused of his murder . . .

For this was young Harry Ascre's fate: arrest, incarceration, arraignment, trial, sentence. And then the almost unavoidable end of those charged with murder. The first two links in this chain had already been forged, and the third was about to be. He didn't remain long in the locked chamber on the ground-floor of the house. By late afternoon of the following day the coroner had arrived from Salisbury. A jury, composed of men from Rung Withers and two or three other small hamlets beyond the bounds of the estate, had been hastily convened by Sam the bailie in advance of the coroner's arrival. As soon as that gentleman appeared they got down to the task like good citizens, sitting in the very room where we'd held our rehearsals and, unsurprisingly, found that an indictment for homicide should be made. The coroner had evidently been expecting this – indeed it was hard to see how any other conclusion could have been reached – for he had travelled to Instede House together with two justices. They immediately bound the young man over for trial and returned with him to Salisbury that very evening, riding off with an escort into the dusk to reach their destination. In all of this Justice Adam Fielding took no part because, I presumed, of his friendly connections with the Elcombe family.

The speed of the process was surprising but it was a reflection of the grave nature of the crime and the rank of the victim. There was also the consideration, no doubt, that it would be better for everybody if Harry was removed from Instede as soon as possible to a more appropriate location than his father's house. This location was Salisbury gaol where he would be detained until the next assizes, due to be held in a week's time.

At some point in his examination young Harry had claimed that he'd discovered his father in the garden early in the morning and that, during the process, he must have got blood on himself. After that he would say nothing. This continuing silence seemed to accuse him of more than complicity in his father's death, quite apart from the evidence of the bloodied shirt and hose. Added to this was a supposition which, having not been much talked of, suddenly became hot in everyone's mouth: it was that young Ascre hadn't really sought marriage at all, but was being pushed and bullied into it by a tyrannical father. Finally, matters had reached some kind of a head on the very morning of his marriage. It was said that he'd encountered Lord Elcombe, either by design or by chance, in the hornbeam garden. Perhaps he'd made one last attempt to persuade his father to be allowed to escape from the yoke of matrimony. Perhaps he'd accused his father of being concerned only for his own interest (and fortune) and having no care for his son's well-being. Perhaps the father sneered at him and told him not to be such a fool as to expect to love or even to like the woman he was about to marry. What were whores for, after all? Perhaps the father cast aspersions on the son's bed-skills.

Perhaps . . . perhaps.

No-one knew anything but almost everybody thought they were in possession of a fragment of the dialogue which had passed between father and son before the latter had struck out at the former or shoved him backwards. By ill chance the father was standing with his back to the sundial and its upright brass gnomon. As the "dagger" found its way between his ribs and pierced his heart, what did the son do? Did he stand there, aghast, spattered with blood, while his father writhed in agony. Did he wait impassively to see what would happen next? Or clamp his hand over his father's mouth to seal up the cries and screams? Or did he, in blind fury, seize the moment and ram his father's body further down onto the flat surface of the dial until its point protruded, slick and bloody, from his sire's chest?

All these versions of the event were current and probably others besides. The gossip, whispered, sorrowful but somehow heated as well, agreed on only one point: that young Harry Ascre hadn't deliberately set out to kill his father on that fine midsummer morning. For one thing, if you were planning to commit a murder you would hardly do it in so open a place as the hornbeam garden and with so cumbersome and strange a weapon as the tip of sundial. For another, all agreed that he did not have the "character" of a murderer, whatever that might be. He was, however, a moody, intense young man, and plainly a deeply unhappy one, the more unhappy as his nuptials drew closer. I'd glimpsed something of this for myself when I'd seen him mumbling and cursing away in the garden.

Whether he'd intended the death of his father or not made little difference. He was headed in one direction only. True, he'd be tried at the Salisbury assizes but would be lucky if he received a hearing that lasted more than half an hour. There were no witnessess against him, but there were none for him either – and even if there had been they wouldn't necessarily have been listened to. Against Harry Ascre were arrayed his almost complete silence, his proximity to the place of the murder, his bloody garments, his known difference with his father in the matter of the marriage. Taken together, this was, or would be, conclusive. There was only one destination for Ascre. He would be turned off in public like a common felon, dangling on the end of a rope. No traitor, he would be denied the axe and the privacy of the execution yard that is the nobleman's prerogative. Only the Queen could pardon him. Equally, there was no reason for Queen Elizabeth to reprieve a wicked young man who had snuffed out the life of one of her principal courtiers, even if that young man was the courtier's son. It would have been better for Harry Ascre (I thought cynically) if he'd possessed some of the address, some of the grace, some of the buoyancy of youth which our sovereign was susceptible to. But he had none of these things. No, he was as good as dead in his Salisbury cell.

What would happen then? I presumed that Cuthbert Ascre would come into the title and the estate. Well, if he would never be able to tread the boards he would at least be free to act the part of patron to the players to his heart's content.

Everything that I've put down here took a couple of days to become evident. And, of course, in the interim a kind of life continued in this miserable house. Preparations were made for the interment of Lord Elcombe in the family vault at Instede. He would lie beside his father, the first holder of the title. Lady Elcombe stayed shut up most of the time, though a couple of times I glimpsed her black-shrouded form passing a door. Sometimes she was reported to be with Brown the parish priest, sometimes with Oswald the steward. Chalk and cheese those two. I knew who I'd rather have to console me. Oswald took on himself an even more central role in the running of the place, seeming to believe not merely that he spoke for his dead lord but that, in the interval while the current holder of the title languished in gaol and before the next one might be confirmed, he actually was master of all he surveyed. His expression reminded me of frosted ground on a winter's morning. His long arms hung by his sides like withered black bladders.

I'd assumed that the Chamberlain's too would quit Instede, there being no reason for us to remain any longer. Everybody had naturally forgotten the *Dream*; no one had any interest in any further diversion (although, from one aspect, that was exactly what was required). But our seniors Richard Sincklo and Thomas Pope consulted each other at length and spoke to one or two others before announcing that we'd be staying until the obsequies for Elcombe were done. This was because, they said, he'd been a loyal patron to us and therefore we should repay the favour by presenting our last respects to him in death. I'm pretty convinced that Sincklo and Pope believed in their own argument. To do one's obsequies was the honourable course of action. We were not tradesmen whose dealings with customers were confined to the account-book. Our connections with our friends and patrons ran deeper. Also there must have been the thought that any ties to the Ascre family were not severed with the death of the head of the household. Another would come to take his place. And, of course, in Cuthbert we already possessed a good friend of the drama.

Despite this, the younger members of the Company were eager enough to escape, except for the two or three like Will Fall who'd formed local attachments – although he complained to me that his kitchen drab Audrey had clammed up under the pretext of grief.

Laurence Savage took a somewhat cynical view of why we were hanging around. "It's because the bastards haven't paid us yet, and aren't likely to now with Elcombe's death and all. So old Sincklo and Pope've got together and decided that we'll get a little recompense by eating and drinking at their expense a bit longer, particularly since there's a funeral in the offing. A funeral's a great provoker of appetite. Come to think of it, they'll probably use some of the left-overs from the wedding feast."

"The opposite of what happens in *Hamlet*," I said. "This time it'll be the marriage table which is providing the funeral baked meats."

"You do know that play, don't you, Nicholas," said Laurence.

As for myself, I wasn't altogether unhappy that we weren't leaving straightaway. It wasn't exactly that I still had hopes of making progress with Kate Fielding ... but, such is the eternal delusion of the lover, neither had I absolutely abandoned those hopes. And sometimes it is enough merely to gaze and adore from afar. More I could not expect.

Although Adam Fielding had not been involved in the arraignment of Harry Ascre, he remained at Instede together with his daughter to offer whatever help and consolation he could to the bereaved household. Or so I interpreted his continued presence.

Of course I had my own story to tell in connection with Elcombe's death. That moment in the early hours of midsummer morning when I stood clutching the parapet and gazing down into the enclosed chess-board of a garden, where the black piece and the white piece swirled about each other, moved by invisible hands – all this retained its dream-like quality in retrospect. The blanched moonscape, the fountain's soft oplach, the curiously stealthy manner in which the shadow had advanced on the white form, the blanking out of this enigmatical scene by the cloud which crossed the moon, the thin shriek which came after. Had I actually witnessed this? Or was it some reverie, perhaps induced by Laurence Savage's story of dark-suited men coming to offer blood-money for the death of a little child?

But in my guts, rather than in my head, I understood well enough that it was no dream. Instinct, not reason, told me so. There *had* been figures in the garden, and some ... transaction had occurred between them. Was this the actual moment of the killing of Lord Elcombe by his son? I tried to recall the position of the figures in relation to the sundial and the summer-house. But all that appeared to my mind's eye was an obscure picture where nothing would stay still long enough to be named. It was very troubling to consider that I might have witnessed a killing, and I preferred to find another explanation but couldn't. Suppose, then, that this had been the case, that murder had been occurring while I looked on, should the black shadow be identified with Harry Ascre and the white form with his father? This seemed the wrong way about. The swift, covert movement of the shadow was much more in keeping with the nature of the father while something about the white form suggested the hapless son. Although I hadn't seen what happened afterwards, I had the strong feeling that the dark form had, as it were, swallowed up the lighter one. And if there'd been a contest of any kind between father and son, this was surely the direction in which it would have gone.

Yet when his body had been found, transfixed by the sundial, Elcombe was dressed in his usual dark garb. And when Harry was sighted ambling up a walkway he was wearing a white shirt and pale hose against which his father's blood showed all too clearly. So, if the father had crept up on the son and there'd been a fatal encounter, the ambush had gone wrong, the white piece had taken the black. But why would father be "creeping up" on son anyway? Hadn't Elcombe got his way with his first-born? Young Harry was about to marry and so secure the cash which his father needed. Why should Elcombe jeopardize this by a middle-of-the-night rendezvous with the boy?

And there were questions of time to consider. All of this took place at about one or two in the morning, before the slightest trace of midsummer dawn showed in the east. So the son and heir of Instede had killed his father and then remained for a further four or five hours in the hornbeam garden, wandering up and down its walkways, shivering in the early morning dew while the blood-stained clothes clung to his body. It was possible, I supposed. It was the kind of behaviour which a man who was not in his right mind would succumb to. The kind of behaviour which a man who'd recently killed his father might enact. After all, what was time to him? He'd just killed time, hadn't he, by ramming his father onto a sundial's point. The sundial was useless now until it had a new gnomon. I didn't think that anybody would be in a hurry to replace it.

Father ... time ... father time. Perhaps young Ascre wanted to arrest time, to put off the moment of his wedding – for ever.

Thoughts like these, if they could be dignified with the name of thoughts, wandered about in my head. Yet this thinking was merely a way of delaying doing anything about what I'd witnessed. My moon-vision couldn't exonerate Harry Ascre; rather the opposite, it tended to confirm his guilt. On the other hand, I didn't consider I could stay silent. And the obvious person to approach with my tale must again be Justice Adam Fielding.

First, however, there was a different, though related, matter to be cleared up. Before and after our *Dream* performance Laurence Savage had told me the strange tale behind his loathing for Lord Elcombe and for Oswald the steward. True, he hated his mother even more for accepting silver on the death of little Thomas, but his contempt for Elcombe had been apparent ever since the Chamberlain's arrival at Instede. What had he said of the two men? "I hate them both for it and will do until my dying day." Well, it was the master who died first. And it was a natural enough notion to cross one's mind, wasn't it, that Laurence himself had the clearest motive for murder. The last I'd seen of him, he was blundering off into the night, heated with drink and heated too by memories of his brother's death and his mother's treachery.

Was it not conceivable that Laurence had fallen down somewhere not far from the playing-area, overcome with drink, and then awakened after a few hours to discover Lord Elcombe also wandering restlessly about the grounds? There followed a confrontation betwen the two men. My co-player would have forcibly reminded our patron of that incident many years before by the Fleet Ditch when a brace of hurrying horsemen knocked aside a young lad. Perhaps Elcombe had claimed to have no memory of the accident. Perhaps he brushed it aside carelessly (he had, after all, important matters to attend to: the imminent marriage of his son, his daughter-in-law's dowry). Perhaps he joked about it. A joke would be in order. What is a poor child to one of the highest men in the land? Something that he said sparked off the fury in Laurence and, in that fury, the player pushed the nobleman so suddenly, so violently, that he fell onto the spike of the dial. Then Laurence shoved down harder – or stood by impassively to see his enemy squirm – or staggered off, unaware of what he had done. Any of the reactions, in short, which had been attributed to Elcombe's son.

I knew Laurence Savage, not well, but as a fellow toiler in the playhouse. His bland looks were useful when an unobvious villain was required, although comedy was really his line. In general, his nature seemed to stand in ironic relation to his name: he was mild, easy-going. That was the reason I'd been surprised, even slightly shocked by the tale he'd told of his little brother's death and what he'd hinted at of his family history after that. It did not seem appropriate that he should have grown out of such sad soil. But then I thought, unfairly perhaps, of the part he had played in *A Midsummer Night's Dream*. Bottom is transformed to an ass, although he doesn't know it, and grows high-handed. This is a love-change. But hate can work equal transformations, and to a shape uglier and less comic than an ass's. Had mild Laurence become murderous Savage, impelled by his loathing and fear of Elcombe?

To be honest with you, I didn't think so. I still trusted to my instinctive knowledge of the man. *But I couldn't be sure.* There was only one way I could have been confident that Laurence was nowhere near the hornbeam garden in the middle of the night: to have seen him at the time in the top-floor room where we'd all been sleeping. Or most of us had been sleeping, at any rate. I couldn't quite place the whereabouts of Laurence's bed. On the opposite, the window, side of the chamber, four or five down from mine? I rather thought so. But as to whether his crib was occupied on the night of the murder, I had no idea. Two or three of my fellows, especially after the excitements of the play and with an eye to the openings which a touring performance provides for diversion, were definitely absent from their cots. To ask where they'd been or whether they'd noticed Laurence Savage while they went about their business would be asking for a justified punch in the nose. We may be responsible for each other in the play but, except in extreme cases, each man's recreation is his own concern.

So there was only one way to get to the bottom of this. I'd have to ask Laurence straight out. I tried various unsatisfactory formulations in my mind: "Well, Laurence, I expect you're glad enough that his lordship is dead . . . " or "I saw something rather strange when I was standing on the roof the other night, Laurence . . . " But in the event Savage saved me the trouble by coming straight to the point. It was apparent that the question had been troubling him too.

"A word, Nicholas."

"I have been wanting to talk, Laurence."

We were walking on the south side of the house, a stone's throw from the garden where the murder had occurred.

"I can guess your theme. It is to do with . . . with the other night and the tale I told you, is it not? Concerning my mother and my brother and Lord Elcombe and his steward."

For an instant I thought that Laurence was going to admit that he'd made it up. That it was all a story.

"I would not want to be held accountable for my words," he said.

For sure, he had invented the story.

"I do not mean to deny what happened by the Fleet Ditch. I was there. Nor do I mean to deny that I . . . hate . . . hated Lord Elcombe. What I have said I have said. But when I spoke of the accident, I was carried away by drink and by a . . . contempt for the man which has been building and building inside me ever since we set eyes on this pile. It was a relief to have your ear, Nick. You're a good listener."

"Thank you," I said, not knowing how else to respond.

"True, I wished him dead and his steward as well, and it has occurred to me since that one should be careful what one utters, even in drink and anger, especially perhaps in those two states."

"You may put your mind at rest, Laurence. Elcombe was killed by human hands and by a sundial's point, not by any harsh words."

"Oh thank you." He grasped me by the shoulder and I saw relief in his face. He had evidently been suffering in mind, forging a link between his words and his enemy's fate. It takes a player or a poet to have such a deep faith in – and fear of – the power of words.

"In his time Lord Elcombe must have garnered up a whole heap of harsh words, given his nature," I said.

"Oh yes," said Laurence eagerly. He looked even more relieved. He'd have to be a good actor to be simulating this condition. (But then he was a good actor.)

"What happened to you on midsummer's night, Laurence?"

"Why do you ask?"

"For my own private curiosity, no more."

"I can't remember clearly. I'd had a deal to drink and then after we'd spoken together, a deal more. I suppose I wandered unhappily about the grounds for some time. I must have chosen to lie down at some point for I recall waking up and finding myself on the grass. Then the next I knew I was lying fully clothed on my bed in our chamber and it was already beginning to grow light."

"So somehow you must have climbed the stairs to the dormitory and found your bed in the dark and lain down on it."

"Well, Nick, I wasn't carried up there by Peascod and Mustardseed. I am Bottom only in the play even if I have made something of an ass of myself."

"Not at all, not at all," I said, wanting to avoid even the faintest resurgence of anger in Laurence. "When you were, er, wandering around here, did you notice anything . . . anybody . . . in the region of this garden?"

I gestured towards the hornbeam enclosure. Through the windows and arches cut in the branches, the flanks and limbs of the statues gleamed whitely in the sun.

"There were plenty of people about that night, I think. But I was hardly in a fit state to see them clearly . . . or to remember who they were if I did see them."

"No, of course."

"What did *you* see?" said Laurence suddenly, sharply. "For sure, all your questions have been directed at something."

"I was on the roof," I said. "I thought I saw figures in that garden over there. But it was all imagination, I expect."

Laurence was curious to know what I'd been up to on the roof of Instede, so I briefly sketched in the essentials. Since he'd been so open with me I owed him some explanation. But he could shed no light on the figures in the garden, and even hinted that I'd perhaps consumed more liquor than I remembered. Either that or it was a trick of the moonlight. All imagination.

The more I thought about it, however, the more convinced I became that I had witnessed something. But what? There was no alternative but to talk to Justice Fielding about it. I was chary of approaching him for a second time about a suspicious death. After the last occasion when, following our interview with Lord and Lady Elcombe, he had abruptly told me that I was being needlessly curious, I wondered how he would receive my latest account.

I caught him writing, as usual, and felt guilty for disturbing him. However, he encouraged me to speak and didn't dismiss me as a fantasist. Instead he seemed to take my words most seriously and, two or three times, made me go over what I had seen from the top floor of the house. Now it was my turn to be close-questioned. He quizzed me about the hour, and why I'd concluded that it was the dead middle of the night. He wanted to know what had roused me: was it a cry, a scream . . . a night-noise of what sort precisely? I repeated that if there had been a sound it was locked up in the vault of my brain. The only thing I remembered was waking to the cold light of the moon. Why had I gone to the window then? I didn't know. Why had I opened it? No reason for that either. (In truth, I was prompted by a line of Master Shakespeare's, or rather Bottom's: "Why, then you may leave a casement of the great chamber window, where we play, open." I did not mention this, however, because no reason at all sounded better than such a silly one.) Why did I step outside? What exactly did I see when I looked down at the formal garden? How long had I stood there? Two figures did I say, or three?

In the end, I was induced to imitate the guarded posture in which the black shape had advanced towards the white form. In a crouching run I made my way across the floor of the Justice's chamber, stopping now and then to look round with cocked head before gliding forward again. As a player, I must briefly become that which I play and now I was transformed into the night-shadow stealing towards its prey. Fielding clapped his hands, either in terse commendation or as an indication that he'd seen enough. Then he made me stand and wait in the posture of the figure in white. So I did, shifting and shivering and not daring to turn right round, and all the time with the unpleasant sensation that I was somehow creeping up on myself.

I protested that I wasn't certain I'd seen *anything*, let alone two figures with such clearly defined roles as pursuer and quarry. Yet the remark was for form's sake only. Even as I crouched down in the part of the hunter or stood, uneasy, in the position of the hunted, I knew that this was an acting-out of the reality in the garden, not a midsummer night's dream, not a moon-vision. "Knew" not with my head but with that more infallible guide to truth, my guts.

"Sir?" I said when this was finished. "Adam?"

Fielding sat slumped in an uncomfortable-looking chair.

He looked as solemn as I'd ever seen him. His grey gaze was directed inwards and his beard had a workmanlike squareness, but every so often a kind of shadow crossed his honest features. It was not surprising, I suppose, that the death of Elcombe and the incarceration of Elcombe's son had hit him so hard, given his long friendship with the family. The despondency and turmoil of the house seemed distilled into this good man.

"What, Nicholas?" he said distractedly, as though he was still taking in what I'd shown him moments before.

"I brought this story to you with some trepidation, since the last time we spoke, about the business of Robin, we did not quite, ah, see eye to eye. Yet now when I come to you with something that even to me is cloudy, you quiz me close and appear to accept my words."

"These are terrible times for Instede and the family and all who know them," said Fielding, seeming to avoid my implicit question. "To lose the head of a family is hard enough at any time but to lose him in such violent circumstances is a grievous blow. Then to have the son indicted for the murder of the father . . ."

He shook his head as if mere words were inadequate.

"We must also," he continued, "remember the suffering of Penelope, and of Cuthbert. They have lost a husband and father – and are in danger of losing a son and brother as well."

I thought of Lady Elcombe, the black-shrouded figure passing the door. Who knew what was going through her heart? Only the parson Brown perhaps – or Oswald, who was in constant attendance on her. As for Cuthbert, he too had scarcely been seen since his father's death.

"You are certain that Harry Ascre killed his father?" I said, visualizing that young man sitting in Salisbury gaol.

"What is your opinion, Nick?"

"I have been trying to square what I witnessed in the garden with what actually occurred. If my eyes weren't deceiving me, I saw a person clad in dark clothes mount some kind of ambush on a figure dressed in lighter material. But I don't know what the outcome of it was."

"Because the moon was covered, the light went out?"

"Just so."

"This is not in absolute contradiction to what happened, then," said Fielding. "There must have been a struggle between Lord Elcombe and whoever killed him. You might have seen the first stage of it, the prologue."

"I am not sure," I said.

"Why?"

I was reluctant to tell Fielding that I'd identified the black shape in my mind with Elcombe and the white form with his son, and that in any such encounter it was almost certainly the father – that ruthless man, one brooking no obstacles – who would gain the upper hand, rather than being left pinned on a sundial's point. What I said was, "Because this took place in the middle of the night and the body was not found until the early morning. If it *was* Harry and his father that I saw, then the son must have remained in the garden for the next several hours, shivering and bloody."

"Rather than going inside, cleaning himself up, destroying his garments and so on?"

"Yes."

"Those are the actions of a careful man, a man who has the wit and will to protect himself. Suppose that Harry Ascre had lost that wit and will."

I nodded. This was very close to my own notion of the older son's character. After all, the very fact that he'd been discovered wandering, bloody and confused, in his father's garden, though evidence of his apparent guilt, was also evidence that he wasn't a calculating killer, wasn't the kind of person who'd take care to cover his tracks.

"Nevertheless, he did not kill his father. I am convinced of that," said Fielding quietly. "I have known the boy since he was small and watched him grow. He is a strange lad, moody and inward-looking, but he is no murderer."

"What can we do about it, Adam? He is bound to hang."

Fielding stood up. The inward expression was replaced by a look of determination.

"We can apply our own wits and wills to ensuring that he is acquitted of this charge."

By virtue of his position, Justice Fielding must have a high regard for English law and English courts, but even I, inexperienced in these things, was aware that once someone appeared at an assize then it was pretty well all up with them. Indictments were laid only against the guilty, everyone knew that.

"How?"

"By finding who really killed Lord Elcombe."

Minutes later Fielding and I were standing in the hornbeam garden by the fatal sundial. All that remained was the stone pedestal, the brass plate with the clock-face and gnomon having been removed or become detached when Elcombe's body was lifted off it. There were dark streaks and splotches down the side of the pedestal which might have been blood, just as there were blotches on the green grass. Birdsong filled the garden. Butterflies fluttered through the mild mid-morning air. The sun shone with his customary indifference.

It had been Adam Fielding who required my presence by this now timeless, faceless lump of stone. As we walked towards the garden, he explained that he wanted me to try to "place" the figures which I'd glimpsed from the top storey of Instede, to put the pieces into position on the "board", for I had mentioned to him the likeness between the garden and a chess-board. It was no good saying I'd already attempted this in my mind and failed. We had to go over the ground together.

As he did when examining the spot where Robin died in

the woods, the Justice spent some time on his hands and knees inspecting the ground around the base of the sundial. The ideal circumstance would presumably have been soil which was soft or damp, receptive to footprints, but there'd been no rain since we arrived in the country. I was puzzled, however, by a couple of deep indentations in the turf on either side and slightly in advance of the sundial pedestal. Fielding enlightened me.

"Those are the marks of Henry Ascre, of the father I mean. The last marks he left on this earth. Imagine. Pinned down on top of this base here, he cannot get free, for he is without the strength or leverage to push himself up from the place where he has been run through. In his death agony, he drums on the ground with his feet, drums so hard that he leaves these deep prints of his heels. Poor man."

I winced at the image.

"But there is no sign of anything else here. The ground is marked for some yards round about but that is to be explained by the large, agitated party of servants that was required to free the body and then transport it inside. There is nothing overlooked here."

"Overlooked?"

"From my first inspection. I came out on the morning of the murder to see what I could see. A second glance sometimes pays. You never know whether you've missed something. "

I thought of the combination of sharp sight and sharp thinking in this man, the way he had anatomized me when we first met at his house in Salisbury. Some of these qualities had been passed to his daughter, for sure. Perhaps it was Fielding's presence that stimulated me to try some deductions of my own.

"I believe that Lord Elcombe knew the person who killed him," I said. "I mean, even if it was not his son, he knew him."

"How so?"

"Knew and trusted him . . . or her perhaps," I added as the possibility suddenly occurred to me.

"Let's not make things even more complicated, Nicholas. We will assume it was a man. Now speak what's on your mind."

"Bear with me, sir. I am not as quick as you are. There were no marks of violence on the body, were there, apart from the single blow with the tip of the sundial."

"I don't think so," said Fielding.

"And Henry Ascre the younger, Harry, he was covered in his father's blood, but there were no marks on him either, no marks of violence. His face was unbruised, his arms and hands unscathed."

"I see where you are headed, Nicholas. You mean that there was no struggle between father and son or between them and anybody else."

"Yes, " I said, not feeling as sure as I sounded.

"And yet a man died."

"Without expecting to, without being prepared for it. Elcombe was unarmed, wasn't he? Unattended too. If he came out here to meet someone – or met them by chance in the early morning – he did not foresee any danger to himself. He allowed that someone to come close to him. Which argues familiarity or friendship."

"I am with you so far. Then . . .?"

"Some words must have been exchanged, some insults traded, but the two were still standing close to each other. Close enough for the other to have lunged or lashed out suddenly so that Elcombe was caught off guard . . . and pushed back here on top of this pedestal. Or perhaps he wasn't even pushed. He stepped back, slipped and fell. In that case no violence would have been required to cause Elcombe's death, merely the shadow of violence."

"A raised arm would have done the job," said Fielding. "It would have been enough for the other to look threatening."

"Which is why I said him or *her*, just now."

Although even before the words were out of my mouth I conjured up and almost dismissed the image of Lord Elcombe being outfaced by *anyone*, let alone a woman.

Adam Fielding stroked his spade beard while he considered what he had heard. "So, if we are searching for an alternative culprit to the young man, you are telling me that we must look within the circle of individuals whom Elcombe trusted or at least those he would allow to come near him. Because in your, ah, reading of the situation, he died or was killed, unsuspecting, at close quarters – and only a person known to him would have been permitted that liberty."

"Yes, I think so," I said, suddenly uncertain now that my formulation was exposed to the warm light of day.

"Therefore what you saw in the middle of the night had nothing to do with Elcombe's death? You talked of an ambush, of one dark shape creeping up on a white one. That's very different from the scene which you've just described."

"I don't know how, but I think it was connected," I said.

"What tells you that?"

"My gut," I said.

"Well, that is no more unreliable a guide than any other – sometimes."

"Sir, I have a question for you. That death of Robin the wood-man now, which seemed to me – seems to me – not to have been a case of self-slaughter, that is connected to . . . all this, is it not?"

I gestured round, taking in the spot where Lord Elcombe had been discovered, pinioned, but also the larger area of the garden where I'd witnessed one figure swooping on another.

"Of course it's all connected," said Fielding tersely.

"My father has a good opinion of you," she said.

"He does?"

"Of your acuity and imagination. He says you are most imaginative."

Was this a compliment? Or was I being subtly rebuked for being a fantasist?

Kate Fielding and I were lounging near the margin of the lake in the Instede grounds. Lounging in complete propriety, I hasten to add. Regret to add. Fully clothed, propped up on our elbows. We had taken a stroll around the water and, finding a shady slope, settled down to admire the view. From here the east face of the house stood up clear, its entrance draped with black baize. Despite this token of mourning, the sun beamed down as it had since we first set foot in the country. The light sparkled off the lake.

"No imagination now, Nicholas? No poetry? That's what we usually talk about."

I registered her use of my first name, as I'd registered the care she'd taken to convey her father's "good opinion" of me. While welcoming Kate's warmer mood, I couldn't help wondering if there was an ulterior motive. Something in the air of Instede bred suspicion – which was hardly surprising, perhaps, in a house of murder. The heart-beating pleasure I took in her presence had abated slightly, perhaps because of the general sobriety and gloom of the last few days. Yet my palms felt moist while my mouth was dry.

"I'm afraid I haven't brought Master Richard Milford abroad with me this morning. He remains tucked under my pillow."

"Where he sleeps sound no doubt. But you, you could improvise some verse?"

"I am no true poet, Kate, no poet at all really . . . I cannot write or hum to order."

"Despite that imagination."

"I have to be inspired," I said, desperately hoping that she would not insist on a test of my (non-existent) poetic faculty, yet unwilling to abandon this promising line of banter.

"And what inspires you?"

"Oh, you know, the usual things . . . transience and beauty

. . . the curve of an eyebrow . . . the breezes of spring . . . the decay of autumn . . . my mistress's lips."

"You have a mistress?"

I hesitated for an instant and that must have given her her answer. But what I said aloud was, "You said to me once about my friend Milford and his lines, 'I don't suppose there was a woman in the case at all.' So that is my answer to your question."

"Haven't we heard enough of spring flowers and autumn leaves?" she said, shifting the ground of our dialogue and also turning to look out across the water. "If I lived in the city I think *that* is what I should write about . . . if I wrote at all. Its sights and smells. Its greatness, its press of people."

"But you have an aunt in London, don't you? So you are familiar with the city."

"Only as a visitor."

"I'm a visitor also, of a couple of years' duration, no more."

It was odd that I so readily made this admission, smacking of provincialism, to a woman I wanted to impress. Usually I was eager to be taken for a born-and-bred Londoner. Perhaps I sensed that plainness, straightforwardness, was the way to reach her.

"Yes, I remember you come from down here. Your parents are country people."

"My father was a parson in a Somerset village. My mother was his wife. They are both dead."

"My mother died when I was quite young but not before I committed her to memory," said Kate. "My father often talks of her. He tells me that I look a little like her now."

"She must have been a . . . beautiful woman."

The little pause was not for effect, I swear.

"He is a partial witness," she said, smiling.

"All witnesses are partial," I said meaninglessly, "particularly when they think they are not."

"I hear that you witnessed something strange the other night."

I felt suddenly confused – and not a little irritated – to realize that Adam Fielding kept no secrets from his daughter.

"Yes, I told your father of something I saw, or thought I saw. But I would not like the story to get abroad."

"Why not?"

"Because it was in the nature of a dream or a nightmare . . . a shifting, uncertain image. You wouldn't like your dreams spread among strangers."

"Am I a stranger?"

"I didn't mean it like that. Shall we talk about something else?"

"I'm sorry if I've angered you, Nicholas."

She reached across and half-grasped my hand. It was worth being irritated to have her touch me. She looked away.

"What's that in the water – over there?"

I followed her gaze. All I could see was the glint of the sun on the surface. Kate rose to her feet and moved a few paces nearer the rushy margin of the lake. She shaded her eyes with her hand and peered intently at a stretch of water. I got up and joined her.

"Where?"

For answer, she pointed. I saw nothing except the gentle ripples and the swaying, feathery plants on the bank. Then at once something seemed to stir in the deeper, darker water beyond the place I'd been looking at. A rash of bubbles erupted on the surface, together with a queer hissing sound. At first I took it for a fish coming closer to the surface – a surprisingly large fish – a monstrously large fish. In Kate's presence I steeled myself against stepping back from the lake edge. Whatever was down there, it could hardly clamber out onto dry land. It was no submarine beast, however, but something more like a long colourless bundle, cylindrical in shape, which appeared to be dragging itself up from the bottom of the lake, twisting slowly round and round and trailing ragged streamers behind it. The reflected sun and the muddiness of the water combined to make the object indistinct.

Kate clutched at my arm. I heard her draw breath sharply. Just as the bundle seemed about to break the surface and disclose itself, it abruptly dropped down out of sight, as though a water-sprite or something worse had tugged it back to the lake-bed. There was a momentary flurry above the spot where the bale-like shape had disappeared, then all was flat and calm again.

We stood there for some time, Kate still holding hard onto my upper arm. In other circumstances I would've been glad of this, glad of the chance to reassure and comfort her. But the truth is that I was shaken myself.

"What was it, Nicholas?"

"I don't know." I shivered. "But there is something rotten here at Instede."

"You must come and see this, Nick," said Will Fall.

"So you've said already."

"We look to the Paradise Brothers to provide something special."

"*We?* Will, you speak like a member of the laity, if I may say so," I said, hardly troubling to keep the annoyance out of my tone. "Anyone'd think that you had never seen a band of players before, let alone been part of their mystery as a member of the Chamberlain's."

The three of us – Will and I, together with his kitchen drab Audrey – were ambling towards the great barn where the Paradise Brothers were due to put on a new "play" for the edification of the estate workers. I was a little surprised that, in this delicate period before Lord Elcombe's interment, they should have thought themselves licensed to act. Still, they were evidently driven by some species of spiritual fervour, rather than baser commercial considerations like the rest of us.

"I mean no aspersions on my own company," said

Will, "but the Paradises remind me of an earlier period of playing."

"You're not old enough."

"An era that was more direct," he went on, ignoring my comment. "An era without so many refinements."

"You mean crude and clumsy."

"I mean rough-hewn and honest."

"Then we agree," I said.

"Anyway, Nick, I look forward to seeing what miracles they can work with bits of cable and harness. We enjoyed Judas a-hanging himself last time, didn't we, Aud? Nearly as good as the real thing."

The short red-faced girl stumbling along beside Will seemed surprised to be addressed and muttered something incomprehensible in reply.

"I wonder who they'll kill today?" he said.

I considered the remark out of place, given what had recently occurred at the great house, but it was no use rebuking Will: there was an honest, rough-hewn quality to him too. He said what he thought, without thought.

When we got to the barn there was the same crowd of besmocked and breeched workers who'd gathered a few days earlier to watch the drama of Judas. Among them, I noticed Sam the grasping bailie and keeper-of-the-rope, as well as Davy, my informant in the household. It was interesting to see that, for all the makeshift circumstances of this presentation, an air of expectation, even of excitement, gripped the little audience. I wondered what Peter, Paul and Philip Paradise were going to divert us with this time. For sure, it would involve murder or self-slaughter – just like real life.

Perhaps in deference to the tragic events at Instede, however, the Brothers had chosen a story without violence: the parable of Dives and Lazarus. You know the one. The rich man in his castle, the poor man at his gate. Then, later on, the rich man is shoved down into hell while the poor man is raised up into heaven, where he rests smug and snug in Father

Abraham's bosom. This is consoling for all of us poor (or not so rich) folk since it tells us that we shall ultimately be rewarded for our privations on this earth. And, more important, *it tells us that the wealthy will suffer for their prior comforts.* Most men, having to choose between pampering themselves or punishing their enemies, would surely choose the latter. So it is, I say, a satisfactory parable.

I wondered at first whether the little rustic audience was going to be disappointed at the absence of murder and suicide – as if there hadn't been enough of these things a few hundred yards away from where we were standing. But the Paradise trio were skilful. They knew how to draw an audience in, with simple or crude colours and effects: the arrogance of Dives and the humility of Lazarus; the descent into hell of the former, the ascent into heaven of the latter. This last trick was nimbly achieved by means of the same harness and pulleys which had been used to hoist aloft Judas Iscariot. As Paul "Lazarus" Paradise rose slowly into the air towards the heavenly cross-beams of the barn, where the sun shot his rays through some ragged places in the roof, so did Philip "Dives" Paradise sink down towards the hellish straw-strewn ground, where he writhed gratifyingly. This double movement, of a man rising and a man sinking in unison, brought little gasps of appreciation from the crowd. Even I was forced to concede that the Paradises, with their mastery of rope and pulley, knew a trick or two.

Then Peter Paradise, playing the part of Father Abraham with protruding beard and furrowed brow, told us all of the gulf which divides Heaven and Hell and how none could cross it. Still "brothering and sistering" as if his life depended on it, he instructed us to turn our backs on wealth and pleasure and to preserve our immortal parts safe and uncor-rupted. Among this raggle-taggle crowd this struck me as odd. What would they ever know of wealth? What would I ever know of it, come to that? As on the two previous occasions when I'd been present at a Paradise performance, it was the parson's share of the show. The trio of players, or Peter Paradise at least, were thwarted preachers. I remembered my father's little tricks and turns in the pulpit. Well, no great distance separates the two trades.

But Peter Paradise, with his white robes and his rabble-rousing delivery, went rather further than was wise. At some point – when exactly I couldn't quite pin down – he shifted from those sermon-generalities which don't really offend anyone to a direct attack on the late Lord Elcombe. *There*, he thundered, was a Dives, *there* was wealth in all its power and arrogance. And now where was this great, proud man? Where was he? Peter's brows furrowed more furiously, his beard protruded more proudly. He looked about as if he expected Lord Elcombe to emerge from the crowd. Then he pointed at Dives still writhing around among the straw. Elcombe was where he deserved to be, that's where. In Hell he surely was, languishing in anguish.

I grew a little uncomfortable at this. *De mortuis nil nisi bonum*, they say, don't they (if they've had the benefit of a Latin education)? Concerning the dead, we should speak nothing but good, if only for fear of what others will say about us after we've gone. Whatever Lord Elcombe had been or done in his lifetime, he was not yet below ground and here was his memory being traduced by there forthright players I wasn't the only one to feel uncomfortable. The crowd of workers who'd watched the parable with approval – and even enjoyed being told to eschew the wealth they didn't possess – now started to shift and stir where they stood. There were murmurs and whispered asides. As Peter Paradise ranted on, there was even the odd voiced comment.

"'t'aint right."

"'e weren't so bad, the master."

"Wealth's a curse to them as have it, without a doubt."

A responsive player would have tailored his delivery to these signs of unease and protest, would have been better advised to shut up altogether, but Peter had too much of the fiery parson about him to be deterred by mere disapproval. Remembering the brawl in Salisbury, I feared trouble. These Paradise people seemed to cause a stir wherever they went, as if their name promised not harmony but turmoil. Just as they weren't really brothers, according to Cuthbert Ascre, so their message was anything but fraternal.

As I'd done on an earlier occasion I tugged at one arm of my companion. But Will had his other arm fastened about his doxy and was too absorbed in palping her tit to pay me any attention so I turned to leave. And walked straight into Oswald the steward.

I don't know how long he'd been standing there by the barn entrance, regarding the antics of the Paradises and listening to Peter's hell-fire talk. His long cadaverous face registered disapproval, though in truth it never registered anything else. My colliding with him seemed to prompt him into motion, into protestation.

"Players, are you mad? Or what are you?" he said. "Have you no wit or manners to talk and act thus in a house of mourning?"

For an instant I thought he was talking to me before realizing that his anger was aimed at the trio on stage. That peculiar dry voice, like a leaf rustling across dry stone, had an enviable carrying power. It scraped down the barn. Heads jerked round in surprise and then alarm. Sam the bailie shrunk into himself. There was a general air as of schoolchildren caught truanting. To emphasize his message, Oswald stretched out his long right arm and directed an accusing finger at the stage.

Peter Paradise had already stopped in mid-rant. Now he pretended to have just noticed the presence of an intruder.

"Who is he who interrupts the word of God?"

There was a fraught silence. Most of the little audience did not come directly under Oswald's control, but everybody on the estate recognized the stick-man. I suspect that Peter Paradise did too. Oswald's next words confirmed it.

"As you well know, I am Oswald the steward of Instede, and I tell you that you have no respect of place or person or time."

You had to admire the dry, assured tones of the man, even as they intimidated you. And you had to admit that he had some justification on his side. The crowd in the barn evidently felt it too, quite apart from their natural fear of the steward.

"We respect only the word of God, brother."

The shafts of sun which shot through the looped and ragged sides of the building suddenly turned hotter. The air, flecked with motes of dust and wisps of straw, grew heavier. There was a collective sigh from the audience. Here was true drama!

"No, player, here you will respect my word. And I say that you have no manners to rant in a house of mourning."

There was some fervent nodding and yessing among the audience, and not simply because they wanted to look good in Oswald's eyes. Rather, the steward had brought them back to a sense of what was right and proper. It was a question of manners. Lord Elcombe might have been Old Nick himself, but it still wasn't the done thing – it wasn't the *English* thing – to kick a man when he was dead and down.

Even Peter Paradise, armoured in his white robes and his whiter righteousness, sensed that he'd lost his grip on the crowd. His two fellows, Paul and Philip, had long since scrambled from their respective heaven and hell, and stood flanking their more solid brother. They made a formidable trinity. But, for all that, I considered Oswald was a match for them. Peter stepped off the raised area at the end of the barn which served for a stage, and strode through the audience which parted for him. Unobtrusively, I put a little distance between myself and Oswald. I noticed that Will Fall and Audrey had absented themselves altogether at some point during the last few minutes. They had better things to do.

Now at the entrance to the barn Peter and Oswald stood

face to face, mingling breaths, tangling eye-beams. The preacher-player gave an inch or two of height to the steward but he made up for it in bulk. Oswald's garb was even darker than usual, in tribute to his late master, while Peter Paradise wore the white robes that signified him as one of the self-chosen chosen. Behind him were his so-called brothers, ready to follow his lead wherever that might take them.

There was a long silence while each man waited for the other to do something first. To flinch, to speak, to raise a fist.

Finally, Peter said, "Have a care, steward."

"You think that because you are virtuous, player, you have a licence to say what you please."

"We have my Lady's licence, brother," boomed Peter.

"No longer. She has sent me to give you your dismissal."

"We will hear that from her lips alone."

"She has other business on her mind at the moment."

"There is no business greater than God's, Oswald. Certainly not yours."

"While the late master was alive," said Oswald, "he suffered her to entertain raggle-taggle groups like yours because what pleased her pleased him, but there is no need of that – or you – any longer."

Paradise looked abashed at this answer. At any rate, his beard drooped. If their patroness had indeed withdrawn her favour, then there was no place for the Paradises at Instede. Perhaps not knowing how else to respond, he repeated, "Have a care, steward."

He who is forced to repeat himself in a dispute has already half-lost (Revill's law). Perhaps sensing this, the senior Paradise continued, with the same resonant boom, "Have a care I say, or you may find yourself making your bed out in the dark – like your master."

Then Oswald the steward did something very curious – very curious for him, that is. He laughed. He opened his thin mouth by more than a margin and from it emerged a crackling sound, rather like that made by dry thorny wood thrown onto a fire. It set my teeth on edge.

It affected Peter Paradise too, affected him worse than words might have done. If you regularly play God, Moses and Abraham, I suppose you get used to being treated with respect. Paradise retreated a step and raised his arm, as he had in Salisbury when he went to brand Cain. But Oswald held his ground. And Paradise, lowering his arm, resorted once again to obscure threats.

"I tell you, steward, that as God found out your master so too will his dart strike you, and that when you least expect. God alone looses the arrow of time, and no man controls his bow."

Oswald stood unmoved by this minatory if poetic outpouring. Eventually, realizing that he was not going to face down this man, Peter stepped around him and out into the clear sunshine. Philip and Paul followed. There was a collective sigh in the barn – of relief and, possibly, of regret that it had not come to a physical trial of strength between these two men. (My money would have been on Oswald.)

The steward, who apparently had his own sense of theatre, waited a moment or two before casting cold eyes on the estate workers. No one dared to meet his glance. Then he said with weary contempt, "You are idle, shallow things. Get back to your work."

Meekly, they trooped from the barn, like chastened schoolboys. I remained behind, wanting to differentiate myself from the others. Oswald's gaze rested on me for an instant but, just before I would have broken it and looked down, he turned away and exited the barn.

After a time I wandered out, musing on what I'd seen and heard. The day continued fine, the birds sang blithely, but my heart was full of murder.

The murder of Lord Elcombe, that is. I pursued the ideas which I'd outlined to Justice Fielding, in particular the notion that, because they must have been standing close, Elcombe had known the person who killed him. However, as I'd just seen in the encounter between Peter Paradise and Oswald, enemies stand close too – when they are about to join battle.

And Paradise's final words filled my mind. All that talk of darts and arrows of time. A figure of speech, obviously, for time itself has no dart or arrow. Time has nothing, although it takes all that we possess. *But a sundial has a kind of dart –* in the shape of its gnomon. If we are to search for time's arrow anywhere then it should be on the sundial's face. Was Paradise's choice of words just coincidence? Or was he making some subtle jest about the manner of Elcombe's death? If so, it was in keeping with the disrespect of the remainder of his performance. Plainly, he did not mourn the death of Elcombe, that rich and godless man.

Another thought struck me: if you regularly played God, then how long would it be before you really played God, as it were. How hard would it be to grow into the belief that one was God's agent on earth, entitled to loose off time's arrow prematurely? No, not how hard but how easy? To bring to a close a life of which you – and more importantly, God – disapproved?

I stopped in my wanderings through the little copse which bordered this edge of the estate. Was I seriously saying to myself, I said to myself, that the Paradise Brothers had taken upon themselves the right to judge, to condemn and to punish. I looked about. Nearby was the cottage of Sam the bailie, where I examined the noose which had pinched Robin's neck tight. If so – if the Paradise trinity had taken upon themselves the right to judge – then how did Robin fit into the scheme of things? I had Fielding's opinion that everything was connected and my own instinct told a similiar tale.

Robin's ramblings about the devil recurred to me. Talk of the devil might well be offensive to someone who thinks he's God. Offensive enough to make one want to close the speaker's mouth? I considered the expertise of the Paradise Brothers, their handiness with rope and harness as they hoisted each other aloft. When had the trio arrived at Instede? Was it before or after the woodman's body was discovered? A little before, I thought. Some dark suspicions hovered on the edge of my thoughts.

Then I heard giggling and other sounds from a dense pack of undergrowth. I tensed, but relaxed after an instant. I recognized the deeper laugh that underpinned the giggling.

"Will?" I said.

A small girlish shriek, then silence, then a male voice: "Nick?"

"No, a wood spirit come to curb your licentious activities."

"Go away, Nick. Audrey and I are discussing country matters."

Another bout of giggles. However much distress she felt for her employer's death, Audrey had evidently come unclammed.

I crept away.

Well, I suppose it's reassuring to know that some activities persist regardless of time's arrow.

The air of Instede was getting oppressive. Sudden death seemed to hang about us, just as the house was hung with swags and bows of black. For all the beauty of the place there was something rotten at its heart, as I'd said to Kate.

The day before the funeral I set out to escape from the estate. While preparations continued for Elcombe's interment, Instede House was possessed by a gloomy stir and I felt my own face set in a miserable mask. It was hard to remember what it was like to laugh or smile. I exaggerate, but not much. As I wandered through the grounds I even thought of whistling – but it would have been an act of defiance not a natural thing. And it's as well I didn't because moments later I glimpsed Lady Elcombe with her son Cuthbert and Kate Fielding, deep in talk. I was pleased enough that she had youthful company until I noticed Oswald making for the group. The stick-man bent forward to whisper in my Lady's ear, no doubt to recall her to her mourning duties, and she broke away from the others. I passed Adam Fielding too, looking grim and furrow-browed like the rest. He scarcely gave me good morning.

Well, I thought, a moment comes when you've had enough of the world's woes and of tasting the cup of grief, particularly if it's not your own preparation. The world – or the unwoeful part of it – goes on. Thank God.

My spirits lightened as I strolled down the great ride which formed the main approach to Instede. It was like slipping out of a prison or, in Cuthbert Ascre's image, through the bars of a gilded cage. I was heading nowhere in particular but soon found myself in the hamlet of Rung Withers, which lay just outside the estate boundaries. After the magnificence of the great house, there was a comfort in the homely cottages with their pinched windows and lop-sided doors. Even the hovels spoke of plain Englishness while the midden at the entrance to the village exuded an honest, direct stench in the mid-morning sun. There was a modest church and a no-nonsense tavern which rejoiced in the name of Ye Clod Pole, a farrier's, a bake-house and so on. Gossips clustered in the high street (the only street) and occasional wagons trundled through. The straightforward feel to the place reminded me a little of my home village of Miching.

Yet it was not so easy to escape from trouble after all. Not the Instede variety this time but a return of the Salisbury business. I spied an individual weaving down the street in my direction. There was something faintly familar about his gait. What was it? In his right hand there was a bottle which, even in mid-stagger, he tilted towards his mouth. But it was form's sake only and nothing emerged, not even a dribble. Then there came out of his mouth another kind of dribble: "Snof-fair. Snorright. Snoffair." Where had I heard *that* before? Why, for sure, from the Salisbury scaffold when the Paradises had for a moment been upstaged by this inebriate. It was the soused farmer – Tom, was he called? – who'd been clouted over the head by Cain. Obviously, drunkenness with Tom was not just an evening treat but a morning requirement.

He wasn't causing heads to turn as he passed down the high street. They were used to him. Perhaps he lived here. I made to steer clear of him. As we passed each other I saw him casting his little eyes about in that watchful way drunks sometimes have, always on the alert for anyone making aspersions on their sodden selves.

"Hey youse."

I didn't look back.

"I said youse – stranger."

Yes, apparently he was talking to me. I put on speed to travel through the village, hoping that, like a bad-tempered cur, he'd leave me alone when I got out of his domain. But no such luck.

"Stop, youse."

So I did stop and turn about to give him a piece of my mind. By now half a dozen of the gossips and other passengers had gathered in the hope of an argument or something worse (and what could be better from their point of view than something worse?). The gentleman came swaying up to me. With his piggy eyes, he looked no more fetching in the glare of day than by the flaring torches in Salisbury market. I moved back, keeping out of reach of that empty bottle, fists handy in case he swung out with it. He shambled to a halt within a few feet of me and I was enveloped by the vapour of small beer. He held out a scroll.

"'syours."

It was.

"My Lysander," I said recognizing this tight cylinder of paper by the tell-tale tear at one end.

"Lyshander?"

"Yes, that's me."

The scroll was neatly secured with string and marked NR

on the outside together with the initials of earlier Lysanders. Of course my lines were of no particular use after the *Dream* performance, but on tour you're supposed to keep your part carefully and give it back to the book-man on the return to the Globe. Fair-copying a player's lines is a chore and, if you lose your copy or drop it in your supper, the book-man is entitled to deduct the cost of replacing it from your wages. As the drunk – now transformed from a lout into a good Samaritan – thrust the scroll at me, my hand automatically flew to the pouch on my belt. It had come undone, causing Master WS's words to fall out onto the dusty high street of Rung Withers.

"'sallright, Lyshander," he slurred, apparently thinking I was actually the part I played.

I took the scroll from his grubby hand. Fortunately my purse was still inside my pouch and I fumbled for a penny to reward sottish Tom for his services to the drama. He held the coin up to the sun's rays, bit it (something which I'd never seen anyone do before), then lurched off without another word in the direction of Ye Clod Pole to spend the penny before it might evaporate. The small knot of people in the street broke up, disappointed at this peaceful outcome. All except one man who now approached me.

"You must be Master Revill," he said.

"And you are Parson Brown," I said.

It was the priest. The small, plump priest of Rung Withers, Lady Elcombe's comforter. I'd seen him during the wedding feast and subsequently at the great house.

"How did you know me, sir?" I asked. He didn't have to ask how I knew him. For one thing he was wearing the dark colours of his trade.

"I was struck by your playing the other night. I asked your name. From Justice Fielding. Before the terrible business."

Now, although the context of this compliment was the tragic affair at Instede House, it was still a *compliment*. And a player would accept compliments from the very devil. So if a

parson praises your playing you have an almost holy obliga-
tion not merely to accept but to revel in it. Besides, I still
have sufficient respect for the cloth to be – to be honest – a
little in awe of it. My father, you see . . .

"You enjoyed the play?"

"No, Master Revill. Or if I did, it was so overshadowed by
what came after that enjoyment would be out of place."

I felt rebuked, a little.

"Of course," I said. "Forgive me for asking."

"That is no slight on you players. You did a good job. Do
not reproach yourself now."

This was better. There seemed something open, something
confide-able about this short, round individual. So within a
brief space of time and under the prompting of a couple of
questions, my life history was tumbling out of me. How I'd
been born and raised not so far from here in the parish
of Miching, had had a parson for a father, how my parents
died during a visit of the plague after which I'd gone to make
my fortune in London, not that you'd ever make a fortune
on the stage, no you couldn't expect that, only plain wages,
but it was an honest or perhaps honourable calling, I'd say,
even if my parson-father didn't approve of the playhouse. I
babbled on. Perhaps it was the effect of being away from the
oppressive air of Instede.

"There's no great harm in the playhouse, I think," said my
new companion as we strolled together through Rung Withers. I noticed that he was greeted cheerfully and with just a
dash of respect by the passers-by.

"The pulpit is often the enemy to the stage," I said.

"Not provided the good are rewarded. The wrongdoers
punished. Then pulpit and stage are fashioned from the same
wood."

Parson Brown had a clipped way of speaking. His was an
educated accent, of course, but underneath it there was a
strain of something neither local nor London-y.

"They always are, the wrongdoers are always punished," I

said, remembering a similar conversation with Cuthbert Ascre. "Or almost always. Though sometimes the innocent must suffer."

"Then we must believe they have their reward in heaven, Master Revill."

"Yes. You have been at Instede recently?"

"There's a poor house. A poor house."

"Poor? Oh, I see . . ."

However clipped his manner, Parson Brown spoke in tones of genuine pity. This was the man who'd uttered a few words over the corpse of Robin the woodman. "There is much need of consolation," he added.

"My father did not have such a, ah, range in his parish of Miching. From great house to hovel. From high to low-born."

"Perhaps it was more that he did not distinguish between them."

"Because they are all the same in God's sight, you mean," I said, attempting piety.

"I don't suppose they are the same," said this odd cleric. "Who's to say that God's not in favour of the low-born. In their hovels. Tell me of your father's parish."

So I did, haltingly, in fragments. Of my father's sexton John, of Molly who lived at the end of Salvation Alley, of my boyhood friends like Peter Agate. Parson Brown and I walked slowly up and down the Rung Withers high street. And at the end of my recital all he said was, "I had a parish like that once – in the north."

So that accounted for the trace of an accent in his voice. Any more conversation was interrupted by the reappearance of Tom out of Ye Clod Pole. He'd evidently drunk his way through the penny I'd given him and now burst onto the street in search of fresh charity. He was still clutching the empty bottle as if it was a kind of charm.

Slurred shouts resounded down the street. It was Tom's battle-cry: "Snoffair. Snorright. Snoffair." Then, spotting Parson Brown and me, he cried out, "Snoffair, parson. Taint right."

I was surprised by the speed and decisiveness with which Brown acted, at least considering his tubby shape. As I stood and watched, he approached Tom, saying conciliatory things like "Of course it's not right. *You're* right." Then when he was within a couple of feet of the drunk, he reached out abruptly and wrested the bottle from the other's hand. Tom hardly seemed aware of what was happening. Then the priest put a friendly hand on the drunk's arm and, braving the clouds of small ale which now hung almost visibly about the man, he led him gently up the high street, talking low all the time. Before he went he waved cheerfully in my direction to signify our meeting was over.

Where he took the sot I don't know. He might have walked Tom round the houses and then pitched him into the centre of the stinking midden. He might have shown true Christian charity by taking him back to his own dwelling. He might have seen him safely incarcerated in the village lock-up. Whatever Tom's destination I couldn't but be impressed with the docile way he'd allowed himself to be escorted away by the parson. What was it Brown had said? "There is much need of consolation."

The funeral of Lord Elcombe was a sombre affair. I mean, particularly sombre because of the violent circumstances of his demise and the fact that his elder son was still awaiting trial for his murder. The date of the Salisbury assize drew closer but before the son could be found guilty and hanged, the father had to be sealed up in the family vault till doomsday. And before that, all the inhabitants of Instede must pay their formal respects to their late master and employer. On the morning of the funeral, we stood in a solemn line which stretched from the lobby of the couple's apartment and down the stairs. Elcombe's coffin, covered with a black velvet pall decorated with his coat of arms, stood in an inner chamber. The rooms leading to it were draped with black baize and the mirrors in them had been turned to the wall. The summer light streaming through the great windows struck the walls, and stopped dead.

As I shuffled along in the mute file of my fellow Chamberlain's walking past the coffin, I couldn't help reflecting on the previous occasion when, together with Adam Fielding, I'd passed through these very rooms. Then a wedding had been in prospect; now a funeral was in preparation. Some of the same high-ups – those counties and cities of England – who'd been invited to the ill-fated nuptial had come back to Instede for the burial, although these great guests would pay their respects to Elcombe after the common folk. I noted that neither Marianne Morland nor any of her family were here. Whether they were staying away out of tact or grief or whether their absence indicated that whatever else the match might have been it hadn't been a love one, I didn't know.

Standing at a short distance from the covered coffin and with the light from a window at their backs were Lady Penelope and Cuthbert. Not far away was Parson Brown. He inclined his head slightly when he caught sight of me. I wondered anew at the range of his ministry, from powerful lords and ladies to village drunks. Oswald the steward was not far away either. He was inspecting the face and manner of every man, woman and child who walked by the coffin and paused for a second to cross themselves or bow the head before passing on. Oswald already had one minor victory in the bag. He had succeeded in ridding the estate of the Paradise Brothers. Shortly after Peter's encounter with him in the barn, the trio had loaded up their handcart and trundled off the estate although I'd heard that they'd merely set up again somewhere on its fringes. The steward was in the right, of course. The occupants of Instede should have other, more pressing business on their minds than the antics of those pious rousers.

As it came my turn to approach the coffin, I glanced at the widow and her son. Lady Penelope's face was concealed by a veil while Cuthbert's normally equable features were frozen into an unreadable mask. He looked impassively at me. Brown pursed his plump lips. Crossing myself at the head of the swathed bier, I moved on. I noticed that Laurence Savage was not with us players; evidently his loathing for Elcombe extended beyond the grave. Or perhaps he was afraid that he couldn't comport himself with sufficient seriousness near the coffin but would skip with pleasure at the death of the man who had destroyed his little brother.

Once outside the Elcombes' quarters I was accosted by Adam Fielding, who was waiting his turn to go in. Kate was with him. She looked beautiful; mourning became her. We hadn't spoken since the previous day when, wandering by the lake, we'd glimpsed that object in the water.

"Nicholas," said Fielding.

"Your worship."

"A sad occasion this. And the interment will be sadder still."

His expression showed that this was no mere form of words. He looked genuinely grieved.

"Yes," was all I found to say.

"You are leaving soon?"

"There's no reason for us to stay once the funeral's done. The Chamberlain's will have completed their duty after that, our seniors say. We shall go early in the morning, so as to get a full day's travelling."

"You will stop in Salisbury tomorrow?" said Kate.

"Probably. I don't know."

"At the Angel?"

"All those arrangements are in the hands of Richard Sincklo."

"Well," said Kate, "wherever the rest of your company lodges, *you* will stop in Salisbury tomorrow night with us. At our house."

"You are too kind," I said, feeling absurdly pleased by her words, which were more order than invitation.

"But first, Nicholas," said her father, stroking his beard and looking grave, "I have a request to make."

"Sir?"

"You know your fellow players well?"

"We work and breathe and sleep together. That should be enough."

"Then, after the funeral, you could select me some three or four among them, trustworthy men, reliable ones? Yourself included of course."

"They're all trustworthy. Well, pretty well all."

"Of course, Nicholas," said Fielding, a spark of light appearing in his expression for the first time. "All trustworthy, all reliable. But the ones you pick, they must be strong too."

"There you show your ignorance if I may say so, sir. A player has to leap and dance and fight for a living. Strength is a first requirement."

"I am glad you stand up so strong for your profession."

I noticed a glance of amusement passing between father and daughter.

"After the funeral this will be?"

"There's a feast which we must attend for form's sake. But as soon as you can decently gather your little band after that, we will set off while the others are distracted in feeding their grief."

"Set off where? And why do you need this little band?"

"I would prefer not to say yet," said Fielding.

"There are plenty of strong men hereabouts on the estate who you could doubtless recruit for yourself."

I was pushing him, to get at his intentions.

"I would rather have players."

"For a little drama?"

"Oh, there may be drama," said Fielding. "But not of the kind you're familiar with."

Seeing I wasn't going to get anywhere with my questions about the purpose of this expedition, I confined myself to more ordinary enquiries as to the time and the place we should meet.

Somehow I wasn't surprised by what Justice Fielding told me. I wasn't too enthusiastic about it either but it was too late to back out.

If the funeral was sober the feast which followed was more sober still. My experience of these events is not extensive. As a boy I preferred to be out in the fields or even hunched over my books rather than watching my father officiate at a burial but I have at least noticed that, while the interment may be a grave enough matter, a lighter mood often prevails later in the day. Indeed, to see and hear some people in the wake of a funeral, especially when they've been well fed and liquored, is enough to persuade you that you're eavesdropping on a new race of immortals. They act and talk as though they will never die themselves, so loud and swaggering do they grow. And, come to think of it, I recall as a child at a country feast going upstairs to escape the press and buzz, and discovering the new widow Blakeman all hot and fresh in the . . .

Well, that's another story, not fit or necessary for this moment.

The Elcombe funeral and its aftermath had none of this spiritedness. Parson Brown presided in tones of the utmost solemnity. There was obviously something about his straightness and plainness which appealed to my Lady. There was some thin singing and whispered prayer. But little noise otherwise. No sob escaped from under the widow's veil, no cry issued from her lips. Cuthbert and three of the most important mourners carried Elcombe's mortal remains into the family vault, next to the chapel. The priest and a few others, including Lady Elcombe, processed into the vault while the rest of us waited mutely. When the chief mourners had again emerged into the body of the chapel, the doors of the vault were closed with a ponderous clang as if they were the marble jaws of death itself. I shivered.

The wake took place in the same banqueting hall where the wedding had been celebrated and at the same time, late afternoon. But it was a subdued shrunken business, without that lifting mood which, as I've noted, often follows on from a country funeral. No one present could have forgotten that earlier wedding-feast, or failed to realize the painful contrast with the present. And I suppose that, while it might be acceptable enough to lose a husband (as the widow Blakeman lost no time in showing), it must add greatly to the family's sorrow to know that the son of the household so loathed or feared his father that he had been driven to kill him. There was a double grief here, for a sudden death and for the treachery at the heart of the family.

Of course, I knew that Justice Fielding, convinced of Harry Ascre's innocence, had set himself the task of discovering the actual killer. The reason he'd required me to gather a little band of players was, I assumed, connected to his investigations. But I couldn't for the life of me see where these investigations were headed. Nevertheless, trusting Fielding and his judgment, I had done what he asked, by enlisting Jack Wilson and Will Fall, both strong young fellows. I hinted at the mysterious mission in which we were involved, knowing that a hint is often more potent than a fact. (I didn't let on to them that I didn't know anything myself.) Will's preoccupation with Audrey seemed to be on the wane, perhaps because he didn't consider that bit of country worth ploughing again, otherwise he might have pleaded more urgent business.

Michael Donegrace, who'd played Hermia to my Lysander in the now-distant *Dream*, was sitting close by us and immediately volunteered himself. I was about to tell him that he was too young but this would have been a pointless rejoinder. Too young for what? – since I was ignorant of what Fielding required of us apart from sinews. Apprentices are tough and wiry. They have to be, to take up the women's parts. So Michael made one of our number. I said that they were to await a signal from me while I, in turn, looked for a word from Adam Fielding during the latter part of the feast.

But first I had to listen to some unexpected words from Cuthbert Ascre, who suddenly loomed up at our table, black-suited, white-faced. We hadn't talked together since the the night of the *Dream*, when he claimed that he'd willingly throw everything over in order to join a playing company like ours. I still remembered the bitter way in which he'd said his father would never have permitted it. This, I quickly discovered was the very thing he wanted to talk of. He leaned forward confidentially.

"Master Revill, you will remember the last time we spoke?"

"Indeed . . . my lord. It was after your triumphant personation of Demetrius."

"It pains me to remember that – in the heat of the moment, in all the, er, excitement of playing – I may have said some things which would have been better left unsaid."

"About turning player?"

"Yes." A slight twinge crossed his face. "And about my father not allowing it."

"I remember. And golden cages and so on."

He winced again.

"Well, Master Revill, perhaps you would do me the favour of forgetting I ever made such foolish remarks."

"What remarks?"

"Thank you. I am grateful."

Cuthbert turned back and made his way towards the high table where the chief mourners were sitting. Naturally, the effect of his words was to make me remember – and wonder about – something which I had in fact almost forgotten. In any computation of winner and loser in this situation, it was easy to see that Cuthbert Ascre came out ahead. He might not have been able to follow his dream of becoming an actor, but with his brother in gaol (and as good as dead) he stood to realize a rather more substantial dream, that of inheriting Instede, debt-ridden as it might be. As widow, Lady Elcombe would have a life interest in her husband's property but the ultimate control of it would fall to Cuthbert.

So, picking at the funeral baked meats, I sat and wondered.

There must have been something dark and fertile in the Instede air, for all its sweet and summery qualities, which caused these suspicions to take root in one's mind. For, to suppose that Cuthbert Ascre welcomed the family fortune which was about to fall into his lap was also to suppose that he acquiesced in the idea that his brother was a murderer. I tried to put myself in his shoes. If I possessed a brother, would I consider a fine estate to be sufficient recompense for the family dishonour – the personal grief, even – which that brother's execution would bring? I wasn't naive enough to imagine, of course, that every family is alike. Not all are bound by ties of duty and affection, especially perhaps in the airy regions inhabited by the Ascres and their like. Nor is there any law which says that brother must love brother. In fact, for some, fraternal hatred must grow from the very cradle. That line from the story of the first murder popped into my head, the one where Cain inquires of God: *"Am I my brother's keeper?"*

And now I looked down the table to where Laurence Savage was tearing into his food and drink, perhaps driven by the desire to make inroads into the stores and lay a little waste to his enemy's house. Even though that enemy was dead. *"Am I my brother's keeper?"* Laurence had tried to be his brother's keeper, hadn't he? His little brother Thomas. And failed. I saw suddenly that part of his anger, as he recalled the tragedy, was directed against himself for not keeping young Thomas safe.

So absorbed was I in these reflections that I almost missed the glance from Justice Fielding as he passed our table. He'd told me to make it look like a casual exit, so the four of us –

Jack, Will, Michael and I – ambled outside at intervals as if for a serial piss. But there was enough coming and going of guests and servants to make our departure unremarked. As Fielding had explained to me, without explaining exactly what it was we would be doing, it wasn't so much that he required secrecy as that what he wanted would be more easily accomplished without curious bystanders. From this aspect, the funeral feast provided a good distraction.

Once outside we made our way eastwards across the lawns in the direction of the lake. For the first time since our arrival at this great and melancholy house, clouds had started to blot up the sky and there was an edge to the air. Adam Fielding was waiting for us by the lake-edge. He nodded in acknowledgment as I introduced the others, then swiftly explained what he wanted us to do. The expectant look on the faces of my fellows showed that, for them, this was a big adventure. Probably I looked the same.

Anchored close inshore was a frail rowing-boat, rocking gently as the breeze ruffled the water. Some canvas sacking lay on the bottom of the boat, which scarcely looked large enough for two. I was all for staying on the bank while my fellows pushed off into the waves, but it was evident that Fielding had appointed me captain to this little crew. Why is it that I'm always fated to end up on water? Or in water? Those same fates must surely know I have a cat-like aversion to this treacherous element – which is the reason why it happens, of course.

What made it worse was the facility with which the other three clambered into and then made themselves easy on the boat. They might have been Thames ferrymen (and you can't offer a more serious insult than that). I slipped and almost plunged underwater while I was scrambling over the side – or gunnel, as I believe it's called. The boat grew no larger while I established my dripping and spluttering self in its back end – or stern, as even landlubbers know to call it. The crested surface of the water seemed to stretch out to the horizon.

Jack lifted a corner of the canvas sacking to display several coils of rope and a collection of hooks and grapnels. Will, our company carter, picked up the oars as delicately as a pair of reins. Michael Donegrace perched up at the front end. I hadn't thought to ask Fielding how he'd obtained the boat. Presumably, objects needed salvaging from the Instede lake from time to time, and the authority of a Justice was sufficient to commandeer craft and equipment.

We waited, bobbing on the water, while Fielding stayed on the bank, glancing over his shoulder rather anxiously. After a time my heart beat a little faster to see Kate walking across the grass towards us. Resolving to act the part of an experienced sailor and glad she hadn't seen me tumble in the water, I sat more upright in the back end. I intercepted one or two knowing glances between my fellows. Well, what did I care who knew my feelings? Kate smiled at the four of us in the rowing-boat, though to my mind she singled me out for a particular beam. Then, clutching her father by the arm, she led him off round the margin of the lake.

Without a word, Will dug in the oars and we slid out into the open water, rocking alarmingly. Our overfraught little craft kept up with the brisk pace of father and daughter. A brace of duck clattered up from the rushes and we all started in surprise. The wind blew cold on my neck and the wet hose clung to my shivering shanks, which, I now saw, were garlanded with bright green weeds. High above all of this, stately argosies of cloud traversed the sky. We skirted several patches of water-lily and reedy clumps before our beautiful guide halted on the bank and pointed in our general direction. I told Will to stop rowing.

"Here?" said Jack Wilson.

"It's not so easy to see when you're down at water level," I said.

"It is here, Nicholas, isn't it?" said Kate Fielding. Her voice carried clear across the few yards of water. "We were sitting talking yonder, under those trees."

More covert glances among my friends.

"Yes, I think so."

"You know what to do?" said Adam Fielding.

For answer, I took one of the grapnels which Jack had already fastened to a length of rope and threw it over the side with landlubberly carelessness. The boat rocked violently and we nearly overturned. Water slopped across the side. I grimaced at the others, as if to say: don't worry, I know what I'm about. Will Fall cast up his eyes in heavenly appeal. Meanwhile Kate's hand flew to her mouth and she cried out between splayed fingers, "Oh take care, Nick!" Believe me, that gesture and those words would have been worth a ducking.

"What about the rest of us?" said Jack, quite loudly. "We may go drown, I suppose."

"What fish are you hoping to get, Nick?" said mischievous Michael Donegrace.

"Dead human ones," said Will, "by the time our master mariner in the stern has finished with us."

"So what should I be looking for?" said Michael. "All the Justice said was to search."

"A white thing," I said.

Jack looked curiously at me.

My friends had been told only that we were going to try and retrieve something sunk in the bottom of the lake. Not that I'd been told much more myself. The single difference was that I (and Kate) had actually glimpsed that mysterious item which, for reasons best known to himself, Fielding considered it necessary to salvage – if we could.

"Row a little more, Will," said Jack, hoisting up the rope that held the grapnel so as to give it some play. "Go in a small circle and then a larger one. We shall see whether this snags."

My little foray with hook and line had nearly sunk us, so I was happy enough to leave the mechanical business to him. Better to do nothing since, above all else, I desired to avoid looking foolish in the eyes of Kate Fielding. Will plied the oars expertly as we went round in widening circles. Michael Donegrace craned forward like a female figurehead. Jack lofted the rope, trying to keep the hook off the lake-bed. I sat there, picking weed from my hose, glancing down occasionally, and wondering how deep the water was. From captain I had been demoted to cabin-boy.

Suddenly the boat stopped and rose up as if arrested by a giant, invisible hand. Jack Wilson was near pulled off-balance as the rope went taut in his grasp. There was some gasping and cursing before quick-thinking Will reversed his strokes so as to get some slack back into the line. At first we thought it must be a fish but this was not so, because the line hung down limp in the water where a fish would have been pulling away and making it taut. Kate and Adam Fielding watched attentively from the bank.

Jack tugged at the cable, not hard. Nothing. Tugged again, more forcefully. Nothing, except for a scatter of air-bubbles breaking the surface and a dank, rank odour which kept them company. The nape of my neck went chill. But I took command of my fear and of the boat again.

"Michael, Will," I said, "lean over to the other side for weight, and then pull again, Jack. I will help."

I took hold of part of the greasy rope while Jack kept his grip and together we pulled. Concentration on the task eased my fear. I had a sense, too, that whatever was on the other end of the cable, whatever was attached to the grapnel's hook, would sooner yield to gentle persuasion than violent jerks. Just as some persons – and animals – can be coaxed but not bullied, so this "thing" would offer itself up to us if were gentle . . . but insistent. Or perhaps my telling myself this was no more than a peculiar way of soothing my nerves.

"She's coming," grunted Jack.

I too had felt the line give. There was less resistance down there now, less resistance and more weight.

A column of bubbles whooshed to the surface and glittered malevolently in the sunlight.

"Well done, lads," called Justice Fielding, and his voice and presence were oddly reassuring.

"Go steady now," said Jack. "Steady."

We hauled manfully on the line, hand over hand, for all the world as if we really were bringing in a large (and somewhat docile) fish. Most of my fear had gone now in the eagerness to see what we had on the end of our line.

There was a final noise, something between a belch and a slurp, and then Jack and I pantingly reeled in our great prize while the boat rocked.

A mat of greeny-brown weed bobbed to the surface, like a giant phlegmy bolus which the lake had at last seen fit to bring up. The rope and grapnel were tangled up in the weed. This was our valuable catch. Easy to see now how the rope had snagged on it and how it had eventually yielded to our insistent tugs. It was massy but not so heavy when detached from its resting-place on the bottom. Still powered by our efforts, it drifted towards us until it fetched up against the boat. It smelled rank.

I glanced up at the Fieldings and made some sort of apologetic movement. What now? But they were not looking at me or the little rowing-boat. Their eyes were wide and they were fastened on a point over my shrugging shoulders.

I turned round.

A little further out, perhaps a dozen feet or more, a fresh chain of air-bubbles rattled up from the lake depths. All at once, there burst from the water a man. His white head emerged first followed by his shoulders and trunk. He had a face, a ghastly face, and it was all swollen and slimed with green.

The surprise and terror in our boat were so great that we again came near to overturning, as we scrabbled to get away from this being from the depths. Fortunately, the island of weed which now sat snug alongside acted as a kind of anchor and prevented our capsizing.

"Jesus save us!" gasped Jack.

Michael Donegrace had turned white as a corpse. Will Fall's mouth hung open. I could read my own reaction in their faces.

On the bank Kate was staring with horrified fixity. But Adam Fielding showed his presence of mind by calling out, "Steady, gentleman. He can do you no harm."

Afterwards I wondered whether he'd known – or had a fair inkling of – what we'd find. Whatever the case, he was correct. The body in the water was beyond harm, either given or received. It was only the way it shot up from below that gave it the semblance of horrid life. It must have been roused from its green grave by our circling movements and by the disturbance caused by the rising island of weed. Once on the surface the body showed no signs of sinking again but bobbed in the wavelets with its chest protruding like a barrel. I knew instinctively that this was the massy pale shape which Kate and I had seen arrive near the surface and then drop back down out of sight. I suppose that then, a couple of days earlier, it wasn't ready to rise. Everyone knows that the drowned, for all that they lack animation, possess a will of their own, coming and going as they please. The white streamers we'd observed were tatters of cloth tangled round the bloated form. They served only to emphasize its naked- ness, at once waxy and greenish. Trailing fronds hung down like a sea-nettle's.

Once we'd gathered ourselves, Fielding did not have to tell us what to do next. This was the "something" which we'd been despatched to harvest from the lake-bed. And now the body had done us the favour of turning up more or less unprompted.

With none of the banter which marked the beginning of our boat trip, in fact without another word except the odd muttered monosyllable, we disentangled ourselves from the raft of weed and paddled with oar and hand in the direction of the bobbing body waiting for us.

We'd misjudged our speed and thunked flabbily against the corpse. It seemed to twist about in the water and for an instant I thought it was going to sink down once more. But it promptly righted itself with all the unsinkability of a cork stopper. What did I say about the drowned and their determination? The wide, engrossed face gaped up incuriously, and I saw with a spasm of disgust that both of the eye-sockets had been emptied. But in that brief instant I had seen enough to know that, whoever this was, I did not know him.

I looked down and away, glad that its privities were still modestly swathed in cloth; a titbit for minnows there, otherwise. With a deal of effort, Jack and I got a couple of the ropes wrapped about the upper and lower portions of the corpse and Will Fall pulled with a will towards the nearest reed-free patch, which happened to be close to our starting-point. Young Michael Donegrace did a thing I would not have thought of and thus respected him for, when he clutched onto one of the trailing arms so as to reduce the drag on the boat and keep the body in a more or less steady position. Even so, with this mortal anchor, our progress was slow.

In the time it had taken us to secure the body and begin the return to dry land, Kate (presumably at her father's request) had run back to the house to collect a handful of helpers. Meanwhile Justice Fielding walked round the shore, gravely keeping pace with us and every so often stroking his beard. Word of what was happening must have spread quickly through the funeral feast because a mixture of mourners and servants soon crowded to the water's edge. With the sun behind them they looked like so many great black carrion birds. I couldn't help wondering – wondering not then but later – what must have gone through their minds when they were summoned from despatching one body to attend to the unlading of another.

Closer to, I saw stamped on the ring of pale faces confu-

sion, anxiety and dismay. Was there to be no end to the ill
fortune afflicting Instede? At the front of the group was
Fielding, looking no less troubled than the rest. As we drew
into shallower water several men jumped in to assist with
pulling the boat the last few yards, almost swamping us in
the process. By the time the four of us were ashore we were
almost as water-logged as the corpse. Luckily, others now
took over the task under Fielding's direction of hoisting our
cargo out of the lake and onto the bank. Whereas in the
water this unfortunate being had seemed bloated and gross,
now, laid out on the grassy bank, he appeared small and
pitiful. The onlookers made a wide half-circle about his form.
Fielding and several others made a cursory examination of the
body but, perhaps repelled by the empty eye-holes and gaping
mouth, stepped quickly back. Apparently nobody knew this
individual or, at least, nobody was prepared to lay claim to
him. From the state of the corpse it did not seem to have
been under the water for that long.

I don't know the reason for what happened next. Perhaps
it was the effect of this unsettling discovery in the lake.
Perhaps it was the sight of those figures – those black carrion
birds – gazing bemusedly at the waxy form on the ground.
But I felt suddenly as though some kind of screen had
interposed itself between me and the mourners, and that I
was looking at a species, a race of beings, I did not know.
Here was a dead man, naked except for a few wisps of cloth.
There was a band of sable-suited mourners, gathered to grieve
for the death of Lord Elcombe but finding themselves face to
face with a superfluous corpse. It was plain that none of them
– none of us – knew what to do. I was reminded of a sight
I'd once seen in a field in my father's parish, of a herd of
cattle grouped about the prone body of a calf. The calf was
dead. One of the cattle, presumably its mother, was licking it
in a futile effort to restore it to life. But the rest of the herd
stood about, unmoved, unmoving.

The scene by the lakeside lasted for only a few seconds but those seconds seemed to stretch to eternity.

So we all stood. All except one.

Glancing away I noticed a figure detaching itself gradually from the edge of the crowd. Without having been completely aware of his presence before, I knew at once that it was Oswald the steward and knew also that, if anyone was in a position to enlighten us in this business, he was the man. Knew it by instinct, in the gut.

At about the same moment that I came to the decision to see what he was up to, there was a shifting in the group. It was as if a spell had been broken. A dozen voices started up. Someone went to get the canvas from the bottom of the boat to shroud the body while half a dozen men made preparations to carry it off.

I also detached myself from the group. Oswald had more than a head start and already I saw his figure diminished against the house which, through some trick of the evening light, seemed to loom larger than ever. As I moved off, I passed Adam Fielding and we exchanged a look of . . . awareness, understanding.

The entire series I've just described – the summoning of help, the hauling-up of the body onto the bank, the uneasy moments when we'd stood mutely around our find – all this had occupied fewer minutes than it takes to tell. Consequently, there were still people making their way from the main entrance of Instede and down towards the lake to see what all the commotion was for. Only two men were going against this tide, Oswald the steward and Revill the player. Not once did the stick-man look back and it was this, rather than any mark of stealth or even great urgency in his manner, which convinced me that he was about some business which he preferred to keep private.

His steady, single-minded progress made it easier for me to keep him in sight as he skirted the southern side of the house and then walked down the west-facing slope fronting the wood where Robin had lived and died. At one point he stopped and scanned the woods then moved on with a slight shift of direction. It's as if he's searching for somebody, I thought, and realized that this was probably the reason he hadn't looked round: all Oswald's attention was to the front. As he neared the trees his stick-form seemed swallowed up in shadow.

There was little opportunity for concealment in the open stretch of ground between the house and the wood so I hung back at the top of the rise, noting the place at which Oswald entered the trees. When he'd disappeared into their gloom I waited a few moments before descending the slope at a run. As I approached the trees I slowed and tried to calm my breathing. Once again, the wood stretched in front of me, a low green cliff, unsettling and formidable.

It seemed to me that Oswald had made his entry a little to the left of where I was standing, not far from the spot where I'd first encountered Robin and close also to the elm where he had strung himself up. I walked forward and crossed the boundary between the meadow and the trees, and wondered what to do next. I didn't have to wonder long. From somewhere off to my left there came the whisper of conversation. The voices were low and it was impossible to make out any words. Only one way therefore to discover who they were – or rather who the other man was and what business he had with Oswald.

I moved ahead slowly and with moderate care. In fact, the woody gloom made any other kind of progress difficult. From the tone of the conversation up ahead, however, it seemed that the two individuals were more absorbed in their own concerns than on the look-out for spies. Their exchange continued, somehow both hot and subdued at once. Carefully pushing aside low-hanging branches, I drew nearer to the speakers. And here was a tiny cleared space in the middle of which stood two shapes, one dark and one pale. I stopped

well back from the edge of this and squatted down on my
hams in the shadow of an anonymous bush. My clothes were
still slightly dank from the lake. In the natural darkness of
the wood, it was difficult to discern things clearly. But I had
the advantage of knowing one of the pair. Oswald stood
facing the other man and more or less opposite to my hiding-
place. The other had his back to me, and I glimpsed only his
stocky shoulders.

"You have reached the end of your road here," said
Oswald.

"You summon me only to tell me that?"

"There are no more pickings for you at Instede House."

"That does not concern me. Pickings and leavings."

There was something familiar in the voice. Who was it?

"How shall you live then?" said Oswald, with a kind of
sneer.

"As birds do, brother."

Of course! It was Peter Paradise. That thick-set build, the
application of "brother" to all and sundry. But why was
Oswald talking to this player whom he'd so lately cast out of
the estate?

"As birds do – what, with worms and flies?"

"With what we get, I mean. With what God sends us,"
said Paradise with a weary dignity.

"How if he sends you . . . this?"

So saying, Oswald raised one of his long arms as if to strike
out at the other but he let it fall after a moment. I was
surprised to see the steward, normally so impassive and
controlled, give way to the threat of force.

"I tell you that you have outlived your welcome here,
Paradise."

Oswald almost spat out the player's name.

"Buzz buzz, that is an old story."

"And you know what happens to those who outlive their
welcome? In your own words? They will find themselves
making their beds out in the dark."

"Like the wild woodman who was found dangling in here?" said Paradise.

"Like him."

"Like your master?"

"Do not speak of him."

"And he who did not grow gills yet would live under the water?"

I was amazed that Peter Paradise had heard so quickly of the discovery of the body in the lake.

"You can see that Instede is a . . . dangerous place," said Oswald.

"It is a place of sin and corruption, I can see that," said Peter Paradise. "But as for all your talk of going into the dark – there are more out there than there are in here. The dead must always outnumber the living, brother, if it comes to that. And remember it will not be dark for all. No, you cannot fright me so."

Indeed, it seemed from his tone that Peter Paradise was as unaffected by the steward's words as by the offer of violence. What I was watching was essentially the same scene of confrontation between Oswald and Paradise that we'd witnessed in the barn after the Dives and Lazarus performance. Threat and counter-threat. Then it had been Paradise who'd first raised his hand in anger before retreating, but now the boot appeared to be on the other foot. There was a long pause, then Oswald swung on his heel and struck more deeply into the wood, apparently trying to make some sort of exit.

Peter Paradise waited a moment longer then turned about and blundered past the very bush where I'd hidden myself. His straggling white beard and furrowed brow floated through the twilight. If he'd looked aside and down he would have seen me. But he didn't.

I too waited for an instant. Waited and thought. Then set off in pursuit of Oswald. Of the two men he seemed the more promising quarry. I could hear the steward crashing deeper into the wood, and I suppose I was curious to know what he was about.

This questing among the trees was turning into a habit, and a foolish one at that. So it proved on this occasion. You've probably heard enough about N. Revill getting lost in the woods before, so I'll cut it short and simply say that there came a moment – a couple of minutes after I'd started off on Oswald's trail – when I became aware that there were no more clumsy, blundering sounds coming from up ahead. I stopped, holding my breath.

All was quiet, apart from the little sounds of little night creatures.

So I'd lost him. Well, I was no hunting dog.

Then, all at once, a twig snapped behind me, and I knew that Oswald, if it was he, had somehow managed to move round in a half-circle and finish up at my back. There's a world of difference between the thrill of the chase and the terror of being pursued. I knew Oswald for a dangerous, perhaps a desperate man. Had he seen me? I was wearing dark stuff (that funeral feast). I did not dare look round for fear he might catch sight of my pale face in the gathering darkness. But I knew he was there. The back of my neck told me so.

I could feel the first touches of panic. My breathing started to come fast and I had to fight to restrain it. I cast frantic glances around. It was almost full night down in the heart of the wood, although it was barely mid-evening up above. The sky was sullen and overcast. We had shrugged off the fine weather of midsummer. The shapes of the trees overhead seemed to be cut in a familiar pattern. I recognized Robin's hiding-place, his den, or rather the great belt of trees which topped the bank under which it lay.

Behind me, there came a rustle of leaves, a pause and then another rustle. The very caution of the sound seemed to tell its own tale of stealthy approach. Without thinking, I dropped to my hands and knees. Perhaps instinct made me assume an animal posture. On the floor of the wood, I tried to penetrate the darkness with my eyes, to find the hole which led to Robin's lair. There it was! I crawled forward but found nothing more profitable than a flat patch of shadow. A shift to the left. No safety there either. Things seemed noisier at ground level with its scuttlings and scufflings. Like a cornered animal I swung my head from side to side. Get up and confront your enemy like a man, I told myself, but did not move. I sensed rather than saw a shape up ahead and rapidly shuffled in the reverse direction. Entirely by chance I found I was backing into the woodman's den. This stinky, muddy hole now felt familiar and comforting. The tight passage widened into the cleared-out hollow beneath the bank. Very faint glimmers showed through the lattice-work of roots.

Here I remained, at first staying on all fours and then shifting to a more comfortable sitting position. My situation was that of an animal cowering in its lair while some larger beast prowls round the outskirts, sniffing for a way in. I strained my ears but could hear nothing more than the sounds of the wood. Perhaps I'd been mistaken, maybe Oswald had not cunningly circled round to take me by surprise, and what I'd heard and glimpsed was no more than the fuss and fume of an overheated brain. Even so, I decided to stick it out a bit longer in Robin's hole. Whereas on earlier visits I had been, frankly, frightened by the place, now it seemed the safest spot in the woods.

Reaching back to prop myself on outstretched arms – if I was going to stay here I might as well be at ease – my hand hit something hard which shifted at the touch. By feel rather than sight I established that it was some sort of container. Naturally I remembered the box which Robin had shown me and which I'd later retrieved and shown to Fielding, its contents proving to be animal (beetles) and vegetable (rags of paper) but otherwise unrewarding. Had Robin secreted a whole hoard of little boxes in his lair? I shook it. Something inside. I took firm hold of the box, intending to examine it later on.

After a time I grew tired of crouching in the dark. The sounds beyond the woodman's den – rustlings, scrapings, little soughings and sighings – did not resolve themselves into a definable human threat and I judged that, if there had been anyone there, he would have grown as tired of waiting as I'd become and gone elsewhere.

So it proved. No one leapt on me as I crawled out of the smelly den. No one fastened himself to my heels as I once again tracked through the twilit wood, resolving not to enter it again under any provocation. I reached the open ground with relief. It was mid-evening. There was no sign of life in front of the west face of Instede. I glanced down at the box which I was holding. It looked like the original leathern one, the one which had disgorged beetles and paper and which had broken on the ground. In fact, it seemed to me that a crude repair had been made to fasten the lid back to the box. This was, well, odd.

Standing in the meadow between wood and house, I gingerly opened the box. No beetle stirred in its innards. But there was a wad of paper, tidily folded away. Evidently, in this adventure, it fell to Revill to make these finds – and then, usually, to make a fool of himself.

But before I hared off to tell Justice Fielding of my latest discovery, I should ensure that there was actually something to report. So, removing the wadded paper, I carefully placed the box on the turf. Then unfolded the sheets. There were half a dozen of them, crisp and quite clean. My heart beat a little faster to see how each was covered with large writing. Not a cultured hand, I'd say, but legible and clear enough.

Clear enough for the purpose. Which was . . . plain and not plain. I read the papers once. Then, with growing bafflement, read them again. It was a story of sorts. A picture began to emerge in my mind. It was like a landscape glimpsed through mist, mist which thins from time to time to let you see the outline of hills and plains before closing once more and leaving you uncertain and confused about where you are, where you're going.

I carefully refolded the sheets and replaced them in the box, tucked it under my arm and, yes, hared off towards the house and my guide in these matters, Justice Adam Fielding.

"I have a painful tale to tell, my lady."

Lady Penelope sat stiffly in her chair in the inner room of her apartment, the quarters which until so recently she'd shared with her husband. She was veiled and garbed in black, as she would be for many months to come, although the black would soon begin to transmute to a fetching dark purple. Unbidden, I found myself thinking about her prospects of remarriage. I rated them as good. Though she'd endured some harrowing days recently and although there were others still in store – the violent demise of her husband, the incarceration and imminent execution of her son – she retained a drawn beauty. There'd be quite a few attracted by her name and her refined looks. Besides, I've observed that marriage has in it something of the quality of an old, comfortable habit. If it's temporarily shrugged off on the death of a spouse, with most people it seems only a moment before they shrug themselves into another suit of clothes, as though they cannot bear to wander all naked and by themselves through this large world. Needless to say, I speak without experience in this business, but one day . . . no doubt . . .

"Believe me, Penelope," continued Fielding, "that I would not have requested this assembly if there had not been the most pressing reasons. Reasons which concern all of us."

I noted that he'd called Lady Elcombe directly by her given name. Enlightenment only came later.

Lady Penelope gracefully – almost coquettishly, it seemed – inclined her black-cowled head towards Fielding. Yes, I thought, you will surely remarry and soon, at the same time marvelling at the extraordinary capacity of women to bear up through trials which would flatten men.

"I wonder that there can be anything more painful," she said.

Adam Fielding looked round the room. There were half a dozen of us gathered there. In addition to Lady Elcombe and the Justice and myself there was Kate, of course, and Cuthbert Ascre and Oswald (who gave no indication that he'd lately been wandering in a wood). Night pressed against the windows. In his hand, Fielding held the collection of paper which I'd given him scarcely two hours earlier. What the sheets told him was so startling that he'd at once called this meeting with my Lady and her son and the steward, apologizing for breaking in on her mourning.

"My young friend here found these sheets this evening in the wood-hole belonging to Robin. Rightly, he brought them to me. They tell a story which only you, my Lady, can confirm. And while it may be painful for you to have to do so, be assured that – if this tale is true – then we can clear your son Harry of his father's death."

I saw Lady Penelope's hands tighten on the arms of the chair where she sat stiff, upright. She said nothing, though.

"My Lady, you will remember that shortly before the, ah, day of the wedding, I talked with you and Lord Elcombe about the death of Robin."

"I remember."

"Your husband said that that unfortunate individual had been born on the estate and then departed with his mother, only to return at some uncertain date, since when he had been dwelling in the Instede wood – for many years perhaps. It seemed that Robin had returned to his birthplace when his mother died, although nobody knew whether this was so or not. That is, nobody knew whether Merry – that was the name she was known by, was it not? – whether Merry was alive or dead."

"Why should they?"

Lady Elcombe's voice revealed how the strains of the last few days had taken their toll. She spoke barely above a whisper.

"Indeed, why should they?" Fielding echoed. "She was only a simple woman, with something of a name for herself among the estate-workers."

"This was before my time."

Again the whisper.

"Not quite, my Lady. Even if she did leave Instede not long after your arrival."

"Are you sure of your ground, Justice Fielding?" said Cuthbert. He had moved in the direction of his mother, perhaps with an impulse of protection. Kate's face wore a look of troubled sweetness, though whether for her father or Lady Elcombe I could not tell. Oswald looked on as impassively as an obelisk.

"Not altogether sure of my ground," said Fielding. "That is why I must tread carefully. Perhaps . . . perhaps it would be less painful if I told a story. After all, what is in these sheets may be just that, a fiction."

"Tell your story, sir, and be done with it."

"Very well, my Lady. There was once a woman who came to a great estate as a new bride. Within the space of half a year or so she had done her duty by her husband and produced a male heir. The child came early and for a time they thought he wouldn't survive. But he did, in fact he daily grew stronger and healthier. Hourly. Their rejoicing was short-lived for, although it was evident that the child was likely to thrive, it was also plain that all was not well with him. Not in body but in mind. The mother knew this soon enough, and the father – even if he could not bring himself to see it straightaway – knew it too.

"Now this couple were tender-hearted, at least in that they did not at once expose the child or abandon it to the elements as our forefathers might have done. But they could not accept the idea that this ... simpleton, this natural ... would one day grow up and come to man's estate. The odds were that he would die. Many children do. The unwanted ones especially. But this one was different. However feeble he was in mind, he showed every sign of health – rather as if all his strength was being diverted from his wits to his sinews. Who can blame them for how they felt? Who can blame them for what they did next? They were helped by the fact that few people were aware of the birth. The child had come early, as I say, and when it became plain that all was not in order, pains were taken to keep him out of the public eye."

There was a profound quiet in this dark room, illuminated only by a clutch of candles. I wondered at Master Fieldings's cruelty and had to trust that he had some higher purpose in mind. Lady Elcombe had half turned in her chair but, like the rest of us, she was hanging on the Justice's every word.

"There was also living on the estate a working woman who'd got a name for herself as loose and careless. She possessed a son too, a long lolloping thing who ran wild. She'd had others no doubt, ones who'd run wild to their graves. In particular she'd very recently borne a child which cried its way through half a dozen days before giving up the ghost. It was to this woman that the mother and father turned ... or perhaps it was the father only. Many children are put out to the wet-nurse. Now, the wet-nurse may be poor but she should be a woman of good character since everybody knows that children imbibe the character of their nurse together with their milk. This woman was poor, certainly, but not virtuous. She was a slattern. Careless, neglectful, loose in the hilts. Which was the very reason why the mother and father ... or perhaps it was the father only ... surrendered their baby to her. They knew she would not be over-concerned for her charge and that, even if she didn't actively seek to end it, she would take no great pains to keep it alive. So the baby was put in the care of Mary, this was her name, and the mother and father washed their hands of their first-born."

"No," said Lady Elcombe. She spoke in the same low tone, looking away from us. "No, please do not think that the mother forgot her child. She believed that she was cursed for her action. She thought God would strike her down – or at the least make her barren."

"But he did not," said Fielding in a gentler tone. "Within the allotted space of time she gave birth to two more sons who were well enough in mind and body. The father was pleased. The succession to the estate was assured. As a sign of this, the parents gave to the older son the same name as had been given to the first boy. The wife had performed her duty. The wet-nurse Mary did her duty too in a way, or she did what was expected of her. Not so long after she accepted the charge of the baby, she vanished altogether. Went away with that great lolloping son of hers and perhaps with the young child. Nobody knew whether the child was still alive or whether he hadn't died and been buried, hugger-mugger, in the woods. Whatever was the case, her disappearance must have been a great relief to the mother and father. Perhaps they'd even paid her to disappear . . . or perhaps it was the father only . . . At any event, it seemed to solve the problem.

"The wet-nurse went to live a long way off from the estate. What she did there, how she sustained herself in another town, the story does not say. But the son, I mean her own boy, at some point quit his mother and came back to the one place he'd known from his childhood. Accustomed to a rough, hand-to-mouth existence, the lad – now a young man – took up residence in some woods on the edge of the great estate and there wore out a long succession of summers and winters. He dressed himself in animal skins, he fed off roots and berries and what the charity of the great house provided him with. He took the title of Robin or was called Robin. The outlaw, the woodman.

"Mary did not continue for ever in her casual, slatternly course. In the story she reformed herself or was reformed. She became a God-fearing upright citizen of the town. She looked back on her early wild days with remorse and shame. Eventually she died peacefully in her bed – at least, I hope that she did, since the story that I am telling is hers and was composed by her, and the one thing we cannot recount in our own narratives is the manner of our death."

Adam Fielding brandished the sheaf of papers. He was pacing slowly about the room as he talked, speaking ruminatively, almost as if he was drawing the narrative from out of himself rather than rehearsing what was on the paper. Lady Elcombe had not stirred where she sat. The rest of us stood, attentive, appalled.

"Before Mary, the wet-nurse, died she wrote a kind of . . . confession. Touching briefly on those early years. But chiefly she wrote about the child. Not the gangly lad who'd returned to live in the woods but the noble baby which had been entrusted to her and which she'd taken away with her. Because, you see, he had not died and been buried huggermugger in the woods. No, he had lived . . . even though it was not especially to his advantage or anyone else's that he should live. Far from putting an end to her charge with neglect, the wet-nurse cared for him tenderly, by her lights. She grew into a mother, of sorts. And all the while he grew up strong, healthy – but no more capable in mind."

There was an abrupt sound, a kind of barking sob, from the woman in the chair. She seemed to shiver then grew still again. My heart went out to her and I pitied her exposure. But she was beyond caring about that, I think.

"He had a name. Of course he had been baptised by the parents. He had the name they'd given him. It was Henry, his father's name. He was not a complete natural. He owned some glimmers of understanding, he had a little sense. Sufficient to take in fragments of what his 'mother', his nurse, told him. And what stories she told him! He retained something of the little child's love of stories well into the years when, by computation, he was an adult. She told him tales from the good book. The story of Cain and Abel perhaps. And she must have repeated again and again the tale of where he had come from, the great house, the noble family. I think she must have talked often about this because Robin the woodman used to talk about it as well. Indeed, I have heard from another *player* in this tale how the woodman apparently believed that *he* was heir to some great estate. With Robin it was imagination surely – all those years living out of doors had addled his wits. But with Henry, it was quite true what his nurse told him. Was he not the scion of a fine house, the child of a great man, the first-born of a powerful man, a wealthy one? He was each of these things. Much use they were to him! Maybe she told him that his father had cast him out when he was little. Or did she say that she was his mother – as, in some sense, she had a right to say. Who knows?

"All that is certain is that in the shadowed parts of his mind, Henry conceived the notion of returning to the great house and family which he had heard about so often. When she died, there was nothing to hold him back any longer in that far-off town. Clutching his mother's dying confession he sped southwards. He was coming home. He travelled by day across open country and forest, finding whatever shelter he could at night, keeping out of men's way. He was wearing white, because to his simple mind that was the colour of mourning, or because that was the garb which his nurse-mother dressed him in. By the end, of course, after nights of sleeping rough and days of travelling wild, the white garments were speckled and grubby. There was no longer a mother to care for him."

Again there came that strange sob from the upright chair. I wondered at the fluency and assurance of Fielding's performance and considered that there was more than a touch of heartlessness in it. Later I realized that it was the only way he could steel himself to get through this very painful interview:

to treat it as a narrative, to be shaped, polished and delivered with address. He continued with the tale.

"And now the story becomes a little obscure," said Adam Fielding, "but we must strive to get the picture whole and clear, if necessary by piecing it out with our reason and our imaginings. A man's life is at stake. When Henry reached the outskirts of the place where he'd been born he recognized it – not from memory of course but from his nurse-mother's stories. The great house set on a rise, the lake and all the other appurtenances. Home. Yet now he was home who was there to acknowledge his existence? He was wary, mortally wary like an animal, as well as simple. He had no words to announce himself, and for authority only a dying woman's confession, words which he could not read but which he somehow knew were vitally important.

"He took shelter in the woods. And now you can see that there is only one direction for the story to go. In the woods he naturally encountered that strange creature Robin. They shared a mother, a mother of sorts. They were, in a manner, brothers. Henry lacked the wit to read but he could still announce who he was, that is, the heir to a large estate and a fine demesne, and he found among the trees a counter-claimant, another strange being who'd for years believed himself entitled to some great inheritance."

Cuthbert Ascre let loose at this point a violent . . . laugh. Like the rest of us, he was stretched to breaking-point and this was, I suppose, his way of manifesting it. I noticed that Kate's gaze flickered constantly between her father and Lady Elcombe.

"Two claimants, whether they are men in a wood or rival emperors, will eventually come to blows. No realm can endure two kings. They will fight until the business is settled and the victor is sole possessor. So it was in this case. Henry may have been simple but he was strong, stronger apparently than he who I have called his 'brother' – an individual who was some years his senior and whose strength had been sapped by all those years of living unhoused, unroofed. It is not comfortable to imagine what happened after that. Within a few days of Henry's arrival in the woods, the hatred between him and Robin had grown so great that the men were mortal enemies. If Robin had a superior knowledge of his surroundings, then to Henry we may attribute the greater strength . . . and ferocity.

"We know the sequel to this. One summer's night or early in the morning Henry surprised Robin and put an end to him. He hung him from a tree. Remembering those stories of his nurse-mother from the good book, the hatred of Cain for Abel, or how David's son Absalom hung from an oak-tree, or how Iscariot swayed from the elder, he hanged Robin from a tree."

Adam Fielding paused. He stopped his pacing. His voice had grown old and hoarse. He hardly troubled with the pretence that he was telling a "story" now. Rather he spoke direct to the matter. I looked down and was surprised to see my hands balled into fists. Outside, the dark pressed on the wide windows of Instede and I wondered when the dawn would come again.

"But even this is not the end of a painful tale. Again, I cannot be sure of what happened afterwards, no one can. But I believe that there was an . . . encounter between the lord of the great house and the woe-begone son who had returned to claim his place in it. Master Nicholas Revill here was a distant witness to the business and he can tell us what he saw on a moonlit night."

I started to hear my name and to realize that Fielding was calling on me to describe the dream-like vision of the chessboard garden and the black and white figures. With none of Fielding's fluency or assurance, I haltingly recounted what I'd seen or thought I'd seen, all the while regretting I'd ever been drawn from my bed to the window that night.

As I stumblingly came to the end of my brief witness, Fielding took up the reins again. He spoke softly, with difficulty now, almost forcing the words out between his teeth. Of all the terrible speculations of this night, what followed was surely the worst.

"So, my Lady, it seems as though there must have been a meeting between these two, father and disowned son. There can hardly have been an argument since Henry – I mean Henry the son – was incapable of sustaining conversation of that kind. Whether words of any kind were exchanged, no one will ever know. In the middle of the night the white spectre of a long-lost son rose up before his father and the father, horror-struck, faced the child he had farmed out all those years ago. Did Henry somehow identify himself? Did his father know him, by instinct or otherwise? I do not convict the son of malice, poor lack-wit. He did not know what he was doing, what effect he was having. Somehow the father backed into . . . he stumbled . . . he fell onto the great sundial in the middle of the garden. The gnomon pierced his heart and he perished after a short struggle."

Fielding paused again. He sighed.

"This is all very well."

The voice, surprisingly firm, belonged to Cuthbert Ascre. He moved from a position close to his mother's seat. There was little enough light in the chamber, and what little there was came from a candlebeam hanging in the middle of the ceiling. Into this subdued circle Cuthbert stepped.

"All very well," he repeated. "But what proof have you, your worship?"

I detected a slight sneer in the appellation. Adam Fielding was quiet for a moment. He reverted to stroking his beard.

"As I said, there is much here that we must piece out with our reason and our imaginings. But there is no doubt of the substance of the story. No doubt, my Lady?"

He spoke gently, in appeal.

Lady Elcombe looked for the first time straight at the speaker. She pushed back her veil. When she spoke her voice, like her son's, was surprisingly composed. It was that, I think, which confirmed to me the notion that there really is such a thing as blood and breeding.

"No, Justice Fielding, you are right. There was such a child . . . and he was put out to wet-nurse in the circumstances you have described. But I would deny before the throne of God that it was ever – ever – with the intention of securing his death. On – on – my part anyway."

Adam Fielding bowed his head in acknowledgment of what she had said.

"When the woman went away, though, I was of the common opinion that the child had gone, I mean, died. Then other children came, to succeed the one that was . . . no more."

"Penelope," said Fielding, with the same mildness in his tone, "did you know that Henry, the first Henry, had returned?"

"I had inklings of it."

"No more than that?"

"To see us at such a time as this!" she suddenly exclaimed in a hiss. "To impede us!"

It took me a moment to see that she was referring to the wedding, and a moment longer to realize that she had been as disturbed as her husband that the lost boy had come back to haunt them. Instead of a mother's gladness (and turmoil) at the restoration of what had long been forgotten, she too perceived Henry as a threat, an "impediment", to Instede. After all, there was another Harry already in place and his marriage was imminent! The shocking reappearance of the simpleton threw everything into doubt. In law, he was surely the rightful heir. His arrival threatened to overturn all. No wonder the mother could not be glad. In any case, she had connived at the boy's removal all those years ago, hadn't she?

As well as composure, I observed that there was a steeliness in her nature, in her blood.

"Well, he will offer no more impediments now," said

Fielding in a tone in which sadness and anger seemed to be struggling for the upper hand. "He lies at the bottom of the lake. Or rather he is laid out, my Lady, in some small downstairs room in your house. Perhaps, given who he is, he should be better accommodated. After all, he will eventually join his father in his resting-place."

"Nonsense," said Cuthbert. "How do we know that this . . . person is who you say he is? I tell you, Justice Fielding, that you are imposing on my mother and myself at this time and that the body from the lake is nothing to do with us, merely some Tom o'Bedlam or vagrant. Even if what my mother has just said is true, it does not mean that – that – thing in the chamber downstairs is my brother."

Where Lady Elcombe's distress registered itself in silence or terse comment, Cuthbert's showed itself in anger. And I could see why he should feel like this. To hear, of a sudden, that he possessed a surplus brother, and that one a lack-wit, a natural. Then to hear that it was *this* brother who had procured his father's death rather than the Harry who lay in Salisbury gaol . . . it would be enough to disturb Old Nick himself.

"It is your brother," said Lady Elcombe to her other son – now, shockingly, her third son. The silence that followed was broken only by a quiet gasp from Kate Fielding.

"How do you know?" said Cuthbert. "You cannot know after all these years."

"That 'thing', as you term it, I have been to look at. A mother might know her own son by instinct, but there was an infallible mark on him. He had only three fingers on his left hand." She shuddered now. "He lacked it when he was born, he lacks it now as he lies prone and pale. It is Henry."

"You did not say, madam," said Cuthbert. He did not mean the finger, he meant the whole business, the whole lamentable story.

"I thought to keep it concealed now as I did then, but God would not suffer it so."

In the gloom I thought I detected a single tear making a snail's progress down her face. If it was there, she made no move to brush it away.

Once again Cuthbert intervened, either to save his mother from further exposure or to give vent to his own anger and confusion.

"Very well." He swallowed audibly. "Very well. But we do not know that he – he – met my father."

"I can answer you there."

Now Oswald the steward stepped forward into the circle of light. His long, dry face was of a piece with his voice – dry as old parchment.

"I did not witness my master meeting his son, but I believe that Justice Fielding's story is correct. An encounter had been, ah, fixed between Lord Elcombe and this person. My master was gracious enough to admit me to his confidence, to an extent. The outcome of that encounter must have been as the Justice tells it."

I waited for Fielding to press this man. Who had fixed the "encounter"? How could one have a rendezvous with a simpleton who presumably took no account of hours or days? And to what end? It didn't make sense, or not completely.

Fielding surprised me by not pursuing these questions. Instead, he said, "Thank you, Oswald. You will swear an affidavit to that effect, that you knew your master's intentions in this matter and so on?"

Oswald said nothing, merely nodded.

"My Lady, will you also sign a statement giving an account of how things stand with your family? To the existence, that is, of an older son who is now deceased."

Lady Elcombe neither spoke nor nodded.

"To save another son from the gallows," Fielding urged.

"I see that we must be exposed before the world," she said with resignation.

"And Nicholas?"

"Uh, what?"

My mind was elsewhere, trying to work out what was going on.

"You too will depose under oath to what you saw in the garden?"

"Of course, your worship. But it is little enough."

"This is a tale made up of little pieces. Together, these pieces will be enough to secure the release of Harry Ascre from Salisbury gaol. It is as good as certain that the dead Henry is guilty of his father's death. A dead man cannot go to the gallows but he may step in the way of a living one."

"But how did – did – Henry finish up in the lake?" I said (since no one else seemed to be asking such questions).

"After his father's demise, I imagine that he wandered away in confusion from the scene," Fielding explained in an almost cursory manner. "He must have had some blood on him. Perhaps he was attempting to wash it off in the lake. Or perhaps he threw himself into the water in despair. Does it matter? It is almost over now."

"Yes," I said.

But it wasn't over, of course.

I could see that.

You can see that too.

Waning Gibbous

The next day Adam Fielding and I rode away together from Instede House. I was never so glad in my life to turn my back on anywhere. The Chamberlain's Company had arrived to celebrate a marriage and to contribute our mite towards the festivities by staging WS's *A Midsummer Night's Dream*. But, instead of the harmony of Hymen, we had attended a triple feast of death. The demise of Robin the woodman was the harbinger for the killing of Lord Elcombe and the subsequent death, whether by accident or suicide, of his sad simpleton of a son.

But the fates were not to be satisfied with this catalogue of misery. A poor drowned soul lay in a downstairs room of the great house, lifeless testimony to the ruthlessness of his father all those years before and an agonizing reproach to the living mother now. The older son of the family, now revealed to be the middle child, was still imprisoned for that same father's murder even if Justice Fielding seemed convinced that the clutch of affidavits he carried in his saddle-pouch would secure the young man's release. There was yet more: a marriage had been disarranged, and two families violently disappointed in their hopes and ambitions. One of those familes had been as good as broken.

I wondered whether, even if Harry were released from gaol, the union with Marianne Morland would proceed. It seemed doubtful. The Morland parents had looked, from my glimpses of them at the wedding feast, to be more interested in the gloss of rank than anything else. They already had the money, you see. (With the Elcombes it was apparently the other way about: they possessed the rank but not the pecuniary means to support it. All these things are relative, I suppose. Instede House and its occupants certainly looked pretty prosperous to me – unhappy but prosperous.) It seemed unlikely that the merchant family from Bristol would consider allying itself with a noble house in which shame and the prospect of the scaffold figured so prominently. In any case there'd been little enough enthusiasm on Harry's part for the match. Now, without Elcombe's insistence, there seemed no reason for the alliance to be concluded.

Justice Fielding and I were riding across the open plain which lies to the north and west of Salisbury. The larks still sang beneath the blue bowl of the sky, summer's good humour restored. It was afternoon. A deal of time had been spent at Instede taking depositions from Lady Elcombe and Oswald, each being heard in private. I don't think they would have agreed to it without Fielding's assurances that their witness was necessary to quash the indictment against Harry Ascre. He had also taken a statement from me about what I'd seen from the players' dormitory on midsummer's night. Although I several times repeated that my vision was confused and wavering, Fielding insisted it would contribute towards the task of freeing young Ascre. "Part of the picture," he said. "An item in the pattern."

All this business of witness-taking meant that my departure from Instede was bound to be delayed so, by prearrangement, Adam Fielding and I journeyed back together. My fellows set off early that morning as planned, the funeral obsequies for Lord Elcombe being complete and our respects paid to a valued patron. (Of course, nobody apart from me knew anything of the inner history of this sad family.) The Chamberlain's were on foot but, since it was late afternoon by the time the Justice and I started, we didn't expect to overtake them. In fact, they'd most likely reached Salisbury and the Angel Inn already.

Kate Fielding had also set off early for Salisbury to prepare things for her father's return. She assured me that the invitation to spend the night in their house still stood. For companionship and safety, Kate travelled back with the Chamberlain's. She was given pride of place beside Will Fall on the cart, Messrs Sincklo and Pope graciously conceding their shared position to a lady for the duration of the trip. As I saw her being handed up to her place, I thought that whatever the lack of refinement in our mode of transport, there was an ample courtesy in the Chamberlain's men attending on her.

Will Fall, for sure, would keep her well amused on the drive. A pang of jealousy pinched my heart, but then I reflected that Kate was hardly mine – hardly anybody's, I hoped – to be jealous about. In any case, Fall's tastes ran more to wenches and drabs like Audrey of the kitchens. Audrey exchanged many broken sentences with her paramour before permitting him to climb up alongside the lady from Salisbury. Perhaps she was jealous too. Even drabs have feelings. I wondered what reassurances Will had given to his country girl: undying love; eternal remembrances; the promise of an infinity of kisses; until the next town and the next girl. He wouldn't be returning to Instede. Safely installed beside Kate and with a knowing grin at her, Will whipped up old Flem. The draughthorse looked to have been well cared for in the Instede stables, and with nary a cough or a wheeze the jade jerked into motion.

No, Will wouldn't be returning. Not one of us would be returning to Instede, I profoundly hoped. A few of the household had gathered to see the Company off and now stood gazing at the disappearing column. Surprisingly, Cuthbert Ascre was there to shake the hands of our seniors and to be told once again that he would have made a player . . . yes, a good player. He seemed to have shrugged off the anger and turmoil of the previous evening and to be his usual pleasant self. Oswald was nowhere in sight. Nor was Lady Elcombe. Not that I would have expected to see either of them. But some lesser beings, like Sam the bailie and my servant friend Davy, appeared and seemed genuinely regretful at the departure of the players. Partly, no doubt, this was to be explained by the pall of gloom which must once more descend over Instede. But it was also a tribute to the flash and fanfare which we players bring with us wherever we travel – we just can't help it. Life must seem so dull after we've gone.

As I say, I was one of those left behind, to assist Fielding in gathering the evidence which would acquit Harry Ascre. Now we were ambling across the plain on a fine late afternoon, following the track which we'd traversed on foot not so many days before. It was almost possible to leave behind, with the house, all thoughts of sudden death, suicide and murder. Almost, but not quite. Mind you, I was helped in my desire to keep my head out of the gloom by having to keep my mind on my horse. This mean beast had been lent me by one of the Instede grooms at Adam Fielding's request. The Justice himself rode his own palfrey, in keeping with his rank. Nicholas Revill, meantime, was required to master and direct a short creature with white legs and a body of indeterminate colour, which took an inordinate interest in Fielding's dignified mount, either out of friendliness or mischief. "Sweathland" was the breed, I was told, or some such name – why do those in the know always delight on inflicting their jargon on the ignorant and the indifferent? Though country-bred, I have never grown familiar or easy around horses. And they know it. My attempts to control this particular nag – which was supposed to answer to the name of Napper but in fact answered to nothing at all, not even cries of "bastard!" or "Jesus!" – caused Fielding some amusement and, I dare say, kept my mind partly away from the last few days.

Even so there were matters that I wanted to discuss with the magistrate. For all the explanations given in my Lady's chamber the previous evening and for all the statements which he'd gathered and which he hoped would unlock Harry Ascre's cell door, I was not absolutely convinced by Fielding's reading of events, by his "story". There were too many loose ends and things sheerly unexplained. Or matters never understood in the first place. For example, to start with something relatively minor, I couldn't see why Harry Ascre had been so opposed to marriage with Marianne Morland. Now that that union seemed unlikely to proceed, I ventured to ask Fielding for his thoughts on the young man's obstinate reluctance. Given his old acquaintance with the Elcombe family, he might have something fresh to offer.

He took some moments in consideration, stroking his beard with one hand while keeping loose hold of his reins with the other. Meantime I held on fearfully to Napper's strings.

"Not all young men are eager to rush into matrimony," he said finally. "And before you go on to say it, the reason is not that they want to continue with their life of lechery and whoredom. Nor that they prefer their own gender. This is not the situation with young Harry, so far as I know. Perhaps he is simply not ready for marriage."

"Oh."

Fielding, perhaps seeing that this was a disappointingly simple explanation, said, "It is sometimes the case. Are you ready for marriage, Nicholas?"

"Doesn't there have to be a woman *in situ?*"

"Not necessarily," said Fielding. "Those who are disposed to marry will find others of like mind."

"I – don't know, Adam. I suppose that, if I hesitate to answer, then my answer must be no, I am not ready."

I did not say that there was one woman I would have married – and married tomorrow.

"But you have a woman in London?"

"Of sorts," I said. Oh the treachery of those who talk about their friends out of earshot! Believe me, I did not feel *that* indifferent towards Nell. "Anyway, when we first met you described my position precisely. You said that any young man on his first excursion out of town will be, what was it?, 'ready for other adventures'."

"You have a good memory."

"I am trained to recall lines."

"There is another factor in Harry's case, I believe," pursued Fielding. "That is, the more his father insisted on matrimony, the more reluctant he became to embrace it. The higher the family, the less freedom its members have to carve for themselves. Of course, the freedom of daughters is circumscribed – some would say rightly so – but the son too may find himself in a cage not of his making."

It was odd how Fielding, with his talk of cages, was echoing the words of Cuthbert Ascre.

"But sons are not docile creatures like daughters, not tractable. They may rebel against confinement."

"And that's what Harry was doing? Rebelling?"

"Yes, in sullenness and silence, not in killing his father. It is simple enough. We do not always want those our parents choose for us. Remember your play."

"Play?"

"Master Shakespeare's *Dream*. There is an arranged match in that piece – and some resistance to it."

Adam Fielding was right. But the Chamberlain's performance of *A Midsummer Night's Dream* seemed to have taken place in another time, another place, to have nothing to do with two men riding across Salisbury plain and talking of marriage and murder.

"I was a rebel once – of sorts, as you would say," said Fielding. "I did not want she who my father had chosen."

"What happened?" I asked, pleased at the Justice's little revelation. And surprised too, as one always is when a man older and wiser than oneself admits to some youthful indiscretion or defiance.

"Oh, I followed my father's advice – eventually."

"And . . .?"

"The woman and I, we married. We were blissfully happy. Or as near to bliss as one can approach on this side of the door. She was Kate's mother."

Something about his tone discouraged any further comment. Anyway at that moment, my horse Napper stopped. I don't mean that he slowed and halted. He simply stopped, dead. If we hadn't been going at an amble, I would have been pitched forward. Since he'd dug his heels in, I dug mine in too, into the jade's flanks. He'd soon learn who was master. The answer came quick: he was the master.

I spoke harshly, I spoke kindly. I spoke pleadingly. All to no effect. Fielding's palfrey continued to pick his civilized way down the whitened track. I don't think the Justice was aware at first that I'd been left behind. When he eventually turned round, his first response was laughter. "Nicholas, you ride a horse as though you were sitting in a chair." Then advice, shouted across the distance between us: "Abandon all hope, Nicholas. Think that your horse will never move again. And let him know that you do not care. Whistle or something."

So I folded my arms, whistled a country air and acted all blithe and unconcerned. Eventually Napper, piqued by my attitude, lumbered into motion once more. When I caught up with Fielding, he was struggling to keep the grin off his face. But I hadn't finished quizzing him. There were other matters, Instede matters, to be explained.

For example, what was the connection between Peter Paradise, the leader of the pious players, and Oswald the drama-hating steward? I described to the Justice how I'd followed the stick-man away from the lakeside and down into the wood, and also repeated some of the fragments of dialogue as far as I could remember them.

"That is easily enough explained, I think," said Fielding. "Can you keep your horse at a little distance, by the way."

"I'll try but he is not very responsive."

"It is a question of command – and the indifference of command. Do not worry whether you will be obeyed."

I yanked Napper away from his attempts to nuzzle Fielding's palfrey, at the same time trying to get the conversation away from my rotten riding and back to the subject of Oswald and Peter Paradise.

"It may be easily explained," I said irritably, "but it's a mystery to me."

"Rather like horsemanship, I suspect," said Fielding. "But if you come to Oswald and the leader of the Paradise players, it is yet another case of brothers. Oswald Eden is Peter Paradise's brother. Peter changed his name when he started touring in this part of the world. He warns of purgatory but he advertises paradise."

"What? Oswald?" I said, surprised and yet somehow not surprised. It's only a short hop from an Eden to a Paradise, after all. "Oswald is related to that pious crew?"

"Not to all of them. They aren't real brothers anyway. I believe that only Peter is officially blessed with the name of Eden – or Paradise. But Peter calls the other two 'brother' and doubtless they're all happy enough to live under the heavenly banner of his name, his assumed name."

"So when Peter was saying 'brother' to Oswald he wasn't just saying it, he really meant it . . .? Wait! Whoa there!"

My little horse, my little Napper, now took it into his pinhead to go off on a personal circuit across the plain. Eventually, by dragging on the reins and with a mountain of curses, I brought him back to the straight and narrow. Or rather he elected to come back to it in his own good time.

"Is that why the players were tolerated at Instede?" I asked, when I'd recovered my breath. "Because of the fraternal connection between pious Peter and Oswald?"

"As fraternal as Cain and Abel, I should think," said Fielding. "No, it was rather my Lady who encouraged their presence. She turned pious herself after her young days. Last night we heard the reason why. She thought she might be damned for causing . . . for allowing her first child to be removed from her. This was her way of making amends, one of her ways. She is a good woman at heart."

"A case of brothers . . . " I repeated Fielding's earlier words to myself. Then a sudden thought struck me under the open sky of the plain, and several things came together in my head at once.

"Adam," I said, in my excitement. "Did you ever see Robin the woodman? The man who hanged himself or did not hang himself – or who was suspended by his simple brother or who was not suspended – or whatever may be the truth of that . . . did you ever see him?"

"He was a shy creature of the woods. How should I have seen him? Why?"

"It's just that he looked a little like Elcombe. They shared the same bony features."

"So?"

"He uttered all that talk about being heir to a great estate."

"Living among trees addled his brains."

"And when you questioned Lord Elcombe about Merry," I pursued, undeterred, "you remember what he said about her? That she was open to all – what was it? – 'any fellow on the estate might have covered her'."

"And so?"

Fielding's dismissive attitude irked me. After all, I had listened to enough of his ideas. So I went on. "Lord Elcombe's father, of whom I have heard only a little, no doubt behaved with the . . . the licence that fitted his rank. Suppose that he 'covered' this woman on his estate – in his youth maybe. That would account for the likeness between Robin and Elcombe, perhaps even explain why the one suffered the other's presence on his land."

"You could be right," said Fielding after a time. "The same idea occurred to me almost at the instant that Lord Elcombe gave that reply."

"Oh, well then . . . " I was obscurely disappointed.

"No one would be helped by the discovery, though," said Fielding. "You are right about old Elcombe's behaviour. There was a greater licence in those days, a memory of the late king, I expect. It is *possible* that old Elcombe was the father of poor Robin. But in the present circumstances, a certain knowledge of this – even if it were obtainable – would only increase the family's pain, to no good purpose. We should rest in doubt, we should leave well alone. Let sleeping bodies lie."

I might have debated this with him, even though it was really none of my business. But at that instant Napper again chose, maliciously, to take off. On this occasion, instead of travelling in a circuit, he elected to go in a straight line. But not the straight line in which Fielding and I had hitherto been moving. Rather we shot at a slant across the great plain. I was barely conscious of where we were going, my steed and I, because I was busy clinging for dear life to reins, mane, pommel, anything. At every instant I could have been pitched or tossed onto the hard, shardy ground, there to make acquaintance with one of the many little hummocks of rock which dotted the plain.

The landscape blurred past. The horizon leapt up and down as I bounced around on top of Napper, every jolt and jerk jarring my bones. The horse's hoofs thundered on the turf, pounding it into submission. Though my steed was short and somehow peasant-like in his overall demeanour, he could move fast. Very fast, faster possibly than any animal had ever moved or human being been moved before. I became convinced that Napper was travelling so rapidly not for his own pleasure but in order to put me in fear of my life. I became convinced that the Instede stable-lad had deliberately foisted on me the most wilful, vicious animal in his stalls. I shouted curses and imprecations to the air and, when those didn't work, whispered endearments in the horse's ear (on those occasions when I found myself close to it), trying to soothe and flatter the beast into slowing. But Napper raced on in his own sweet way. I dared not look round, couldn't look round, so didn't know whether Fielding was aware of my predicament. He was most likely sitting at ease on his immaculately behaved palfrey, roaring his head off at my discomfort.

To my jumping vision, something white and blockish now seemed to be gathering form in the distance. As we drew closer I realized that it was the strange collection of standing stones which we had passed on the way to Instede House. The stones which had reminded me of the uprights and cross-pieces of a giant's house and which, according to Richard Sincklo, had been transported to this place and erected by the magic of Merlin in Arthur's age. Last time, walking with my fellows, we had not approached the stones so near as Napper now seemed determined to take me. From a distance, the pillars and cross-pieces were imposing enough, partly on account of their strangeness and the mystery of their origins, partly on account of the way they stood up against the large sky. Close to, they were as alarming as God's teeth.

Close to ... and closer to ... and closer to still! Jesus, when was this horse going to stop going, or slow down, or swerve aside from a course which must bring us – me! – into the most immediate bone-snapping skull-shattering meeting with hard stone. "Napper! Napper!" I shouted, screamed, pleaded. "Napper!"

But to no avail. The mighty blocks of stone reared up like fragments of cliff-face. Evidently my mount, deciding that neither of us deserved to live any longer, planned to fling himself headlong at an immovable object many times larger and harder than himself. I clung low round his hot neck while a few prayer-like phrases rushed pell-mell through my head.

At the last instant Napper swerved and came to a stop so abruptly that I was almost somersaulted forward over his neck. Then, without a pause, he began to crop at the grass which grew in thick tufts near the base of the stones, for all the world as though we'd been out for a gentle amble. I scrambled off his back before he changed his mind. My legs were simultaneously stiff, from clinging tight to the horse's flanks ever since Instede, and trembling from terror, and I near buckled to the ground. The horse went on grazing contentedly, his white legs planted foursquare on the turf as though nothing would shift him this side of doomsday. I was quite glad he hadn't looked up to witness my weakness. I dare say he was aware of it, though. Animals are like that.

After a time I'd recovered my wind and wits sufficiently to start inspecting my situation. I was standing just outside the perimeter of the great white teeth. Another couple of seconds and we'd most assuredly have collided with that monster over there, and Revill's brains – to say nothing of Napper's lack of them – would be spilled all down the stone. Well, it was just a matter of waiting for Adam Fielding to catch up with me. Then, pleading the intractability of my horse, I'd beg a hoist up onto the back of his civilized grey palfrey for the last few miles to Salisbury. Napper could stay grazing, or make his own way back to Instede, or go to the devil, for all I cared.

I waited. At my back the wind whistled softly through the stones, and I couldn't help thinking of someone whistling through their teeth. I listened for the distant clop of hoofs but heard only the lazy murmur of a summer's afternoon, insect buzz, bird song. Where was Fielding? Surely he must have seen the direction I'd taken off in? Scattered around the edge of the upright rings were fallen slabs and tumbled blocks. I clambered on top of one of these slabs and was surprised at how much better a vantage point it gave over the surrounding plain. Shading my eyes, I gazed out to the hazy west, ready to shout and wave whenever Justice Fielding hove into sight. But he did not appear. Gentle mounds and humps disturbed the grassy spread. The wind whoo-whooed mournfully among the stones and the grasses bent to the breeze. I shivered slightly, to think once again of the mighty race which must surely have had a hand in the cutting and shaping of these mighty stones, unless Merlin's magic had done it all. In such a spot, it is easier to believe in magic.

It was lonely out on the plain under the bare sky by God's teeth. Even Napper, that browsing self-destructive steed, had shifted out of my line of sight and was presumably munching grass round a corner. Well, I told myself, I'll give it another few minutes and then I shall set off back to Salisbury relying on that never-failing mode of transport: human legs. It was no more than a handful (or legful) of miles to the city. In *that* direction, I rather thought, turning round, an easterly direction . . . so if I kept my shadow more or less in front of me . . . I should arrive well before nightfall.

But it wouldn't be necessary after all to trust to the Revill legs because, turning back, I now saw in the distance a mounted figure making his easy progress across the plain. I was more relieved than you might think. I called out, I waved my arms in the air, and was pleased to observe the figure making a slight alteration in his course to steer towards the stone circle. I sat down on the slab, then lay down on my side, keeping half an eye on Fielding's unhurried advance. The surface of the stone was warm and its mossy indentations might have been shaped to the body, my body at least. I closed my eyes. The westering sun warmed my face and limbs. I allowed my mind to drift, imagining how I'd fend off Adam Fielding's jibes at my poor horsemanship, then moving on to think of his daughter Kate. I hoped she hadn't grown too familiar with Will Fall on the drive to Salisbury. Surely the daughter of a Justice, with her impatient wit and sharp eye, would find Fall, well, a bit common? He was used to drabs after all and should not aspire higher, being only the son of a carter (not that I'm normally disdainful about origins, of course). And he was short of stature. Short Fall.

I must have fallen asleep for a moment. Because when I next looked at the sky the sun had slipped down a notch and the figure on the plain had grown bigger. The air between us was thick and dazzling, and he and his mount shimmered in the gathered heat of a late June afternoon. I almost made to sit up and wave him in over the final two or three furlongs but he was obviously heading in this direction without my aid, so again my eyes closed, involuntarily. Seconds later, it seemed, they flew open to discern the black figure larger, much larger, as if he'd suddenly put on speed in the intervening period. But that couldn't be, because he was still travelling at the same leisurely pace.

Once more, I made to sit up but an instinct caused me to stay still, to lie close along the top of the slab.

There was something about him . . . what was it?

It's easy enough to recognize someone on foot, from their pace, their posture and outline, even if you're only halfway familiar with them. It's harder with a person on horseback because together they make a new shape. However, I saw — now that the figure was only a couple of hundred yards off — that it was not Adam Fielding. I'd expected to see him, and that expectation had conspired with the hazy dazzle of the afternoon to make me believe that the approaching shape must be him.

Instead, it was Oswald the steward, Oswald Eden, riding a pale horse.

There was a gentleman I had no wish to meet.

I wondered whether, if I lay very still atop my slab, he might pass me by altogether. Foolish Revill, to have stood up earlier, shouting and waving. Then, in front of my eyes, pranced that treacherous beast Napper, fresh from his grass-cropping and ready for another bout of running, almost as if to draw attention to my presence among the stone rings. For, even if Oswald wasn't sure of my exact whereabouts, he'd know that I wouldn't be far from my horse.

I didn't doubt that Oswald had come to harm me. Or, if that sounds too self-concerned, I didn't doubt that he was up to no good and that when he found me in his way he would not scruple to harm me if he could. I thought of leaping off the slab where I lay stretched out like a sacrificial offering but he would have seen me shift for certain, if he hadn't already noticed me.

It was Napper came to my rescue. That doughty little beast, all skirring white legs, saw in the distance an equine fellow. The fact that it happened to have a human being on top of it was immaterial. They say horses are sociable beasts, don't they? Just as he'd earlier tried to make friends – or mischief – with Fielding's dignified palfrey, so Napper now set off to make hay with Oswald's pale mount.

The steward was a much better rider than I'll ever be, and probably didn't have much difficulty in controlling his own mount and seeing off the unwanted little Sweathland. I didn't wait to find out. Oswald was distracted for a space, sufficient to let me stage an unobtrusive exit. I half rolled, half jumped off the far side of the slab, putting it between me and the rider. I landed awkwardly on the turf and a protruding stone stabbed me in the ribs but I took no account of that and scuttled further into the stone circles, sometimes on hands and knees, sometimes at a crouch. The monumental grey-white columns and cross-pieces, which had previously seemed alien, now offered shelter. Out on the plain I could hear whinnies and whee-hees and the odd shout. Good. Oswald was still occupied. Perhaps he wasn't such a good horseman after all. Near the centre of the rings, I found a pair of fallen blocks angled together, perhaps a cross-piece and an upright. Even in their fallen state they stood taller than me. The grass here was longer and some straggles of bramble had thrown themselves across the slabs. Oblivious to the brambles, I snugged myself into the sunless corner. Huddled down here, I hoped to go undiscovered, at least if Oswald made only a cursory search. Then, when he'd ridden away, I would emerge from my hiding-place and walk to Salisbury, walk briskly, to get back to cities and men and civilization.

I waited. The sounds from the plain had died away. Again, I waited. I seemed to have been waiting among these stones for ever. The rings might have been magic circles inside which time was halted. But time had not stopped. I observed the shadows lengthening on the grass and inching up a facing stone. There was no sound, apart from insect hum and bird calls. A rabbit scuttered across the rubble-strewn centre of the circle. The place was pocked with their holes. Still silence.

I made to move. I was stiff from having huddled in the stone angle, and my hands and face tingled from bramble scratches. I was almost upright on my feet when I froze.

A clink of stone and a kind of shuffle somewhere behind me.

Quicker than thought, I dropped back into my hiding-place.

"Are you there?"

I had my mouth open to answer – it's very difficult not to answer that question if it comes at you out of the blue – but stopped myself before any sound emerged.

"Are you there, Master Revill?"

It was Oswald. The dry, parchment-y tones sounded incongruous out here on the plain, away from Instede House where they properly belonged.

"I know you are there."

If you know, then why do you need to ask? I thought irritably to myself.

"Master Revill, you can hear me for sure."

It was easier now not to call out, not to respond. I schooled myself in silence. Although Oswald Eden's words might indicate an innocent game of hide-and-seek, his tone suggested otherwise.

"I have something to give you."

The voice shifted, seeming now close at hand, now more distant. I guessed that he was wandering randomly among the upright stones and the fallen blocks. I squeezed myself further into the angle between the two great slabs. Their scabby roughness, garlanded by strands of bramble, gave the illusion of shelter. The sun was in my favour, throwing its shadows outward from where I was cornered. If it came to it, I could probably hold my own in a tussle with Oswald, but I did not know what weapons he was equipped with. More to the point, I didn't know what violence he might employ, how desperate he might be. For sure, he intended me harm.

There was a silence for some moments. Then, without being able to see or hear anything, I knew that the gentleman who sought me was on the far side of one of my slabs of stone. I *knew* he was close by. Perhaps it was that intuition which is nature's way of balancing the scales between hunter and hunted. Confirmation came almost at once.

"Come on, Master Revill, no more games."

Then the sound of scrabbling on the far side of the slab, coupled with a little emphatic breathing as Oswald hoisted himself on top of it. Presumably he was doing this for the same reason as I'd climbed one earlier, to get a better viewpoint.

There! I saw his shadow elongated on the grass. I saw and heard him pacing along the slanting surface of the stone as if he was walking on a stage. When he reached the end he stood and gazed around. I stayed stock-still in my hiding place. Oswald, in his customary suit of solemn black, appeared to nod to himself a couple of times before wheeling about to return the way he'd come. I looked down, perhaps out of the simple belief that if I didn't see him he couldn't see me.

Then he was above me.

His footsteps ceased; "aah", he went; then he must have stooped down to pick up something because it made a scraping sound.

"Master Revill?"

I kept looking down.

"I can see you."

Don't move. Could be a trick to get me to move. Like a clever child. But not a child. Dangerous, this man Oswald. Now overhead. Will go away soon. Don't look up.

"I can see you, Nicholas. What did *you* see that night? I fear you saw too much."

I looked up from my pit, squinting through the strands of bramble.

His stick-shape, limned by sunlight, tapered up into the air. From where I cowered he looked ... dangerous. In his hands he held a large round stone.

For some reason, I felt myself to be the wrongdoer, caught out, trapped, exposed. I smiled placatingly. At least, my mouth pulled vaguely in that direction.

"I say again, what did you see?"

"Nothing," I said.

"That wasn't the story you told in my Lady's chamber."

"I never named you."

"But what did you say in your deposition before the Justice?"

"Whatever I said, it's too late now. Justice Fielding has the depositions in his saddle-bag."

I regretted the words before they were out of my mouth. I'd just given Oswald the perfect reason to stop and assail Fielding as he rode across the plain ... *if he hadn't already done so*. My stomach lurched to think how long I'd waited for Fielding's palfrey to amble into view. Perhaps the steward had already disposed of the Justice and was now about to eliminate the last witness against him. For – even if I hadn't said as much to Adam Fielding in my statement – there was little doubt in my mind of Oswald's involvement in the dark doings of a midsummer's night. Indeed, did not his words and behaviour now confirm his complicity?

I saw him raise both his long arms and stand with straddled legs, the stone held above his head. It must have been heavy; his arms were braced against the weight. The top of the slab where he stood was about seven feet above me. He couldn't miss. Oswald mightn't kill me outright when he let it fall but he'd certainly injure me badly enough to be able to finish me off at leisure. Nor could I get out of the tight corner where I was wedged, or not quickly enough before he launched the stone at my head. I have seen boys stone a wounded waterfowl – have done it myself, I'm ashamed to say. It is not difficult to achieve a strike.

I flinched in expectation of the blow. There flashed through my mind the idea of curling up into a ball so as to protect my head and delicate parts. But that would be to surrender to my assailant, to present him with a hapless, hopeless target, and something in me instinctively rejected this. Seconds seemed to lengthen to hours, to eternities. Still Oswald stood poised overhead, as though he had been turned to stone too.

"Wait!"

He had flexed his arms, preparatory to a throw. When I shouted, he paused. I suppose that throwing down a large chunk of rock on a poor defenceless individual is not *that* straightforward. You may be checked, for a moment, by notions of humanity and other fripperies. Even the hardest heart can house a scruple. So it was with Oswald. Or perhaps it was simply my arresting shout. Whatever the reason, he paused.

And this allowed Justice Fielding to get close enough to the steward to take him by surprise – or almost so. I'd spotted Fielding edging along the top of the slab and shouted out to distract Oswald's attention (and with the minor aim of preventing his braining me). Oswald spun round, sensing a presence behind him. In simple self-defence Fielding pushed at the steward. Or it may be that the latter simply lost his footing, overbalanced by the awkwardness of his posture as well as by the stone which he still held above his head.

Whether he fell or was pushed, the upshot was the same. Oswald toppled backwards and fell into the narrow angle where I lay. As he descended his head struck the facing slab. Somehow he appeared to slither down the stone wall, ending up on the grass. He lay there in a curiously restful position as though he was taking a nap, arms and legs fully extended and head propped up against the base of the slab. His head lolled in a way that I have never seen a head loll before. In the centre of his chest sat the round ball of stone with which he had intended to dash out my brains.

"How do you feel now?"

Oh it was worth nearly having one's brains dashed out! To have Kate Fielding ministering again, as she had tended to me after my first escapade in Salisbury. True, my injuries weren't exactly severe. Cuts and scratches, and a dramatic many-hued bruise on my side where a protruding stone jabbed me when I landed on the ground. Nothing to complain of. After all, others in this adventure were not bruised but dead – dead by rope, by drowning, by falling from a height, dead even by sundial.

"Hmm," said Kate, looking at the discoloured area below my ribs, "that looks nasty."

We were sitting in the parlour where I'd talked with her father less than two weeks before. It was a bright morning in Salisbury, and fresh country sun and country air streamed through the open casements, only a little admixed with the smells and noises of the town. Kate had insisted on giving me a thorough inspection, within the bounds of propriety of course. I was pleased enough to have her play the part of nurse, believe me.

"It's not so bad," I said, manfully.

"It's a pity you didn't get it seen to earlier. Then we could have applied the traditional remedy for this kind of bruising."

"What's that?"

"Fried horse dung."

"Oh, a pity."

"Of course it has to be put on almost straightaway otherwise it's not much use. So we'll just have to fall back on plantain again."

"Never mind," I said. "I'll live."

Later on, when she was palping and prodding my lower

limbs, she encountered the scar of the stab-wound I'd received the previous winter on the roof of Whitehall.* After I'd stopped wincing, I could see that she was impressed. At least, that's how I interpreted her expression.

"Another adventure," I said casually. "Someone tried to kill me."

"It seems to be a habit with you."

"London, you know," I shrugged.

"Oh, that is the wicked city you warned me about. With the wild apprentice boys and the desperate veterans."

"I didn't know you knew it, at the time."

"I shall be there again quite soon."

"You will?" I couldn't keep the smile out of my voice or off my face. "With your aunt, the one in Finsbury Fields?"

"You've got a good memory, Nicholas."

I wanted to say, how could I forget anything material to you, Kate? But instead I contented myself with some remark about actors and memory, as I had with her father on that fateful ride back from Instede.

"And since you are to visit there, Kate, I insist that you come and see the Chamberlain's in performance."

"I have already watched you do the *Dream*."

"But you have not seen us play in our home."

"Home?"

"The Globe playhouse, I should say."

"Your friend Will Fall was urging me to do the same."

Again, the little twinge of jealousy.

"Ah yes. How did you enjoy your ride to Salisbury?"

"Well enough. He is a lad, isn't he, Will."

I couldn't quite interpret this. Approval? Or disdain? Or amusement? So I went on to urge her attendance at the proper playhouse, explaining that the Instede experience wasn't to compare with it.

"And besides when we were playing at Instede, everything

* see *Death of Kings*

was overshadowed by what happened afterwards," I said, echoing the words of Parson Brown in Rung Withers. "It was no occasion of joy, but the prelude to melancholy. No, you must see us as we should be seen."

"I think you mean I should see *you*, Nicholas."

I could not meet her eye, and found myself growing red like a schoolboy. This was the moment surely. Seize it, Nicholas. Kate meantime bent forward to apply some ointment to a particularly vicious flesh-tear on my forearm.

"Of course I do," I said.

"Well, I will come and see you play. That is, unless you endure any more adventures in the interim. You might not survive another adventure."

She looked up at me with those clear, candid eyes.

"No adventures, I promise, until you are come to London."

Greatly daring, I leaned forward and kissed her on the lips. The touch, the taste stayed with me for several hours afterwards. Or rather, I tried to ensure it did by allowing no drop of liquid to pass my own lips – just like a green, lovesick schoolboy.

Around the dinner hour, Adam Fielding returned from the gaol, where he had been in conference with the two justices who had originally ridden over to Instede for the inquest on Lord Elcombe and who had committed young Harry Ascre for trial. Armed with the depositions which he'd gathered from Lady Elcombe and (the now defunct) Oswald, as well as myself, he had succeeded in persuading his fellow magistrates that the charges against Ascre should be abandoned.

Adam Fielding had saved my life. For I had no doubt that, if he hadn't had crept up behind Oswald Eden and caused him to topple to his death, the steward would have launched his stone missile at the unprotected head of one N. Revill, whose pate is no harder than the average mortal's. It was not likely that Oswald would have missed at such close range, and – even if he hadn't disposed of me at the first strike – he could have finished me off straight after. Then I would have remained lying outdoors in the midst of the stone rings on Salisbury plain, for crows and other carrion to peck at.

Approaching the mighty stone rings, Fielding had sighted Napper the nag cantering in circles. Worried that I'd fallen off and injured myself, he had put on speed. (When he told me this, I was touched by his concern and forgave him for his mockery of my poor horsemanship – like sitting in a chair, indeed!) Next Fielding spotted Oswald's horse, tethered on the outskirts. Whether he recognized it or not I don't know, but the sight made him uneasy. Dismounting, he walked in the direction of the voice which carried over the grass. Curiously, it echoed the question on his own lips: "Are you there, Master Revill?" Then, seeing the black stick-figure stalking among the stones, he had grasped my danger and set to stalking Oswald himself. For all his years, Adam Fielding was a fit, limber man. To clamber atop a six-foot high slab was no great challenge, to creep up behind a man preoccupied with his own quarry was a reversion to child's play.

I owed him my life.

Afterwards, we'd walked and ridden back to Salisbury from the stone rings, with Fielding and I taking it in turns astride his dignified palfrey. The late Oswald was draped over the crupper of his own mount, the pale one he'd arrived on. There was no sign of my Napper. I guessed he was half way back to Instede. If I owed Fielding my life I owed the nag a debt too, for he'd enabled me to slip away more or less undetected as Oswald rode up. Now the steward's head lolled on one flank of his mount and his feet waggled on the other. My legs were still shaky and it seemed to take a particular effort to put one in front of the other during my spells of walking. Fielding was uncharacteristically quiet, so it was a silent little trio, two living and one dead, that paced city-wards across the plain while the thumb-print of a waning moon rose into the sky. We reached Salisbury in the middle of that summer evening.

I was relieved that arrangements were in the hands of an

important citizen of the town. I was relieved I did not have to face such things as the bestowal of the body, the sending off next morning of a messenger to Instede with the news of Oswald's demise, or the inevitable explanations required from various quarters. My fellows were lodging at the Angel Inn in Greencross Street and were due to set out on their return to London later that day. I spoke to Richard Sincklo and outlined some of what had happened without going into much detail. I asked that I might remain behind a day or two longer since my witness might be required. My friends like Jack Wilson and Laurence Savage were eager in their questions and I promised them that I would unfold the whole story when we were together again at the Globe.

But what was the whole story?

Fielding explained that, like me, he considered Oswald to have been somehow implicated in the series of Instede deaths. The steward had claimed no more than that he'd been aware of his master's meeting on midsummer's night with his cracked older son. But there was a closeness between them – Fielding held up his hand with the index and middle fingers wrapped about each other – a closeness which suggested Oswald knew much more than that simple fact about Elcombe's plans and intentions. Whether he, that is Elcombe, had gone out to silence Henry the simpleton, and so keep the way clear for the second son's marriage to proceed . . . or whether he had attempted to bribe or trick the natural into leaving the estate . . . but had himself perished in the course of the business . . . whatever had occurred, Fielding was sure that Oswald had been up to the hilts in it.

"Oswald couldn't be certain what you'd seen that night," said Fielding. "After he'd given his testimony, he was suddenly seized with the belief that he'd given himself away. Or that you might have said more to me than you'd let on. Accordingly he decided to waylay you on the way back."

"And then you?"

"I dare say. Travellers are robbed on the plain from time

to time. Wild rogues and rakehells. It would have been easy enough for Oswald to cover his tracks."

"He must have been very devoted to the memory of his master."

"He was. But devoted mostly to the memory of himself. Also, I believe that he had ambitions . . ."

"In the direction of the Lady Penelope?"

"Yes, Nicholas. You too noticed that."

I hadn't before that instant, but sometimes you don't realize what is the case until you say it aloud.

"He was at her side after her husband's death, often at her side. Everyone saw that. He kept her husband close company too. But a steward!"

"There is precedent," said Fielding. "The Duchess of Suffolk married her Master of the Horse."

"And Master Shakespeare created an ambitious steward in one of his plays. But he was a figure of fun."

"That was not Oswald. Well, Nicholas, I am in high hopes that young Harry Ascre will be freed tomorrow and returned to his family. At least something will have been salvaged out of this wreck."

Something was salvaged. Adam Fielding's hopes were realized.

Young Ascre was released to go back to a house in mourning. Lady Elcombe might be relieved that she had two out of three sons left, even if the eldest had been momentarily restored only to be snatched away. But then how deep could her grief be for a simpleton she hadn't seen since he was a baby? Given what was known of that unfortunate's life (and the hand he'd played in procuring his father's death), it couldn't altogether be regretted that he now lay in the family vault.

No doubt the family would knit together, eventually. Lady Elcombe might expect to remarry in time, when her widow's weeds turned to purple. Harry Ascre wouldn't be compelled to marry Marianne Morland, wouldn't perhaps be compelled to marry anyone at all. Cuthbert might be able to indulge his passion for the stage . . . though I judged this unlikely. With noblemen, such passions are essentially pastimes.

Nicholas Revill's hopes, on the other hand, weren't realized.

I must confess that my heart had swelled at the invitation from Kate Fielding to spend the night at the Justice's house in Salisbury. I'd thought – such was my green-sickness – that she desired to have me on her home territory, there to take advantage of a young player. Yes, all right, I know, the wish was father to the thought . . . but you must admit it was not completely out of the question.

True, when her father and I arrived home in the middle of a midsummer's evening, shaken and exhausted and leading a horse with a corpse draped over its cropper, this did not seem the most propitious beginning to a romantic idyll. And then the next day there were my wounds to worry over, when Kate seemed all too happy to play the nurse's part but nothing else. I'd kissed her! (But the kiss had not been returned, really.) After that there was only a little more business to attend to. I had to give a formal deposition before the two justices respecting Oswald Eden and his intention to brain me, and to testify that Adam Fielding's arrival had saved my life.

I heard too, by the way, that Peter Paradise, being informed of his brother Eden's death, had charitably attributed it to the hand of God. The Paradise "Brothers" were now on the road to Exeter, there to inflict upon the citizenry their violent sermons.

Meanwhile I had to get back to my business of playing. My fellows would have reached London already and I was eager to see my city again. Before I quit Salisbury, however, I extracted a promise from Kate Fielding that she would visit the Globe playhouse to see the Chamberlain's when she was next in town. And I got from her what I'd been angling for in return, that is, an invitation to visit her at her aunt's Finsbury house. All was not lost, quite.

I enquired at the Angel Inn and discovered that a party of carriers was leaving the next morning to travel to Kingston. I was reluctant to cross the open countryside by myself. Ordinary prudence urged company, and my late experience made it seem more desirable. Accordingly, I hitched myself to their wagon. The wagon was metaphorical only, for the carriers were using pack-horses to transport their gammon and razes of ginger and turkeys and the rest, and their progress was slow. Nevertheless I fell in with them easily enough and they were glad enough too – if I don't flatter myself – to have a real live London player in their train. At Kingston we parted company near the river, and I made my lone way over the last few miles.

As I drew nearer London the air thickened. There were straggles of tumbledown houses by the road and the country-side wore a battered, put-upon air as if it knew that its time and tenure were strictly limited. Coming up from the south, I passed close to Broadwall where I'd spent a few uncomfort-able months lodging with the weird sisters the previous winter. Then I took an eastwards turn and found myself on this fine afternoon strolling along Upper Ground by the river and in the direction of Paris Garden and the bear-pit. Familiar sounds – church bells, shouts from the watermen, the trundling of carts – greeted me. The passengers I met seemed to wear an extra air of sharpness and intelligence, which I could only attribute to their Londinity (to coin a vile phrase). The river sparkled as though God had newly laun-dered it. You would hardly think that the waves concealed all manner of filth and detritus. And, indeed, on that afternoon I did not think of it, I was only too pleased to be back on my native ground.

At long last, over the tops of the lesser buildings, I sighted the high white sides of the Globe playhouse. Seeing it there, glowing in the sunlight like the fabled walls of Troy, brought a lump to my throat. It reminded me of my first glimpse of it on my first arrival in London. Then it had been the height of my ambition to stand on those bare boards and play my part. And now . . . well, not all dreams are beyond reach.

And now I was crossing the small bridges which spanned the many channels on this side of the Thames shore, and now I was ambling up Brend's Rents, and within a few moments more I was home again among my fellows.

Waning Crescent

"Look, Nick, I have something to show you."
"Oh Nell, haven't you shown me enough already?"
"Not that, this is different."
I tried to summon up enthusiasm but in truth I was a little wearied after a strenuous bed-bout. This was by way of being a welcome home, and I must say that Nell greeted me as if I were an Odysseus returning from a twenty-year absence. Or so it seemed to me. We went at it with a will in my lodgings in Dead Man's Place.

Not long before, my lascivious landlord, Master Benwell, had also given me a particular welcome home. He was all agog to hear of my adventures among the country gentry, particularly as he'd picked up something about the tragic happenings at Instede House. Indeed, the death of Lord Elcombe and the thwarted marriage of Harry Ascre and Marianne Morland was hot in people's mouths. That's what happens when tragedy strikes the high and mighty . . . the low and meek rub their hands with glee and lick their lips. I assured Master Benwell that he'd hear about it in due course, and made a mental note to refer to it the next time he grumbled that I was only paying a shilling a week in rent.

To Nell I had given a truncated version of the Instede events. I left out almost any mention of Kate Fielding – although I wasn't as troubled by my friend's jealousy as I would have been in our earlier days together. Nell was oddly uninterested, however. Perhaps she thought that country folk, of whom she (like me) was one, went round all day hanging and drowning themselves or stabbing each other with sundials.

"Sounds a dangerous place, Nick," was all she said.

"The country?"

"Yes, a dangerous place."

"Oh it is, full of bears and wolves and dragons."

"Is it?"

But her mind was somewhere else, not on my teasing. She swung out of bed as naked and unabashed as Eve before the fall. She rummaged in a bag she'd brought with her and produced some paper and a pencil. Then, returning to bed but sitting up, she rested the paper awkwardly on her crooked knees and proceeded to scrawl something, breaking off now and then for thought. I say "something" advisedly because when she handed me the sheet I had some difficulty in deciphering the words.

"Very good," I said.

"You can read it?"

"With ease."

"What have I written then?"

"Er . . . this is your name at the head, is it not?"

"Yes yes, and . . .?"

"What does this say? 'Hips'? It looks like 'hips'. I'm not quite sure."

"Give it me again."

She snatched the paper, almost tearing it. "I will read it if you cannot. It is some lines of verse."

She cleared her throat.

"It begins thus:

'*Her lips are as the coral red,*
Her eyes are precious stones . . .'"

"Lips," I said. "Oh, I see. *Lips.*"

She hit me on the shoulder. The blow wasn't altogether playful.

"Whose lips and eyes are these?"

Her own lips and eyes gave me the answer which I expected – and suspected.

"And did you write this?" I quizzed.

"You have just seen me do it."

Her tone ought to have told me to tread carefully but, equally, something in me no longer cared so much.

"I mean, did you pen these lines about yourself?" I asked.

"Someone taught them me."

"Ah yes, one of the sisterhood."

"It is better than what *you* write . . . about Puck and Bottom and the others."

I might have protested that I'd merely been doing what Nell herself had requested of me – that is, to provide details of the *Dream*. Evidently, during my absence, the whore had grown quite refined in her notions.

"So she is teaching you to read and now to write, it seems."

"Oh I am sorry, Nicholas, very sorry indeed that I cannot write a fair court-hand like yours."

"I didn't mean it that way. Who is it?"

"Who is who?"

"Your instructress. Your co-worker."

"Jenny," she said with suspicious promptness.

"I thought it might have been one of your . . . visitors."

"What an if it were? Would there be anything wrong with that? You've never wanted me to read and write."

"So we're back to that again," I said.

All the delight – or, if I'm to be strictly honest, the delighted and desperate appetite – of our recent encounter had flown out of the window. Nell seemed to feel this too. She swung out of my bed once more, with a flick and a flounce as if to indicate that she wasn't going to return to it in a hurry. Dressing quickly and claiming she had business to attend to (a very plausible pretext), she exited my room. She did, however, condescend to give me a quick peck on the cheek together with a half-reproachful look before she went, so that I almost got out of bed as the door shut and made to call her back again.

Almost but not quite.

Instead, I lay back and stared at the low, lumpy Benwell ceiling. I couldn't pretend to be alogether sorry at the way things were turning out. Nell and I had been keeping company for . . . some time now. Perhaps our frantic love-making had been a sign of things ending rather than of a fresh beginning.

I stretched out with the contentment of a cat atop a sunny wall. I thought of Kate Fielding. I would not care to be seen by her in a whore's company. She might have got hold of the wrong idea – although exactly what that wrong idea was I could not specify.

Not that I had any title to the Justice's daughter, I was quick to remind myself. *No title at all.* Only a kiss's worth. A kiss largely unreturned. But it helped, didn't it, to be unencumbered. To be un-Nelled. Just in case. You never know.

I must visit Kate soon. She was due in London about now, to stay at her aunt's in Finsbury. I could tell her about the forthcoming presentations at the Globe. I could advise her of the size of N. Revill's parts therein, and indicate which pieces would justify her patronage. She had promised to attend the playhouse.

Idly, I held up the sheet on which Nell had written out those lines of poesy. What was scrawled at the head? "Hell", was it? No, "Nell" of course to signify that the lines which followed were hers, were about her. She could scarce write her own name clearly. Then below that name: *Her lips are as the coral red* . . .

I groaned at the cheap verse and imagined some love-struck brothel-creeper laboriously sticking together shards and fragments from his table-book and, while he recited them in Nell's ear, grasping hold of her fingers as she made her big r's and long p's . . . *Her eyes are precious stones* . . . all the time employing his other hand to play with her . . .

Perhaps I'd been a bit hasty in welcoming Nell's departure.

If I'd been a little more circumspect in my choice of words I too could now be playing with her . . .

To cool down, I envisaged her new poet-friend. And succeeded in heating myself in a different way as he sprang into instant existence in my head.

Obviously what *he* wrote was preferable to my scribblings. Revill couldn't pen poetry, he only made rude quips. Though she'd found the jokes about Bottom and Puck funny enough when I was last in London. Perhaps I'd been relegated to the role of Bottom, the asinine lover, the one to laugh at, the substitute, the scapegoat . . .

Something snagged in my mind, like a thread catching on a nail.

Scapegoat.

And something else: "Nell" – not "Hell".

Well, well.

Sighing, I turned on my side and fell into an uneasy sleep even though it was only mid-evening. In my dream, black and white figures chased each other across a chess board while the moon played peekaboo behind the clouds.

Although we were in the middle of the summer season, a period when companies often took to the road, the Globe was still expected to provide enough fare to satisfy its home audience. So when the touring group of the Chamberlain's returned to London we were plunged straight into rehearsals for three or four pieces. One in particular I liked, for the naked reason that I had a bigger part in it than in the others.

The play was *Love's Disdain*, and the author William Hordle. It was a nice piece about love requited and unrequited, unions celebrated and thwarted, vengeance threatened and averted. A tragi-comedy, in short. I had a good, solid role as an unrequited lover, one of a duo, a male and female duo. Now, in the way of dramatic things, an unrequited twosome would normally make up a cooing pair by the end of Act Five, but William Hordle was made of sterner stuff. He granted happiness to two out of the three couples – not a bad average for the real world perhaps but a little below par for the playhouse. The unhappiness which I was scheduled to play was in contrast to my Lysander in the *Dream* whose desires were finally fulfilled. This time, in *Love's Disdain*, they would not be. Most players enjoy misery more than they enjoy happiness. It is easier to play sad, to pull faces and speak dolefully. It comes more natural, except to our clowns, and offers us more of a chance for showing off. I thought it would be a good occasion for Kate Fielding to make her promised trip to the theatre and to see Revill's mettle.

Accordingly, I took advantage of a free morning to hasten northwards towards Finsbury in quest of the Justice's daughter. I even carried with me a play-bill. The aunt's house lay beyond the city walls in Finsbury Fields. I walked through fenny Moor Fields, where the pastures were criss-crossed with what in my part of the country we called rhines. These channels, with their stiff scummy surfaces, were fringed with feathery water-plants. On a warm day like today they gave off a not unpleasant smell of rot which took me back to Somerset. This was a familiar enough landscape to most players anyway because two playhouses, the Theatre and the Curtain, lay in the area of Finsbury Ditch. It goes without saying that they had little of the grandeur or the address of the Globe, even if they were well enough in their way.

Even though I was outside the stone girdle with which London encircles herself – and inside which a modicum of safety and protection is offered to her citizens – most of the scattered houses in this northern quarter were a world away from the lawless confusion of Southwark to the south of the river. Set behind substantial walls and guarded by lodges, these mansions had more of the rustic than the urban. London was within reach all right, for you could glimpse her smoky stacks and hear the bells from her spires, but round about were grasses and trees and unencumbered clouds.

I recognized the house from the griffins on the gateposts, which Kate had described to me, and glimpsed a satisfying red-brick frontage through the greenery. Kate's aunt, Susanna Knowles, was married to a well-to-do merchant, very well-to-do judging by the style and size of their residence. She had two or three offspring from an earlier marriage, as did her husband, Kate said, but now the couple had reached that dry land which lies beyond the child-bearing years. Once inside the property, I negotiated for a little time with the gatekeeper in the lodge before I saw a familiar figure strolling with another woman in the shade of a great oak.

"Kate!" I called.

She waved, smiled and came towards me. We exchanged a chaste kiss, but she held my hand for a moment or two longer than necessary. She turned her head and said to the woman now emerging from the shadow of the oak. "Master Revill is here. He I told you of, the player."

My first thought was, why should Kate need to identify me to Lady Elcombe? – for it was she who was now approaching the spot where we stood on the lawn. I must have stood there, mouth ajar, like a mammering idiot for I couldn't work out why Elcombe's widow should be here in Finsbury Fields, and not dressed in mourning either but in something light and cheerful for a summer's day. When she drew close, however, I saw that it was not Penelope Elcombe but a woman very similar to her in appearance. This one shared with her country mirror the same imperious manner, offset by the same generous mouth. But she was older than the Instede lady, her hair streaked with grey and her face a little more lined. For all that, though, she wore an expression of content which I didn't remember to have seen on Lady Elcombe's face during any of our brief acquaintance.

Kate Fielding introduced this lady as her aunt, Susanna Knowles, and we passed a few pleasant minutes in conversation, during which I was gratified by her interest in and knowledge of the London players and playhouses. Kate had noticed my little discomfiture. She must have guessed its cause, surely. But I'd have to wait for enlightenment – even if one or two glimmers were already breaking through into my darkened mind, like the first streaks of dawn.

I produced my playbill advertising *Love's Disdain*. Mrs Knowles said, "Master Revill, you are in this thing?"

"Indeed, madam. I play a lovesick individual."

"One who finds happiness in the end, I expect, though?"

"I don't want to give away the play – but I think I may say that if you come to see it, you and Kate, you could be in for a surprise."

"I promised, aunt," said Kate. "I said I would go and see Nicholas next time I was in London."

I felt a little glow in my stomach which was only slightly diminished when she added, "And the rest of the Chamberlain's Company of course."

"Well, we shall all go together," said Mrs Knowles.

I was a bit baffled by the "all together" but assumed she was referring to her husband or something. Then aunt Knowles went to attend to some indoor business, and I was left alone with Kate. It seemed to be our fate to wander round lawns and gardens, without approaching what I would have liked to make our own indoor business. Nevertheless, I was pleased enough to have this woman's company on any terms. And, besides, I had something quite specific to ask her about now.

"I had no idea, Kate, that Lady Elcombe was your aunt."

"It's no secret, Nicholas."

"But you never said so, you never called her aunt."

"Unlike with aunt Knowles, you mean. I saw the way you were looking at her. I suppose they are quite alike, Penelope and Susanna. When you have grown up with people you do not see these things, or rather you forget them early on."

"There is not so much likeness when you are close to."

"Oh Nicholas, that sounds ungallant." By this time we were sitting in a nook or roosting-place in a corner of the garden.

"I didn't mean it that way," I explained hurriedly. "I mean that your aunt, your London aunt, looks happier with life than your country aunt."

"Her husband Knowles is most devoted to her."

She left unsaid – didn't need to say – that Lord Elcombe had, by contrast perhaps been not so devoted to *his* wife.

"But you never said, about Lady Elcombe," I said reverting to the subject and probably trying Kate's patience.

"The reason I don't refer to her as my aunt is not deliberate. Just that I don't see her in that light. She is a great lady, with houses and lands at her disposal, and she has . . . well, to be round with you, she has always had a distant air with me ever since I was a child. Perhaps it was because my father had once been a favourite with her."

I must have started slightly because Kate added, "Long ago, before he married my mother."

"You know this?" I said, surprised that a daughter should be so familiar with her father's amours or preferences.

"My mother occasionally mentioned it," said Kate. "It was a joke between them, my parents. I mean, a pleasant joke. To show that, we were often enough at Instede and I would play with my boy cousins. I received few nods or smiles from Lady Elcombe though. So it's no wonder that I prefer my aunt Knowles."

There was so much here that I hardly knew what to take first. Cousins. Cuthbert and Harry. Trawling through my mind I remembered that she'd called Cuthbert "coz" at some point. After the play, was it?

"We? You said, *we* were often at Instede."

"My mother and father, of course. And me. I passed the time with Cuthbert and Harry, well Cuthbert especially. Harry was always rather moody and solitary."

"Therefore your mother is – was the sister of Lady Elcombe and Mrs Knowles."

"Well, of course, Nicholas. Would you like me to draw you a family tree to make things easier?"

"It might be useful," I said before realizing the absurdity of the remark.

Kate looked at me curiously. She'd been making a joke, of course. We were sitting at opposite ends of a garden seat, our usual position in relation to each other. At opposite ends. There was a statue in the nook, Cupid with his bow and arrow and a scarf wrapped about his eyes, to signify that he had no idea who he was shooting his love-darts at. The presence of this little marble darling was apt (and predictable) but at that moment I didn't quite feel in the mood for flirtatious banter – not that I'd ever got very far with Kate in this respect. At the moment the only parallel between myself and the blind boy was just that: blindness.

"So your mother . . . was the youngest of the sisters?" I said tentatively.

"The middle one. Aunt Knowles is the oldest while my Lady Elcombe is the youngest."

"You told me you remembered your mother?"

"Oh clearly, even though she died many years ago. My mother and father were very close and I was included in that closeness, not shut out from it as childen sometimes are."

Adam Fielding had said about his wife, about Kate's mother: "We were blissfully happy." As often, when the subject of her father cropped up, Kate's face softened, and I reflected on what an unusually close and happy family hers had been and still was.

Then I spied another familiar figure approaching from the region of the house, and it was as if by referring to him, by thinking of him, he'd been conjured up. It was the Justice of the Peace. I had said farewell to him in Salisbury only a few days before and he had given no inkling that he was coming to London with his daughter – but then, I told myself, why should he have done? He noticed the two of us sitting in the roosting-place and came over.

"Well, Nick, it's good to see you again," he said, grasping me warmly by the hand.

"You too," I said, looking at the man who'd saved my life on Salisbury plain.

"I have just now heard that young Harry Ascre has been restored to Instede," he said. "The indictment against him has been annulled."

"So justice has been done," I said.

"It would seem so," said Fielding, stroking his spade beard thoughtfully and gazing appraisingly at me.

"And all is clear as day."

Fielding said nothing but continued to regard me

"Has Cuthbert arrived?" said Kate.

"Why yes," said her father. "It was he who brought the good news about Harry up from the country. He is even now talking to his aunt."

Obviously the house in Finsbury Fields was turning into a gathering-place for the members of the Fielding and Ascre families. I felt a little, well, excluded. And other things were weighing on my mind. So I made to leave at about the same time as Kate smilingly indicated that she was going indoors to say hello to her cousin. Once again, we kissed chastely – but what else could it have been under his cool grey gaze? – and I held her hand between mine for a couple of instants longer than was necessary.

"We are going to see Master Revill and our other friends from the Chamberlain's tomorrow," she said. "You are playing in, what is it?"

"*Love's Disdain*."

"*Love's Disdain*, then," she said

"At the Globe," I said to her departing back. "Tomorrow afternoon."

When she'd left there was a short silence between me and Justice Fielding. A breeze shivered the tops of the garden trees. Cloud was building up to the north-west.

Finally he said, "You're going back to London, Nick?"

"This very moment."

"You would not object if I accompanied you some of the way?"

"I would be glad of it."

We paced out of the garden without speaking and turned together into the path which led back across Finsbury Fields. In the distance was the city wall, and beyond it the chimney-stacks and church spires glinting in the morning air. Being summer, the road was relatively dry. Occasional carts trundled past, forcing us to step onto the grass verges.

We'd still said nothing. I sensed that Fielding was waiting for me to break the silence.

I took a deep breath.

"Did you rely on my finding that – that document – in Robin's den? Mary's last 'confession'. Or were you going to go and search for it yourself? Play at searching for it, that is."

Fielding was too shrewd a man to pretend not to know what I was talking about. The only sign of his unease was that he avoided glancing at me as we walked side by side.

"It was chance that you found it so soon – I'd only put it there that afternoon," he said quietly. "When you went off in pursuit of Oswald Eden I'd no idea he'd lead you into the wood or that you'd end up in Robin's hole. And to answer your question, Nicholas, no, I had not then decided exactly how I was going to recover the confession. Perhaps I would've asked you to go and have one final look down there, so that you were the one to bring it to light. Perhaps I would have 'found' it myself. In the event, you did it without being prompted, though rather earlier than I'd planned."

"Hence your hurried conference with Lady Elcombe and all the rest of us. Now the papers had been discovered, you didn't want to waste any time in making use of them."

"Yes. My one concern was to help poor Harry Ascre. To keep him away from the assize. I knew that once he'd been tried, his execution was almost certain to follow."

"Innocent men have been hanged before and will be again."

I was being deliberately harsh.

"But I am a Justice," said Fielding, simply and sadly. "I – I could not allow that to happen if it could be averted."

"You could have owned to the killing yourself," I said.

"I could," said Fielding. "Yet it was no true killing."

"Surely that is for a jury to decide?"

"Of course it is, Nick. You are right to be so rigorous. Well, a jury may still decide on the question."

"How was it not a true killing, then?"

"Elcombe's death was pure accident – almost pure accident. Yet the death which took place earlier that evening was not. *That* was murder, impure as it could be. I mean the murder of Henry Ascre, the poor simpleton, the natural, the figure in white."

For the first time, Fielding's voice rose above a soft, sorrowful note. This time there was anguish in his tones – and anger.

"There was indeed a meeting between Elcombe and Henry Ascre in the middle of the night. Not that the poor boy knew anything of times and meetings and engagements. It was rather that at some period during the night he was accustomed to creep out from his hiding-place in the woods and gaze at the splendours of Instede House. Perhaps there was some confused idea in his head that this was where he belonged, even though – as we heard – his wet-nurse had removed him from the scene when he was little more than a year old."

"According to her 'confession'," I said, "which *you* wrote."

"I wrote only what was true or, at the least, likely," said Fielding. "I knew a little of what happened to Mary and was able to find out more. The rest I pieced together."

"Using reason and imagination."

"Just so. There is no conscious lie in the whole account."

"One can still deceive without lying."

"*Suppressio veri*," said Fielding. "Yes, by suppressing the truth rather than spreading an outright falsehood one may still deceive. I will not add to my other crimes by being disingenuous in front of you, Nicholas. Even so, it is the case that Mary did leave Instede with the young Ascre and her much older son. *He* returned and became Robin the woodman. Henry waited many years until the wet-nurse's death. Then he too came back to haunt the place of his birth."

"And was it the case that she lived and died piously?"

"I have it on good authority from one who knew the woman and her story. From a cleric who was once in Cheshire."

"Oh holy authority. You can't controvert that," I said, thinking of Parson Brown. He'd come from the north. He'd known Fielding.

"I tell you," urged Fielding. "I wrote only what was true — even if it was meant to mislead."

"You told the story which she couldn't tell herself. Because she was unable to write."

"Just her name and one or two things more."

"Even her name she couldn't write properly," I said. "It looked like 'MERCY' but what it actually said was 'MERRY'."

"Henry had brought back those papers with him and given them to Robin the woodman for safe-keeping. There must have been a trust between them, not enmity. The papers were Henry's nurse-mother's last remnants. But they said nothing of value."

I thought of the discoloured, smeared documents which I'd found in Robin's lair. I thought of how my Nell had writen "hell" instead of her own name, or rather of how I'd misread her hand.

"I couldn't use those documents, the ones you retrieved from Robin's lair," said Fielding. "They were worthless. So I had to supply new ones. I disguised my hand slightly, but it's hard to cover your traces completely. Your hand gives you away, willy-nilly."

"It wasn't only that," I said. "You hardly gave anyone a

chance to look at the 'confession'. You were very quick to take it out of my hands when I brought it to you that evening and nobody else was permitted to examine the papers. But it wasn't just that. It seemed ... unlikely ... that a woman would have gone from being a simple wench on an estate, gaping and grinning, to being someone who could pen her life-story. I could believe in her conversion, believe that she was overtaken by piety. That's easy enough, or not uncommon anyway. But I cannot believe that she suddenly learned to read and write. Or anything more than her name. 'Merry'. Why should she learn to write? *Cui bono?* you said to me once."

"You are in the right," said Fielding.

The image of Nell flashed through my mind again. For sure, she was learning the art of writing. But then she was young and bright and ambitious, not silly and gaping like an unlettered wet-nurse.

"I saw what happened that midsummer night," said Fielding. "Or had glimpses of it anyway, like you, only perhaps a little less obscure. I was out and about, couldn't sleep. Elcombe and Oswald knew that the poor natural was in the habit of coming out to gaze on the moonlit splendours of Instede. Elcombe decided once and for all to put an end to this witless threat to his estate. One – or both of them – rushed at Henry, overpowered him, smothered him. Some of this I saw, as you did."

"Then they took him down to the lake," I said.

"I didn't realize that. They had a body but I didn't know what they'd done with it," said Fielding. "Not until you and Kate described what you'd witnessed by the shore. The white object floating up to the surface then sinking down again. I understood that it must be Henry's body, and I couldn't rest until it was recovered."

"You confronted Elcombe over this. *You* were the one who approached him in the hornbeam garden."

"I couldn't find him for a time. I was wandering, sleepless, about the house and grounds, pondering on what I'd seen and what to do about it. Eventually, as it was getting light, I saw Elcombe again. He must have returned from the lake. He and his steward had finished their dirty work. Oswald was nowhere in sight. I said nothing to Elcombe but my eyes and face must have told the whole story because as I advanced on him he backed away in alarm. He looked ghastly. Even ghastlier than I looked, most likely. He stepped back and stepped back, and then fell onto the sundial. I was within a few paces of him. Even if I'd wanted to do anything to help him, it was too late. He writhed and struggled but the point had pierced him through. I saw, and could not be sorry. He was not a good man."

"He deserved to die?"

"We all deserve to die," said Fielding. "Or none of us deserve to die. Some days I incline to the latter, but not often. No, Elcombe was an especially vicious example of his species. He would kill to safeguard his wealth and standing. He would compel his other son into a marriage he didn't want. He would do everything necessary."

"Including the killing of Robin?"

"Yes, I am, almost certain that he and Oswald between them strung Robin up. Perhaps to scare Henry away. Like a farmer who dangles a line of dead crows to frighten off the others. Elcombe and Oswald knew of the link that bound Robin and Henry. They got rid of the one, then when they found that the other was still there they moved to destroy him too."

"You were content to blame Henry for that," I said.

"Not content, no. But it – it seemed the most convenient story to tell at the time."

"Convenient for yourself," I said, rigorous again.

"I accept that too," said Fielding. "After Elcombe had fallen on the dial, I hardly knew what I was doing. I wandered about the Instede grounds like the first murderer. When I eventually returned to the spot it was to be told that young Harry had been discovered and – and caught."

"Whereas he had been out and about early on his wedding day," I said, applying my own reason and imagination to the situation. "A sensitive and solitary young man probably pondering on the tyranny of fathers. And then he had stumbled across his father's corpse pinned to a sundial, gone close to it, got covered in blood and staggered off speechless."

"Yes. So from that moment it became my prime concern to exculpate Harry Ascre."

"Even at the cost of implicating his unfortunate namesake, his brother, the first Henry."

"He was already dead by then," said Fielding roughly. "What harm could it do him?"

"His memory?" I ventured. "It harmed his memory. Did he have no name to preserve?"

"A lack-wit's name," said Fielding.

"A person," I persisted.

"I suppose a father may be allowed a greater latitude than others in this matter."

There was a pause while I misunderstood him. Then it grew clear, and I felt myself go a little weak in the legs. All the time the walls of the city drew nearer. We were now traversing the marshy area of Moor Fields, with its green-mantled ditches and sweet smell of rot. Clouds covered more than half the sky. The afternoon would not be fine after all.

"You know?" I said, and the question struck me as strange even as I put it, because he should have been saying it to me. "You know it for certain? He was your son."

"Oh yes, there is no doubt about it."

Adam Fielding stopped on the path for the first time since we'd set off from his sister-in-law's house. He looked direct at me.

"I went to look at him after you and your fellows dragged him out of the water. When he was laid out in that little room. If a mother may know her child by instinct but infallibly, I suppose that a father may as well. It was our son. I told you once that I had a moment of rebellion when I was young. I wished to marry Penelope before – before she became Lady Elcombe. We would have married too, if my father had not stepped in and directed that I should marry her sister Elizabeth instead. And the aftermath of that . . . was a happy marriage. Brief but blissful perhaps, as I said to you. Besides, Kate came out of our union and she would redeem anything. My father knew better than I did. Or more likely it was luck or fate, I don't know. Whatever the sequel, I went to my wedding-day an unhappy man, like Harry Ascre.

"But before that day, some time before, Penelope and I had done what youngsters will generally do if they're left to themselves. She found herself big with child. By then she was married as well – to Elcombe. She too had a father to direct her in her choice of spouse. The child came a little early, if not as early as she pretended to her new husband. He never knew. He thought it was his, she believed it wasn't but of course said nothing. And the rest you know. Their discovery that the baby was not . . . normal. I think that Penelope saw it as a punishment for our sin and for her deception of her husband. And then there was Elcombe's decision to farm Henry out to a wet-nurse who would be negligent, even murderous. What he hadn't reckoned on was the child actually being well cared-for and growing up strong and healthy enough to return one day to the family home. When he did and Elcombe realized the full extent of the danger – well, my lord took what he would see as a justified action to protect his interests."

I looked round. By this time we were close to Moorgate.

"There, Nicholas," said Fielding. You have it all, or as much as I can think of to tell you. The rest is yours."

"I do not catch your drift," I said.

"Come now," said the Justice. "What did I say earlier? A jury may still decide on the question."

"No," I said, returning his look, candid, unabashed as it was. "*You* must decide."

"I already have," he said. "I can live with my conscience. Not easily but I can live with it and I have resolved to do so."

"When we first met, your worship," I said, "we talked about what I do for a living."

"I remember."

"You said that play-acting would save no souls from the eternal bonfire and I said I wasn't concerned with that."

"Well, you are now," he said with a touch of grim humour.

I turned in the direction of the city gate, making it clear that I did not expect – or want – Adam Fielding to accompany me any further.

"I am due for a rehearsal. It is the piece that your daughter and her aunt are coming to see tomorrow. *Love's Disdain.*"

"You will not see me there, I think," he said.

"No. Well. Then there is only one thing left," I said.

He looked a query.

"To thank you for preserving me on the plain. From Oswald. I would not be here now, breathing in this slightly rank air round Moor Fields and enjoying the prospect of going off to rehearse with my fellows, if it wasn't for you."

"You have already thanked me, Nicholas, and no more is necessary. Let it not colour your thoughts – or affect your actions, whatever you decide."

And he strode off down the road which we'd so lately walked together, talking of murder and lost sons and blame.

Why wasn't I surprised the next afternoon – as I scanned the Globe audience in the intervals of playing – to see in one of the private boxes in the upper part of the house a family group which consisted of Susanna Knowles (together with an amiable-looking gent who I presumed to be her husband), Kate Fielding and Cuthbert Ascre? Of Adam Fielding, though, I saw no sign. When we'd finished *Love's Disdain*, done our little jig &c., I caught another glimpse of the quartet, or of the significant half of it to be precise. Cousin Kate and cousin Cuthbert were rounding the corner out of Brend's Rents while I was gazing from one of the small casements in a back passage behind the tiring-house, perhaps in the very expectation of seeing them.

They were walking as a couple and talking as a couple and laughing as a couple, and I thought of those other occasions when I'd glimpsed them together – without thinking anything of it – as at Harry and Marianne's pre-wedding feast. So. But I'd already known, hadn't I? From the way that Kate's face had lit up when her father announced in the Finsbury garden that her cousin was come to town. From the way she'd been eager to quit our company to join him. And from half a dozen other little episodes or moments, now I came to review the last few weeks.

Fool, Revill! ever to think . . .

Well, I wished them well . . . and that seemed to me to be a mark of the fact that I truly loved Kate Fielding . . . that I was able to wish her well. I couldn't even bear a grudge in my heart against Cuthbert Ascre, or not much of a one anyway. Just as long as he didn't think he could become an actor as well.

They married in the following spring. At Instede House. The nuptials must have done something to atone for the abandonment of the other match, the Ascre–Morland one, not least in that this was a couple who were truly matched, properly in love (I can write this with only a small tremor in the hand).

Two marriages took place within a fortnight of each other, in fact, and together they must have helped to erase the shadow of the past, the shock of a sequence of violent deaths and a tale of sons lost and found. Justice Adam Fielding and Lady Penelope Elcombe were joined in matrimony, so that it seemed as if my lady had, like her namesake, Odysseus's wife, waited twenty years or more before she was reunited with the man she had once loved. Whether Justice Fielding ever told the full story to his second wife of that midsummer night or whether (like me) he decided to let sleeping bodies lie, I do not know.